Angels of
Bourbon Street

Books by Deanna Chase

The Jade Calhoun Novels
Haunted on Bourbon Street
Witches of Bourbon Street
Demons of Bourbon Street
Angels of Bourbon Street
Shadows of Bourbon Street (March 2014)

The Crescent City Fae Novels
Influential Magic
Irresistible Magic
Book Three in the Crescent City Fae series (June 2014)

The Destiny Novels
Defining Destiny (Dec 2013)

Angels of Bourbon Street

A Jade Calhoun Novel

Deanna Chase

Bayou Moon Publishing

Bayou Moon Publishing
dkchase12@gmail.com
www.deannachase.com

Printed in the United States of America

Acknowledgments

This book is for all the readers of the Jade Calhoun Series. Thank you so much for your enthusiasm. It means the world to me.

Also a special thanks to Chauntelle Baughman, Lisa Liddy, Rhonda Helms, Angie Ramey, Susan Sheehan, and Lynn McNamee. This book would never have gotten done without you.

Chapter 1

You'd think after dealing with a lunatic ghost, breaking into Hell, and surviving having your soul ripped in half, planning a wedding would be a piece of cake. Right?

Wrong.

"I'm so sorry about this," I said to Ms. Bella, the seamstress I'd found to alter the wedding attire. "I'm sure they'll be here soon."

Ms. Bella checked her delicate wristwatch and pursed her thin lips. The wrinkles around her eyes deepened. "I have to leave for another appointment in twenty minutes."

A small dose of panic pushed me into action. My brides-maids, Lailah and Kat, hadn't arrived yet. They were supposed to be meeting us here at Summer House—my fiancé Kane's family house in Cypress Settlement, thirty miles south of New Orleans. We had back-to-back appointments with wedding professionals all day. Their dresses needed the most work. Both were at least two sizes too big. They'd been purchased off the rack, sight unseen, each shipped from a different sister store of a local boutique. With only five weeks left until my wedding, we didn't have time to find anything else.

"I understand." I glanced at the garment rack Ms. Bella had wheeled in. The most important dress, mine, was suspiciously absent. It hadn't come in yet. Instead of wowing my friends in my beaded silver dress, I was decked out in a cotton skirt and a long-sleeved green T-shirt that matched my eyes. I felt like a slug.

"Maybe you can fit Pyper first?" I waved at Kane's best man—er, best woman. She was wearing an ill-fitting ladies tuxedo and had her phone pressed to her ear. "Pyper," I whispered, trying to politely interrupt her phone call with Charlie, the manager of Kane's club on Bourbon Street.

She waved an impatient hand and scribbled in her appointment book. "Which day?"

I leaned over her shoulder. She'd written *Body Painting* on the second Sunday in February. Pyper owned The Grind, the cafe next door to Kane's club. Recently, I'd learned she was also an accomplished body paint artist who was in heavy demand during festivals.

After scratching down a name and number, she pushed back her shiny black hair and hung up. "Sorry. Charlie's taking care of making my appointments for Mardi Gras week, and I just landed a gig for a huge exclusive celebrity party."

I raised my eyebrows. "Celebs are getting body painted?"

"Uh-huh." Her voice was low and husky. "It's confidential, but let's just say someone mentioned the names 'Hugh' and 'Gerald' as two attendees." Her face flushed, and she fanned herself.

"Hugh? As in Wolverine?"

Pyper nodded with overzealous enthusiasm.

The seamstress grinned and her eyes twinkled. "Oh, Hugh. Now there's an inseam I'd love to get my hands on."

Pyper swept her gaze over the spry seventy-year-old and let out an appreciative whoop. "Ms. Bella, you're naughty."

The older woman laughed. "It's not like I haven't lived, darling." She placed a capable hand on Pyper's arm and tugged her to a riser in the middle of the parlor. "Step up here and let me pin these pants."

Pyper did as she was told, phone still in her hand.

"What day is the party?" I asked.

"Fat Tuesday," Pyper said, sucking in her already flat stomach.

I felt my lips form into a tiny pout. That was the last day of Mardi Gras. "And I'm going to miss it."

She rolled her eyes. "You're getting married. You won't even be here." Her smile turned mischievous. "I'm sure Kane can find plenty of ways to keep his new wife occupied."

My cheeks heated as I envisioned my soon-to-be husband distracting me with his considerable talents. Then panic rose in my chest, and I tapped my foot nervously. "If we ever get this done. No way are we going to be ready in five weeks."

"We'll make it happen. Don't worry. We'll have everything done before Hurricane Shelia arrives from the Caribbean." Her sneer did nothing to calm my nerves.

I grimaced. Kane had proposed in November, and I'd imagined a late fall wedding. But when we'd informed Kane's parents of our plans, they'd balked, insisting they had prior commitments in Europe for the second half of the year. His mother, Shelia, had said, "Darling, you know how busy we get. Can't you plan it for next fall?"

There was no way either of us were waiting that long. Kane had politely declined and wished his parents well.

Then she'd shocked us by announcing they'd be in town for Mardi Gras. I'd stupidly, impulsively insisted we throw the wedding together so everyone could be present. Kane had protested, saying it didn't matter. The only one he'd miss was his mamaw, who had unfortunately passed a few years ago.

But they were his parents. They were going to be here. We had the venue. We'd already decided to get married in his family plantation home. It was gorgeous. All we needed was a caterer, invitations, the wedding gown and bridesmaid dresses altered, a cake, decorations, linens, tables, chairs, a band, flowers, dishes, a minister, and about a million other things that were going to be impossible to find during Mardi Gras. What the hell had I been thinking?

"Where is everyone?" Pyper asked, craning her neck toward the stairs and smoothing the lapels of her black jacket. Before I could answer, her phone dinged. "Wait a sec," she said to me and pressed the phone to her ear.

"That's a good question," I huffed.

My maid of honor, Kat, was missing in action. She was an hour late with no phone call. Lailah had at least gotten in touch. She had some angel emergency that, for once, did not involve me. She was a guardian angel, and in addition to watching over Bea, my mentor, and Dan, my ex, she apparently had a new charge to deal with. Still, she wasn't sure she was going to make it today.

All the amusement vanished from Pyper's face. Right as Ms. Bella was pinning the back of her jacket, Pyper jumped off the riser, grabbed her appointment book, and headed across the room. "Sorry," she called over her shoulder to an irritated Bella and shot me a weird look I couldn't decipher.

I gritted my teeth to keep from yelling. What about *five weeks* did they not understand? "Take your time," I said with a fair bit of sarcasm. Only, Pyper was already too far away to hear me.

Dammit! I grabbed my phone and dialed Kat again. Voicemail. I took a deep breath. "Kat, I don't know where you are, but you promised you'd be here at noon. It's one o'clock now. If you don't call or show up in five minutes, I'm going to perform a finding spell on your ass." I tossed my phone down in angry satisfaction. A second later the phone rang. "Kat?"

"Jade! I'm driving. Don't do that finding spell. My car will take someone out."

"Where are you?" I demanded. "The seamstress has to leave in fifteen minutes."

"Five now," Ms. Bella corrected.

Shit! "Make that five," I said.

"I'm so sorry. I'm not going to make it in time. The traffic on 90 is horrible. A semi overturned, and we've been backed up forever. Hopefully, I'll be there in another half hour and we can work on some of the other details. Hang on, all right?" A horn blared in the background. "Oh, shut up, you old coot!"

"Umm…"

"Sorry. Some geezer thought I wasn't going fast enough. I'm not going to make the fitting, but I'll be there as soon as I can for the rest of the appointments."

"Okay. Drive safely. And don't flip off any old people."

She laughed. "I'll try to keep myself in check."

I tossed the phone back down on the table, scowled at Pyper's back, and gave Ms. Bella an apologetic smile. "Sorry about this. Can I call you this afternoon to reschedule?"

Ms. Bella tucked her pins and chalk into her bag and nodded. "We'll need to get the first fitting in by the end of this week if I'm going to have time to refit once more before the big day."

I sent her a grateful smile. "I'll make sure it happens. Thanks again for coming. I appreciate it."

She clasped my hand and smiled. "Anything for Eloise's grandson."

I forced another smile. This woman was Kane's grand-mother's best friend. I hated that we'd wasted her time.

I helped Ms. Bella carry her stuff to her car. On the way back in, my feet dragged with weeks-old fatigue. Ever since I'd gotten back from my trip to the angel realm a month ago, I hadn't quite felt like myself. I was rundown, and not even Bea's herbal pills were making it better. I headed into the kitchen. "Gwen?"

My aunt straightened in front of the oven, sugar and flour covering her red T-shirt and overalls. "The cookies are in the oven. Don't they smell wonderful?"

The aroma instantly took me back fifteen years to Gwen's kitchen in Idaho. Despite my irritation, I smiled. "Smells like home."

She passed me a warm snickerdoodle. I took it and sighed as I bit into the mouth-watering goodness. My aunt ran a hand over my arm. "Relax, sweetie. Everything will be fine. You'll feel better after a cookie or two."

"I doubt baked goods are going to fix anything."

A trace of hurt flashed in her eyes.

Crap. I squeezed her hand still resting on my arm. "Sorry. It's just that Kane's mom grew up here." I tugged her out of the kitchen and waved a hand, indicating the gorgeous house. "I wanted everything to be perfect. At this rate, we'll be eating barbeque off paper plates."

"Jade, darling. Kane isn't impressed with his parents' life. He doesn't expect you to compete with them."

I swallowed the self-doubt rising from my chest and shook my head. "I'm just nervous. I don't want them to look at me like the country bumpkin from Idaho."

She wrapped an arm around me and led me to the table. "They won't. And even if they do, it's their loss. Kane loves you, and that's all that matters."

A buzzer sounded from the kitchen, and Gwen disappeared, leaving me alone. Pyper laughed from the other room. I frowned and snatched my phone again. Missed call from Kane. Some of the turmoil eased from my chest. Smiling, I touched his number.

"Hey, pretty witch," he said, his voice low and seductive. "I've been thinking about that dreamwalk we shared last night. How about we recreate that scene when I get home?"

"Hey, yourself." I licked my lips, picturing him naked and making love to me in the water. Kane was a dreamwalker and could slip into my dreams whenever he wanted, which was usually nightly. "We don't have a pool."

"I'll call a contractor as soon as we hang up."

I laughed. "Okay then. Sounds perfect. Did you call for anything specific or just to flirt with me? "

"I heard maybe you could use some good news."

"Oh?" I glanced behind me at Pyper. She was busy scribbling in her notebook again. I hoped whatever she was booking was damned important. If not, I was going to strangle her. It wasn't as if one got married every day. "Did Kat call you?" I asked Kane.

He chuckled. "Maybe."

Shaking my head, I smiled. My best friend always knew what I needed. "Okay, what's the good news?"

"Other than the fact that I have plans starting in exactly seven hours that involve the shower and stripping you down to—"

"Excuse me," a soft feminine voice called in the background. "Mr. Rouquette?"

"Damn it," he muttered. "Hold on a sec, Jade."

Static filled the phone for a moment before Kane spoke again. "Hey, babe, I've got some paperwork I need to complete, and the courier is waiting for it. Can I give you a call back?"

So much for my good news. "Sure. I'll talk to you soon."

"Love you." The phone went dead.

Slightly mollified from the sound of Kane's voice, I rolled my shoulders, trying to relax, and went in search of my mother. The house was big but not that big. What could she be doing for forty-five minutes? I sent Pyper a frustrated glare as I made my way up the stairs. She gave me an apologetic smile, the same expression she'd been wearing when she'd first answered her phone. The one I'd been too irritated to decipher. Well, at least she felt guilty.

Had I really just thought that?

Oh, jeez. I was about five seconds from crossing over into bridezilla land. I took a deep breath, and the rest of my tension disappeared instantly. They were all making an effort, even if it wasn't working out as planned.

I used to always know exactly what my friends were feeling, but with my empath ability now gone, I'd been having a hard time adjusting. When you spent your life privy to your loved ones' emotions, it was rather disconcerting when the gift vanished.

Last month, the angel Meri had managed to gain access to my soul, and we ended up sharing it—a fate that would have eventually killed one of us. The angel council stepped in and decided to award my soul to the angel. In the transfer, my soul split, leaving each of us with half. The half Meri got also included my empath gift.

At first, I'd been relieved. I'd had peace and quiet for the first time ever. No other energy was affecting my moods. It was bliss. Until I realized how much I'd relied on that sense to help me cope with the people around me. I was like a deaf person trying to read lips without any training.

At the top of the stairs, I paused, listening. Where was Mom? Silence. Hmm. I headed right to the room we'd turned into an office for me. The door stood slightly ajar. Inside, the dark walnut desk gleamed to a shine, my laptop still sitting closed in the middle. Not a pen was out of place. The following two guest rooms were empty. I slowed as I neared the lilac room. A rustle of paper sounded from inside. Oh, no.

I pushed open the door. Mom stood in front of the antique dresser, her arms out and five candles lit. With her eyes closed, she recited, "Lost. Found. Lost. Found. Open my sight. Let the lost be found." It was the finding spell she'd taught me so long ago.

"Mom!" I cried and ran forward. "No." The last time I'd lit those candles, the resident ghost, Camille, had surfaced. She'd caused all kinds of mayhem at the Christmas engagement party Kane and I'd thrown a few weeks ago. Bea said there was some sort of summoning spell connected with the candles, but we hadn't had a chance to neutralize them yet.

"Reveal yourself!" Mom commanded.

Shit, shit, shit.

The candles flickered, and a second later the flames extinguished. The remaining five trails of smoke shot out the door. Mom barreled past me into the hallway. I followed her and the smoke down the stairs and into the kitchen. The smoke curled near the pantry and sucked its way in through the edges.

She flung open the door, and right there among the canned goods was my wedding planning book. "Finally. Thank the Goddess. I've been looking for this all morning."

Just as her hands wrapped around the leather binding, a chill crept over my body. My limbs went numb, and I gasped for breath, unable to fill my lungs with the icy air.

Mom spun around, holding the book out to me. Her triumphant smile fell, and she took a step back.

"Hope?" I heard my aunt's faint voice from somewhere far off. "What's going on?"

Static rang in my ears. The chill crawled up my spine, down my legs, and prickled over every inch of my skin, paralyzing me in place. Then, with sudden force, my muscles spasmed as the ice raced through my veins straight to my heart. Panic screamed from the depths of my brain, but I couldn't move. Couldn't talk. Couldn't even think.

The one thing I could do was feel. Foreign joy and triumph sailed to my heart, conflicting horribly with my own confused fear. Giddy elation seized me, and my numb limbs moved on their own.

Frustrated tears gathered in my eyes, the only form of protest I could muster as something, someone clumsily carried my body past Gwen to the warm snickerdoodles still cooling on the rack.

My trembling hand reached out and grabbed a cookie. Without any will from me, my hand stuffed the entire cookie in my opened mouth. A high-pitched moan of ecstasy escaped from the depths of my throat as the cinnamon sugar melted on my tongue. Involuntarily, I swallowed and licked the excess crumbs from my lips. Another satisfied groan. And then in a high, giddy voice, words tumbled from my mouth. "It's been a hundred years since I tasted anything so delicious." I giggled and added, "Or anything at all."

No, no, no, I screamed, but the words went nowhere. They stayed locked away in my head.

"Jade?" Gwen prompted in a far-away voice, trembling with concern.

My mother's eyes narrowed, and sudden fear replaced the joy filling me. My heart sped up as my mother raised her arms once again. Green energy crackled at her fingertips, her earth magic clinging to her hands in a spidery electric conduit. The magic shot out at the same time she shouted, "Release her!"

The ice melted a fraction of a second before the magic hit me right in my gut. Fire exploded through me, knocking me back with such force that I rose through the air and slammed into the nook wall. I seemed to hang there for a moment then crumpled to the floor, gasping.

"Oh, no, Jade!" My mom's voice was clear now, no static, just a ringing from having my clock cleaned by a very powerful earth witch. "I'm so sorry, honey," she said and kneeled beside me, checking for damage.

I tested my arms, then my legs, and rolled my neck. Everything was mine again. "I'm fine, Mom," I said and nudged her out of the way, staring right into the face of the ghost who'd just managed to possess me. "Camille," I said in a low, dangerous tone.

"Hello, Jade," she said in her high, tinkling voice. "I'm so glad to see you again."

Chapter 2

The tall, dark-haired woman floated beside me, her beaded satin ball gown flowing gracefully to her feet. I took a few steps backward, trying to escape the chill in my bones. Gwen put a protective, warm hand on my arm.

Camille, Summer House's resident ghost, floated closer, smiling serenely.

"Stop right there!" I demanded.

The ghost reached out, her icy fingers wrapping around my wrist. I trembled, bracing myself for another possession. How was I going to keep her out? I could already feel her excitement racing up my forearm.

My magic sparked in my chest. From the depths of my inner being, a blast of heat raced toward her icy probe. The sensations joined together in some sort of mystical standoff for a few beats. I met Camille's faded gray eyes. Our gazes locked, and I struggled to fight her hold on me. My strength faltered as my power slipped from my mental grasp. I let out a frustrated growl, and my magic fled, vanishing as her energy plunged back into me.

Through blurry vision, I spotted Gwen and Mom hovering, my mom's hands sparking with magic. I shook my head frantically, afraid she'd blast me across the room again. I wasn't sure what was worse—the ghost or the concussion.

Intangible thoughts formed in my mind. Revenge. Death. A woman holding a limp child, tears falling on the little girl's angelic face. A deep terror seized my heart as I realized none of these thoughts were mine. They were Camille's. She was invading not only my body but my mind.

Hate slithered like tendrils along my subconscious, latching into my heart, body, and soul. I vibrated with it. Somewhere deep inside, I recoiled from the horror washing through me. "Lizzie," I said, my voice high-pitched and definitely not my own as I focused on the memory of the beloved girl.

"*Eximo!*" The powerful voice penetrated the gray haze of my world. An anguished cry ripped from my throat, and I crumpled to the floor as my limbs went from frozen to numb to blazing hot. The gray faded. Cream tiles stretched out in front of me. Three frantic voices filled the kitchen, their words streaming into my awareness in snippets. Possessed. Ghost. Black magic. Bea.

Firm hands clasped my shoulders, making me flinch. My muscles screamed in protest, my nerve endings alive like a hot wire. I curled into a fetal position, rocking back and forth, trying to shake the awful sensation.

"Stand back."

"Mom?" I whispered. Was that her?

Something soft as velvet inched over my skin, soothing the fire burning beneath the surface. I opened my eyes, blinking to see through the early afternoon sun streaming in from a nearby window. After a moment, her green eyes came into focus. "Mom?" I said again.

"It's okay now, Jade. You're fine. Everything's going to be just fine." She sat beside me, one hand on my shoulder, the other caressing my hair back away from my face.

"What happened?" My thoughts were unfocused. A child was hurt. Someone needed help. I scrambled to sit up.

"Take it easy, shortcake," Mom soothed. "It's all over now."

"But…" *Lizzie.* She needed me. I had to get to her.

A loud banging, like a door slamming into a wall, sounded from across the room. Someone else hovered over me. A sheet of blond hair fell into my view.

"Jade," the woman said. "What was that? What happened?" I recognized her voice. Lailah. Ice-blue eyes narrowed as her intense gaze tried to command my focus.

"Lizzie," I repeated. "She's hurt."

"Who's Lizzie?" Mom asked quietly.

"Jade." Lailah gently took one arm, pulling me to my feet. "Who did this to you?"

I stared at her through glassy eyes.

"She was possessed," my mother said, her voice echoing in the distance. "A ghost."

Lailah let out a shaky breath. "Okay, let's get her off the floor and settled somewhere comfortable."

The pair of them lifted and half-dragged me, my head spinning and eyes unfocused. I vaguely recognized the smell of leather as they settled me on what must have been a couch. Pyper and Gwen whispered behind us, but my mind couldn't focus. All I saw were the wide, pleading blue eyes of the helpless child.

I buried my head into one of the cool cushions as grief sprang up from the depths of my tattered soul, and I had to choke back a sob, unable to control the foreign emotions.

"Hurry," Lailah commanded. Footsteps shuffled around me. Then a warmth settled deep in my bones, and it was as if a veil lifted. The room came into focus, bright with natural light.

I sat up, glancing around at the worried faces of Mom, Gwen, Pyper, Lailah, and even Kat. When had Kat shown up? "What happened?" I asked, wiping away tears I hadn't known I'd shed.

Frowning, Lailah sat beside me. "A ghost possessed you."

I closed my eyes and shivered. How had she done that? I jerked and stood on wobbly legs, frantically searching for the ghost. "I know that much. Is she still here? Where is she?"

"No, sweetheart." Gwen guided me back down onto the couch. "Lailah banished her."

Kat moved to stand beside me, putting a light hand on my shoulder. After all these years as best friends, my body responded to her intentions without me even reaching for my magic. I glanced up at her gratefully as her tingling energy flowed into me, shoring up my strength.

Before I'd known I was a witch, I'd always considered this unusual gift of energy transfers as part of my empath ability, probably because it happened to come with a heavy dose of the other person's emotions. This time, I didn't get any of Kat's calm, only a vague restorative current that stopped my trembling at once. Now I knew how other people felt when I transferred energy to them, except I missed Kat's steady emotional energy. I could use it right about then.

"That's not all." Lailah paced, her footsteps muffled by the fleur-de-lis–patterned area rug. She stopped, placing her hands on her hips. "I felt it happen."

I leaned back against the sofa, studying her, a little stunned. Lailah was an angel. She saved souls, could see auras, and wield spells. She wasn't a psychic or an empath. She shouldn't have been able to feel what was going on with me.

"Whoa," Pyper said in a hushed tone. "Is it the angel connection?"

Lailah nodded, a lock of her honey-blond hair falling from her hastily tied bun. She tucked it back and sat in a chair across from me. She leaned forward, eyes worried. "The binding should've faded by now."

Two months ago, Lailah had asked to step in and be assigned as my guardian angel. The request had been granted, but only with the condition that her fate was tied to mine. When the angel council awarded my soul to the ex-demon Meri, Lailah had felt my soul split right in two as if it had been her own.

"I thought that was temporary," I said. "I mean, you haven't felt anything else, right?"

Heat crept up my neck, and I knew I must be blazing red. *Please, Goddess, don't let her be privy to my private life with Kane.* The intensity of our love life was enough to spontaneously combust on its own. If there was still a link between Lailah and me…I shook my head, dislodging the thought. I didn't even want to go there.

Lailah's lips twitched as she fought back a smile. "No. I haven't. Your love life is safe from me."

I sucked in a relieved breath.

All the amusement vanished from her face. "But I did feel Camille possess you. That means she's very dangerous and incredibly powerful." She pulled out her phone, tapped a few times, and put the phone to her ear. "We need to talk to Bea."

Again? Every time something went wrong, the first thing we did was call my mentor, the former New Orleans coven leader. You'd think we could at least discuss the issue first.

Lailah scowled and put the phone down. "No answer."

"She's at her shop," I said. Bea owned The Herbal Connection, a supply store specializing in witchcraft.

"I know." Lailah sent me an irritated glare. "I just came from there."

My mom moved to sit next to me, and she placed a hand on my knee, a subtle way of keeping me silent. She trained her gaze on Lailah. "Tell us what you experienced."

The angel dropped her gaze to her hands, visibly contemplating what she wanted to say.

"Spit it out." Irritation rang in my voice.

"Jade," Mom warned.

"No, Jade's right," Pyper agreed from behind me. "Lailah knows more than she's letting on." She stalked to Lailah's side and gave her an unfriendly smile. "Maybe you'd like to fill us in before things turn ugly."

A bubble of laughter rose in my throat. Pyper never pulled punches. It was one of the things I loved most about her. But I swallowed the chuckle. There was no sense in pissing off Lailah when she had information we needed. Not to mention we'd finally become friends after a rocky start. She'd tell me, eventually.

Lailah didn't even acknowledge Pyper's request. Instead, she stood and stuffed her hands into the pockets of her peasant skirt. "What happened right before the ghost appeared?"

Mom's hand flew to her throat. "Oh, dear. I'm afraid I must have summoned her by accident."

"Camille?" Lailah asked.

I nodded.

"Is this the first time you've seen her since the party?"

"Yes."

Lailah held out a hand to me.

I stared at it quizzically and then quirked an eyebrow.

She gave a terse jerk of her head. I suppressed a sigh and took her hand. She yanked me to my feet and pulled me toward the door. "We've got to get you out of here."

She had me halfway to the front door before I managed to grab the stairwell railing and yank my hand out of hers. "I can't leave now. The caterers are on their way. There's food to sample and decisions to be made."

"Jade." Lailah placed her balled fists on her hips. "It's too dangerous. The ghost was banished but not to another dimension. She's strong. She could come back at any time."

"You know what's going to be dangerous?" I raised my voice, almost yelling. "If one more person tries to thwart my wedding planning." Narrowing my eyes, I pinned her with a stare. "Do you have any idea how hard it was to find vendors willing to squeeze us in at this late date and during Mardi Gras? As it is, these people are only accommodating us because their grandparents were friends of Kane's family. I can't leave. I won't."

Lailah tensed and her nostrils flared. Actually flared. It didn't take my empath ability to realize just how pissed she was. She took a deep breath and opened her mouth, no doubt ready to tell me off. But then her gaze shifted to the stairwell, and her face went white. All the anger that had rushed to her cheeks disappeared in that second.

"What is it?" I whispered, almost afraid to follow her gaze. I turned my head but was pushed from behind as Mom yelled, "Move!"

I pitched forward and slammed into Lailah, who thankfully saw me coming and half caught me in her outstretched hands.

Behind me, Mom chanted a spell in Latin, her power pulsing with enough magic it sparked my own. I tried to turn back to her, but this time Kat caught my other arm, and she and Lailah dragged me out of the gorgeous plantation house.

"Stop! Let go." I flailed, trying to twist and turn, but neither gave an inch. Once we were outside, I expected them to drop their hold. They didn't. Instead, they marched me to Kane's car and shoved me into the passenger seat.

"Hey. Watch it," I said when my head grazed the top of the doorframe.

"Sorry," Kat said. "This is for your own good."

I would've stood, but both of them were blocking me in the car. It took all my willpower not to kick either of them in the shins. "What the hell was that?"

"The ghost, Jade," Kat said, her eyes wide with disbelief. "She was coming back down the stairs, and with every inch, she was getting more and more solid. It's like you were feeding her energy."

"That's exactly what's happening," Lailah said, backing off and pacing once more.

Then Pyper ran out of the house. "Lailah, Hope needs you!"

Lailah looked me dead in the eye. "Stay!" She nodded at Kat. "Sit on her if you have to."

"Will do." Kat shifted to stand directly in front of me, only moving when Pyper appeared

"Oh, my God. That was freaky." Pyper sat on the grass in front of my feet and pulled out her phone.

I snatched it from her. "No one's calling anyone until I get some answers. What's going on in there?"

Kat held her hands palms up. "I don't know. All I'm doing is keeping you away from the ghost."

Pyper reached for her phone and scowled when I wouldn't give it back. "Well, I don't know either. It sounded like Hope was trying to bind her or banish her. I'm not sure. But damn, wasn't that weird how she almost looked alive? Except her eyes." Pyper shuddered and gazed at me. "Life with you around is never dull."

Her phone buzzed and instead of answering it, I turned it off.

"Hey!"

"Whoever it is, you can call them back."

"What if it was Kane?" Pyper held out her hand as if her question solved everything.

"Again, you can call him back."

She pursed her lips and shook her head. I was trying to figure out if she was getting angry or if she was amused. It was impossible for me to tell.

"He's going to be pissed, you know." This time she smiled. A genuine one. "When he finds out you're playing with ghosts again."

"I'm not playing with anyone." I scowled, wishing I could shove the key in the ignition and drive off, leaving my pain-in-the-ass friends behind. But the caterers were coming. I couldn't stand them up. "Move, I think they need my help."

"I don't think so." Kat shifted aside, revealing Lailah, Gwen, and my mom moving toward us.

I climbed out of the car and sidestepped Pyper. "What happened? Is she gone?"

Mom and Gwen nodded, but Lailah shook her head.

"Oh, Lailah, no," Mom said. "Really?"

"I'm afraid so." Lailah turned to me. "I'm sorry. The ghost is somehow connected to the house. We tried to banish her from the premises, but even though I could feel the spell working, it failed in the end."

"All right." I took a calming breath. "I've lived with a ghost before. It can't be that bad." A tremor ran through me as I remembered the dull, lifeless little girl in my arms. "Other than possession, I mean. Is there a way to guard against that?"

"Sure," Mom said. "There are spells and wards. We can whip something up."

Lailah shook her head again. "Not this time, Hope. I hate to say it, but I think Jade and Kane are going to need to find a new wedding venue."

A new venue? Hell no. This was Kane's family house. We had to get married there. "Lailah." I grabbed her arm and shook her slightly. "What aren't you telling me?"

We all stilled and went silent, waiting for the answer.

"Shit," Lailah mumbled. "I wanted to talk to Bea first, but this is too serious to wait."

I stared her down, my arms crossed over my chest.

"It's your soul," she said weakly. "The ghost can possess you because Meri has the other half. You're an easy target."

My stomach dropped to my feet. I knew the soul-splitting thing would come back to haunt me. I didn't realize it would be literally. "So you're saying anytime a ghost is near, it can possess me?" Lovely. What if I got an evil bastard like Roy again? Jesus. Life just kept getting better and better.

"I don't know about *any* ghost. But this one can. And it's full possession. That's what I felt in the car on the way over here."

I furrowed my brows. "Why is that, do you think?"

Lailah's shoulders slumped. "It's the angel directive. I'm still connected to your soul. Because the ghost is trying to use yours, I feel it."

My chest constricted, and I struggled to suck in a breath. "Are you saying the ghost could steal my soul?"

Her sad eyes met mine. "It's possible."

Why did this crap always happen to me?

I slammed my hand down on the roof of the car, barely noticing the pain racing up my forearm. "Goddamned son of a bitch! Can't a witch catch a break?"

"Fuck me," Pyper whispered.

"So this is why you can't stay for the caterers. Or be here at all. We need Bea. She's our best shot for exorcising the ghost," Lailah said reasonably.

"But—"

"Pyper and I will stay," Kat said. "We'll let them know you had an emergency. We'll sample everything and bring you the best of the lot to choose from. Would that work?"

"What if the ghost tries to possess someone else? I mean, right now I'm the easy target, but with me gone, she might try one of you."

Lailah shook her head. "They're all too strong. She can't get in. Their souls won't allow it."

"Oh." I furrowed my brow. "What about Meri? Is she in danger too?"

She shrugged. "I don't know, to tell you the truth. She's an angel, so it might be different for her."

"We need to call her."

"I'll do it," Mom said.

Pyper stood next to Kat and smirked. "As much as you know I *love* ghosts, I'd be happy to help Kat deal with the caterers. Want us to meet you back in the city in a couple of hours?"

I sighed, wishing none of us had to be there. Pyper had been tortured in another reality by Roy, the evil ghost, some months back. She was dealing with it by helping her boyfriend, Ian, hunt ghosts. Sort of like ripping off a bandage. But this was much more terrifying than anything Ian dealt with.

"What's the point?" I threw my hands up in defeat. "If we can't get married here, we might as well start over. And no venue is going to be available at this late date." I closed my eyes and tried not to cry. This was where Kane's grandparents had gotten married. It was where he'd always wanted his ceremony. It was what I wanted too. I gazed at the beautiful house, sorrow filling my heart.

Lailah put an arm around my shoulders. "I don't think there's reason to lose hope. I'm confident there's a way to get rid of your house guest before the wedding. Let Pyper and Kat do the initial testing, and you can do the rest of your planning from Kane's house. Five weeks is a long time to get rid of an unpleasant ghost."

"I guess." I let her stuff me into her car, and I handed Kane's keys to Pyper. "Be careful. If anything strange happens, just get out. Okay?"

"Don't worry, shortcake," Mom said with a soft smile. "Gwen and I will be here. We'll watch over your friends."

Mom was a powerful witch. If she was strong enough to take on a demon and survive, she was strong enough to take on a ghost. "Thanks, Mom."

The four of them stood under the moss-filled tree, watching as Lailah and I sped off down the driveway.

I turned to her. "If you ever keep information like that from me again, I'll curse you into next year."

She laughed. "I'd like to see you try."

Chapter 3

Lailah drove through the gate of Bea's family home in the Garden District and pulled around to the back, where her carriage house sat among the rows of blooming azaleas.

I peered out the window and frowned. "Her curtains are shut."

Lailah shrugged. "Maybe she was vacuuming naked."

I sent her a flat stare. "Funny."

"I thought so." Lailah smiled, put the car in park, and opened her door.

Slowly, I followed. Besides my half-soul and the danger of being possessed, there was something very wrong. Over the last seven months, I'd never once seen Bea's house closed up. She loved cheerfulness and sunshine. The inside was even painted yellow, and practically every soft surface was covered with sunflower fabric.

"I don't think she's home," I said, dragging my feet across the cement.

"Her car is here." Lailah gestured at the gray Prius and then knocked on the door.

I stood at the bottom of the porch. For some reason, I couldn't bring myself to move any closer. The whole house seemed to be vibrating with bad juju. My mind tingled as if I could sense its energy, but not quite. I narrowed my eyes, trying to place the sensation.

When no one answered the door, Lailah stepped to the side, trying to peer through the covered windows. What? Did she think she had X-ray vision? Or did she have some weird angel gift I didn't know about?

Something foreboding grew in my gut, making my stomach churn. It was as if a dark force had crawled into my soul and manifested into an early warning system. "Lailah," I said, my voice low, but commanding, "step away from the door."

"I know she's here, Jade. Give me a minute."

I pressed my palm to my stomach as the ball of trepidation grew in my core. I squeezed my eyes closed and focused. This wasn't someone else's fear. This belonged solely to me. Every instinct was on high alert. And right then, deep in the fiber of my being, I knew danger was lurking in the shadows, just moments from striking.

"Lailah!" With two steps, I bounded up the stairs, wrapped my arms around her middle, and yanked her backward.

"Oomph!" she cried, stumbling into me.

My foot slipped off the top step, and with yelps of alarm, we both tumbled off the porch.

Shit, that hurt! Darts of pain screamed through my elbow and my hip as I tried to roll Lailah off me. "Move!" I pushed her away and scrambled to my feet, ignoring the twinge in my ankle.

"Jade! What the hell?" She pulled herself up on her knees, not appearing hurt in the least. Of course not, she'd landed on top of me.

"Look." I pointed toward the window.

She almost had her feet under her when she glanced up. Then she froze. "What the…?"

Right there on the porch, in front of the window, stood an ethereal couple. He was tall and thin with a narrow mustache, wearing a three-piece suit. She was a foot shorter, adorned in a sleeveless sheath dress and long pearls. I could see right through them.

"Get in the car," Lailah ordered, backing up.

I was already pulling open the passenger door. Holy Jesus. Was I going to see ghosts everywhere I went now? The pair floated inches from the ground, their eyes fixed on me. I couldn't tear my gaze from them. The fear gripped my stomach, making me catch my breath. "Get me out of here," I whispered to Lailah once we were both in the car.

Her tires squealed as she whipped the tiny car around and sped down the driveway.

"Are you all right?" she asked when we stopped a few minutes later at a red light.

I took a deep breath, willing the unease in my stomach to settle. "Just take me home. To Kane's, I mean." Kane and I were already living together in his shotgun double in the French Quarter. Well, when we weren't at the plantation house. I used to live in the apartment above Kane's club on Bourbon Street. Technically, it was still mine. My furniture was still there. So was my ghost dog, Duke.

Duke.

Was he okay? Would these new ghosts have any effect on him? Maybe he could protect me. Oh, God. Would he be able to possess me? I did not want to go through life drooling like a golden retriever. I slumped against the window. "Since when does Bea have house ghosts?"

Lailah shook her head. "I've never seen them before. But that doesn't mean they haven't always been there."

"They're new." I closed my eyes, trying to block out the creepy figures burned in my mind. "Wouldn't I have noticed them when I was staying there?"

After my soul split, I'd spent a week recovering at Bea's house while she watched over me. Absolutely nothing out of the ordinary had happened during my stay. It had been the most peaceful week of my life.

"Maybe," Lailah mumbled and took a sharp right onto Saint Charles. "But Camille has always been in the plantation house and this is the first time she's come after you. Haven't you and Kane been spending a lot of time there since Christmas?"

I chewed on my lip. "Yeah."

"Something's different, then." Lailah gripped the wheel. "Something's changed."

I let out a hollow laugh. "Yeah. A ghost tried to take my body." A shiver ran through me, and I curled inward, wishing I were in bed with the covers pulled over my head. "We need to find Bea and make sure she's okay. What if the ghosts are terrorizing her, too?"

Lailah sped through a yellow light. At the last second, she swerved left.

I eyed her. "Where are you going?" We shouldn't have turned for another dozen blocks.

"To get answers." A few moments later, she pulled the car into a narrow driveway and parked between two brick buildings.

"The Herbal Connection? I thought you said Bea wasn't there." I pushed open the door and climbed out.

"She could be in the back working on spells. If not, her plans might be written on her calendar." Lailah hit the remote on her key, and the car beeped, signaling it was locked. "Let's go. I don't want you on the street any longer than necessary. Anything could be hanging around out here."

I glanced around. "Like what? Tourists?" The French Quarter was always full of people, and definitely a lot of odd people, but it was rare to run into another witch or angel. There just weren't that many of us.

She let out an impatient huff and grabbed my arm. "*Ghosts*, Jade. Ghosts. You know the Quarter is haunted."

Jesus Christ on a cracker. Of course there were ghosts. My heart thundered. Would I be safe anywhere in the city? What about Kane's house? Or my apartment? It had already been haunted once. The ghost had left, but what if there were others hanging around? I let Lailah pull me to Bea's shop and waited as she unlocked the door. In addition to being Bea's guardian angel, Lailah was also her shop assistant.

We shuffled into the dark store. The smell of fresh rain and sea salt permeated the air, and for a brief moment, my shoulders actually relaxed. It was the welcoming charm Lailah had invented, unique to each patron, bringing the person whatever his or her favorite scent was. Mine happened to be the beach and Kane's cologne. In any case, the calm was short-lived. I tensed. What if the store had lingering ghostly visitors?

"This way." Lailah tugged on my arm, pulling me through the neatly organized rows to a door marked *Witches' Sanctuary.*

At least I thought it was a door. But there wasn't a knob. Lailah placed her hand flat on the surface and whispered her name. The area around her hand glowed blue and then turned white as it melded with her aura.

I squinted, fighting the desire to shield my eyes. Holy crap, her inner light was bright.

The door gave a soft click and swung open.

"Illuminate," Lailah said. Hundreds of candles lining the walls flickered to life.

"Wow. I guess that's one way to keep the electric bill low."

Lailah rolled her eyes and strode to the writing desk farthest from the entrance. While she rummaged around, I stood in the middle of the room, noted this side of the door had a handle, and then took in the two stainless steel work stations. The one to the right was impeccable, not a beaker or jar out of place. The one to the left had half-filled jars of brightly colored liquid weighing down a bunch of scattered notes. I moved closer, eyeing the concoctions. Each one had a label naming the contents, and upon careful inspection, I realized the papers beneath were detailed notes of the experiments.

"What's Bea working on?" I asked, sniffing the beaker with the electric blue liquid.

Lailah turned and raised one eyebrow. "Nothing, apparently." She tilted her head toward the empty work station.

Ah, I should've known. Lailah had once mentioned that she was a skilled inventor. I put the liquid down and jammed my hands in my skirt pockets. "Any luck?"

She tossed the day planner on the desk and shook her head. "No."

I leaned against the counter. "Now what?"

She frowned, pulled out her phone, and called Bea. Sighing, she left a short message. "It went straight to voicemail."

Damn, where was she?

Lailah stared at her phone and then closed her eyes, rubbing her forehead with one hand as if praying for strength.

"Lailah?"

Her calm, take-charge attitude had left the building. She gave her head a little shake. "Sorry. It's just I haven't talked to him since the hearing."

"Who?" I asked with no small amount of suspicion. "You're talking about Philip, aren't you?"

The pain in her eyes told me everything I needed to know. I took three long steps and pulled her phone from her hand. "No. You don't need to call him. We'll wait here for Bea. Or Lucien, he might know. Or hell, even Ian. He's a ghost hunter. He knows a few things about keeping them away."

She placed a light hand on my arm and led me back to her work station. "See this?" She pointed at the blue liquid I'd asked about.

"Yeah."

"The scent tricks you into thinking everything's fine. It's a soothing potion. And this one?" She picked up the scarlet-red potion. "Its scent is an aphrodisiac. Guaranteed to lower your lover's inhibitions."

I eyed it, and an image of Kane stepping out of the shower, wet and warm, and smelling of fresh rain, flashed through my mind. Hmm. What exactly would happen if I—

"Jade." Lailah waved a hand in front of my face. "Now isn't the time."

I swallowed. "Sorry." Heat flooded my cheeks, and I smiled sheepishly.

"For the love of...never mind. The point is, my skills lie with illusion. I can trick the brain into thinking pretty much anything. It's quite useful for healing enhancements, actually. If the brain thinks you're well, then it usually provides the body with what it needs to get better. But I can't keep ghosts away from you or trick your soul into being more than it is. Even if your brain believes, your soul has its own power. It isn't ruled by your mind."

"So? What does any of that have to do with calling Philip?" He was an angel who guarded souls. Well, technically he was supposed to guard mine, but he was sort of MIA. Lailah had taken over. And good thing, too. If I saw him, I'd likely curse him into another dimension. The traitor.

"He's been your soul guardian for twenty-seven years. No angel is better equipped to help you than he is."

"You are," I said dismissively. No way was I dealing with Philip. He'd tried to give my soul to Meri, the angel who'd turned demon and then turned angel again. And Philip still thought he'd made the right decision.

Lailah reached out, hesitated, and then took my hand.

I stared at the union with more than a little shock. Lailah and I had become friends since our stint with the angel council, but we weren't close. Not close enough to be touchy-feely, anyway.

She squeezed my fingers. "I can't protect you from possession. Remember what happened last time with Pyper?"

Six months ago, Lailah had tried to perform a ritual to free Pyper from her evil spirit. Only it had gone horribly wrong, and Pyper had ended up in an alternate reality. "That was different. Roy was evil. You couldn't tell what was going on."

"And I can't now, either! Look, as much as I hate to admit it, Philip does know something about ghosts. He'll probably have a decent idea of what to do."

I scoffed. "Oh, really? Then where was he when I was being haunted by Roy? Huh? According to him, he's been my guardian since I was born. But he sure as hell wasn't around then."

She shrugged her shoulders slightly. "The thing is, you weren't haunted by Roy. Pyper was. You were haunted by Bobby, who was protecting you. As far as Philip could see, Bobby would've gone on protecting you if I hadn't trapped him with that spell. There wasn't anything Philip needed to do."

Shit. She was right. While Pyper had been suffering at the hands of Roy, I'd had Bea's brother haunting me. And it hadn't been unpleasant. Not in the least. Except when Kane was around. The ghost had been a little jealous. But he'd moved on when he realized I wasn't who he thought I was.

I ground my teeth, hating that I needed to rely on the good-for-nothing piece of angel turd. "Can we go home first? I'd really like to be on my own ground if we're going to have to endure the bastard."

Lailah glanced around the work area. "It appears safe here."

"I know, but I want to see Kane." God, I was starting to sound like one of those clingy housewives. What was wrong with me?

The frustration lining her face made me take a step back and study her. The one thing about Lailah was that, even though I no longer had my empath ability, I pretty much always knew how she was feeling about me. She was almost always either exasperated or angry. Our relationship was special like that. Except now, she appeared a little scared. "Lailah?"

"What?" she huffed out.

"What are you frightened of? A ghost possessing me, or seeing Philip?"

Her nostrils flared, and right away I had my answer.

"Philip," I confirmed confidently. "And you'd rather see him on your turf, right?"

She jerked one shoulder in a quick acknowledgement.

"Okay. We can have him come here. But let me call Kane... and Ian," I added reluctantly.

Lailah gave me a skeptical look. "If you say so."

I frowned. Of all people, Lailah should be one who believed in the ability to banish a ghost. Heck, we'd done it together when we'd kicked Roy's ass into Hell. "Do you need food? Is your blood sugar low?"

She straightened. "No. Why? Are you trying to say I'm cranky?"

"If the shoe fits..."

Chapter 4

"Dammit, Kane." I hit the End button on my phone and scowled.

"No answer?" Lailah flipped through one of Bea's spell books.

I shook my head. Where was that fiancé of mine? I'd already called his office, but the receptionist said he'd left. Now he wasn't answering his cell phone. Sighing, I hit Ian's number and sat on a stool behind the store counter.

"Jade?" Kane's frantic voice carried over the connection.

"Kane?" I pulled the phone from my ear and squinted at the screen. Ian's number stared back at me.

"Where are you?" he asked. Muffled voices filled the background.

"Bea's shop. Why do you have Ian's phone? And why aren't you answering yours?"

"I left it at the office. I'll be right there." The background noise vanished.

"Kane? You there?" I glanced at the screen. *Call ended.* My hands started to shake. Why was he so worried? What was happening that I didn't know about?

Lailah slammed the book closed. "There's nothing in here about warding off ghost possessions."

"It's a spell book. What did you expect?" I pressed Ian's number again. It went straight to voicemail. My heart sank.

Kane was *never* unreachable. And where the hell was Ian? "Son of a...ugh."

"Witches have been known to deal with ghosts before," Lailah said idly.

I turned to stare at her. "What's going on?"

She shrugged. "How should I know? You're the one calling all your boyfriends."

"Ian is *not* my boyfriend. We went on one date. One horrible, awful date. He's with Pyper now."

"Yeah. Whatever." She spun and headed down an aisle toward the back of the store.

"Lailah." I put my phone on the counter and followed her, irritated at the snide remark. She stood in front of a display of essential oils, pretending to inspect the labels. "What's wrong? Ten minutes ago, we were forming a plan. Now you're acting as if this is the last place you want to be. Do you have a problem with me or Ian?"

"No."

"Kane?"

"Of course not." She pulled the cap off one of the bottles. The sweet scent of lavender tickled my nose.

I inched closer, wondering how I was going to get through this relationship without my empath gift. "Do you regret being my surrogate soul guardian?" Technically, Philip was still my assigned angel, but Lailah had asked permission to watch over me. I'd thought it was temporary, but she'd informed me we were bound unless she petitioned the council. And neither of us was in a hurry to see them anytime soon.

"No. Not at all. It's just..." She put the lavender oil back on the shelf and faced me.

I raised one eyebrow.

"I called Philip." Her eyes were too bright, filled with a deep hurt she rarely showed anyone.

"Oh," I breathed. I took her hand and led her back to the counter. Philip and Lailah used to have an on-and-off-again relationship after his mate, Meri, had turned demon. The problem was that, once an angel mated, he or she couldn't fully commit to another. And yet, Lailah had fallen for him. She loved a man who could never truly love her back. And I thought prior to meeting Kane I'd had unhealthy relationships. "You don't have to stay when he gets here."

She stiffened. "Yes, I do."

"Lailah—"

"No, Jade. He betrayed you. I don't care what his motive was. I'm not letting you out of my sight when he's around." Her lower lip quivered slightly, and she bit down on it and gave a short shake of her head. "It's just hard. That's all."

"Okay. I hear you." I scanned the shelves, and when I found what I was looking for, I led her to a locked case filled with small vials of potions. "Then we need to get one of these resistance elixirs in you."

She snorted out a laugh. "Seriously? You, the queen of never taking magical enhancements, are suggesting I arm myself with an anti-love potion?"

"Yes," I said indignantly. "You make the stuff, not me. If anyone should feel comfortable taking it, it's you. It doesn't matter how *I* feel about ingesting them."

She chuckled again. "True enough." Then she shrugged. "You might be right." After producing a small key from beneath the counter, Lailah opened the case and plucked out a small vial of red potion. Without any hesitation, she popped the cork and downed it.

"Better?" I asked after she relocked the case.

"Oy, that stuff is strong." She shook her head, her eyes watering a bit. "I won't know until he shows up."

"He's on his way then?" I hadn't known he was still in the area. Though that made sense since Dan, his son, was living across town, sharing a house with Meri. Where else would he go?

"Yes," she said softly and then shuffled into the small restroom near the back of the store.

In the candlelight, I flipped through one of the spell books Lailah had left on the counter, pausing when I came to one titled *Summoning the Spirit.* I scanned the incantation and recognized it as a modification of the one Lailah had performed the day she'd tried to rid Pyper of Roy. I took a bookmark and stuck it between the pages. If Camille or anyone else did possess me, this spell might help. It called upon Selene, the moon Goddess. She was ruler of those who walked the shadows.

Could she help me? Maybe we should call her in advance. The thought sent a tendril of apprehension straight to my gut. That night the Goddess had actually possessed Lailah. Talk about unnerving.

Get a grip, Jade.

A brief appearance by a Goddess was hardly anything to get worked up over. I mean, I'd fought a demon, almost died from black magic, and lost half my soul. How could things get any worse?

The door rattled, followed by an incessant knocking. "Jade! Open up."

Kane. Thank heavens. I ran to the door, struggled with the sticky lock, and finally wrenched it open.

He swept in, grabbing me in a tight embrace. "I'm so sorry, love," he whispered into my hair.

I clutched his broad shoulders and melted into his safe embrace, breathing in the traces of his crisp cologne mixed with his musky male scent. "For what?" I whispered back.

He pulled back just enough to plant a tender kiss on my lips. "For subjecting you to some crazy ghost. Pyper told me what happened. Are you okay?" He scanned my body from head to toe, inspecting every square inch of me. "That's twice now a ghost has tried to harm you." Crushing me to him, he let out a frustrated groan. "Maybe we need to live in a brand new house, one guaranteed to be void of all spirits."

I gently pulled myself from his embrace and closed the door. "It's not your fault. I'm the one who—" I stopped midsentence. "She only surfaces when those candles are lit. Maybe we're overreacting."

"Not likely," a deep voice said from behind Kane.

I jumped, and Kane turned, positioning himself in front of me. I peeked over his shoulder and suppressed a frown. Philip stood in the open doorway, the late afternoon sun bouncing off his light brown hair. His emerald-green eyes were trained on Kane, who no doubt had fury streaming off him. He practically vibrated with it. I placed a tentative hand on Kane's shoulder, a silent request to not kill the man standing before us. His muscles tensed under my fingers.

Philip nodded an acknowledgement to Kane and then met my gaze. "Jade, it's good to see you again."

A low rumble reverberated from Kane's chest.

"Philip," Lailah said, her tone welcoming, "come on in."

I studied her, noting the sudden spark in her eyes. Was that potion working? She looked entirely too happy to see him.

Kane glanced at her, his arms flexing in barely constrained control.

"Kane, move aside and let Philip in. Jade, lock the door, will you?" Without saying a word, Lailah waved one hand around the room. Candlelight flared to life in the sconces on the wall.

Philip glided past us to Lailah and wrapped one hand around her waist as he kissed her cheek in greeting. She tilted her head and smiled up at him. I clenched my teeth at his audacity and moved to flip the deadbolt.

Kane's hand stopped me. "Pyper and Ian will be here in a minute."

"Oh, yeah. Why did you have his phone?" I glanced at Lailah, who was now leaning into Philip, and scowled. The spell most certainly wasn't working.

Kane followed my gaze and shook his head. "Pyper and Ian were getting out of her car when I got home. I helped them carry in the stuff from the caterer, and Pyper had just finished filling me in on what happened at Summer House. Then Ian's phone buzzed. It was lying on the counter, and when I saw your name, I grabbed it."

"Ah." I shook my head. "Understandable, but you didn't let me talk to Ian. And when I called back, it went straight to voicemail."

He narrowed his eyes. "What did you want Ian for?"

"His ghost experience, of course. He says he can exorcise a ghost now."

Kane shook his head. "Right. Because he did such a great job last time."

I took a step back and studied him. Kat had recommended Ian when I'd realized my apartment was haunted. All I'd wanted was peace and quiet, and all Ian had wanted was to study the ghost. Unfortunately, he'd never actually gotten around to trying to expel the ghost. Bea and Lailah had done that in the end. "You know he's had some success lately. Just last week, he managed to cleanse a jewelry shop on Saint Peters."

"Or so he says," Kane mumbled.

The bells on the door chimed, and Pyper rushed in, followed by Ian, who had his hands full of equipment. I refrained from rolling my eyes. I had wanted him to come, after all. But the ghost wasn't here. She was back at the house.

Kane turned the lock on the door and guided me back to where Lailah and Philip stood, laughing.

"What's so funny?" I demanded, gaping at them.

Lailah let out another gale of laughter and placed a limp hand on Philip's chest. "Oh, Jade," she gasped out, "you're going to die when you hear this."

Her response triggered a deep chuckle from Philip, and both of them cracked up.

Crossing my arms over my chest, I glared at her. "Lailah."

"Hold on a sec." She sucked in a breath, tried to speak, and fell into Philip, hanging on as she struggled to collect herself.

"Jesus. Is she drunk?" Pyper asked, her eyes wide with disbelief.

"Not unless she was guzzling booze in the bathroom." I turned my attention to Philip.

Noticing my glare, he sobered and clasped Lailah's shoulders, steadying her. "Sorry. Now isn't the time."

"But—" Lailah started.

"Later." He smiled down at her and placed a light kiss on her nose.

Her eyes lit up, and she gazed at him with lovesick wonder. What. The. Hell? What happened to that potion? She seemed more like she'd taken ecstasy instead of some resistance drug. Good Goddess.

"Um, I hate to interrupt," Ian hedged.

"Please do." I waved an arm, hoping he'd distract me from the disturbing pair.

"Thanks." He gave me a sheepish smile. "Do you mind if I set up my equipment? I want to get a reading as soon as possible."

"The ghost isn't here," I said. "She's at Summer House."

"Right." Ian glanced at Pyper. She nodded her encouragement. He cleared his throat. "You know I've been gathering a lot of data the last six months."

"Yeah." The word came out clipped, almost hostile.

Kane's hand tightened on mine. He pulled me closer and placed a soothing kiss on my temple. "You did call *him*, love," he whispered in my ear.

"Right." I met Ian's frustrated gaze. "Sorry. I'm a little on edge. You were saying?"

He cleared his throat. "Well, before the soul-splitting, we already knew you were susceptible to spirits. They affected you more than the average person."

"Yeah," I said again, only this time I stretched the word out in hesitation. "Lailah, too, because of our gifts."

Ian nodded enthusiastically. "Yes. But since then, I haven't had a chance to get a read on you. I think it's best we do that before another ghost shows up, so I have a baseline. Do you mind? The sooner the better."

I glanced at Lailah. She was pressed against Philip, rubbing her hand over his chest. My stomach turned. "Okay. Fine. There's a lab back here." I moved to the door, desperate to get away from Lailah's embarrassing display. Had she taken a harlot potion by mistake? I'd never seen her act so odd before. I glanced at Ian. "That'll be better, right?"

"Perfect. Otherwise, we'd need to kick everyone out."

The twitch of Kane's right eye told me he wouldn't be going anywhere. I smiled at him. "We'll be right back."

"I've heard that before," Kane ground out.

Pyper slid to stand next to him. "Chill, Captain Cranky Pants. All Ian is going to do is turn on some equipment and take some readings. It'll take less than ten minutes, and we'll be right here."

Furrowing his brow, he bent his head, his dark locks covering one eye. "Captain Cranky Pants?"

She grinned.

I shook my head at the ridiculousness in the shop and stalked into the lab.

Ian followed, juggling his cameras and EMF readers. Once he got inside, he kicked the door shut and moved to the clean work station. "What the hell is going on with Philip and Lailah?"

"Her resistance potion went haywire."

His eyebrows shot up. "What was she supposed to be resisting?"

"Philip."

He laughed. "I think the label must have been switched. Her behavior looks like the inhibition blocker Aunt Bea's been working on."

Wonderful. "I'll be right back." I stalked to the door and pulled it open just enough to poke my head out. "Pyper?"

She slid past Kane and joined me. "What do you need?"

"Do whatever you can to keep Lailah away from Philip. She accidently took some potion that's making her act crazy. When she comes out of this, she'll be mortified by her behavior."

A sly smile moved over Pyper's lips. "Sure. Consider it done."

"Thanks." I gave Kane a tiny wave and disappeared back into the lab.

"Ready?" Ian asked.

I glanced around, noting the three video cameras, an old-fashioned tape recorder, his 35mm camera, and a notebook. "Wow, you're getting proficient at this."

"It's been a busy six months."

"I guess so." My feet were silent on the carpeted floor as I moved to his side. "Want me to do anything special?"

"Nah. Just hang with me. I might have you say a few things, but other than that, this really is just for a baseline. I don't expect to catch anything here."

"Gotcha. I'm ready."

Ian set his notebook down, took my hand in his, and said a protection prayer, the one he'd used in my apartment the last time I'd been haunted. I squeezed my eyes shut, trying to block out unexpected memories of Roy and the glass box I'd been trapped in while he tried to torture me. Every muscle tensed as I fought the rising panic.

"Relax, Jade," Ian soothed. "It's just a prayer."

I let out a long breath. "I know."

With his hand on the small of my back, Ian guided me around the room, pausing for a moment in front of each of the cameras and the recorder. When we came full circle, he stepped back and grabbed his notebook. "Repeat after me."

I nodded.

"Visitors of the afterlife, we seek your acknowledgement. If you're here with us today, please make yourself known."

I hesitated. Inviting ghosts to do anything other than leave made me uncomfortable, especially after what happened at Summer House.

"Jade?" Ian questioned.

"Do I have to? I really don't want to invite trouble."

He pursed his lips. "Understandable. I just wanted a clean baseline. You don't have to."

I breathed a sigh of relief. "Good. I don't think I could take another possession, not after what Camille—" An icy-cold presence stabbed me right below my heart and spread with a gust of fury through my core. I groaned, clutching the edge of the worktable.

"Jade?" Ian's worried voice seemed far off in the distance.

"Camille," I grunted out. "She's here." The fog took over, blurring my senses. Ian's form went translucent as everything else faded to black and white.

A faint "What?" reached my ears. I tried to respond, but my mouth wasn't mine. I was so cold my teeth should've been chattering. Instead, I stood tall and composed, frozen and trapped inside my own mind by a ghost.

Camille! I shouted, though I formed no words. *Get the hell out of my body.*

Chapter 5

A faint No answered my demand. With Camille at the controls, my body moved forward, stopping inches from Ian. It was as if I were a marionette, totally helpless.

Damn you, Camille! Get the hell out of my body!

She gazed at Ian intently and then reached out a tentative hand and gently caressed his cheek.

He jumped back. "Jade, what are you doing?"

It's not me you, idiot! Are you a damn ghost hunter or not? Jesus. Wasn't my touch cold? Weren't any of his devices registering anything?

Foreign longing and sadness filled me up and pressed on my heart. A tall, lanky blond man, somewhat resembling Ian, played in my mind. He held hands with the small girl I'd seen in Camille's earlier vision, only this time, the girl was very much alive and staring adoringly up at the man. He wore a brown tweed suit, and the girl wore a simple cotton long-sleeved dress. Church. They'd just come from church. I was sure of it.

A tiny high-pitched whimper escaped my lips, and Camille pressed closer to Ian.

He froze, glancing past me. His edges started to blur. All I could make out was his monochromatic form as he tried to side-step me.

"Stop." Camille's high-pitched voice was gone, replaced by a lower register, but it still wasn't my own. She brought both of my hands up, resting them on either side of Ian's face. "I've waited so long. Don't deny me now."

No, no, no, I cried again.

She moved in, tentatively touching his lips with mine, and pressed my body against him, wrapping my arms around him in a lover's embrace.

In an odd, detached universe, I felt my tongue dart into Ian's mouth and my hands run through his soft hair. Camille's pleasure shuddered through me, while I mentally recoiled. This was Ian, Pyper's boyfriend, and some crazy ghost was using me to have her way with him. Why was he letting me kiss him? I made a mental note to kick his ass later.

Her kiss deepened, turning more heated, and she moaned. The sound seemed to trigger something in Ian, and his hands shot out, knocking my body backward.

"Hey," Camille scolded gently.

Ian grabbed his backpack and pulled out some sort of smudge stick. "Stay back! I don't know who you are, but you aren't Jade."

Finally. It took him long enough.

He rounded on me, forcing Camille deeper into the lab, and then he backed up, clutching the doorknob.

"No!" Camille cried, her now high voice full of panic. "Don't! I just wanted a little time with you. Please."

Ian's eyes narrowed as he studied me. After a moment, he nodded and released the door handle. "All right. Let's sit." He nodded at the stool in front of Lailah's work station.

"Oh, Branson. Thank you."

"Who's Branson?" Ian asked.

She didn't respond. As she walked, I felt as if I were floating in a bubble. Mentally, I pushed against Camille's spirit, straining to regain even a tiny bit of control. Nothing. My effort met a brick wall and bounced back at me, causing vertigo and more shades of black and white.

My head started to pound, and I realized all the fighting I was doing was with myself. She had me fully contained while she maintained complete control over my body.

I wanted to scream. Cry. Pound my fists on someone. But I couldn't do anything other than witness the scene with Ian and the crazy ghost who thought he was someone named Branson.

Ian slipped his hand into his pocket and pulled out a tiny recorder. Pressing a button, he placed it on the counter. "Who are you?"

"You don't know me?" she asked, pouting. "But we spent so much time together at Summer House."

"Camille." Ian nodded.

A tingle of happiness rippled through me. It made me nauseated. *Camille, he's not Branson. He's Ian. A friend of mine. Get out of my body!*

The ghost paid me no attention and straightened, holding her head high. "Branson," she cooed.

"How long has it been?" Ian asked. "Since we've seen each other, I mean?"

Camille moved us closer to Ian.

He put out his hand. "Let's just talk for now. It's been a while, hasn't it?"

Darkness clouded my already altered vision, and I felt her tense. "You've been gone too long."

Ian nodded. "I thought so. Do you know when I left?"

What in the world was he doing? Shouldn't he be trying to expel her from my body, instead of having a freaking conversation?

"I…" She glanced at the carpeted floor, confusion mixed with anger swirling in my body. Heat burned through to my skin, and my head snapped up. "You left us. She died. You were gone, and she died!" Camille leaped toward Ian, nails brandished like a feral banshee. "It's your fault, you no-good bastard. Lizzie's gone, and it's your fault."

Ian was on his feet faster than Camille could maneuver my body. Jumping to the left, he grabbed his smudge stick and lit it with one of the candles nestled in a sconce on the wall. "That's enough! Spirit of the other world, you do not belong here. Release Jade and return to your place of rest."

Camille slowed and came to a stop in front of Ian. She breathed in the sage, not even affected one little bit.

Shit! Now what?

A high-pitched giggle flowed from my lips. "You don't understand."

Holding the smudge stick high, Ian waved it again. "By the power of the moon Goddess, I command you to release your host. You are no longer welcome here."

Hot anger slithered from the depths of the ghost and crawled over my skin, making me recoil deeper into my mental cocoon. With a surge of venom, Camille whirled, grabbed a liquid-filled jar from Lailah's station and hurled it across the room. "Never! Her body is mine."

Ian flung himself to the floor as the jar whizzed inches from his skull and shattered against a metal cabinet.

Then, all hell broke loose. Liquid dripped from the cabinet and pooled in a small puddle. A vapor rose from the potion, forming dark shadows. They twisted and writhed as they split off from one another into six distinct forms, each one becoming more solid with each passing moment.

"Fuck!" Ian cried, scrambling to his feet. He'd just reached my uncooperative body when the door slammed open.

In poured Mom, Philip, and Lailah.

Mom. Please don't let anything happen to her. She'd been home from Purgatory for over three months, but due to the time I'd been held captive in the angel realm, we still hadn't had much of a chance to reconnect. And here she was, battling Goddess knows what.

Philip stopped beside me, while Mom and Lailah rushed to contain whatever Camille had unleashed. Phillip placed one measured hand on my shoulder, and Camille whirled. "Branson?"

Oh, Jesus Christ on toast. Did she think every male was this Branson character?

"Yes, sweetheart," he said soothingly. "I'm here."

If I'd had any say in my body's functionality, I would have gaped. A smile tugged at my lips, and Camille glided me into his arms.

Philip pulled me close, running a light hand through my hair. "It's all right now, darling. I'm here. Whatever it is, I'll fix it."

Camille's tears filled my eyes, and I sniffled. Across the room, voices chanted, and I sensed a strong magic current humming somewhere nearby.

"You'll find her now?" Camille asked Philip.

"Yes, darling." His voice was low, whispering in her ear as a lover would. "Shh, don't be upset. She'll be home soon, I promise."

"Home." She sighed. "Can we go there now? I want to get the house ready for when you find her."

"Sure. In a moment." He pulled back from the embrace, staring over my shoulder.

Magic materialized, seemingly from thin air, and filled me like an electric shock. It rushed into my mind. Frantically, I grappled for it, but it slipped away as fast as it had rushed in. Only a trickle of the magic thread remained. I focused on it, somehow keeping the spark connected to my mind. The tiny bit of power seemed to give me a modicum of strength. I held on tightly, praying I had an opportunity to use it.

"Branson," Camille whined. "I'm tired. Take me—"

"*Pello Pepulli Pulsum!*" Philip's voice rose above the commotion, filling my ears.

Heavy magic pressed in on me from all sides, stabbing and testing, forcing its way under my skin. Searing heat rippled through my blood, frying me from the inside out. My silent screams echoed in the recesses of my mind. I had a sudden vision of a mental patient bound and drugged. That was what I'd become: a prisoner in my own mind.

Camille carried us backward, screaming everything I wanted to but couldn't. "No! What have you done? It hurts. Make it stop. Branson, make it go away."

Frantically, she ran about the room and headed straight into the cluster of black shadows Mom and Lailah were containing.

I was doomed. But the tendril of magic still played in my mind. Maybe if I got the chance, I could zap one of them. I squinted through the hazy fog, catching sight of Mom. She stood tall and strong, watching me. So did Lailah. Why weren't they doing anything?

Then Philip and Ian joined them, forming a circle around me, Camille, and the shadows. Together, they raised their arms and shouted, "*Pello Pepulli Pulsum!*"

The dark shadows clung to me, their invading fingers reaching deep, passing through me, searching while Camille writhed. "Nooo," she whimpered and fell to my knees. The dark shadows froze, and then, as one, the six of them slithered inside of me with white-hot stabs of heat. My muscles constricted, screaming in protest at the agony scorching my body.

I mentally curled into a ball, wishing I could rock the pain away. The magic sparked in my mind, and when a soul-wrenching spasm hit me, I released it, hoping to find a small dose of relief. But as soon as the magic sparked, the shadows vanished, and my body convulsed as it tried to rip itself apart right there on the floor of the lab. The world snapped back to color, so bright my eyes watered. Or was that from pain? I couldn't tell. All I knew was that Camille was gone and there was a fire in my sternum, right where I could usually find my soul.

Kane's face floated over mine right before the world flashed white, and suddenly, everything was blissfully numb.

"Jade?" The faint sound of my mom's voice entered my awareness. "Honey, wake up."

Pain stabbed in time with my heartbeat just below my breastbone. I winced but didn't open my eyes. Something told me even fluttering my eyelids would hurt.

"Jade?" Mom said again.

I tried to moan an acknowledgement but couldn't seem to manage even that. Hushed voices mumbled in the background.

"I thought you said your plan was harmless?" Mom snapped. "Look at her. She's black and blue."

"I can help with that." The southern drawl of my mentor rang in my ears.

"Bea," I croaked out through barely movable lips.

"Jade!" Mom exclaimed.

I cracked my eyelids enough to make out Mom hovering over me.

She smiled and pressed a gentle hand to my head. I winced. "Sorry," she said and scowled at someone on my other side. I didn't bother to find out who.

"Bea," I said again.

"Yes, dear. I'm here." She took Mom's place and gazed down at me, her eyes bright with concern.

"Herbal enhancements?"

A smile cracked her worried expression. "You're not going to fight me this time?"

"Not today." I'd had a bad habit of refusing Bea's enhanced healing herbs right up until I'd come back from the angel realm with half a soul. She hadn't given me much choice after that, and I'd kind of gotten used to them. Now she couldn't help teasing me after all the months I spent shunning them.

"I have one right here." She turned, holding out her hand. Someone handed her a cup of water and a little green pill. "Here."

"Just the pill," I said and opened my mouth. Pulling myself up to deal with a cup wasn't an option.

Bea scanned my body and frowned.

"It's bad. The pill?" I prompted.

Bea nodded and placed the enhancement on my tongue. The miracle drug started to work instantly, dulling the agony to almost tolerable levels.

"Hey, where have you been?" I asked her. "We were afraid the ghosts got you."

She raised a skeptical eyebrow. "What ghosts?"

"The ones at your house."

She frowned. "There aren't any ghosts at my house."

"We saw some today," I said, "me and Lailah. Outside your house. We were afraid you were in danger."

"No, dear. I was out visiting a friend. I'm perfectly safe." Her tone was light, but worry lines crinkled around her eyes. She placed a sure hand on my arm. "Are you okay?"

I nodded out of some weird sense of appeasement. I clearly wasn't all right.

"Jade?" Kane said, gently caressing my hand.

I turned my head and met his soothing chocolate brown eyes. "Take me home?" I asked quietly. My mind was too tired to process anything else. I pushed the rest of my questions aside and reached for Kane. "I don't want to be here any longer."

"You've got it, love." Without hesitation he picked me up, gently cradling me in his strong arms. I pressed my face into his chest and breathed. The faint trace of fresh rain filled my senses, and just the scent of him helped clear the angry darkness still clinging to my heart.

Kane had me out of the lab and halfway through the store when Philip stepped in front of him. "You can't leave."

"Watch me," Kane said in a low dangerous tone.

"It's not safe."

"Pearson, I'm only going to say this once." A muscle in Kane's neck pulsed. "Get the fuck away from my fiancée before you find out what it's like to have your soul removed with my fist."

Oh, Jesus. Kane wasn't joking. It was Philip's fault I'd lost half my soul. And he'd testified against me at the angel hearing last month. He'd wanted to give my soul to Meri, his former mate. Yeah. Kane wasn't going to let that go.

Philip held his ground. "I know how you feel, man. I really do. If I were you, I'd have already done the same or worse. But Jade is very vulnerable. If you take her home now and she comes into contact with a ghost, any ghost, I fear she'll be possessed again. She isn't strong enough to ward one off."

Mom took a place beside Kane. "I'll be with her. I can ward off a spirit."

Philip eyed her. "For how long? And what if there's more than one? She already said she saw some at Bea's house. It sounds as if they are following her around. You can't keep a twenty-four-hour vigil. And worse, if Camille shows up again...you saw what happened in there. It took three of us to break her hold."

Mom crossed her arms over her chest and set her jaw stubbornly. "I'll get Bea and Lucien to help me set up wards. Lucien is Jade's second in command of the coven. Surely he and Bea can handle it."

"And if one is already haunting Kane's house? What then?"

Lailah, who seemed subdued and her normal self again, put a tentative hand on Kane's arm. "I know you don't want to hear from Philip right now, but he's right. Jade isn't safe."

Kane clutched me tighter. He stared at the shop door, his body vibrating with restrained action, and for a second, I thought he was going to ignore them both. But then he met Lailah's eyes. "What do you suggest we do then?"

Philip and Lailah shared a glance. Lailah nodded and turned to me. "We need Meri."

"No," I said automatically. Even though Meri had asked the council to restore my soul to me, the fact remained that she was at the center of almost everything, starting with when my mom was abducted and taken to Hell. I understood she'd fallen and the person she was today wasn't responsible for everything that had happened. Still, I found it hard to be around her without all the pain of years past overtaking me.

"But, Jade—" Lailah started.

I pulled back from Kane's chest and twisted to meet her worried gaze. "I said no. She took my mother, Kane, you,

Dan, Bea, and half my soul. Whatever she has to offer, I don't want any of it."

"You don't have a choice," Philip said evenly.

Kane's whole body tensed, and his left hand squeezed my arm so hard I winced. "Sorry," he whispered and relaxed his grip, though his murderous gaze stayed trained on Philip. "Don't ever tell her what to do."

Lailah took a deep breath. "He's not." Then she turned to Philip. "Go in the other room. Your presence isn't helping."

Philip hesitated, but after a pointed look from Lailah, he nodded and retreated to the lab where Ian was still taking measurements.

"Look," she said to us. "The problem is Jade's soul."

"It's fine," I said stubbornly.

"It's not fine. It should be, but it isn't. The reason Camille is able to possess you is because she's able to invade your soul. Philip thinks, and I agree, that if you and Meri are together, your soul will be stronger, and you'll be able to fight any spirits off yourself."

"There's got to be a better solution," Kane said. "What are they going to do, spend every waking hour together?"

Lailah's shoulders slumped. "I don't know, but it's the best answer I've got right now. At least until we can come up with something more concrete."

Mom moved from the shadows and caressed my hair. "I think you need to do this, honey. The three of us got rid of Camille for now, but she's very strong. We won't last in another fight."

The worry in her eyes made me close my own and press into Kane once more. He was heated, barely holding back his frustration. I glanced up at him, a silent question on my lips.

He pressed a kiss to my forehead. "We can try. At least I'll be able to get you home and to bed."

Bed. That was all I really wanted right then. I nodded. "All right."

"Good," Lailah breathed. She hit a button on her phone, and not thirty seconds later, the front door opened, and in walked Dan—my ex—and right behind him was Meri, her board-straight mahogany hair hanging in a sheet down the length of her back.

"They were outside this whole time?" I shot at Lailah.

"Put her down, Kane," Meri said in a soft, commanding tone.

He stared at her with one raised eyebrow.

"Trust me," she said, and I had to hold back a snort. "In order to get her home safely, the two of us need to join our energies. I can't do that with yours in the mix."

The storm raging in Kane's eyes told me he'd rather do just about anything other than listen to Meri. I sighed and nodded at Kane. The sooner we got this over with, the sooner I could lie in his bed with his strong arms keeping me safe. He frowned but gently placed me on my feet.

My knees instantly buckled.

Kane caught me and pulled me to him. "This isn't going to work."

"Trust me," Meri said again and reached a hand out to me.

I stared at it as if her fingertips were fangs.

"Jade," Dan said. "Please, Meri's only trying to help."

Yeah," I huffed. "Every time someone tries to help, all hell breaks loose."

"You want to go home, don't you?" Meri smiled at me, her deep gray eyes almost appearing kind.

Damn, I wished I could read her to make sure I understood her current emotional state. She could be totally faking. But it was either take her hand or stay in the store all night. And I had catering samples to taste.

I reached out my right hand and clasped hers. The effect was immediate. My heart fluttered, and the space below my breastbone seemed to swell. All the masked pain dissipated, and for the first time in a month, I felt normal, one hundred percent myself, ready to face anything. Just the way I had before I'd lost half of my soul.

"Feel better?" Meri asked, her eyes going wide with surprise.

"Yes."

"Me, too. Let's go figure out how to make this permanent."

I was so alive. So happy. So myself. I turned to Lailah with a look of wonder, ready to ask why she hadn't told me this would happen, but her shocked expression stopped me. "Lailah? What is it?"

She blinked. "You're...holy shit."

"Whoa," Philip said softly.

"What?" I demanded, getting more irritated by the second.

"It's your aura," Lailah said. "It's just shifted from purple-tinged to pure white."

"Yeah, so?" Purple was the sign of an intuitive. I was somewhat surprised the color hadn't changed as soon as Meri had taken my empath gift. "Mixing with an angel could certainly mask the purple or wipe it out altogether."

"No, Jade. Meri's is still purple-tinged. Yours faded to pure snow white. Something's changed. It's the sign of a full-fledged angel's soul."

Chapter 6

Everyone decided to meet us back at Kane's house except Bea. Concerned about our ghost sighting, she opted to go home and strengthen the wards around her house. And to also research ghost possessions. With three angels and my mother watching over me, I had more than enough keepers.

"A full-fledged angel?" I whispered from Kane's couch for the third time and glanced at Meri sitting in the chair across from me.

She craned her neck to check on Dan, who was sitting by himself in the dining room. Normally, I wouldn't invite my ex into the home I shared with Kane, but she'd given me no choice. She'd insisted he come with her. She seemed to sense my gaze and stared back, studying me.

"Do you think they're right? Is it possible that I have some sort of angel gene?" I asked her. She was an angel, after all, and a former demon. She should have some knowledge.

Kane shifted beside me and squeezed my leg.

Slowly, Meri shook her head. "No. I've never heard of a witch turning angel. Besides, the soul you and I share is exactly what I'd expect from a powerful witch, not an angel."

Angels existed to protect souls. It made sense she'd know what mine was supposed to feel like. "What about whatever you did to me back at the shop? We shared some sort of energy. You could've transferred a part of you."

"It doesn't work that way. I was only letting our souls connect so they could restore themselves. Nothing more."

Good. I did not want to be an angel. After my experience with the angel council, I wanted as little to do with them as possible. Present company excepted.

The door rattled and swung open, bouncing with a crash off a stone umbrella stand. Pyper bounded in, Ian at her heels. He had his bag slung over a shoulder, a camera in one hand and his EMF detector hanging from another. Without stopping, he headed into the middle of the room, dropped his bag, and sank to one knee. A second later he had the rest of his equipment spread out around him.

I stiffened. "What are you doing?"

His head jerked up at my harsh tone. Frowning, he put down his equipment and stood. "I'm going to take some readings so we know the house is safe."

"No." I stood on shaky legs, staring him down. "Not after what happened at Bea's shop."

Kane rose, positioning himself to my right but just behind me. I sent him a slight smile in recognition of the gesture. He was there if I needed him, but he'd let me handle this.

"But—"

"No. You've already done readings here once before. Nothing was found, and I'm sure as hell not letting you invite anything else into Kane's home."

"*Our* home," Kane interjected.

"Jade." Pyper touched my arm. "He's only trying to help."

I turned on her. "Like he tried to help by kissing me after the ghost possessed me and I couldn't do anything to stop it?" I clapped a hand over my mouth. Had I really just blurted that? *Shit.*

Kane's hand tensed on my shoulder as my words hung in the air. Pyper gaped at me, and then hurt clouded her bright blue eyes. She turned abruptly to glare at Ian. His face flushed bright red.

Oh, double shit. I'd planned to tell Kane, but I hadn't wanted to hurt Pyper. Before Kane and I got together, Ian had made no secret of his interest in me. But he'd been dating Pyper the last few months. I'd truly thought he was over his fascination with me.

"You did what?" Pyper asked through clenched teeth.

Ian backed up, his expression resembling a deer in the headlights.

Kane bent close to my ear. "A heads-up would've been nice."

I turned to him and wrapped my arms around his waist, burying my head in his chest. He straightened, his body turning rigid. When he didn't return my embrace, a tiny piece of my heart shattered.

I sucked in a shaky breath. "I was going to tell you after everyone left. I didn't mean to blurt it out like that. He just made me so angry..." Tilting my head up, I prayed he saw the truth echoing in my eyes. "I really didn't have any control over the situation. You know I don't harbor any feelings for Ian. I never have." And right then, I had a fair amount of contempt for the ghost hunter. "You don't honestly believe I would hurt you or Pyper like that, do you?"

Kane sighed and wrapped one arm around me. His other hand came up and brushed a stray lock of hair behind my ear. "Of course not. I want nothing more than to deck the asshole, but it looks like Pyper might beat me to it."

She'd backed Ian up against the front door and fisted his T-shirt in her hands. Visibly shaking, she gave him a verbal lashing in a hushed tone, making it impossible to hear what she was saying. But the expression on his face made it obvious whatever she'd said wasn't pleasant. He didn't even try to defend himself. He just stood there and took her wrath.

Smart move, considering how pissed she was.

"Bastard," Pyper spat and shoved him against the door. "Get out."

He reached a tentative hand out toward her, but she knocked it away. With her hands clenched in tight balls, she lowered her arms to her sides and took a step back.

Ian's eyes never left hers as he reached behind him to open the door. He took one step forward and paused. "I do have an explanation when you're ready to hear it." He glanced at me and Kane.

Heat radiated from Kane, no doubt the anger he was trying to control.

Ian closed his eyes in defeat, and when he opened them he grabbed his bag of equipment, nodded once, and slipped outside.

Pyper slammed the door on his retreating back. "Shit," she said and stalked back to the kitchen.

"That was…uncomfortable," Meri said.

"I bet," Dan said, sending her a look of sympathy. He leaned against the wall with one leg crossed over the other. Meri smiled at him and crossed the room, following him back into the adjoining dining room.

Twenty minutes later, I was sprawled on the couch, too exhausted to move, when Lailah, Philip, Mom, and Gwen showed up. They'd stayed at Bea's shop to cleanse the space, making sure Camille and any other potential ghosts were gone. Everyone was too busy arguing to pay any attention to me.

"She's not an angel," Mom insisted, talking over Philip as they moved deeper into the house. They gathered in the dining room where there were more chairs. "There's no possible way."

"But her aura says otherwise," he replied in a patient tone. "Whether she was one before or not, it's clear she shows signs of being one now. I want to find out why."

I grimaced at Philip's words. I *wasn't* a damn angel. White Witches could have white auras. Mine had happened to be tinged purple due to my empath gift. But I wasn't an intuitive anymore. No wonder my aura had changed.

Kane emerged from the kitchen. "Hot chocolate?" he asked, holding an oversized red mug out to me.

I propped myself up on the pillows, smiling at him. Through all the chaos and uncertainty, he was there, offering me my comfort drink of choice, complete with homemade whipped cream. Tucking my feet underneath me, I gestured to the couch. "Sit with me."

Kane settled in beside me, his strong, capable arm pulling me close to his body. He kissed the top of my head. "Looks like our brief reprieve has come to an end."

"Where's Kat?" I asked him.

He shrugged. "Maybe she went home?"

I raised my eyebrows and cast him a side-long glance.

He chuckled. "Okay, probably not. When they calm down, you could ask someone."

"Yeah." I stared into his gorgeous toffee-flecked chocolate eyes, remembering the gleam that had been there this morning, and shook my head sadly. "We'll never get this wedding planned. And now, unless we find a way to banish Camille, I can't go back to Summer House."

His arm tightened around me. "Don't think for a minute I'm letting my angel get away from me. The wedding will go on as planned." His lips curved in a half-grin. "Even if I have to snatch a justice of the peace and marry you in the street."

I ignored his taunt. "But Summer House…" I trailed off, not wanting to say the words. It was where he'd proposed, where his grandparents were married. Part of his history. He deserved a grand, elegant wedding, not some half-assed Bourbon Street tourist attraction. What if Camille possessed me the day of the wedding? Would Kane be married to her? I shook my head, banishing the thought.

Kane's hand slid over mine, warm and reassuring. He leaned in, his breath tickling my ear. "Summer House is only a house. I told you before I don't care where we live, and I'm telling you now I don't care where we get married. I only want you." His lips brushed lightly over my temple. "No matter what."

My mother's voice rose from the other room. "I already told you, Jade is not an angel. It's impossible. Find a different explanation!" Her footsteps rang through the house as she stomped toward the kitchen. A second later, the back door slammed.

"Hope," Gwen called and followed her.

I sighed and turned my gaze to Lailah. She stood with her hands jammed in her cargo pants pockets, watching Philip watch his ex-mate. Meri had moved back into the living room and sat as far away from everyone as she could get. Her eyes were closed, and the pained expression on her face made me tense with alarm. But when Mom stormed back into the house, ranting at Gwen about my supposed angel status, Meri's face pinched even more, and I realized she was just having trouble processing the high emotions running through the room.

It was bound to happen. She hadn't grown up being exposed to everyone's emotions from birth. I'd developed ways to shield myself. From the looks of it, she needed help.

"Mom," I said evenly.

"It's no one's business but mine and Jade's," she carried on.

"Hope," Philip said, "I'm just trying to find out why her aura changed suddenly. That's all. It could be a clue to help figure out the possession."

"Maybe it's because she only has half a soul," Mom snapped. "Thanks to you!"

"Mom." I raised my voice.

She spun and hurried to my side, placing a tentative hand on my shoulder. "What is it, honey?"

I sat up. Kane's grip eased, but he didn't let go. At one time, that would have annoyed me. Now his actions were reassuring, as if I had support in anything I did. "You need to calm down." I nodded toward Meri. "She's having issues controlling my gift."

Mom jerked her attention to Meri. She watched her friend and then slowly lowered herself to the arm of the couch. Rolling her shoulders, she reached one hand behind her neck and kneaded her muscles. "Sorry," she said to Meri.

The tension in Meri's face eased a bit. She nodded at Mom.

"If you need a reprieve, you can go outside for a few minutes," I offered. Sometimes nothing worked but solitude. Experiencing everyone else's emotions was as physically draining as it was emotionally. If you couldn't block people out, "emotional vampire" took on a whole new meaning.

Meri shook her head and stared at me pointedly. "I can't."

Frustration welled in my chest. "Seriously? You'll be, like, twenty feet away." Then a sinking horror coiled in my gut. "Are you saying we have to stay in the same room until this is figured out?"

"No, just the same building. The walls absorb energy, giving you more breathing room. But when one of you goes outside, the other needs to stay close. It's more of a risk," Philip said.

That was something at least.

Meri got to her feet, waving off Dan, who sprang to her side. Where had he come from?

"Dan," Mom said, sounding just as surprised as I was, "you're still here."

He nodded and hunched his shoulders. "I wanted to make sure Meri was okay." He glanced at her, and I wondered, not for the first time, what kind of relationship they had. It skeezed me out to imagine a romantic one. Meri had been his dad's mate. I shuddered with the thought. Too gross.

"I'm perfectly fine, Dan," Meri said with a slight grimace. "Really, stop worrying."

Dan hovered, and Meri turned to him, her gray eyes flashing with irritation. When he didn't take the hint, she used both hands to shove him sideways.

"Hey!" he protested, rubbing his arm. "Watch it, will ya? You didn't need to put any angel power behind the blow. Jeez. You gave me a dead arm."

She smirked, something I hadn't seen her do before. A sense of recognition washed over me. For the first time since Meri had come into my life, she was behaving like a living, breathing human, not a demon or an angel.

As I watched them, I realized I'd never seen her or Dan touch intimately or share a lover's glance. No, they interacted with each other much more like the way Pyper and Kane usually did. Fiercely loyal and relentless. Just like brother and sister. A vision of Dan helping Meri find her strength so they could leave Hell came rushing back. I'd witnessed their struggle through a dream while I'd been sharing a soul with Meri. Ah, their relationship became clear. They'd bonded while fighting for survival.

Meri glanced toward the dining room, where Lailah and Philip sat talking quietly. Philip lifted his head to meet her eyes. Meri glanced away without any acknowledgement.

Lailah's lips formed a thin line as her gaze darted between Philip and Mcri.

He abruptly pushed his chair back and stood. "There isn't anything else to do tonight."

Lailah rose, still watching him. "You're leaving?"

"I have research to do. Jade should be safe as long as Meri's here." He nodded his goodbye to Lailah and strode over to where I sat with Kane and Mom. "I'll be by tomorrow to let you know what I find."

I suppressed a scowl. I didn't want him around or working on this new development. It was my dumb luck he was still my guardian angel. If it were up to me, I'd have let Kane rip a limb or two off, but that would've only gotten Kane imprisoned in the time-warp room and me back in the angel court, trying to free him. Philip wasn't worth it. The back-stabbing piece of angel turd.

It was much easier to deal with him when I pretended he didn't exist. Reluctantly, I gave him a short nod, indicating my consent. Without saying another word, he left. The room gave a collective sigh of relief as soon as the door slammed shut.

"Where's Kat?" I asked Lailah this time.

She glanced around. "She's not here?"

Dan got to his feet. "She said she'd be a few minutes behind us but"—he glanced at the wall clock—"that was an hour ago."

My heart pounded with fear. I grabbed my phone, but before I could hit Send, Dan was already speaking to her voicemail.

"Damn," he said, shoving his phone into his pocket. "No answer."

I jumped up and grabbed my purse. "Meri, let's go."

She startled. "Where?"

"We're going to backtrack to the store, and if we don't find her, we'll head to her apartment. Something's wrong. Nothing would keep Kat away on a night like this. Not even if I begged her." I strode to the door and turned to give her an impatient glance when she didn't move. "Well, hurry up."

Kane moved in front of me. "Maybe it's better if Lailah and your mom go."

The magic in my chest tingled and electric sparks sprang to my fingertips. Shocked, I stared at the blue-tinged glow, overwhelmed with the desire to blast him out of my way.

Holy crap, Jade. Get a grip.

Horrified, I backed away from everyone. I'd almost zapped Kane.

Mom's hands covered mine. Her soothing earth magic stifled the electric desire. "You're too weak after what happened, sweetie. It isn't your fault. Magic can take on a life of its own when your body has been through so much."

Kane reached out a hand to guide me, but I jumped out of his grasp. I was too dangerous to be anywhere near him.

"Jade?" he asked.

"I'm sorry." The words came out choked. "Go find Kat. I know something's wrong. Please," I begged him. "I'm going to go eat something, try to shake this off."

"Promise?" he asked, his concerned eyes boring into mine. "Dan's going." He waved at my ex already striding out the door. "So's Lailah."

She hovered near us, car keys clutched in her hand.

"Yes. Just go. The more the better. Meri and I will be fine here. Call as soon as you know anything."

Kane ran a light hand down my arm, and I struggled not to flinch, grateful when my magic didn't electrify him. Then he followed Dan, Mom and Lailah out the door. That left me, Gwen, Meri, and Pyper, but Pyper was still hiding out in the kitchen. Gwen sat beside me and took my hand in hers.

"Don't worry," she soothed. "I have a feeling she's going to be fine."

"Going to be?" My voice rose with each word. Gwen was a psychic. She didn't talk about her visions usually, but *going to be* fine was a far cry from actually being fine.

Gwen ran a sun-weathered hand over mine. "The message is vague but strong. 'Going to be' is good enough for now."

I didn't care for that answer at all, but what could I do? I grabbed my phone and called Kat again. Straight to voicemail. "Damn," I said, echoing Dan's sentiment.

The three of us sat in silence, Meri curled up in an oversized chair, her eyes closed, and Gwen and I huddled together, waiting. I didn't wait well.

After five more attempts to reach Kat, I got to my feet. "I'm going to check on Pyper."

"That's a good plan," Gwen said. "I bet she could use someone to talk to right about now."

I nodded and retreated to the kitchen at the back of the house then paused in the doorway. Pyper stood at the sink, clad in yellow rubber gloves, scrubbing the dishes Kane must've left from breakfast.

"Hey," I said softly. "You okay?"

She whirled around, a plate clutched in her hands. Her too-bright eyes found mine and then narrowed as her lips turned down into a deeper frown. Without warning, she threw the soap-filled sponge right at me. It landed smack dab in the middle of my face.

I sputtered, spitting out dishwashing soap. "Pyper! What the hell?"

Her mouth dropped open in a surprised O, and then she started to giggle, followed by bone-shaking laughter. Tears streamed down her face. "Oh, God," she gasped. "I'm sorry. I was just...so mad." Another bubble of laughter sprang from her lips.

"At me?" I asked, more than a little pissed. "What did I do?"

"Nothing," she wheezed as she tried to sober. "Nothing at all, and that's the problem."

Chapter 7

Eyeing Pyper with caution, I reached over and pulled open a drawer full of dish towels. I wiped the water dripping from my chin and asked, "What are you talking about?"

"You." Her amusement faded and she huffed with exasperation. "You do nothing, yet everything revolves around you. Everyone drops everything to deal with the crisis of the week. It's no wonder everyone's so fascinated with you."

Her words were a sucker-punch to my gut. Crisis of the week? Everyone drops everything for me? As if I *asked* for these things to happen to me? Hell, I'd even saved her ass once. Everything about me? What the…? I narrowed my eyes. "By everyone, do you mean Ian?"

"Obviously." She bent down and picked up the sopping sponge from the floor. Her fingers curled around it and a puddle formed at her feet. "And Kane. And Kat. And Lailah. And your coven. Jesus, even your ex-boyfriend shows up."

My mouth hung open, and as her words sank in, my vision blurred a hazy shade of red. "Are you kidding me right now?" After all I'd done to help her, I couldn't believe what I was hearing. "Are you saying you'd rather be stuck in an alternate reality with Roy? Or that I should've let Meri keep Kane and Kat in Hell? Or that I should've given up my soul to a demon?

Because all of those options sure as shit would've been a lot easier to deal with. In fact, none of us would be here right now to even argue about it."

"Oh, fuck you, Jade!"

The sponge flew again, but this time I ducked.

A startled gasp sounded from behind me. I whirled to find Gwen standing in the doorway, her red shirt darkened with sponge water. She held the sponge in both hands. "Ladies, is there a problem in here?"

"No," we said in unison.

I turned angry eyes on Pyper. She'd just nailed my aunt with a sponge, and she hadn't even apologized. "What's wrong with you?" I demanded, scowling at Pyper.

"You!" She threw a wooden spoon into the sink and stalked toward Kane's bedroom. My bedroom now. The door slammed shut, rattling the glassware in the cabinets.

I threw down the dish towel and forced out a breath. None of this was my fault, but I still couldn't help feeling guilty. I'd kissed Ian. So what if I'd been possessed at the time? It was still awful. My whole body started to shake with delayed adrenaline. Clutching the counter, I hung my head. "Goddess, Gwen. Is that what she thinks of me? That I invite this crap to happen so I can be the center of attention?"

Gwen's strong, capable hand wrapped around my arm. She gently tugged and led me to the table. "Sit."

I did as I was told and buried my head in my hands. First, I'd been possessed—twice. Then Kat went missing, and now Pyper was ready to delete my number from speed dial. What a fucked-up day.

"Want to talk about it?" Gwen asked.

"No," I mumbled, not lifting my face from my hands. "I'd really like to have a moment to myself if you don't mind."

I felt Gwen hovering, clearly not wanting to leave me alone, but then she nodded and squeezed my shoulder. "I'll be in the living room if you change your mind."

As her footsteps faded into the other room, I dropped my hands and leaned back in the chair. Damn Pyper. Why'd she have to take my room?

"Jade?" a deep female voice said quietly.

I jerked, finding Meri standing just inside the kitchen door. Her head was tilted to the side as she studied me. "Yeah?"

"Do you mind if I join you?" Her tone was quiet, cautious.

Now what? Frowning, I waved a hand at the chair next to me.

She chuckled. The chair skidded across the tile as she pulled it out and took a seat. "I'm not the enemy, you know."

"I never said you were."

"You didn't have to." She leaned in, her eyes locked on mine. "I'm not the demon who did all those terrible things to the people you love."

No. She wasn't. But she used to be. "I know."

She shook her head. "I don't think you do. Not where it counts."

Goddess, save me from smacking her. I did not need this right now. "What are you talking about?"

She leaned back, her eyes sparkling with a knowing glint. "You're so busy looking backward you don't see what's in front of you."

My exasperation exploded with an exaggerated huff. "Meri, I'm sorry, but I can't do this right now. I don't think we're going to be able to work out our *issues* in one night anyway." I pushed my chair back and stood.

She shrugged. "Fine. This isn't about you and me anyway. But you might want to think about what I said."

I gave her an incredulous look as I stalked out of the kitchen and then stopped in the middle of the dining room. Pyper was in the room I shared with Kane. Gwen was in the living room. Meri was in the kitchen. That left the guest room if I wanted solitude. What I really wanted was my little apartment on Bourbon Street and my ghost dog, Duke. But Kane would kill me if I left. And I'd have to take Meri if I didn't want to end up possessed again.

Shit.

I spun and headed back toward the master bedroom. I could hole up and wait for a phone call, or I could get to the root of the problem with Pyper.

Dragging my feet, I forced myself down the hallway and paused outside the bedroom. *Just get it over with.* What was the worst that would happen? She'd throw something else at me? It wasn't as if she could kick my ass. After all, I *was* still a witch.

Not that I'd actually use magic against her. I shook my head, knowing it wasn't a physical outburst I was worried about. Time to woman up. I knocked gently on the door. "Pyper?"

Silence.

I knocked harder and pressed my ear to the door. "Pyper, I'm coming in."

My words were met with the sound of running water. She was in the bathroom. Fine. I'd be waiting when she came out. Slowly, I opened the door just to make sure I hadn't misinterpreted the noise. The bathroom door was shut with light seeping from the gap at the bottom. I glanced at the empty bed then headed for the armchair in the corner.

With my feet tucked under me, I waited.

I stared at the bedside clock and counted as the minutes passed. One. Three. Five. What was she doing in there? Just as I was about to get up and check on her, the door eased open. Pyper emerged, a tissue clutched in one hand as she wiped fresh tears from her cheek.

"Oh, Pyper, no," I breathed and hurried to her side. I'd only seen Pyper cry once. And that was after she'd been used as a punching bag by an evil ghost. She stiffened as my arms came around her, and despite my instinct to back off, I pulled her into a hug. She resisted for only a moment then leaned into me, sniffling.

I placed my hand on her back, rubbing gently. "What is it?" This couldn't be about me. There was something a lot more serious going on.

She took a ragged breath and gently pushed me back. "I'm sorry."

"It's okay." I tugged on her hand and led her to the bed. Sitting, I patted the space beside me.

"No, it isn't. I threw a sponge at Gwen."

I laughed. "You threw it at *me*."

She snorted and then frowned, her eyebrows pinched as she struggled to keep the tears at bay.

Wrapping an arm around her shoulders, I pulled her into a half-hug. "Don't worry. Whatever it is, I'm sure everything will be all right."

"No." She yanked back and dabbed at her eyes, reeling in the tears. "It's not going to be all right. Ian kissed you, the asshat. After all this time, and you and Kane getting engaged, he still fucking kissed you!"

I swiveled, staring at her. "Is that what all this is about? I'm not even all that sure what happened. I mean, I was possessed. It was a blur. One minute, I was struggling to regain control of my body, and the next, the ghost was sucking Ian's face."

"What difference does it make?" She clutched at the comforter. "Between his infatuation with you and that reporter chick, I don't know what the hell I'm doing with him."

I raised an eyebrow. "Reporter chick?"

She laughed. A hollow, sardonic sound. "You don't even know about her. Typical."

"Hey, wait just a minute," I said gently, trying to be sensitive. Tears still glistened in her eyes, but I would've bet my last dollar she wouldn't let them fall. "I was gone for a month. How can I know stuff if you don't tell me?"

Her normally bright blue eyes turned stormy. "You don't ever ask. And Kane's too busy watching over you to pay attention anymore."

An ache formed in the middle of my chest. That was what she meant when she said everything revolved around me. Kane was her best friend and the one person who'd always been there for her. Ever since I'd come into his life, she'd taken a back seat. And some friend I was. I'd been so wrapped up in Kane and the wedding I hadn't even noticed something was wrong.

I closed my eyes and took a deep breath. "I'm so sorry, Pyper." Reaching out, I curled my fingers around hers. "You must hate me right now."

I fully expected another humorless laugh, but when her lips curved up, her eyes softened. "I don't hate you. How could I? You make Kane happier than I've ever seen him. It's just…"

"You've been left behind?" My words slipped out so low I barely heard them.

She bit her lip and nodded. "I don't…there's no one around when I need…"

"I'm here," I said. "And Kane's here. I—"

"Where? When?" She glanced around. "When is there ever time for a normal breakdown? When aren't we chasing a missing person or an evil ghost or demon? Hell, even my best dates with Ian include ghost hunting."

"I'm here," I said firmly. "And so is Kane." Before she could deny my declaration, I took her hand and squeezed it. "I know I've been preoccupied. But that doesn't mean I don't care. Pyper, please, all you need to do is say something. You know Kane and I will come running."

"That's the point, isn't it?" She didn't acknowledge the pressure I kept on her hand, but she didn't pull back either. She turned to stare at a blank space on the wall. "Before all this started, Kane always knew when I needed him. Now…" She shrugged. "I gained a sister." Her eyes met mine. "But I feel like I lost my brother. And now my boyfriend, too." She took a deep breath. "He's been spending time with some reporter he dated in high school, and he's clearly still got a thing for you, even though everyone knows you don't want him."

Damn Ian. He knew Pyper was in love with him. The bastard. She'd told him at the Christmas party last month. I couldn't believe he was behaving this way. Sure, he'd been into me once, but I'd thought all that had ended after he started dating Pyper. What the heck had that kiss been about? "Tell me about this reporter. What's her name?"

"Sybil Tanner," she said, misery coloring her tone.

The name rang a bell, and her face flashed in my mind. She'd done a story on the immorality of witches not long ago and outed our coven circle. "The one who reported on Goodwin's rally last fall?"

"Yep. That's her. Perky Sybil."

I frowned. Ian had gone to high school with her? Why hadn't he said anything? It wasn't as if Ian and I were best buddies. Still, Sybil had reported on the coven circle. You'd think he could have warned us her knew her. "What makes you think he's seeing her?"

Pyper clenched her hands into fists as her eyes narrowed. "Well, he *says* he isn't seeing her. But I know they've had dinner together at least twice. Charlie saw him with 'some blond in a pink suit' at The Gumbo Shop last week. And once, on a different occasion, I accidently picked up his iPhone, thinking it was mine, and saw a text from her, confirming drinks."

"Did you confront him about it?" My mind spun in eight different directions, contemplating the ways I could torture the douche canoe. My favorite involved fire ants and maple syrup.

"No. " She stood and paced in front of me. "I was hoping he'd tell me, and when he didn't, I had my answer."

I leaped off the bed. "And you're still dating him? Why?" I grimaced as I heard the accusation in my voice. Dammit. The last thing she needed was me judging her. "Sorry. I didn't mean—"

"Don't worry about it. I was just sitting here asking myself the same thing." She moved to the door.

"Wait." I stood and scrambled to block her exit. "Can you tell me one thing?"

She tilted her head, waiting.

"Why Ian? I mean, I used to think he was a nice guy, but now I don't know. What is it that drew you to him?"

She laughed, true humor shining through this time. "He's quirky. A free spirit. Someone who hasn't conformed to the norm. Just like me. I thought that was obvious." She reached around me for the door and quietly slipped from the room.

I stood there, staring at the deserted hallway and filing away that mental note. Ian had said much the same thing to me once, that he liked me because I made a living as a glass artist, or at least tried to. He liked that I understood his desire to live a nonconformist life and didn't judge him for wanting to make a living hunting ghosts—something most women found unstable at best and downright crazy at worst.

Pyper fit that bill to a T. She'd been a stripper for a handful of years before she opened her coffee shop. She was a body-paint artist. She even helped Ian with his ghost-hunting jobs. He'd be hard-pressed to find someone more supportive of his unconventional goals. And she was sexy as hell. What the fuck was wrong with him? Anger burned in my chest, and the fire tingled at my fingertips again.

I stared down in horror-filled fascination at the flames flickering from my fingers and took a step back from the door. *Just breathe, Jade. Breathe.* As the air filled my lungs, I forced myself to relax. Rolling my shoulders, I exhaled and imagined the tension draining from my muscles. My fingers tingled with cold and when I looked down, the fire was gone.

What was I becoming? My heart thundered. What if I couldn't control my magic? What if I hurt someone? I stumbled back and landed on the bed, too afraid to move. Trembling, I reached into my pocket and produced my phone. I stared at it, ready to scream from the lack of messages. Where was Kat? Why hadn't they found her yet?

Just as my finger touched the button to call Kane, my phone started to vibrate. Lucien's number popped up.

"Have you seen, Kat?" I asked.

"Yes. She's with me—"

I let out a loud sigh of relief, totally missing his next words. "Huh? What was that?"

"Dammit, Jade. We're at Bea's. Just get here. She's barely hanging on."

"What?" I jumped up, running into the hall.

Silence on the other end.

"Lucien?"

The phone beeped twice, signaling a dropped call. Kat? No! He was wrong. Not her. She wasn't even a part of the crazy paranormal world.

"Goddammit!" Tearing through the house, I burst into the living room and spotted Meri lying on the couch, a light blanket covering her legs. "Get up. We're leaving." I glanced back at Gwen. "It's Kat. She's in trouble."

Without waiting to see if anyone was following, I burst through the door. A whisper of ice crept over me, and I froze. Static filled my ears.

Ghost.

Chapter 8

Not again.

"Meri!" I cried, unable to move. My limbs were already starting to go numb again.

My breathing turned rapid and panic took over. This could not be happening. Kat needed me. *Kat.* A sob formed at the back of my throat. Pyper had been right. My life was such a cluster-fuck. I wasn't there for anyone who needed me.

"Jade, what *were* you thinking?" A faint voice penetrated the static filling my ears. My head wouldn't move. I tried to turn but couldn't. I was trapped in my own personal hell. "I thought you were in a hurry?" The voice was slightly louder this time, irritated.

Ice slithered through me, and the fear bursting from my core did nothing to thaw my frozen limbs. I forced my mouth open, determined to speak a fire spell, hoping the flames would burst at my fingertips.

"This is ridiculous," Meri said, her voice distinguishable now. "I'm going back inside."

"Whaaa," I forced out, before my mouth clamped shut. Or I should say Camille clamped it shut for me. My only consolation was that it appeared she couldn't move either. We were locked in a stalemate.

"Jade?" Meri said again, and I thought I heard her move closer. I wanted to warn her or move away, protect her from the ghost possessing me, but I couldn't. I couldn't do a damn thing. "Are you okay?"

My shoulder tingled, and the ice melted. Feeling rushed back into my arms, core, and legs as the rest of the static fled.

I shifted to study her, finally noticing her hand on my arm where the tingling had started. "How'd you do that?" I croaked out, my throat raw from the forced communication. It was as if I'd been screaming for hours at a rock concert.

"Do what?"

I shook my head, trying to clear the cobwebs. "You expelled Camille. How'd you do it?" Whatever spell she'd used, I needed to know it. Maybe next time I could combat the possession before Camille overtook me.

She frowned, confusion lining her face. "I didn't do anything."

"Yes," I said, ignoring the pain in my throat as I raised my voice. "I was possessed, and then when you touched—" Holy crap. What was it about Meri that kept the ghost away? And could I reproduce it? I swallowed and lowered my voice. "It was your touch. As soon as you placed your hand on my arm, you broke the spell, and Camille fled. Do you have some special ghost kryptonite or something?"

She stared at me, eyes narrowed. "Not that I'm aware of."

I grabbed her arm and clutched it to me. "Whatever it was, it worked. You saved me from a full-on possession." I sighed and sent Philip a silent thanks. As much as I hated the bastard, he'd been right about making me and Meri stay together. "Let's go. Kat's in trouble."

I parked Pyper's VW Bug behind Bea's Prius and scanned the grounds. No creepy ghosts. That was something. Then I had to force myself to wait for Meri before sprinting into the house. I wouldn't be any use if Camille showed up and took over again. Hurry up, I wanted to scream when her light sweater got caught on the door handle and she struggled to detangle herself. Clenching my teeth, I seethed silently, my hands glowing with magic again. I rubbed them together, stamping it out. I was sure she wasn't intentionally trying to piss me off.

"Ready?" I forced out after the passenger door shut.

"You know, this isn't fun for me. I could go home." She glared at me.

I turned and ran up the steps of the porch. Over my shoulder, I called, "But you won't because you're an *angel*." Not to mention if the council found out she'd risked the other half of the soul they'd tried to give to her just a few weeks before, there'd be hell to pay.

She let out an audible huff but kept pace behind me. Not bothering to knock, I flung Bea's door open and ran inside. "Kat?" I called, pausing to glance around the brightly lit room. Empty. I took off, taking the stairs two at a time.

"In here," Lucien called from the guest room, the one I'd been a resident of not too long ago. The door stood slightly ajar, and I hesitated for just a moment before I pushed it open slowly, terrified of what I'd find on the other side.

"Jade! Thank God. Get in here." Lucien jumped up and pulled me to the bed.

I stared down at Kat. She was trembling and so pale she almost looked translucent. "What happened?" My voice shook as I forced out the words.

Lucien dropped into a chair next to the bed and rubbed one of his large hands over his haggard face. His mussed blond hair fell forward covering one pale green eye. "I'm not exactly sure."

I sank to the bed and carefully took her hand in mine. "Lucien?"

His haunted gaze met mine.

"Start at the beginning."

He took a deep breath, visibly shaken. "I was at a friend's house when she called. She wanted to talk about what was happening to you. She insisted it couldn't wait, so she came to see me."

"Your friend? Another witch?"

Lucien was my second in command of the New Orleans coven. Kat had been fine when I'd seen her at The Herbal Connection. Whatever was going on with her had to be magic related.

He shook his head. "No. An artist friend of mine. He was having an open house for his work, and I wanted some of his pieces for the gallery. Leaving would've meant missing out. That's why I had Kat meet me there instead of going to your house."

I caressed Kat's still hand and glanced at Lucien expectantly. "What happened after Kat got to your friend's house?"

He blew out a breath. "She was frantic, talking about how you'd been possessed and not making any sense at all. She was so upset I took her outside, and I don't really know what happened. One minute she was babbling, and the next, she went stiff, trance-like. Her speech changed. Her voice went high-pitched, and then she screamed. I couldn't get her to calm down, so I put a mild tranq spell on her."

"What?" I clutched at the side of the bed. A tranq spell should've acted as a mild sedative. Instead, she appeared comatose.

He hung his head, staring at his feet. "It didn't work. Or at least not the way it was supposed to." Pain clouded his eyes when he lifted his head to look at me. "She passed out. And hasn't woken up."

I gasped and covered my mouth with a trembling hand. This had happened while she'd been trying to find help for me. When would my life stop putting the people I loved in danger? Pyper's words echoed in my mind. *You do nothing, yet everything revolves around you. Everyone drops everything to deal with the crisis of the week.* That was what Kat had been doing, dealing with my crisis of the week. My heart squeezed as I took in her appearance. The blue veins in her arms were more prominent than I remembered. Her skin seemed paper-thin, almost as if she'd crumble if I touched her.

Lucien slumped as he whispered, "And now I've almost lost her."

"Don't say that," I snapped. "Where's Bea?"

"In the kitchen, trying to concoct something."

She was? I hadn't seen her when I'd stormed in. I tilted my head, trying to focus on the hushed voices floating from downstairs. Meri and Bea. A tiny bit of peace settled over me. If Bea was working on a treatment, Kat would be fine.

My phone buzzed in my pocket, making me jump. "Shit," I mumbled, realizing I'd forgotten to call off the search party. I quickly sent Kane a text asking him to meet me at Bea's and to let everyone know Kat was found and they should go home. I didn't want the entourage barging into Bea's house. If Bea couldn't heal her, no one could.

Lucien stood abruptly.

"Where are you going?"

He stared down at Kat, his shoulders hunched. "I did this to her. I shouldn't be here."

Two long strides and he'd almost reached the door.

I jumped up and grabbed his arm. "Hey."

He tensed but stood still.

"Please stay. I'll probably need your help." A lump formed in my throat, and I forced out, "She needs you."

He rubbed his neck as he hung his head. Then he straightened, but he didn't look back. "I'll be downstairs with Bea if you need me."

The dejection in his voice was too much. Before he could leave, I wrapped my arms around him from behind and pressed my cheek to his back. "This isn't your fault," I reassured him. "She's going to be fine."

After a moment, his hands covered mine in a comforting gesture. Then he separated himself from my embrace and left without another word.

I sighed and moved back to the bed, determined to stay by Kat's side until she woke up. Sitting beside her, I took deep calming breaths. If I was upset, my magic might spark out of control again.

I ran a hand through her bright red curls and whispered, "Kat, wake up, sweetie. We're counting on you. You're the only one who can talk sense into me." Tears filled my eyes, but I made no effort to blink them back. Kat was my oldest and best friend, the one person besides Gwen I'd been able to count on the last thirteen years, without fail. "I'm going to need you here to help pick out my wedding cake." The word "cake" came out with a sob.

She looked so fragile, as if she'd disappear at any moment. Not knowing how to help her, I curled up on the bed next to her, hoping she was somehow aware of my physical presence.

My tears flowed hot and steady onto the sunflower print comforter as I held Kat's limp hand in mine. Footsteps echoed in the hall. I sat up and hastily wiped my cheeks.

But then Kane filled the doorway, and my resolve melted. He strode to me, pulling me off of the bed and into his arms as he studied Kat. "I'm so sorry, Jade."

"They don't know what happened," I murmured into his chest.

"I know, sweetheart. I talked to Bea. She'll be up shortly to try a potion she's working on." One hand came up, cupping the back of my head.

I closed my eyes, wishing I could erase the entire day. "Is Lucien still here?"

"Yeah, he's helping with the final spell."

"What? No." I pulled away and ran to the door. Kane followed, but I spun and stopped him. "Please stay here just in case Kat wakes up. I don't want her to be alone."

Kane kissed my temple and nodded. "You got it."

I stood on my tiptoes and gave him a soft kiss on the lips, then ran out the door before I could change my mind. Lucien didn't need to be wielding any more magic.

I found Bea bent over a copper sauce pot on the stove in her bright yellow kitchen. "Where's Lucien?" I asked, glancing around.

"Out on the porch, collecting himself." She stirred the concoction with a wooden spoon, her lips pressed into a grim line.

I glanced out the window. Lucien stood slumped at the railing, his back to the front door. Half of me wanted to comfort him, and the other half wanted to curse him with scabies—if I actually knew how to do that. The fact was, his magic had done this to Kat. And worse, he had no idea how to fix it.

Taking a place next to Bea, I peered into the pot. "Can you help her?"

"Yes." Her tone was clipped.

"But?"

"It could be temporary. There aren't any guarantees." Bea doubled her efforts, stirring the potion with vigor. I had the distinct impression her movements were due to her frustration and not a requirement of the recipe.

I'd been waiting for Bea to fix everything, and now it appeared she didn't have the answers. Determined, I straightened my spine and forced all my fears aside. We'd figure it out together if it was the last thing I did. "What can I do?"

"Get Lucien in here. He's the best chance at reversing the spell."

"But…" I was about to say maybe he should stay out there. Instead, I forced the thought down and nodded. Like I'd never made a mistake before? *No one's perfect, Jade. You of all people should know that.* "I'll be right back."

"Wait." Meri uncurled from the couch. "You can't go without me, remember?"

Dammit. No, I'd totally forgotten about her and Camille. This togetherness was really inconvenient. I waved a hand, inviting her to go first.

A moment later, I closed the door behind us and joined Lucien on the porch. Meri retreated to the corner and sat in the porch swing. Though I knew he must've heard the door open and shut, he didn't acknowledge either of us.

I touched his arm gently. "Hey."

He straightened and turned to stare at me.

"We need you in there."

"For what? So I can put her out permanently?" His knuckles turned white as he tightened his grip on the porch railing.

I frowned. "What are you talking about? One spell went wrong."

"One spell. Right," he said, his tone disgusted.

I stepped back and crossed my arms over my chest. Since when had he gotten so self-deprecating? Normally, he was confident, ready to take on anything. "What aren't you telling me?"

"I...fuck." He ran a hand through his hair, frustration lining his normally easygoing expression. His corded muscles and tall frame, combined with his witch powers, usually oozed strength, but tonight he seemed to almost hunch into himself as if he were trying to disappear.

My eyebrows rose in surprise. I didn't think I'd heard him swear more than a handful of times. "Lucien?"

Anguish lined his tired eyes as his pleaded with mine. A sinking feeling made me clutch my stomach.

"I'm sorry. I should've taken her to you. I never should've used that spell." His voice lowered to a strangled whisper. "This can't happen again."

"Again?" I cried. "What do you mean, *again?*" I grabbed him, fisting my fingers in his shirt. "Has this happened before? Did you do this to someone else?"

He gave me one slow, solemn nod.

"What happened? How did you fix it?"

He didn't say anything. He just stood there, staring at me with those tortured eyes.

"Lucien!" I yanked on his shirt, shaking him. "Tell me." Electric magic zinged from my fingers.

Lucien jumped back, rubbing his chest. "I guess I deserved that."

"No. I would never..." I forced myself to step back, trembling with a mix of fear and frustration. I swallowed. "I didn't mean to do that."

Meri rose and stood next to me, studying Lucien. "He couldn't fix it. I can sense the unrest in his soul."

"You can?" I crossed my arms over my chest and balled my hands into fists, too afraid to touch anyone. Then her words sank in. "Are you saying someone died?"

"Only Lucien can answer that for sure," she said.

Our eyes met and held until Lucien finally spoke. "It happened a long time ago. I'd just learned I was a witch when… she was only nineteen. My best friend's sister. She spent three years in a coma." His voice broke, but he pushed past it. "We scattered her ashes on her twenty-third birthday."

Chapter 9

Magic pulsed to my toes. Three years? And then she died? And Lucien used the same damn spell? "What the hell is wrong with you?" I raged, pounding my fists on his chest.

Lucien didn't resist my attack even as each blow sent a shock of power into him.

I only hit him harder, lost in the pain seizing my already battered heart. "How could you?" I sobbed, tears streaming down my face.

I barely noticed the front door swing open.

"Jade Calhoun, stop that right this instant."

A heavy force washed over me. My arms went limp, and despite my struggle to regain control of my limbs, my feet peddled backward away from Lucien. It had to be Bea's magic pushing me back. It was too strong to be anyone else's.

"What is wrong with you?" Bea demanded. "I told you we needed Lucien inside. Kat's life depends on it."

"I don't want him anywhere near her," I yelled through my heartache. "This is his fault."

"Jade." Another wave of Bea's magic prickled over my skin. The anger and uncontrollable power holding me hostage started to fade into oblivion. My feet took another few steps back, seemingly with no help from me.

"Stop it, Bea," I demanded, turning on her. She was manipulating my magic and my emotions. "You have no right to spell me into submission."

"I have every right. We need to work fast to save your best friend." Her voice shook with anger. "Stop acting like a child and get upstairs. All three of you."

An invisible force propelled me toward the door. Goddammit!

Before I knew it, I was up the stairs and staring into the guest room at Kat, lying exactly where I'd left her, Kane at her side.

Footsteps sounded behind me. I gritted my teeth and moved into the room, taking a place next to Kat on the bed.

Kane's arm wrapped around my waist. "Jade?"

I met his worried eyes. He could tell something else was wrong besides Kat's condition. I placed my hand over his resting on my hip and shook my head. Now wasn't the time. When was it ever the time, between saving souls and fighting ghosts and demons?

Bea stormed in after Lucien and stood on the other side of the bed. "Jade, take her hand."

I swallowed the fear rising in the back of my throat and did as I was told. Bea had decades of experience. If anyone could help Kat, she could.

"Lucien, take Jade's hand."

I gulped and met his hooded eyes.

He walked slowly to my side, and as he vacated the doorway, Meri took his place. She studied us with raw intensity, as if trying to work out a problem.

I opened my mouth to ask what she was thinking, but Lucien took my hand and I flinched, almost fighting the familiar magic that sparked between us. He'd done this to her. What if his magic backfired again? What if I couldn't control mine?

Kane suddenly stood and placed both hands on my shoulders. "What's going on?" he asked Lucien. "Did you do something to her?"

"Kane," Bea said sharply, "we'll fill you in later. Time is running out."

"I'm fine," I whispered to Kane.

Clearly shocked at her tone, he dug his fingers into my muscles. Or maybe it was her response. I wasn't sure, but none of us had seen Bea this intense since the day she'd sacrificed herself to the black magic, saving me and the entire coven from sure death.

"What do you want us to do?" Lucien asked.

Bea rubbed a small amount of the potion she carried onto Kat's forehead. "You're going to use Jade's strength to reverse the spell."

"What?" we both cried as Lucien yanked his hand from mine and took three steps back.

Bea stood straight and rigid, her small frame filling the room. Her gaze bored into Lucien's. "You're the only one who can reverse it. So that's what's going to happen. But since Jade's a witch—a very powerful white witch—you'll push it through her. She'll be able to fight anything that goes wrong."

Goes wrong? I leaped from the bed, but Kane stepped in front of me.

"No." He crossed his arms over his chest, his forearm muscles bulging. "Jade's been through enough today. Hell, the last six months. She can't temper a spell that put her best friend in a coma."

"Her magic is out of control now. Containing someone else's seems risky at best," Meri said.

"She can, and she will." Bea scooted around Kane and pulled on my arm. "You are the only one strong enough. I need you to focus. You're strong. Stronger than you think."

I glanced down at Kat, horrified by her gaunt cheeks and wasted body. "But what if Lucien can't handle it?" I whispered. "He's done this before."

"I already know," Bea said softer, more understanding in her tone. "That was a long time ago, and Lucien is a different man now. Please, Jade. For Kat."

My head snapped up. I'd do anything for Kat, and Bea damn well knew it. It wasn't that I didn't want to. I just didn't trust

Lucien, especially since he looked as if he were ready to bolt. But who else was going to save her? If Bea said Lucien was the only one who could reverse the spell, I had to take her word for it. I touched Kane's shoulder. "It's okay. I have to help her. Bea won't let anything happen to us." I met her eyes. "Right?"

"Of course." She glanced up at Kane. "Can you give us some room?"

A torrent of emotions passed over his face, but at my nod, he gave me a quick hug and went to stand near Meri, who was still positioned in the doorway, frowning with her eyebrows pinched.

I wanted more than anything to know what was running through her mind right then, but Bea was already putting my hand in Lucien's. The buzz of coven magic zipped through me as soon as our flesh touched. Though I should have been scared out of my mind, I wasn't. The magic felt right, made me finally feel in control. Somehow our connection had stabilized me. Lucien squeezed my hand tighter this time, though he still appeared as if he wanted to run.

"Suck it up, Boulard. Kat needs you." I gripped his fingers, wanting to crush them, but backed off when I realized I was tightening my grip on Kat's hand as well. Jesus, I needed to calm down. People fed off other's emotions and although Kat wasn't an empath, if I was going to transfer magic to her, my turmoil could very well accompany it. That was the last thing she needed.

"All right, Bea. We're ready." I held my gaze steady and tried to think only about the magic I needed to control.

"You're sure? You're both centered?" She eyed us, holding up her potion.

"Yes," I said firmly. Kat had always been there for me. Now it was my turn.

Lucien cleared his throat. "Yeah."

It took all my willpower not to yell at him. Couldn't he be a tiny bit more confident? What had happened to my second in command? He was a damn powerful witch. I pushed back the guilt filling me. I certainly hadn't helped matters by attacking him. I turned what I hoped were kinder eyes on him. "We can do this. Together we can help her. Whatever it was that went wrong, we'll reverse it."

Surprise and then something close to gratitude flickered over his features. His voice was low and husky. "I couldn't do it before."

"Well, you didn't have me before, did you?" I asked, smiling brightly, though my heart was ready to crack down the middle. "We fought a demon and won. After that, we can do anything. Right?"

He didn't look convinced, but he nodded anyway. I supposed I wouldn't be either if I'd spelled someone and the person…I shook my head, dislodging the thought. *Don't think about that now.*

"Bea?" I prompted.

"I'm ready." She moved to place a thumbprint of potion first on Lucien's forehead and then mine. "Jade, this is going to be a lot like the energy transfers you've done in the past. Once I loosen the spell on Kat, you'll need to draw it through you so Lucien can reclaim it."

Oh, Goddess. I hadn't done much magic since I'd lost half my soul. And then there was the control issue. I sucked in a tentative breath. This was Kat we were talking about. I'd give up the rest of my soul if it meant saving her, and everyone in the room knew it. I nodded and clutched Lucien's hand harder while keeping a light hold on Kat's.

Bea handed the potion to Kane and shuffled him back into the hall. "Whatever happens, do not interfere," she told him. Then she glanced at Meri. "Make sure he doesn't break her concentration."

Meri stretched her arms out, grabbing both edges of the doorframe. "You got it." She glanced at Kane. "Maybe it's better if you wait downstairs."

Kane ignored her and stared at me through the doorway, the question clear in his eyes. There was only one person who could convince him to leave. Me. And I really didn't want him to. I forced myself to nod anyway. Bea knew what she was doing, and if something went wrong, Kane would try to help me. No doubt about it.

"I'll wait right here," he said.

Bea's lips formed a tight line of irritation as she turned toward him. She opened her mouth, but Meri held up a hand. "I can keep him out. I *am* an angel after all."

Kane and Bea locked gazes, and a few moments later, Bea relented. "Fine," she said to Kane. "But stay there unless I call for you."

Dread coiled in my belly. In all the time we'd been wielding spells together, she'd never once demanded Kane or anyone else leave before we started. After Kane nodded, I asked, "How dangerous is this?"

Bea turned to face me. "Very. If you drop the magic, it could bounce back and kill her. Or Lucien."

My heart raced, and I suddenly felt lightheaded. I was going to be holding both their lives in my hands. Literally.

"You'll be fine, Jade," Lucien whispered. "You're powerful. More powerful than anyone I've ever met. If anyone can do it, it's you."

I was grateful for the words but had trouble believing them.

"Focus now." Bea raised her arms. "Goddess of the living, hear my call. We ask for your help, or your mortal daughter will fall."

The air in the room grew thick and heavy with humidity, despite the steady draft of artificial cool air. It embraced me, holding me rooted to my spot.

"Reverse the poison that taints her blood. Help us bring her back to those she loves." Silver light shimmered around Bea's short stature, and I tensed.

The last time we'd called on a Goddess, she'd shown up in Lailah's body.

Bea brought her hands together, studying the ebb and flow of the silver light. When her fingers touched, a ball of silver magic pulsed in her palms. She smiled, said a quiet prayer, and stepped up to the bed. "Jade, when it hits you, slow it down so it filters through your magical spark before transferring it to Lucien. Your essence will neutralize it. Got it?" Bea moved over Kat, ready to touch her chest with the pulsing light.

"Yeah," I breathed, praying I could control it.

Bea reached down and barely grazed Kat's chest.

The effect was instantaneous. White-hot fire rushed into my fingertips, seared through my veins, and shot straight to my heart. I gasped and struggled to keep my hands clutched in Lucien's and Kat's. My knees weakened, and I couldn't stop myself from sinking onto the edge of the bed. It was either sit or fall.

"Concentrate, Jade!" Bea yelled. "The magic is out of control. Slow it down."

The intense pain seizing my arm and chest were almost too much. How had Kat survived this? How would I? Rocking back and forth to distract myself from the horror within me, I thought of only one thing: the magical spark that usually resided just below my breastbone.

Nothing.

Come on. *Where was it?*

The fire rushed into my heart. My eyes bulged, and bile rose in my throat. My chest was exploding. I couldn't do this. Pain shot down both arms, different from the heat burning me from the inside out. My muscles spasmed, and I fell backward, suddenly unable to hold myself up.

"Jade!" a faint voice called. Kat? Or was that Bea? I couldn't be sure. The sound was too far away. My eyes blurred, and a rancid stench almost choked me as the potion took over. Frantic, I reached deep within myself, searching for my spark. The hollow space below my heart was empty. Void. My magic was gone. Lucien's death magic was too much for it. I closed my eyes and shook with equal parts anger and despair.

"Jade!" a louder voice shouted in my ear. Firm hands gripped my shoulders, shaking me. My eyes flashed open, and I focused on the deep gray ones in front of me. They were slanted, piercing, and frantic. "Get control. Your magic is there. Trust me. I can feel it."

"No, it's gone," I mumbled.

Meri shook me harder. "It's not. Now grab hold of it. You're a white witch, dammit. Don't you dare give up now. You're too damn stubborn. If the council couldn't take your soul, then this sure as hell shouldn't."

My soul. Right. She had the other half. Clarity pushed away my despair. I had kept half my soul. I'd refused to die last month. And I wouldn't now. Not when Kat needed me.

"Kane," I said. "Get Kane." Voices mumbled around me. "Now!" I demanded.

The fire was almost burning my hand, which was still attached to Lucien's. If I didn't get it under control, he could die when it slammed into him unfiltered.

"Jade." Kane's deep voice caressed my psyche.

"Don't touch her," Meri advised.

"*You* are," I spat at her, longing for Kane.

"You can't hurt me. It's the soul connection."

I bit back a curse and focused my tear-filled eyes on Kane.

"Jade," he said again, though this time I didn't miss the anguish in his tone.

My burning heart pulsed and there, just beneath it, something fluttered. Kane's mere presence had given me the strength I'd needed. I almost cried out in relief as I grabbed hold of the faint threads of my magical spark. It was there, buried under the magic trying to claim me.

The instant I connected with my spark, the burning rushed to my center. "Oh Goddess," I croaked under the weight of the pressure trying to fill my center.

"What's happening to her?" I heard Kane ask, but I couldn't see him through my blurry vision.

"She's all right," Meri soothed. "She's just getting a handle on the magic. Give her a second."

If this was all right, I would've hated to see what the alternative was. Slowly, the pressure started to seep from my spark down my left arm.

Lucien fidgeted beside me, his nervousness coating me even though I knew I shouldn't be able to feel his emotions. Maybe it was Meri's touch that brought a hint of my old gift back. Whatever it was, he was growing more panicked by the second. If I didn't get some magic into him, he might bolt.

My fingers dug into his, and a moment later, the warm, prickly magic reached our joined hands. I stood once more, fortified by the magic.

Lucien flinched with the jolt, but his nervousness fled, followed by grim determination.

"That's it," Bea coaxed. "Good. Nice and easy now."

The burning magic was concentrated to just my right arm, the poison seeping from Kat. My power swirled in my chest, taming whatever spell Lucien had used, forcing it back into him, though slower than I would've liked. My energy was failing fast. It took all I had to stay sitting upright. By the time the last dregs of magic filtered into Lucien, my breathing was shallow and my eyelids heavy. If I hadn't been so worried for Kat, I could've drifted off right then.

"Kat?" Bea said, leaning over my friend.

I glanced down at her. The fragile appearance of her skin had disappeared, replaced by her usual pale, pinkish tone. Firm muscle tone replaced the gauntness, and she appeared healthy even. The only problem? She hadn't yet opened her eyes.

"What's wrong? Why isn't she waking up?" I stood, my knees buckling under the stress of the spell we'd wielded.

Kane rushed forward and scooped me in his arms, saving me from landing on my backside.

I clung to him, grateful for his support.

"She needs time," Bea said, though I sensed her worry. It washed over me. I glanced at Meri. She'd moved back across the room. How was I still feeling emotions? I shook my head. I'd worry about that later.

"No," Lucien ground out. "This isn't happening. It can't." He sat down in front of me and placed a tentative hand on Kat's leg. "Not like this."

We all stared at him.

"What do you mean?" Bea asked carefully.

Lucien's jaw worked as he tried to force the words out.

I grabbed Kane's hands, terrified of the expression on Lucien's face.

"I didn't know." Shaking his head, Lucien whispered, "I'm sorry."

"Didn't know what?" I asked, fear taking up residence in every corner of my heart and mind.

He stood and walked to the door. With his hand on the knob, he hung his head. "It's my fault. It's a curse." He turned then, anguish lining his face. "I thought once the magic was reversed, she'd wake up. But now, seeing her so perfect as if under glass, I know."

"What are you trying to say?" Bea touched his arm gently.

"It was a black magic curse. I walked into it years ago. I honestly thought it had died with Alannah." He paused, seeming to try to find the right words. "I didn't realize until just now..."

"What kind of curse?" Bea's voice had a tremor of fear and, without warning, tears fell unchecked down my cheeks.

Lucien looked as if he might break at any moment. "A black heart curse. As long as I'm alive, she won't wake up."

Chapter 10

"And you're just telling us now?" My voice was laced with a hard edge. Kat's life was on the line! Magic zipped down my arms, making my fingers ache from holding it back.

"Jade!" Bea scolded. "Take a deep breath and try to calm down. Losing control of your power again isn't going to help."

I tamped down the magic. Pain clutched my heart, squeezing until I thought it would shatter right in my chest. Not Kat. She didn't deserve this.

"Let's go downstairs and let Lucien explain." Bea gently took my hand in hers, but I didn't move.

"No. I won't leave her." I physically could not move. Though Kat was lying down with her eyes closed, a small smile tugged at her lips, her complexion as fresh as if she'd spent a day at the spa. Pink skin and rosy cheeks. Peaceful. As though maybe she was having a really pleasant dream.

"She's fine right now. I promise. Whatever this is, we'll fix it," Bea said.

Kane's warm hands slipped over my shoulders. "Do you want me to stay again?"

My body started to tremble, and coherent thought fled my mind. They were crazy if they thought I'd leave now. I shook my head violently and moved back to sit on the bed beside my best friend. I was the reason she knew witches. If I hadn't come to town, she never would've met Lucien, and this wouldn't have happened. Of course, she could've ended up being controlled by a demon, but that was another matter entirely.

"I'm not leaving," I said again and placed a protective hand on Kat's arm.

Bea stared at me.

Lucien hung his head and moved to the door. "I should probably go."

"Lucien," a faint voice called from the bed.

Startled, I jerked and peered down at Kat. Her eyes hadn't opened, but she'd shifted, and her eyebrows were furrowed.

"Kat?" I asked, praying I wasn't imagining her voice.

"Hmm." Her eyes fluttered.

"Oh, Jesus," Lucien uttered and rushed to Kat's other side. He reached for her but pulled away before he touched her. "Kat? I'm here. I'm so sorry. Can you hear me?"

This time when her eyes fluttered, they stayed opened. She blinked, focusing on him.

Lucien let out a guttural sigh of relief. "There you are," he said softly.

"Thank the Goddess," I whispered and pressed my lips softly to her hand. "Don't ever scare me like that again."

"Hey." She glanced around the room, paused to take me in and once again focused on the man hovering beside her. "What happened?"

"An accident. Something with the spell went wrong. I'm so, so sorry, love."

Love? I narrowed my eyes at my second in command. What was going on here? Hadn't Lucien said a black heart curse? What did that mean exactly?

I brushed Kat's curls from her eyes. "You okay?"

Her hazel eyes met mine, and she gave me a small smile. "You helped me. I can feel it." She tapped her chest. "In here."

Tears burned my eyes again, but I blinked them back.

"I'm okay now. Thank you." She turned her attention to Lucien again. "Would the rest of you mind giving us a moment?"

I sucked in a breath but let Kane guide me toward the door. "We'll be downstairs if you need us," he said.

She nodded but didn't break her gaze from Lucien. He sat there, studying her, appearing heartbreakingly miserable. His entire body was tense as if he were holding himself back. From what? Leaving? Or wrapping her in his arms? I was pretty sure it was the latter.

I forced myself to give them the privacy they obviously craved but paused in the hallway.

"Downstairs," Bea said. "We need to talk."

As she followed Meri down to the first floor, I stayed behind outside Kat's room and glanced up at Kane. My throat closed on a sob. His expression went soft, and he crushed me to his chest. I held on, trembling, but this time my eyes stayed dry.

"What can I do?" he whispered into my ear.

"You're already doing it."

We stood together, me clinging to his sturdy frame and him holding me up after another awful day that seemed to never end.

Eventually, I took a deep breath and pulled away just enough so I could see into his rich chocolate eyes. "Thank you."

"For what, love?" He ran a gentle thumb along my cheek.

"For being here. Letting me do what I need to do without going all caveman on me."

He chuckled. "Don't think I haven't thought about it."

I laughed. "Really? When?"

The amusement faded from his face as he turned stoic. "Every time I see you take your life into your hands to save someone else."

I sobered. He'd watched me do that on more occasions than I cared to think about. But he had as well. A few months ago he'd followed me into Hell—literally. And I knew he'd do it again.

He pressed his lips to mine, kissing me softly.

"Jade!" Bea called, impatience lining her command.

I blew out an exasperated breath. Couldn't we have one moment?

Kane pulled away slightly. "How long do you think it will be before she comes up here and drags you away from me?"

I glanced up into his humor-filled face and shook my head. "Mere moments, I'm afraid."

"That's a shame." He winked and tucked my hand in his as he led me to the stairs. "Time for answers."

I pressed close to his side, wishing I could turn the clock back twenty-four hours. I didn't want to deal with any more supernatural crap. There was wedding cake to sample back at Kane's house. If I'd been the only one affected by the day's crazy events, I would've walked out right then and there. But I wasn't. This was Kat, and I had to know what happened.

As Kane and I rounded the corner to descend the steps, we almost ran smack dab into Bea. Her face was contorted into a frustrated grimace. She stopped on the top step and placed her fists on her hips. "What are you doing?"

"Following your orders and going downstairs," I huffed, but as I studied her, my irritation vanished. She was breathing heavier than normal, her hair mussed, and her hands were fidgeting. I'd never seen Bea act so uncollected before. The realization terrified me. She'd never failed to supply us with competent solutions to all our issues, even when she'd been the one slowly fading away. Now she seemed flustered. Scared. My heart plummeted into my stomach. "Bea, what's going on?"

Her face morphed into part relief, part anxiety. She shook her head and turned around. "Follow me. This requires something stronger than tea."

Once back downstairs, Kane led me to the dining room table. He sat to my right, while Meri followed Bea into the kitchen. The pair of them went to work brewing coffee and slicing a freshly made carrot cake.

"I'm not really hungry," I said, eyeing the cake as if it was the last crumb of food in a post-apocalyptic world.

Kane chuckled. "No one's buying it. Cream cheese frosting? Yeah, that carrot cake doesn't stand a chance."

Bea sent me a hint of a smile. "You don't have to eat it, dear. I'll put it out in case anyone needs something to pick at."

Meri fished plates out of the cupboards, grabbed some silverware, and took a seat at the table.

Bea sat, and instantly we all gave her our attention. She pushed the carrot cake in my direction. "Here."

I shook my head, but Kane reached for the plate and grabbed us both generous helpings.

"Carrot cake helps every situation," he said.

I refrained from rolling my eyes and clutched my warm coffee mug. My insides were cold with trepidation. Whatever Bea had to say, I knew I wasn't going to like it.

She cleared her throat. "For the time being, I recommend you suspend Lucien's magic."

Well, yeah. I'd already figured that one out on my own. I was the coven leader. It was my place to temporarily suspend the magic of any of the members if the need arose. What else was I going to do after he'd almost killed Kat? "Of course. But can you tell me what happened up there?"

She pursed her lips and shook her head. "I'm not exactly sure. I need to talk with Lucien."

I glanced at the stairs, suddenly worried he might accidentally hurt her again. I pushed the chair back and started to rise.

"Wait." Bea put her hand over mine. "We need to discuss this before Lucien comes down."

With my gaze trained on the stairs, I lowered back into the chair. "Okay, but if he takes too long, I'm going back up."

"Understandable. But back to neutralizing his magic. You can't be the one to do it. You'll need to ask someone to take your place." Her amber gaze never left mine.

"Why?" The spell was a simple, yet powerful one.

"Because with your ghost possession problem and what just happened up there, I'm afraid it's too much magic to wield. It will leave you even more vulnerable."

I frowned, not liking the way that sounded at all. "I don't even know if Rosalee is powerful enough to do something like that."

Bea shook her head. "She's not. Besides you, Lucien is the only one who possesses that kind of power, and obviously he can't suspend himself."

"That leaves you then." I grabbed a fork and picked at the walnuts in the carrot cake just to keep my hands busy.

After taking another sip of coffee, she put down her cup and stood. "There's more. If you ask me to revoke Lucien's power, in effect you'll be handing me the coven leadership again."

My body turned cold, and an odd sense of loss filtered through me. Give her back the coven leadership? I slumped in the chair. I hadn't even agreed to transfer power, and I was already having a physical reaction. The shock of it startled me. When had the coven become so important to me? "I don't understand. Why does that matter?"

Kane's hand moved to my neck, his fingers soothing my tense muscles. I cast him a soft glance, grateful for the support.

"You'll be giving me power over your members." Bea tapped her nails on the table, almost nervously. "Remember when you reinstated Lailah's power? You were already the coven leader. You had to do it. If I'd tried, it would have undermined your leadership, weakened it, and left you all vulnerable. The same will happen if I take over without a power switch."

"And if we were to switch roles for just long enough for you to neutralize Lucien?" I held my breath. I wasn't sure why I cared so much. I hadn't wanted it when she'd given it to me. But the current that ran through me when we worked together was comforting. More comforting than almost anything, except my connection to Kane.

"We could do that." She eyed me thoughtfully. "But are you sure you want to?"

Anger flared deep inside me, an anger that made me almost flinch. Where had that come from? "Are you saying you want the coven back?"

"No. Not at all." She pressed her lips into a thin straight line then picked up a thick leather volume I recognized as a spell book. "I gave you my personal copy because I was ready to retire. I was and am ready to let the coven go. But you're compromised. If something happens to you, if for some reason you end up possessed, that ghost will have access to the coven. With Lucien out of commission, no one will be able to stop her."

Crap on toast. I hadn't even considered that. As much as I didn't want to transfer power, I had a responsibility to keep everyone safe. Bea was powerful and exceptionally knowledge-able, which certainly made her the best choice. "Let's do it."

"Now?" she asked.

"Yes." Before I had time to change my mind, I stood, gesturing to Meri, and we all headed outside to Bea's unmarked circle in her backyard. She kept the marks covered with enchanted grass. That seemed awfully convenient.

Meri paused on the porch. "Is it cool if I stay here?"

"Should be fine," Bea called over her shoulder. "This won't take long."

My feet dragged as I made my way across the perfectly mani-cured yard. The almost-full moon illuminated Bea's flowerbeds. One was full of white and pink blooming annuals.

Bea raised her hands, and a pentagram flickered to life under her feet. I stopped when I was directly across from her in the middle of it.

"Take my hands," she said.

I pressed my hands to hers. The spell was simple. All it took was a declaration of intent and a spark of magic. "Ready?"

She squeezed my fingers. "I know it's hard to give up." Her voice was low enough that I was certain Kane and Meri couldn't hear. "The connection is unexplainable. Trust me. I'm aware this isn't easy, but it's only temporary until we find a solution to the possession."

"Yeah." What else could I say? As far as I knew, until my soul was complete, I'd be forever vulnerable to wayward ghosts. Damn angel council! This was their fault. I tamped down the mounting anger and focused. Bea didn't need to get zapped because I couldn't control my emotions.

I gripped Bea's warm hands with my cold ones and focused. My magic sparked in my chest, warm and familiar. "I, Jade Calhoun, hereby transfer the leadership of the New Orleans coven to Beatrice Kelton, effective immediately." Power zinged from my fingers to Bea's, and I jumped back, ripping my hands from her grip. "Shit! I did it wrong."

Bea's eyebrows pinched, and she took a step forward. "What makes you say that?"

The acute loss of the coven collective left me hollow and raw with emotions, and I had trouble forming words. "Last time…um…" I swallowed the lump in my throat. "When I gave Lailah back her power, I created a connection. I think my magic just did the same thing."

Bea smiled. "No, Jade. It didn't." She patted my arm. "You did it perfectly. The zing is supposed to happen with this transfer. We're no more connected than we were before. Well, maybe a little bit. You're still part of the coven. If I call on you, you'll feel it."

"Oh." I didn't remember the zing from when she'd transferred the coven to me, but we'd been battling black magic at the time. My memory was hazy. "Okay. I guess we better get Lucien so you can bench him before anything else happens."

Bea gave me a sad smile. "I always hated this part of the job." She slipped her arm through mine, and we walked back up to Meri and Kane, who were still waiting on the porch.

"This won't be forever," Kane soothed. "We'll fix this. We always do."

I nodded my agreement but secretly wondered when our luck would run out.

Bea waved for us to sit in the living room while she headed upstairs to deal with Lucien. After a few minutes of complete silence, Bea returned with a sullen Lucien following her. My heart ached for him. I'd lost the coven leadership; he'd lost his ability to cast magic. It wasn't a position I ever wanted to find myself in.

"Have a seat," Bea said to Lucien.

He sat on the chair next to Meri and stared across the room, his eyes glazed over in thought.

"What's a black heart curse?" I asked.

Lucien's head jerked up, and he locked eyes with Bea.

She studied him for a moment. "It's just a name for a specific type of death curse. In this case, it appears to be tied to the spell Lucien used. Though, black heart curses don't usually have longevity. He was correct in his thinking that something like this shouldn't have happened again." She moistened her lips in thought. "I need to do some research to figure out why it's lingering. Lucien, any ideas?"

"No. I've even used the spell successfully after..." He cleared his throat. "I have no idea why this is happening."

Bea pursed her lips and jotted down notes. "That's very unusual."

Lucien nodded.

She put down her pen. "I'll make some phone calls tomorrow."

The room fell silent. Another mystery. What the hell was going on?

A few moments ticked by, and then Bea rose and crossed the room. She perched on her sunflower print couch next to me. "Let's talk about the possession."

"Do you know if Meri and I can do anything other than stay joined at the hip for twenty-four hours a day?" I asked.

"I happen to know a little bit about souls." Bea pursed her lips. "I did a lot of studying over the last few weeks."

I felt my eyes go wide. "You did? Why?"

Bea's expression turned tender. "Would I do anything else? I may have given the coven leadership up, but I didn't abandon you. Souls are nothing to mess with, as you can see. This is part of the reason I warned you to be careful to not give up any of your soul while transferring energy."

I straightened. "You knew I could be possessed?"

Kane's hand tightened on my leg, but he kept silent.

"No, dear." She glanced at Meri. "Angels deal in souls. They have a command over them. For Meri, having half a soul is only inconvenient because her power is weakened. She has less to work with. But for you, your soul is who you are. It's that piece of you that keeps you grounded here on earth. If you lose it, you lose yourself. In turn, if someone takes it over, you're lost inside yourself until you waste away."

Trepidation filled me and my fingernails dug into her chintz couch. "Are you saying a ghost can steal my soul? What about Meri? Is hers in danger, too?"

"There isn't a record of an angel being possessed before. We don't think Meri's at risk. But it does appear that you *are* susceptible to ghost possession. If one is strong enough, she could steal your soul."

I let out a barely audible gasp. "Camille."

Kane perched on the edge of the sofa, staring intently at Bea. "But with Meri around she's safe, right?"

"For now."

Kane stood, almost knocking over the coffee table. "What does that mean, *for now*? Jade's risked everything for a lot of people, including Meri. There must be something that can be done."

The strain in his voice made me want to wrap my arms around him and block out the rest of the world. Intellectually, I knew Bea was telling us my life was on the line again. I should've been freaking out. I should've been asking what I could do to change the trajectory of my path. Ever since I was fifteen, my world had been turned upside down by magic and the supernatural. I was supposed to be marrying my best friend, not trying to dodge a goddamned ghost intent on inhabiting my body. I shuddered at the thought.

"I think I have a solution," Bea said.

I waited for her to continue. When she didn't, I narrowed my eyes at her, frustrated with the buildup.

"Well?" Kane sank back down next to me and grabbed my hand once more. "What is it?"

Meri leaned forward. "We think a spell can be woven around both her parents to help rebuild her soul enough that she'll be able to fend off attacks by herself."

"My parents. As in my mom *and* dad." The bottom dropped out of my stomach. I pressed a shaking hand to my middle. I hadn't talked to my dad in seventeen years.

"Yes. You came from them. They have everything you need to make you whole again."

"Wait. Are you saying there was a cure for Jade's soul this whole time?" Kane asked, anger clouding his eyes. "Why are we only finding this out now?"

"No, we didn't know," Meri said, grabbing some notes from Bea's table. "Like Bea said, she's been doing some research, and combined with my knowledge of how souls are formed, we're pretty sure this will work. It's highly unusual and will mean we need the angel council's approval, but it should work."

He increased the pressure on my hand. "How exactly are souls formed?"

Meri pressed her lips together and then took a deep breath. "We don't talk about this outside of the angel realm, but each individual soul is seeded with pieces of the parent. It's in their DNA. If we can get the council to agree to a small transfer, Bea can perform the spell and Jade's soul should be able to heal itself."

"They won't do it," I said in a small voice. "They'll never agree to an intentional soul splitting." Why would they risk two more souls? Even if we did happen to find Dad.

"They might." Meri passed one of the papers in my direction. "Bea found a mention about an intentional soul healing in the coven records from about two hundred years ago."

The writing was faded on the yellowed parchment paper, but I made out the note about a torn soul healed with the help of the parents. No other details.

I took a shaky breath. "Does it have to be my dad, too? Can't it just be my mom?"

Bea shook her head sadly. "One isn't enough. Do you think it'll be hard to get your dad to come?"

Tears welled in my eyes, and I wasn't sure if it was because I wanted to see him or if I didn't. "I have no idea. I don't even know where he is."

Chapter 11

I sat next to Kat. She was still weak, but sitting up and alert. I forced the thoughts of my dad from my mind. I didn't want to think about him or how he'd walked out on us. Leaning forward, I smoothed her curls from her forehead. "You'll be fine here for the night without us?"

"Sure." She smiled, appearing as if nothing had ever happened. "I don't think there's anywhere safer. Do you?"

"I'm not worried about your safety. Not here. Just your piece of mind."

Her smile faded. "I'm not going to lie. What happened was awful. I mean, I don't even really know what happened. One minute, I was waiting on Lucien, and the next, my whole body felt like it was in a vice grip. My head felt like someone was stabbing it with an ice pick. I know I was screaming, but Lucien's warm magic drifted over my skin. At first, everything was better…" Her eyes shifted, and she stared at one of the Garden District paintings on the wall.

"Then?" I prompted.

She snapped her head back in my direction, her eyes hard and cold. "You don't want to know, Jade. Trust me. It was awful. If I tell you, you'll never think of Lucien the same, and I don't want that. It's not his fault."

"This happened before, Kat. How can you say it isn't his fault?" My chest ached. I didn't want to be angry with Lucien. I liked him. But he'd almost killed my best friend, the one person who knew everything about me.

"I know. And he's really beating himself up about it." She rolled onto her side and propped up on one elbow. "You have no idea the level of self-loathing he experiences for what happened to his friend. After she"—Kat gulped—"passed, Lucien was in a dark place for a very long time. Therapy and counter spells got him to where he is today. He swears he thought the spell died with her. He was only trying to help me."

"But why did he use the same spell? What was he thinking?" I couldn't imagine ever again using a spell that had gone so terribly wrong.

"Please let it go," she said, her eyes pleading with me. "I don't blame him, and I don't want you blaming him either. It happened. It's over. Now we need to find out why and what we can do to help him through this."

Those damn tears were back, burning my eyes again. This had always been one of the things I loved most about Kat—her absolute compassion for those she loved. She saw the best in us and took us for who and what we were, despite the fact that she didn't have one magical bone in her body. She came along for the ride and helped in any way she could. "I love you."

"I love you, too." She smiled through the tears swimming in her eyes. "Now go home and talk to your mom. She might at least have the last known address of your dad."

"What makes you think he'll even agree to see me?" I hadn't spoken to my dad or heard from him since I was ten years old. I couldn't imagine calling him up and saying, *Hey, Dad. Just in case you didn't know, I'm a witch, and my soul's in danger. Can you come down to New Orleans and help Mom put me right?*

Oh, jeez. Yeah, that would go over well. I lowered my voice. "What if he thinks I'm nuts?" Everyone I'd grown up with had. I'd been the class freak. I didn't want to face my dad and feel like that again.

Kat sat up and squared her shoulders, putting on her practical face. The one she wore when she was trying to talk sense into me. "You won't know until you ask."

"Shit. I hate when you're all logical and crap." I grinned, grateful that she seemed to be perfectly okay.

Maybe she was right. I was still furious at Lucien, but I'd try to put it behind us for her sake.

And my dad…I sighed. I really, really didn't want to call him. I'd had enough rejection in my life. I wasn't eager for more. But if it meant living with Meri for the rest of my life or sucking up my pride and talking to the ass who walked out on us, then I'd do my best to track him down. She couldn't stay by my side forever, especially if she had some weird connection to Dan. My relationship with Kane deserved more.

I kissed Kat on the cheek. "I'll talk to Mom."

"I know." Her lips quirked up into a mocking smile. "Get out of here so I can get some rest."

Laughing, I headed for the door. "Call me if you need anything."

I turned Pyper's Bug down the narrow Garden District streets and glanced in the rearview mirror. Kane was following us back to his house. Beside me, Meri was slumped in the passenger seat, staring out the window into the darkness.

"Everything okay?" I asked.

She turned tired eyes on me. "Fine. I was just wishing for my own bed is all. It's been a trying day."

"I'm sorry. I know it's hard to be in other people's spaces."

"Don't worry about it." She reached over and turned on the radio, loud enough to make talking difficult.

I took the hint and drove on in silence. When we hit a red light, I turned down the radio and faced her. "Did we need to stop by your place to pick up anything? Toiletries? A change of clothes?"

She shook her head. "Dan's going to bring some stuff by."

Right. Great, I got to see my ex…again. I suppressed a sigh and turned right onto Saint Charles. Ten minutes later, we pulled up in front of Kane's shotgun double. And sure enough, there was Dan waiting for us on the porch.

Meri's face lit up, and once again, I wondered exactly what kind of relationship they had. Not romantic, but it almost seemed magical, as if something mystical was holding them together.

Dan, dressed in faded jeans and a black T-shirt, met us on the sidewalk. His light brown hair needed a trim, and he probably hadn't shaved in a week. If it hadn't been for the stubble on his face, he would've looked exactly as I remembered him in high school. An intense desire to hightail it into the house clutched at my stomach, but I couldn't leave Meri's side. Instead, I was forced to invite him in. And then I felt terrible for not wanting to. Dan was a decent guy. It wasn't all his fault we'd broken up, nor was it his fault he'd almost been possessed by a demon or that he'd spent time in Hell.

I shook my head and marched up to the front door. "Dan, did you want to come in?"

He turned from Meri, surprise clear in his pale emerald eyes. "You sure?"

I'd certainly never invited him in before, not that he hadn't been in the house a number of times. I'd just never personally invited him. "I know you and Meri need to talk. Come on in so you can get some privacy." Under one roof, they could go into another room where I wouldn't be forced to witness whatever it was they had to say to each other.

Kane pulled his car to a stop behind Pyper's and then came up the steps just as I was opening the door. "Hey," I said as he placed a hand on the small of my back. Once inside, he ran his hand the length of my spine. I closed my eyes for a second, trying to wish everyone away. Too bad I didn't know a spell for that.

Meri and Dan followed us in. I waved them toward the guest room.

"Jade?" Gwen emerged from the back of the house with a plate and a dishtowel. She absently dried it while searching my expression. "How's Kat?"

Gwen took me in after Mom had disappeared into Hell, only a few days before I'd turned fifteen. From the first week I'd moved in with her, Gwen had loved my friend just as much as I did. "She's fine. With Bea's help, we managed to reverse the spell. Bea's keeping an eye on her overnight just in case."

"But is she okay? Really okay?" Gwen's eyes shone with genuine worry.

I searched them, wondering if she'd had a premonition. No, she was usually much more stoic after she saw the future. "Really. Good as new. Bea's just being cautious."

Gwen let out a relieved sigh. "Thank the Goddess." She ran a hand down my arm, then turned and disappeared back into the kitchen.

My steps slowed as I followed the sound of my mom's voice.

"It'll be okay, you know," Kane whispered. "No matter what. I'll give you my soul if I have to."

I stopped and gazed up at him. "You would, wouldn't you?"

His chocolate-brown eyes turned molten with emotion. "It's no less than you'd do for me. And if your deadbeat dad can't be bothered, I'll personally hunt him down and set him straight."

A smile tugged at my lips. "You're too good to me."

"Don't you forget it." He leaned down and brushed his firm, warm lips over mine.

I placed my hands on his broad chest. "I love you."

"I know." His eyes crinkled as he smiled down at me.

"We're going to get through this with both our souls intact. Got that?"

"Yes, ma'am."

"I won't have it any other way." Because the alternative was unthinkable. I wouldn't take his soul anymore than he'd take mine.

"Me neither." He bent down, his lips gently brushing over mine again. He hesitated for just a moment, but when I gently clasped my teeth over his lower lip, his tongue darted, tasting me. I opened to him, and our tongues met, tangling in a slow waltz.

I pressed against his lean frame, wanting to feel every inch of him. It had only been a few days since we'd been together, but after the recent events, it seemed like weeks. Running my fingers up his arms, I stopped when his broad shoulders filled my hands. He was tall, lean, and powerful in his own way, beautiful and all mine, forcing that exquisite ache of desire deep in my center. Strength exuded from him, demanded to possess me with his gentle yet commanding kiss.

I nibbled, biting the corner of his mouth as he turned to trace kisses along my jawline. His sure lips possessed my neck, sucking and teasing until I swayed and my knees weakened. The things he did to me… It was a wonder I didn't combust right there in his arms.

"Jade," he whispered, "I want you."

My breath caught. Goddess, I wanted him too. Wanted to rip his clothes off, make him mine right there in the living room. Feel his touch on my stomach, my thighs as he pulled me to him, as he entered me, claiming me as his, again and again.

"Jade, honey?"

"Shit," I mumbled, reality crashing back down on me.

Kane smiled, his lips still pressed to mine. His tongue darted into my mouth for one last tantalizing taste of his coffee flavor. Then he pulled back, holding me at arms' length with his hands still on my hips.

"Oh!" Mom yelped as she stepped into the room and pivoted to walk back out. "Sorry, didn't mean to interrupt."

Kane laughed.

"Stop it." I swatted his chest and giggled as my face heated. "Mom, nothing's going on. Come back."

"Um, honey, why don't you join me in the kitchen?" she called. "I cut up strawberries."

Kane's eyebrows rose. "I bet she made homemade whipped cream too."

"Probably." Tingles slid through me as I recalled the last time we'd had whipped cream in the house. Yanking him to me, I crushed my lips to his, pouring my heart into the kiss and running my hands through his hair until I had to pull back to take a breath. Winded, I took just a moment to refill my lungs. Then I smiled sweetly. "Consider yourself lucky. No one has ever ranked above homemade whipped cream before."

I left him leaning against the living room wall, his body taut and eyes brimming with desire. Glancing over my shoulder, I whispered, "I'm sending Mom and Gwen to my apartment since Meri's here. I'll meet you in our room in one hour."

"That had better be a promise," he replied, his voice husky.

I gave him a slow nod and forced my feet to keep moving forward. I'd give almost anything to fall into his arms and block out the rest of the world right then and there. And Kane as a distraction would do just that. For as long as I needed.

Liquid heat sent sparks of desire everywhere, and I had to stop in the hall restroom to splash water on my face. I could not have a conversation with my mother until I cooled off. She'd already walked in on us groping at each other like horny teenagers. That was bad enough.

"Hey." I scooted into the kitchen. "What's up?" I glanced around and found Mom at the table with a bowl of berries, whipped cream, and a crock pot of melted chocolate. "Looks like you went all out."

Mom shrugged and lifted her hands in a vague gesture. "I wanted to do something nice after the awful day you had."

Gwen pulled the full coffee pot from the counter, gesturing to a mug. "Coffee?"

I'd already had a few cups at Bea's, but if I was going to gorge on Mom's offerings, I'd need it. I nodded and headed to the refrigerator, nervous energy pulsing through my body. Mom and I never talked about Dad. What would she say when I asked about him?

Mom stood. "What do you need, Jade? I'll get it. You just sit."

I waved an impatient hand. "I've got it, Mom. You've worked hard enough."

Gwen passed me a cup only three quarters of the way full. I smiled. She knew exactly what I wanted. After a quick search behind the orange juice and milk, I pulled out the bottle of Irish cream. Without asking, I added a shot to Gwen's mug and took the chilled bottle to the table. I lifted it in offering. "Mom?"

She glanced at Gwen and then back at me. "I'd better not."

I raised an eyebrow in question, but Mom shook her head. "Okay, then." I set the bottle on the countertop. "I'll leave it out if you change your mind." She might need it after she heard what I had to say.

Mom dished up generous helpings of strawberries and whipped cream, while Gwen and I settled into our chairs.

"Bea knows how to fix my soul," I blurted.

Startled, Mom dropped a dollop of whipped cream on the table. "Oh, shoot." She grabbed a paper towel and went to work on the mess as if it were a red wine stain on white carpet instead of some cream on plain wood.

"Mom." I placed a hand over hers, stopping her from smearing the cream all over the table. "It's fine. I'll get it later."

She pursed her lips at the film still stuck to the table but dropped the napkin and looked at me. "How can she fix it?"

"We need to call Dad."

Chapter 12

Mom didn't even flinch. She just stared at me, her mouth agape.

Gwen glanced between us then stood. "I'll give you some privacy." She brushed a reassuring hand over my shoulder as she retreated to the living room.

I propped my elbows on the table and rested my chin in my hands, prepared to wait Mom out.

After a few beats, she closed her mouth and swallowed. "You know that's impossible."

"Why?"

"You know why." Her tone was hard with an impatient edge to it.

I reached across the table and grabbed her hand. The one that was picking at Kane's linen placemat. "No, Mom, I don't know why. We haven't talked about Dad since the last time he failed to show up for his visitation."

"Yeah!" Her eyes were wide open now, blazing with anger. "Seventeen years ago, he abandoned you. We never heard from him again." She sucked in a breath. "You didn't…I mean, he didn't get in touch while I was…gone?"

Gone. That was one way of putting it. Mom spent twelve years in purgatory after being kidnapped by a demon. It would have been nice if Dad had shown up to check on me when she'd disappeared, but that never happened. The state hadn't been able to find him at his last known address.

"No, he didn't get in touch, and I didn't know how to find him. But we have to now. It's important."

She pushed her dessert away and shook her head, her mouth clamped shut in that tight line again.

I suppressed a frustrated sigh. If she didn't cooperate, my entire existence was on the line. "You haven't even asked me why we need him."

"It doesn't matter. No one knows where he is, and even if we did, he'd be useless. His *work* was always more important than we were."

She must've been thinking that he'd run out on her, too, left her alone to raise a child on a healer's self-employed income. No child support. Nothing. He'd hurt her so much, she'd shut men out of our lives completely. I'd never even seen her date after that.

I took a long sip of the spiked coffee, grateful for the soothing burn sliding into my belly. Then I softened my tone. "If we had a choice, I wouldn't ask you to do this. But if we don't find him, I could end up permanently possessed—or worse, stuck to Meri's side for the rest of my life."

"Good God, don't let that happen," Meri said from behind me, horror in her husky tone. "I'll track the bastard down myself if you want. I knew him once, too."

"Meri!" Mom scolded.

"Sorry, Hope." The angel took a seat next to Mom and wrapped an arm around her shoulders. "But if it makes you feel better, I know a few ass-kicking spells that don't leave any marks."

Mom let out a surprised huff of laughter and leaned back to take a look at her longtime friend. "You'd do it, too."

Meri grinned. "With the way he left you two? It would be my pleasure."

I glanced behind her. "Did Dan leave?"

She nodded and as Mom and Meri chattered about ways to enact revenge on my father, old memories of him surfaced.

A tall, sandy-haired man with a quirky half-smile played like a film reel in my mind. That was one of the few images that had stayed with me through all the years.

I stood at the edge of a creek, holding on tight to a sapling fishing pole while he baited the hook, his eyes twinkling in the morning sun. Clear, kind, blue eyes. That was my most vivid memory. I was eight years old, and Dad was teaching me to fish. The next time he'd come around, I was ten. I'd been engrossed in some cartoon and barely noticed when Mom went to answer the door. Five minutes later, she came back into the room, holding an envelope, her face pinched in anger as if I'd ignored her request to clean my room one too many times.

"Sorry! I'm going." I jumped up and skirted toward the hall." It'll only take a few minutes."

"Huh?" Mom sat on our shabby faded blue couch and glanced at me with confused eyes. "What will only take a few minutes?"

I paused. That fear of getting in trouble vanished at the odd look on her face. She wasn't angry at all. She was acting different, though, and for some reason, her emotions were closed to me.

"Jade?"

I shuffled back into the room and stood in front of her, not sure what to think of her quiet, unnatural tone.

"Come sit with me." She held out her arm, coaxing me over.

Snuggling next to her, I placed my head on her shoulder as she caressed my hair. "What's wrong, Mommy?"

"Nothing, sweetheart. I just wanted to hold my baby for a minute." She breathed deeply, her chest rising against my cheek.

I stared out the front window, and after a moment, I noticed a man leaning against a green truck, his head bowed. Then, almost as if he felt my gaze on him, he turned and raised his gaze to mine. Dad. My heart did a funny flip-flop in my chest because I hadn't seen him in so long. Why was he waiting outside?

Despite the distance, I knew he was troubled. Maybe it was the way he was slightly hunched or maybe the fact that he wasn't smiling. I couldn't remember a time he'd looked at me and not smiled in greeting. Just as I was about to pull away from Mom to run outside, he gave me a jerky wave and climbed in his truck.

"Dad!" I cried and ran to the window. The tires squealed as a puff of smoke spewed behind the retreating truck. I spun back to my mother, hands on my hips. Tears spilled down my cheeks and I sucked in a gasp, my chest aching. "What did you say to him? Why'd he leave?"

The next thing I knew, Mom jumped from the couch and engulfed me in her arms, holding me. "I don't know, sweetie." She pulled me down into a nearby chair and rocked me as we both cried.

"He's never coming back," I said. "Is he?"

Mom shook her head, silent tears flowing from her jade green eyes. "I don't think so."

"Why?" I asked over and over, not accepting that she didn't have the answer. I hadn't seen him in two years. He hadn't even called or sent a card. And somehow my ten-year-old self knew he was gone for good.

I didn't know how long Mom and I stayed locked together in that chair. I could only remember her tugging me off to my bed much later and tucking me in. "Tomorrow, we'll plant a birch tree."

Clutching a stuffed dog, I stared up at her.

"The birch symbolizes a new beginning. We'll have ours, just you and me, shortcake."

I smiled. "Will there be strawberries and whipped cream after we're done?"

She laughed and cupped her palm to my cheek. "Of course. And melted chocolate, too. Now get some sleep. We have a big day tomorrow."

Just as I'd suspected, I never saw or heard from my father again. And after the birch tree was planted, we never spoke of him, either. Looking back, I was pretty sure my empath ability was picking up on whatever Mom must have known but not told me. She'd known without a doubt Dad was leaving for good, but she'd never told me why.

Now she'd have to tell me.

"Mom, I think you need to tell me what was in that letter."

She frowned. "What letter?"

Pain sluiced through me from the unwelcome memory. How could a father walk out on his kid? I'd never understood it. My fingers flexed, wanting to smash something. He'd walked out on me not once, but twice, and hadn't bothered to say goodbye either time. Angry tears burned the back of my eyes. I forced them back and took a deep breath, afraid I'd snap if I didn't get control of my rampant emotions. "The one Dad gave you the day before we planted the birch tree."

Mom's face went white, and I could've sworn something close to terror must have been running through her veins, though I couldn't feel it anymore. And frankly, I was glad. I had enough of my own emotional bullshit to deal with. All I wanted at that moment was the truth.

"There wasn't a letter," Mom said, her voice shaking.

I stood abruptly, knocking my spiked coffee over in the process. The creamy liquid seeped into the placemat, leaving a large, dark brown stain. I stared at the enlarging area, my fists clutched tight. "Stop lying. I saw the envelope that day. I know Dad gave it to you. What did it say?"

"Hope?" Meri asked, confusion ringing in her voice.

Mom's chair screeched against the tile floor as she pushed it back and rose to her feet.

I snapped out of my coffee-spill trance and glared at Mom. "Where are you going?"

Her hand came up and clutched at her neck as if someone was trying to choke her. "I need a minute." She backed up slowly then ran out the back door, slamming it behind her.

Through the floor-to-ceiling windows at the back of Kane's kitchen, I watched her pace, mumbling to herself. She kicked at the decorative rocks, scattering them across his patio.

"Any idea what that's about?" I asked Meri without turning to look at her.

"No." From the corner of my eye, I saw movement as Meri crossed the kitchen. Dishes clattered in the sink before she returned to the table and yanked up the soiled mats.

I tore my eyes away from my mother, who was clearly arguing with herself, and took the linen from Meri. "Thanks." A minute later, armed with a clean cloth, I laid it over the pristine wood table Meri had wiped down. I met her gray eyes with a piercing stare. "You know something, though. You said you wanted to beat him for the way he'd left us."

She met my stare with a hard one of her own. "Yeah, I do. But it's your mother's story to tell, not mine."

My chest constricted, and not because Meri wouldn't tell me. I understood this was between me and my parents. But Mom used to be my best friend. I'd always trusted her to tell me the truth, and up until today, I'd never doubted that bond. Now, she seemed to be holding everything back. Had being trapped in Purgatory for all those years changed that part of her?

Couldn't she see my existence was being threatened? What could be so bad that she couldn't bring herself to tell me the truth?

"She needs time to work it out," Meri said, standing next to me as we watched Mom throw stones at Kane's shed. What was she doing? Having a nervous breakdown?

One after another the rocks ricocheted off the metal siding, the loud commotion filtering through the window. One flew and crashed against a small window, making me wince. The next one sailed right through the window, shattering the glass.

"Shit," I said under my breath.

"Don't worry about it," Kane said from behind me, making me jump.

"Where'd you come from?" I asked, leaning my back against his chest as he ran gentle fingers through my long hair.

"I was in the guest room, changing the bedding."

Jesus, I really was marrying the perfect man. While I'd been demanding my mother talk to me about my father, he was playing house maid, freshening up the guest room for Meri. "Thank you." I turned my head and kissed the back of his hand.

I felt him shrug behind me. "Not a big deal." He leaned in. "Maybe you should go outside and talk to her."

"Probably," I said wearily and eyed Meri. "Care to join me in the backyard so we can try to calm the crazy lady?"

She held out a slender hand. "After you."

I turned and gave Kane a quick kiss. "There's dessert and coffee if you're hungry."

He pressed his lips to my ear and whispered, "I think I'll wait for a private moment with you."

I couldn't help the smile tugging at my lips. Losing myself in him sounded like the perfect ending to the incredibly craptastic day I'd had. But it would have to wait.

"That had better be a promise." Reluctantly, I stepped away from him. The back door was maybe five feet away, but with each step, my limbs felt heavier, less willing to go where I commanded. I slowed, causing Meri to bump into me.

"Go on." Meri's hands wrapped around my shoulders, gently guiding me to the door. "The longer she stays out there, the harder it'll be to get her to talk."

"How did you…?" I didn't finish the question. I knew they'd known each other, but I hadn't realized Meri knew Mom *that* well. Of course she had. Mom wouldn't have risked her life or the possibility of losing me for just anyone. It dawned on me Meri and Mom had to have been best friends at some point. The kind of friends Kat and I were.

"You're right." I opened the back door, and with resolve, I squared my shoulders, ready for whatever secret Mom was keeping.

Chapter 13

The door closed behind us with a soft click. Mom froze, and the rocks in her hand fell unceremoniously back to the ground. She didn't turn to face us, though.

I glanced once at Meri. She waved me off the deck in Mom's direction. The gravel crunched in the silence under my boots. I came to a stop beside Mom, inspecting the shattered shed window in the pale moonlight.

"I'll get it replaced." Her voice sounded tired, distant.

"What's going on?" I asked.

"I failed you," she said quietly. "You were an empath. Do you know how hard it was to keep all my fears hidden from you? I learned to lock them all away in a tiny box in my heart." She made a face and turned away from me when she spoke again. "I was the queen of denial. I realize I really have no idea how you feel about your childhood."

It hit me dead center in the heart. She was terrified she'd messed up the time we'd had together. I stepped around her and met her unsteady gaze. "Mom, you did fine."

"I wanted to do right by you. Prayed I was doing enough to keep you safe and *normal*. You felt everything so deeply. I couldn't tell you. It would've torn you apart."

My brain stalled on her last confession. *It would've torn you apart.* "Tell me."

Tears gathered in her eyes and she shook her head, unable to speak. My heart broke with her obvious pain. I wrapped an arm around her waist and turned us so we were facing Meri.

Mom stared at her feet.

I nudged her gently. "I remember planting daisies and picking strawberries from the neighbor's fields in the moonlight so we could have a midnight snack. I remember feeling safe and warm, even during the worst winter storms." I shook my head. "Not a day went by that I ever felt like I was missing something in my life."

Mom's hand curled around mine and she squeezed so hard I almost winced. Her tears flowed faster, spilling down her cheeks even as her lips broke into the tiniest of smiles. "I'd have done anything for you."

"I know," I said quietly. "And you still would."

She tried to take her hand from mine, but I kept it in my grasp.

"I don't know what it's like to have a daughter of my own, but I do know how you felt about me. No one understands what it's like to be an empath. The sheer depth of your love for me was overwhelming, stifling even, but in the best possible way." I paused and pointedly met her gaze. "I never, for one moment, ever felt unloved. Not once. Not when I was with you. It's what I hope Kane and I share with a child of our own. So I know you never wanted to leave me. I *know*, Mom. Understand?"

Her eyes went wide with wonder, the tears finally slowing to a stop. "I knew you could sense what I was feeling." She frowned. "That sounds ridiculous. Of course you could. I just never realized you felt so much, saw so deeply into someone's soul."

This time I pulled my hand back, and she let me, probably realizing I needed some space to talk about this part of me. I'd never been all that comfortable with my gift, and for good reason. People don't like me invading their private emotions. And Mom had been with me through my early years when I hadn't been able to handle it.

"I don't feel that deeply with everyone. I mean, I didn't before I lost the ability. Only with you, because we always had a bond." I smiled. "Though you obviously learned somewhere along the line to hide some of the things you didn't want me to feel. But that overwhelming sense of loving me and keeping me safe no matter the consequences was always there."

Mom nodded, studying me. "You never told me any of this before."

I shrugged. "I didn't know how to verbalize what it was then. It was just the way things were. Until you left."

Mom's eyes misted again from emotions I could no longer feel.

"It's all right," I said quickly. "I already told you, I understand why you did what you did." I took a deep breath, willing myself to force out what I had to say next. "But now you have to stop protecting me. Tell me whatever you know about Dad. My soul depends on it."

She raised her head and gave me a pained look. "I already told you I don't know where he is. You should drop this, honey. He isn't coming back. Nothing we do can force him to come here."

I let that sink in for a minute, positive she was wrong. We were connected by DNA. A finding spell would do the trick. She had to know that. Maybe she was in denial? I let out a frustrated sigh. "You're not listening to me."

Her green eyes flashed with irritation. "And you're not listening to *me*."

"That's because you're not making sense. Look," I moved to sit in one of Kane's patio chairs. "I need *both* of you here. Camille has found a way to invade my body when Meri isn't around because my soul is too weak to keep her out. When we're together, I suspect we're both stronger, but we can't live our lives attached at the hip."

"What does your father have to do with that?" she asked stubbornly as she headed toward the backdoor. "I can do whatever you need."

"Mom!" I threw my hands up. "It's not a spell I need from just you. I need a tiny piece of both your souls to help mine heal. Both you *and* Dad. I was created by both of you, and it will take both of you to help regenerate my soul enough that I won't be susceptible to possession."

She clutched the doorknob and stood with her head bent, not saying anything.

Why was this so hard for her? He'd left seventeen years ago. Hadn't time healed anything for her? People changed. She'd changed. He must've. "You really haven't had any contact with him since that last day I saw him?"

She shook her head, appearing defeated.

"And you have no idea where he is?"

"No." She forced the word out.

Frustrated, I stood. "Well, unless you know any of his family, I think the best thing to do is a finding spell. I bet Bea will know one that can at least give us a general idea of where he is. Then we can go from there."

"It won't work." Mom raised her head and stood straight with her shoulders back. "There are things about him you don't know. He's powerful, sweetheart. A finding spell is just not enough."

"What things? Why can't you tell me what you know?" I dug my fingernails into my palms in total frustration.

"It's…" She glanced in Meri's direction, a plea of help in her eyes.

Meri sighed. "Jade, can we go inside? I need to have a private word with your mom."

I glanced between them, noting Mom's lips pressed together in a thin line. Shit. I'd lost her. "Fine." I met Mom's eyes. "But I'm not waiting much longer. Either find a way to tell me what you know, or I'll ask Bea for help." I was tired of fighting with her. If she didn't want to tell me why she was so bothered by seeing him, that was her business. But he was my father, and after seventeen years of not needing him, I did now. He owed me a couple of days of his time.

Mom nodded reluctantly. The three of us entered the house, and Meri tugged Mom off to the guest room. I poured another cup of Irish cream and added a dash of coffee just for flavor and then pulled out my phone. I went to punch in Bea's number and stopped when I saw the time. It was way too late to check on Kat, and surely Bea would've called if anything had gone wrong. I tucked my phone in my pocket and went to find Gwen.

In the living room, Kane and Gwen sat together on the couch, their heads bent together as they spoke softly. I smiled. On the table sat untouched slices of five different kinds of cake. Our wedding cake samples. Had the caterers really brought those today?

"There you are." Kane took my cup and set it on the end table and then tugged me down onto his lap. "We were waiting for you."

I smiled. "Looks to me like you two were plotting something."

"We were." Gwen grabbed a couple of plates and handed one to me. "We're trying to figure out how we're going to con you into choosing the mocha mousse cake instead of the cream cheese tiramisu."

I inspected the strawberry-swirled yellow cake on the plate now resting on my knee. "Mocha moose and cream cheese tiramisu are available options, and you handed me some crappy strawberry swirl cake? Have you lost your mind?"

Kane chuckled. "I told you."

Gwen smirked and shoved a generous piece of the offending cake in her mouth. Her eyes closed and she moaned in obvious pleasure. "Oh my Goddess, you have no idea what you're missing."

Dubious, I reluctantly picked up my fork. It couldn't be that good. Fruit-filled cakes never were. Unsure, I held the cake-filled fork up to Kane's mouth.

He grinned and turned to Gwen. "That's two for two. Nice try, but you lose." Then he shifted and wrapped his beautiful lips around the fork. My breath caught in my throat. How I wished I was the fork right then. If anything could clear my head of what had happened over the last sixteen hours, it was Kane and his expert lips.

Gwen cleared her throat. "I should probably get going."

"What?" I twisted and grabbed her arm to keep her seated. "We still have four types of cake to sample."

She shook her head, her eyes crinkling at the corners. "We all know which one you're going to pick." She bent down and kissed my cheek. "Have a good night. I'm going to grab your mother and head over to your apartment. Get some rest. We'll be back for brunch."

Gwen disappeared into the hall. A moment later, the door squeaked as she opened the guest room.

Kane placed the strawberry swirl cake back on the coffee table and pulled me against his chest, gently rubbing his hands down my arms. "How are you, pretty witch?"

"Honestly?"

He kissed my temple, his warm breath sending a shiver down my spine. "Honestly," he echoed.

I turned to gaze into his intense, toffee-flecked eyes, finding all the love I so desperately needed right then. "Exhausted, frustrated, wide awake, and frightened."

He took my face in his hands, cradling me with his palms. "I am all those things too, and all I can think about is carrying you away from this mess, from everyone, and locking us away for a month."

I shook my head. "That won't help if Camille decides to possess me again."

"No," he whispered as he brought his lips to mine. He tasted faintly of coffee and sugar. "That's the only reason I haven't kidnapped you. But I am going to carry you off to bed, where I can tuck you in beside me and keep you wrapped safely in my arms all night."

"That sounds perfect." I relaxed into him and clasped my hands around his neck, content to stay on the couch all night if it meant he never had to let me go.

"Have a good night," Gwen called as she tugged Mom behind her.

At the door, Mom paused and met my penetrating stare. She had information she didn't want to give up, and she needed to know our conversation wasn't over.

She took a calming breath. "I'll have the answers for you in the morning. I…" She swallowed. "It's been a lot of years, honey. Your father…" She swallowed again and pushed her dark bangs out of her eyes. "There are a few things you need to know, but I need a night to put my thoughts in order. Do you understand?"

I found myself nodding, even though I had no clue what she was talking about. He was my father. I deserved to know whatever she knew. But if she needed one night, I could wait that long. It wasn't like we could do anything about it at two in the morning anyway.

"Thank you. Get some sleep. I'll keep Gwen away until at least noon."

I smiled. Gwen was an early riser, and brunch in her world was at nine. "I appreciate that. It's been a long day."

"Goodnight." Mom inclined her head and then scooted out the door after Gwen.

"Finally," Kane breathed. Then he grinned. "Ready for bed?"

"Yes." But I didn't get up. I wrapped my hands tighter around his neck.

He eyed the buffet of dessert on the table. "Do you want to bring any of these?"

I glanced over and shook my head, not at all hungry. Not even for the tiramisu.

He arched one eyebrow. "You sure?"

"Positive." My mind was spinning with half a dozen wickedly hungry thoughts, but none of them included food. "Just take me to bed."

"Hang on." He gracefully rose to his feet, still clutching me in his arms. Glancing down at the cakes, he shook his head.

"I thought I'd never see the day you'd turn down a chance to lick tiramisu off—"

I crushed my lips to his, silencing his thought. Desire coiled in my center and heat burned from everywhere I touched him. Breathless, I pulled back. "I only want to taste you."

Chapter 14

Kane eased back, his chest heaving as he breathed heavily against my lips.

I stared into his intense eyes, my insides turning liquid at the desire smoldering there. "I thought you were ready to take me to bed?" I asked, my voice low and husky.

"I am. Believe me, I'm ready." Slowly, he lowered me until my feet touched the cool hardwood floors. He leaned in and touched his forehead to mine. "It's been an awful day, love. Maybe it's better if we slow down."

He slid his hands up my back, his touch so light, so familiar, so agonizing because I wanted him touching me everywhere all at once.

I shivered.

"Are you cold?" He pulled me against him, intensifying the heat already claiming my pulsing body.

"No."

"You have goose bumps." With sure hands, he stroked my bare arms as if to warm me.

I nodded, his touch sparking over my skin like a live wire. Why was he not recognizing the effect he had on me? "Kane…" I swallowed then bit down on my bottom lip as I stared at his tempting mouth. His gaze mimicked mine, and I slowly moved my tongue over my lower lip.

He took in a sharp breath. "Babe, it's been an awful day."

"You said that before." I clutched his biceps and gazed up at him. "I don't want to slow down. I want your touch to take it all away. Make me feel something other than fear." I pressed my lips to his, kissing him softly. Then I stilled and whispered, "Make it so I'm only thinking of you."

His whole body tensed, and he circled his arms around me, pressing me tight to his chest. I let go of the breath I'd been holding and melted against him, hugging tight. He buried his face into my neck and after a moment he pressed his lips lightly to my collarbone and slowly worked his way up until he nibbled just below my ear. "You're mine, pretty witch. Forever. Don't ever forget it."

I dug my fingers into his shoulders, holding on. Against the warmth of his neck, I said, "Show me."

His hand came up and tangled in my hair as his other hand tightened around me, molding me to him. He clutched harder, letting out a muffled groan. Then his grip loosened, and the slight pressure of his hands left a trail as he worked his way under my shirt. Every place he touched me heated, and a familiar hum took over deep in my core.

Unable to hold back any longer, I opened my mouth and darted my tongue out, tasting the hollow of his throat. My head swam from his male musk mixing with his fresh rain scent. His breath hitched and his hands shifted, clutching my ass as he lifted me up. My legs came around him, and I pressed myself to his solid frame. Then next thing I knew, he was carrying me down the hall.

Pressing me to the door, he kissed me, his tongue sweeping over mine in an all-encompassing possession. My bones started to melt.

Yes.

My mind quieted as my world narrowed to all things Kane—his intoxicating scent, the rough feel of his caress on my bare skin, his hard body demanding my attention. I was in the only place I wanted to be—in the arms of the man I loved.

With one hand gripping my thigh, Kane moved the other up my side until his thumb connected with the base of my breast. A low moan escaped from the back of my throat, and my hand came down clutching the doorknob.

"I want to see all of you," I said and slowly turned the knob until it clicked.

Kane heard it and pushed me into the room. One kick and the door swung closed, leaving us in total privacy. Finally.

I snaked my hands under his shirt, and his muscles tensed and rippled under my touch. I smiled into our kiss. I felt him smile back.

"Off," I commanded, gripping the hem of his shirt.

He grinned. "Anything you say." But instead of releasing me so I could undress him, his hands found the edge of my shirt and slipped beneath the cotton. His fingers rested lightly on my waist as he pulled back and gazed into my eyes.

Love. That was what I saw shining back at me. My chest squeezed, emotion piling up inside me, making me want to cry from the sheer intensity of it.

His expression turned hungry, determined. His hands came up my sides in a steady, controlled movement as he lifted me off him and placed me gently on my feet. Still keeping eye contact, he turned and sat on the bed, positioning me so I was standing nestled between his thighs.

I pulled his hands over his head. As I tugged his shirt up, I whispered in a very soft voice, "I said, this needs to come off."

Free of his shirt, I stared down at Kane, admiring his well-defined chest. I pressed my hand to his rapidly beating heart and sighed with the knowledge that this was forever. He was mine in every way, and I was his.

Kane placed a solid hand over mine and then brought my fingers to his lips. "It never slows down, you know."

"What doesn't?"

"The way it beats when you're touching me. Some days, I feel like it's going to jump right out of my chest." Lowering my hand, he placed it flat against his heart once more as if to prove his statement.

My stomach fluttered. In answer, I placed his other hand over my own erratically beating heart and sucked in a breath when his thumb caressed the swell of my breast. I arched into his hand, my body suddenly aflame once more.

"Jade," Kane whispered and dropped his hands to my waist, yanking me closer. An instant later my shirt lay on the floor and Kane's lips were pressed between my breasts, devouring the exposed skin as he worked the front closure of my bra open. The fabric fell away, and I stilled as Kane cupped me and gently teased both nipples.

Sensation flooded me. I tossed my head back and sucked in a ragged breath.

"You're so damned beautiful," he muttered and leaned in, wrapping his lips around one nipple.

"Oh, God." I clutched his shoulders, trying to keep upright as my knees went weak.

His teeth teased until both of my nipples were hard. One hand shifted to my calf and slowly made its way up my leg beneath my skirt.

"Kane…" Everything pulsed, right down to my toes. I wanted him anywhere and everywhere.

"Hmm." His mouth never left my breast as his arm wrapped around me and pulled me closer. I arched, pressing my breast into his willing mouth. The teasing stopped, and as he sucked harder, my knees buckled. But he held me up long enough to reposition us so I was straddling his lap, my skirt bunched up around my waist.

I could feel him, hard and ready through his jeans. Kane rocked me into him, his hands bracing my back. I stared down into his eyes and moved against him.

"I love it when you do that," he said, his voice hoarse.

"This?" I pressed forward, creating more of that wonderful friction between us.

He let out a breath and met my slow pace but shook his head. "That's not what I meant." His breathing quickened, but he kept his movements achingly slow. "I love it when you stare at me through those eyes. Eyes I know are just for me."

"Oh, that," I breathed. "Yeah, but this is better." I pushed him back onto the bed and dropped my hands to work the button of his jeans. He flipped me before I could get past the top button.

"No, sweetheart. Tonight is all about you." He rolled to his side and ran a gentle hand down the center of my chest, coming to a stop at the top of my skirt, his fingers teasing the exposed skin just above the waistline.

My stomach quivered with anticipation. Kane had really good hands. Exceptional ones. The type that knew what they were doing. And knew how to torture a girl into blessed bliss. I swallowed, trying not to quiver as his hand traveled to my bare thigh, inching its way toward the pulsing need at my center.

I closed my eyes, letting him take control, and gasped as his palm cupped me and kneaded against my sex. I twisted, desperate to feel him, all of him against me and reached for his jeans once more.

At my touch, a small shudder rippled through him. He crushed his mouth against mine, his fingers still pressing against me, driving the pressure higher. I rocked against him, lost in his touch. Then he pulled back.

I whimpered, feeling the aching loss deep inside. A loss that didn't have anything to do with the pulsing between my thighs. I propped up on my elbows. "Kane?"

He stood before me, his molten eyes raking down my mostly naked body. His eyes closed and he took a deep, steadying breath. "I just need a moment."

My skin chilled, and I wrapped my arms over my chest, covering myself.

Kane's eyes fluttered open and he moved over me, gently pulled my arms away. "Sorry," he whispered into my ear as he positioned my arms above my head. "I needed to collect myself. Your touch drives me insane."

I smiled at that. "I like driving you insane."

"I know." He kissed a trail over the crest of my breast, lingering over my aching nipple long enough to tear another groan from the back of my throat. Moving lower, he paused at my hips, wrapping his big hands around me, then gently stripped the rest of my garments, leaving me totally exposed before him.

"Your turn." I admired his bare chest and moved my gaze lower, taking in his jeans riding low on his hips and the indents of his narrow waist. All I wanted to do was touch him. My fingers itched with it.

He shook his head. "Not yet." He kneeled on the floor, his hands once again resting on my hips. "I have something else in mind first." With one tug, he pulled me to the edge of the bed. His head bent, lips connecting with the tender flesh of my inner thigh as his fingers inched closer to my center.

"Oh," I said, my voice hoarse. "I like the way you think."

A deep chuckle sounded from his chest. A second later his finger slipped into me. I clutched at the bed, my head back and eyes closed, concentrating on his magical touch. Slow at first, he worked his mouth, nibbling and teasing where my leg met my hip as he pressed his finger into me.

Holy Jesus. My mind blanked as my entire existence shifted to pure need. My hips jerked, wanting more.

Then his mouth was on me, sucking and teasing my most sensitive spot, his finger still moving inside me.

Pure sensation pulsed through my core. The world faded completely, leaving me in my love-lust haze, completely at the mercy of Kane's touch.

He splayed his free hand over my stomach, warm and gentle, a stark contrast to his fevered lovemaking. My desire only heightened from the feel of his light touch. My hips rocked, desperate for release. His tongue flicked once, twice, and then he clasped his mouth over me once more, sucking with fervor.

I shattered, every piece of me breaking apart as my muscles constricted around him.

He stilled, his breath warm on my stomach, and I knew he was watching me, watching my face for the tranquility to follow. When my muscles relaxed, he placed a gentle kiss on my stomach and stood.

The sound of buttons popping open filled the silent room. I smiled weakly, watching him.

Kane, finally divested of his clothes, lifted me and maneuvered us both onto the bed, my head resting on a pillow. He hovered over me and trailed two fingers over my cheek. "You look…"

"Sated?"

He flashed a self-satisfied smile. "Absolutely."

I mimicked his gesture, trailing two fingers over his stubbled cheek. "I could get used to that, though it might be a little tiring to keep me in this glorious state." Shifting beneath him, I stretched out my tense muscles and sucked in another gasp as he lowered himself to me, his tip pressing against my center.

"Whatever it takes, love." He dipped his head and flicked his tongue over my lower lip as he slowly eased into me.

I wrapped my arms around his shoulders and rose to meet him.

Our eyes locked, and we rocked together, our gazes never breaking.

Kane positioned my leg higher on his hip to bury himself deep. My heart expanded and all but burst with emotion at our joining. Raw and exposed, we belonged to each other. I moaned, reveling in the way he filled me. That one tiny sound broke him and he quickened his pace, thrusting over and over and over again, claiming me once again as his. His mouth crushed against mine and I spasmed, coming hard and fast.

"Jade," Kane groaned as he spilled himself inside me and buried his face in my neck, holding on as if he'd never let go. After a moment, he rolled to his back, pulling me with him.

We lay together, wrapped in each other's arms, not moving. I listened to his breathing until it slowed and then lifted my head, pressing light kisses on his chest. "I love you," I murmured.

He was quiet, and I wondered if he'd heard me. Still lying on his chest, I shifted to gaze up at him and found him watching me through hooded eyes. I smiled. "Hey."

"Hey, yourself." He brought his hand up, brushing a stray lock from my eyes. "I know."

"Know what?" I placed another kiss on his collarbone.

"That you love me."

"Oh, that." I put my hands down on either side of him and lifted myself until we were face to face. My gaze shifted to his perfect lips, and I lowered my head just enough to give him another soft kiss. "It's probably pretty obvious."

He nodded. "It is."

I laughed. "Like you're so sly."

His chest rumbled. "Who said I was trying to be sly?" He shifted again, rolling me on my back, then to my side so I was facing away from him. His lips brushed over my shoulder as he tucked me beside him. He moved his hand in a slow circle over my abdomen. "I've loved you since the day you face-planted on the stairs. There was something about the way you spent the next forty-five minutes staring at me like I was your man candy that hooked me."

"You have not." I shook my head slightly, chuckling at the memory. "You barely even knew me then." I'd only moved into my apartment less than a week before. Love? He was crazy.

"Have too. I knew that moment you were the one."

"How?" I glanced back with narrowed eyes. "No, you were just in lust."

His hand rose to gently cup my breast. "That too," he whispered and ran his tongue down my neck, making me shiver.

"What are you doing?"

He pressed against me, and I felt exactly what he was up to. I couldn't keep the smile from quirking my lips. I *did* ask him to shut everything else out. He had, and now he was ready for more.

"Already?" I whimpered with pleasure as his fingers pinched my nipple.

He paused. "Want me to stop?"

"No. I don't think that will be necessary," I said in a tone a lot cooler than I felt. Heat was spreading again.

"That's what I thought." His body molded to mine and his magic hands went to work once more, pushing everything from my mind but him and the pleasure we brought each other.

Chapter 15

An hour later, Kane hugged me to him once more, and we fell into a deep peaceful sleep. As usual, Kane arrived in my dream, a nightly ritual that made us that much closer. He was a dreamwalker who could enter other people's dreams when he wanted, but these days, he only dreamwalked with me. Not only did we sleep together, we dreamed together. As soon as he popped into my dream, I smiled.

"Long time no see," I said, walking to a railing on the balcony overlooking the French Quarter.

His lips twisted into a half-smile. Turning, he waved a hand over Bourbon Street. "For you."

"Something's different." I glanced around at the empty streets. "Besides all the people missing."

This time he laughed. "It's the smell. I tend to try to forget about that unfortunate reality."

"Ah, yes." I took a deep breath, inhaling the fragrant honeysuckle instead of Bourbon Street's usual rotten orange stench. "It's lovely."

"Isn't it?"

We both stared down at the pristine streets. Light shone from the lampposts through the thickening fog filling the humid air. The eerie glow only heightened the romance of the city. "It's too bad it's never this peaceful."

"It's close enough," he said, wrapping an arm around me.

I couldn't help but wish we could stay there forever, on the balcony of the unknown building. The beauty of the heavy fog building on Bourbon Street, barren of the thousands of tourists and street performers, was a rare treat. It was so lovely. Soul-filling. Something I hadn't experienced since before my soul split with Meri.

The thought weighed on me. Would I always feel partially empty? Or would I get used to living with only half a soul? There was no way to know. We had to find my father, because I didn't want to find out. I squeezed my eyes closed and breathed in more of the fragrant honeysuckle, only to cough as the air turned fetid with mud and mold.

Jerking back, I opened my eyes and stared at Kane. "What was that?"

"What?" he asked, glancing around.

The fog shifted, moving toward us. Dark gray tendrils twisted and reached straight for me. I screamed and jumped behind Kane.

"Jade?" Kane's concerned tone barely registered. The tendrils were growing more solid, slipping right past him. One swirled around me then latched on, wrapping around my chest.

I stumbled back, clutching at the solid fog. "Get it off!" I cried.

Kane spun, ready to come to my defense, but he stopped and looked around in confusion. He took a step closer, inspecting me. "What is it? Where?"

A familiar stabbing ice pricked my skin, pushing me deep into my mind. "No!" I try to shout, but it came out more as a whimper.

"Jade?" Kane gripped me by the arms and pulled me to him, but it was too late. Camille was back and she'd already taken over. I felt as if I were trapped inside myself with a film of haze over my vision, so I couldn't make out the fine details of his expression

"Hi," she said, her voice lower than the high-pitched tone she'd used before.

"Are you okay?" Kane's eyebrows pinched together as he studied me. "What happened?"

"Nothing," Camille said, now in full possession of me just as she had been before. I could feel Kane's touch, the cool night air, and even Camille's excitement, but my mental commands went unanswered. I was trapped, unable to do anything. Somehow in this dream state, she'd been able to penetrate my soul. I wanted to scream, pound on something, but I couldn't do either. Instead, I prayed Kane would realize I was no longer myself.

"I wanted this," she whispered and ground my body into him like a sex-starved teenager.

A smile blossomed on his face. If I'd had control of my stomach, I would've vomited right there. Rage boiled inside my brain. He had to know it wasn't me. But why would he? We'd just spend the better part of two hours doing exactly what Camille wanted to be doing with my fiancé.

How dare she? My thoughts pulsed with the burning desire to smash her face in. But knowing that was impossible only made me that much more frustrated.

Camille placed both of my hands on Kane's chest and giggled. Giggled, for God's sake.

Kane just smiled down at her like we were sharing some private joke. Only there was no joke. This was a nightmare.

"Kiss me," Camille tilted my head up and opened my mouth, waiting for him to oblige.

And the ass did. He bent down and kissed my lips. Only I could barely feel *him*. I felt her and all her nervous anticipation, mixed with wild sexual desire. The faint image of a man dressed in wool pants and a vest flashed in my mind as Camille's excitement grew. She flung her arms around Kane's neck and attacked his face like a mangy dog going after table scraps.

"Whoa," Kane whispered against my lips, pushing me away slightly. "What's gotten into you?"

He knows.

The thought bounced through my mind until I realized he was smiling down at me, amused. Panic filled my mind. He really didn't know it wasn't me. How far was this going to go before he figured it out?

Camille answered by placing my hand on his crotch. "Nothing yet. You have no idea how long I've been waiting."

Kane stilled and then stepped back, putting space between us. His intense brown eyes searched mine. Had something clicked? "I think we should just go to sleep." The scene morphed around us, and my body was back in Kane's bedroom, but my mind was still trapped with Camille.

"Much better," she cooed and moved to straddle him, lifting his shirt and fiddling with the button of his pants.

Oh, hell no! I screamed in my mind. *Don't you even think of touching him, you dead slut.*

"No." Kane's hands gripped her waist, and he shoved me off him. "Something's not right. You're not yourself."

Camille swung my hand and knocked him in the side of the head.

"Hey!"

When Kane dreamwalked, if anything happened, you tended to feel it the next day. He said wounds didn't last, but the phantom pain or pleasure did. The mind didn't know any different. He'd feel that in the morning.

"Of course I'm not myself," Camille squawked in her normal tone. "I'm in that witch's body, trying to seduce you, and you're not man enough to take a woman who's throwing herself at you." She stared at his crotch. "What's wrong with *you?*"

"Camille." Kane's eyes narrowed, and Camille's fear pulsed around me. She didn't know what to do. She'd only come for Kane. But I didn't know why. She wanted to have sex with him—not for pleasure, but for something else.

Oh, Jesus Christ on a cracker. Sex magic?

At least Kane had figured it out. The storm raging in my mind lessened slightly, even though he'd kissed her the way he was only supposed to kiss me. My head spun thinking about it.

Then without warning, I slammed back into myself. My limbs tingled as blood rushed to my extremities. I stretched, realizing I was back in Kane's bed. Awake.

"Jade?" He was standing a few feet from the bed, keeping his distance. "You there?"

I sat up, rubbing my head. Possession gave me a headache. "I'm here. Camille's gone."

He peered down at me, not at all convinced.

"It's really me, all right? I was stuck in my head while that bitch of a ghost rubbed her...*my* body all over you. Only I wasn't really there." I glared up at him. "Took you long enough to realize it wasn't me."

His breath came out in a whoosh and he sank into the bed, pulling me tight against him. "I'm so sorry, love. I didn't... well, I knew something was off, I just didn't know what." He turned his head in the direction of the guest room. "You don't think Meri left, do you?"

I shrugged. "I doubt it. She knows I need her here, but how else did Camille get to me?"

Kane pulled on a pair of jeans and a shirt that was draped over a chair. "I'll find out."

I jumped out of the bed in my full-on naked splendor and placed a hand over his arm. "No. Better let me go."

He raised one eyebrow and swept his gaze from my head to my toes. "Like that?"

I let out an exasperated sigh. "No. Not like this."

A few minutes later, I was dressed in boxers and a tank top, with my robe cinched tightly around me. I headed down the hall and stopped at the closed door of the guest room. I glanced back. What time was it? I had no idea, but the hall seemed lighter than usual, and I guessed it was predawn. Not wanting to wake Meri, I inched the door open just a tiny bit and peeked through the crack.

The bed was empty.

"Dammit," I muttered under my breath. My heart raced. What would I do now? And why would Meri leave? She knew how much I needed her. At least until we found my father. I had to find him before Camille took a permanent hold.

The door was yanked opened with surprising force, my hand still on the knob. I fell forward into the room.

A figure jumped from the shadows, followed by a gasp of alarm.

"Ouch. Son of a bitch!" I cried out as my knees banged against the hardwood.

"Jade?" Meri's voice came out skeptical. "Is that you?"

"Shit." I pushed myself up and clamored to my feet. "Of course it's me. Who else would it be?"

She took a long, steadying breath. "Well, considering I felt you leave, it could've been anyone."

I turned to face her. "What do you mean, you felt me leave? I've been here the entire night."

Meri gave me a dubious glance and then strode out the door. "I need coffee."

Trembling slightly with fading adrenaline, I followed her into Kane's kitchen.

She moved around as if the place was her own, grabbing the beans from the refrigerator, opening the correct cabinet for the grinder, putting her hands on the sugar without even searching. I sank onto the barstool and buried my head in my hands. My eyes watered from lack of sleep. The world spun as darkness closed in, and I jerked upright, blinking away the film blurring my sight.

I shook my head. I needed answers.

Once the coffee pot was brewing, Meri busied herself toasting bagels and setting out cream cheese. I glanced at the clock. Six forty-five a.m. I'd only been asleep for less than three hours. No wonder I was weary.

A scraping sounded on the counter, and the scent of a rich dark roast filled my senses. I opened my eyes and stared down at the oversized mug in front of me. I wrapped my hands around it and let the warmth seep into my flesh. If I drank any

I'd never get back to sleep. Meri picked up the plate of bagels and joined me.

"Thank you," I said, keeping my nose buried in the cup, enjoying the rich aroma.

She shrugged. "I was making some anyway." A few moments went by with the bagels sitting untouched. "Where did you go?"

I cast her a sidelong glance. "I already told you, I didn't go anywhere. I was here the whole time with Kane." Then I frowned. "What do you mean when you say you felt me leave? Are you talking about the empath gift?" Horror settled over me. Had she felt the emotions Kane and I shared? Could she sense farther than I could? My whole body burned with embarrassment.

She shook her head. "No, but you might want to clamp down on what you're feeling now because it's coming through loud and clear."

Shit! Of course it was. My face felt combustible with the amount of heat consuming it. I took a deep breath to settle myself then imagined my glass silo that had become second nature as an empath. The one I used to shut off other people's emotions.

"That's better." She picked at the edge of a bagel. "I meant I felt your soul leave. I can sense it, you know."

I twisted. "You can?"

She nodded. "You can't?"

I shook my head. I'd been aware of a connection when we were sharing the same soul, but now that my soul had split, I couldn't feel her at all.

"Interesting." She dropped a spoonful of sugar in her coffee and stirred. "When you're around, your soul is like some sort of beacon. I can tell where you are within a certain range. It's not imposing, just sort of an 'I know you're there' sort of thing. It's not really a big deal."

"Even when you're sleeping?"

She shrugged.

"What does that mean?"

Setting her mug down, she turned to me. "I'm not consciously aware of your soul while I'm asleep, but I woke up suddenly and you…or your soul was gone. Like it had disappeared."

Of course it had. How could I be so stupid?

"Kane dreamwalked me to Bourbon Street." It was only a few blocks away. But far enough for Camille to follow me. To try to take me over. How odd that she was able to invade my soul without my body. I shuddered. It was creepy enough when she was using me physically, but to take over my soul completely…that was the worst violation ever. The walls closed in on me. I couldn't even go anywhere in Kane's dreams without being in danger.

"That would do it," she said.

Feeling like an idiot, I stood, nearly knocking the stool over. "I'm going to try and get some more sleep," I said through a yawn.

"Good luck. And don't let Kane pull you back into a dreamwalk."

Nodding, I stumbled back to bed.

Chapter 16

I slept fitfully, and after a few hours, I silently slipped from the bed and headed for coffee. When I couldn't take it anymore, I grabbed my phone and called Mom. I was done waiting for answers about my dad. Each attempt went straight to voicemail. I gave up and started texting. Camille had found a way to invade me during my sleep, the time I was most vulnerable.

I shook my head and texted Mom again. When my fifth text in a thirty-minute period went unanswered, I called Gwen. Voicemail. Damn them. What the hell? Did Gwen even know how to turn her ringer off? I sent Gwen a text, demanding she call as soon as possible, and then stormed back into Kane's room.

He was laying crossways, the sheet barely covering his firm ass. The sight instantly drained some of my frustration. I blew out a breath and sat next to him, running a light hand through his mussed hair.

His long eyelashes fluttered and a slow grin spread on his chiseled jaw. "Come here," he murmured. He looked so damn sexy, I couldn't resist. He turned on his side, leaving me a space to curl up next to him. With my head resting on his shoulder, he tucked me close to him and deftly untied my robe, splaying his large hand on my naked belly. "That's better," he said into my hair. "Where'd you go?"

"Coffee."

"Hmm." His fingers traced a slow caress on my sensitive skin, sending familiar tingles through my middle. "Coffee. That could be good." I started to pull away, but his grip tightened. "Wait." And suddenly I felt his warm lips just below my ear as he nibbled. "I don't want to get up just yet."

I smiled. "We can't stay here all day, you know."

"Yeah." His lips trailed lower, leaving a hot trail down my neck. I stretched, giving him more access. "But once we leave this room, reality will take over, and I'd rather not face it any sooner than necessary."

His lips, combined with his touch on my now-naked torso, were more than enough to convince me. After the dreamwalk, I needed something to take away the memory of Camille trying to seduce him. Thoughts of phone calls and texts vanished from my mind as I turned into him, ready to let the world slip away for just this moment. A moment I desperately needed.

I buried my hands in his hair and closed my eyes to the outside world, concentrating on nothing but his hands sending sensation after sensation through the most intimate and personal areas of my body.

Precious moments later, Kane rolled me on my back, my robe discarded. He stared down at me with love and passion radiating in waves.

The intensity of the moment brought tears to my eyes. "I love you," I whispered.

"I love you, too, Jade. More than you know." Then he lowered himself and slowly, gently, lovingly, he entered me.

A shower and two more cups of coffee later, I stood in the kitchen, staring at my silent phone. It was after ten, and I knew Gwen had to be awake, even if Mom wasn't.

"Nothing?" Kane asked, placing dishes into the dishwasher.

I bit my lip and shook my head. "I think we need to go over there."

"Okay, give me a minute, and I'll drive you." He shut off the water and then dried his hands on a dishcloth. I couldn't help but smile. He even did dishes.

"We can walk." I dropped the phone on the counter. "There probably isn't anywhere to park anyway."

"Right." I watched him disappear back into our bedroom and then went to find Meri.

She was curled up on an oversized armchair, surfing the Internet on an iPad.

"Hey." I sat across from her. "I need to go to my apartment. Mom and Gwen aren't answering their phones. I'm worried."

She glanced at the clock and stiffened, then uncurled and stood. "Give me a minute." She disappeared into the guest room, leaving me alone in the living room, fidgeting.

I held my phone, willing it to ring or buzz or flash a Facebook message, even though neither of them used the application much. I just needed something, anything to let me know they were okay. Hell, with the way my life was turning out, they could've been kidnapped by wolves for all I knew. What time had they left last night? The French Quarter was generally pretty safe, but it still had its share of crime. "Damn," I mumbled and paced.

Kane emerged and wrapped his arms around me. "I'm sure they're fine."

I eased out of his embrace, not in the mood to be soothed. "You don't know that. And Mom left agitated last night. What if she pissed someone off? They both could be bleeding out in a gutter right now."

He raised his eyebrows. "That didn't happen." He leaned down and kissed me on the forehead. "I know you're worried, but no use getting worked up until we know for sure where they are. It's more likely your Mom is just trying to give herself a bit of time before she has to deal with the dad issue."

"And Gwen?" I challenged. "She wouldn't ignore me."

He shrugged. "Maybe Hope turned her phone off as well. Maybe she's in the shower? Maybe she went down to the cafe and forgot her phone? It could even need a battery charge. There are plenty of logical explanations."

I bit back a retort. He was right, of course. I knew that. It was just hard to believe.

Meri appeared wearing a black turtleneck, black jeans, and black boots. Her sleek black hair was pulled into a ponytail. She looked more like she was headed to crack a safe than check on a couple of middle-aged women. Not that Mom looked middle-aged.

"After you." Kane pulled the door open for us. Meri went first, and as I passed him he whispered into my ear, "Cat woman." He nodded at Meri, and I stifled a laugh.

If only she had the ears. I didn't know why, but the image managed to settle my nerves for the time it took to walk from Kane's house to Bourbon Street. But once we rounded the corner, the events from the night before flashed through my mind and all I could think about was Camille trying to take over my soul. I quickened my pace. By the time we stopped in front of The Grind, I was slightly winded. Crap, I needed to work out more.

Kane and Meri both appeared to be unaffected by the brisk walk. I cursed them both silently. Kane held the door open for us once more, and Meri and I scooted into the cafe.

"Hey, hey!" Charlie called from behind the counter. "It's the boss man and his beautiful bride-to-be." Her gorgeous smile lit up her heart-shaped face as she winked at me. "How's the wedding planning going?"

I grimaced. "Stressful."

She came out from behind the counter and gave me a hug. I hadn't seen her since our engagement party.

I took a long look at her. She radiated with happiness. "Looks like life is treating you well."

"Can't complain."

"How's the girlfriend?"

Her grin turned wicked. "Fuckin' amazing. And I mean that literally. You should—"

Kane cleared his throat, cutting her off before she delved into too many personal details. Charlie wasn't known for being discrete, especially when it came to the women in her life.

I choked back a laugh. Kane owned a strip club, for God's sake, but he couldn't handle it when Charlie spilled the details of her love life? I glanced around, noting the lack of customers.

Charlie followed my gaze and then turned to Kane. "You're a lot more modest since this one"—she pointed at me—"came into your life."

He shook his head. "Just respectful. You might want to take a lesson." The words seemed harsh, but he said them with a soft smile and plenty of affection for his club manager.

She nodded, not at all offended. "You probably have a point." She cleared her throat. "My girlfriend is gorgeous, laugh-your-ass-off funny, and quite possibly has the biggest heart on the planet." She raised an eyebrow at Kane. "Better?"

He gave her a warm smile. "Much."

I shook my head at them, but my heart swelled at their interaction. Charlie was good people. "Where's Pyper?"

"Upstairs, body painting. Her apartment."

"Oh." That meant Mom and Gwen weren't with her, and they certainly weren't in the cafe. "Have you seen my mom or Gwen?"

Charlie's brilliant smile turned mischievous. "Who do you think she's painting?"

"What?" I all but shrieked.

Kane laughed, and Meri snorted.

"Oh, Jesus." I took off without another word through the back of the cafe and rounded the stairs to Pyper's apartment. What the hell were they up to?

Standing outside of Pyper's door, I took a moment to collect myself. Meri, who'd followed me—thank God—stood beside me smirking. Kane leaned against the wall, clearly prepared to wait outside. If Pyper was really body painting them, they could both be naked. I closed my eyes, horrified at the thought of seeing both my aunt and my mother in the buff. How did Pyper do it?

I knocked.

Nothing.

Knock, knock.

A muffled voice sounded from behind the door.

"I know you're in there. You might as well open up, or I'll use Kane's key to get in." I glanced at him for confirmation. He patted his pocket, indicating he did indeed have his key. He was the landlord and had kept a spare room at Pyper's apartment for the nights he worked late at the club. He didn't stay there anymore, instead opting to sleep with me in my apartment when necessary.

"Come in!" Pyper's faint voice called through the door.

Kane handed me the key. "I'll be in my office." I gave him a quick kiss and watched him retreat. Something inside me didn't want him to leave, but it wasn't as if he could watch Mom and Gwen get body painted.

I slipped the key in the lock and let myself into Pyper's apartment, Meri close behind me. But the room was empty. I headed for Pyper's bedroom until the sound of laughter coming from the kitchen rerouted me. Terrified of what I'd see, I tentatively peeked through the doorway and gasped.

"Holy shit! What's going on in here?" I asked.

Pyper had moved her breakfast table out completely and draped the area with a white sheet. Mom sat on a clear plastic backless chair, her top off, her torso covered in sparkling blue glitter.

Gwen, thank the powers that be, was fully clothed and only had traces of blue glitter on her hands.

Pyper laughed, her whole face lit up with a happiness I'd never seen before. "Gwen's learning to body paint."

"Umm." I glanced at Gwen.

She smiled sheepishly and shrugged. "Your mom offered to be my canvas."

"Of course she did," Meri mumbled behind me.

I shot her a confused look before turning my attention back to my lunatic family members. "I've been trying to reach you all morning. Where the hell are your phones?"

Gwen grimaced. "Sorry, sweetie. Back at the apartment, I suppose. We went down for coffee and got to talking to Pyper about her side business and one thing led to another and… well, you can see how it turned out." Her gaze flicked back to my mom, who was grinning like a fool.

"It's the most fun I've had in over a decade," Mom said, her eyes twinkling.

"I don't doubt it," Meri said under her breath.

This time, I shot her an irritated glare.

"Did everyone forget about my little problem? I thought we were going to work on it today." I spun, staring at Mom intently. "I need to talk to Dad. Whatever it is you're holding back, I need to know about it. Now."

Mom's smile died on her lips, and I had to fight back the guilt clawing at my throat. This moment really was the only time I'd seen her happy and unguarded since she'd returned to us. But why did she have to choose now? My soul was in danger… again. If we didn't find Dad I was screwed. Didn't she see that?

"Maybe we should give them some privacy," Pyper said. She placed a tube of paint on her makeshift painter's table and gestured for Gwen and Meri to follow her. As she passed me, she touched my arm. "Sorry. I didn't mean to cause any problems. I just thought they could use a little reality break. I didn't think we'd be here long."

The concern in her eyes touched me. "It's not your fault. It's no one's, really. Just another crap situation. It's all right. Really."

She smiled, but it didn't reach her eyes, and I wanted to kick myself for taking her happiness away. She'd looked so down the night before, and this morning she'd obviously been having fun. I'd taken that away from her again.

I was going to kick Ian's ass the next time I saw him.

When the trio left, Mom pulled on a terrycloth robe and moved to the kitchen sink to wash her hands.

I waited for a few beats and then blurted, "Mom, you have to tell me what you know."

She spun. "What I know," she gasped out, "is that your father decided he wasn't interested in spending his life with us. He left us alone to fend for ourselves. Do you really think he's going to come back now because you need a favor?" Her eyes were bright with unshed tears. "Do you really want to put yourself through that, Jade?"

My heart sped up as I realized she wasn't talking about me. She was talking about herself. We'd never discussed it before. The first time Dad left, I was told it was for a little while. I understood the military was his job, and he didn't have a choice. The second time, I was already used to it being just Mom and me. While I felt the loss, it was more in the 'Why does everyone else have a dad and I don't?' kind of way as opposed to actually missing mine. He hadn't been around much. Except for that last time he'd come by the house, I'd never even seen Mom upset about him before.

She'd kept this hidden from me. How awful. Who did she talk to about it? Gwen? Meri? Her coven back in Idaho? Or had she locked her pain away and concentrated on our life together? I suspected the latter. Besides Mom's herbal remedies and the small shop she'd ran, I'd been the center of her world.

"Mom." I waited for her eyes to meet mine. "Why did Dad leave?"

She blinked back her tears and a hard expression settled over her face. "You'd have to ask him."

"I'm asking you. What did he say to you that day? The last time he came by the house. What was in that note?"

Her brows furrowed. "I didn't read it. It was for you when you were older. But then I never got a chance to give it to you."

We both fell silent at the mention of her time spent in Purgatory.

I shuffled to the refrigerator just for something to do and pulled out two Diet Cokes. I held one out to Mom, but she shook her head. I shrugged, put it back, and busied myself with a glass and ice. After I was done, I leaned against the counter and gave her my full attention. "Where's the note now?"

She shook her head. "I wouldn't know. It was at the house."

The one we no longer owned. It had been sold after I'd moved in with Gwen and everyone had given up hope that Mom would come back. The letter *could* be in some of the things Gwen had saved for me. Or it could be long gone. My chest tightened. Damn it all. One more question that would go unanswered. I tried again. "What did he say that day?"

"Nothing."

"Mom!" She startled at my outburst. "You can't keep ignoring this. If you don't tell me, I'm going to cast the finding spell. I'll call Bea right now, and then I'll ask him myself."

Her wild eyes blazed in fury. "That won't work."

"Why the hell not?"

"Because Marc Rollins isn't your father." She sucked in a shocked breath and then spun and stalked to the refrigerator. A moment later, she pulled out the can of Diet Coke I'd offered her and popped the top angrily but didn't bother to drink any of it. She just stood there shaking.

An odd sense of confusion wound its way through my brain. I blinked, trying to clear it, opened my mouth, closed it, and then cleared my throat. "What do you mean?"

"Shit," she said so quietly I was sure she didn't think I could hear her.

"Dad wasn't my dad?" My voice trembled and I wasn't sure why. Were those tears burning my eyes? I blinked rapidly, trying to bury my unfamiliar emotions. Dad had walked out on us years ago. I never thought of him. Why did it matter now?

My gut started to ache. And I knew why it mattered. After Mom had disappeared, I'd prayed Dad would show up to take care of me, prayed someone would find him and tell him. All these years, I'd assumed no one knew where he was or that he was out of the country. I'd never really believed he hadn't wanted to be a part of my life. Now I knew.

"He left because I wasn't his, didn't he?" My voice was so low, so strangled, I wasn't sure she heard me.

But the way she twitched told me she had. And the fact that she didn't deny it right away told me it was the truth. A deep-seated fear blossomed from the depths of my being. The one my fifteen-year-old self had worked so hard to overcome. After Mom vanished and I'd been all alone in the foster home, before Gwen had come, before Kat and Dan, that scared, hopeless girl had known no one wanted her. Both of her parents had disappeared without notice, without warning.

She hadn't been wanted.

And that was still true. He'd left seventeen years ago without so much as a glance back. And what about my biological father? Where was he?

"Who?" The word rushed out in a demand. "Who?" I said again, my voice rising. "Mom!"

She turned to look at me with haunted eyes, her face tight with fear.

My words caught in my throat, and suddenly, I had no desire to know who I really belonged to.

Chapter 17

All the buried rejection of my past came rushing back, and I tore out of the kitchen, heading straight for the front door. I'd demanded she tell me about my father, and now that the moment was here, I wasn't ready. I couldn't face whatever she had to say. It hurt too much.

"Jade!" I heard a voice call.

But I had the door open and crashed through it, my brain a solid mass of old rejection and pain. It was a state I was familiar with. I'd grown up with it, learned to live with it. But during my time with Gwen, and the last eight months of living in New Orleans, I'd thought I was cured of the all-encompassing, soul-crushing knowledge that no one loved me enough to stick around. I wasn't good enough for anyone. Not Mom, Dad, Dan, or maybe even Kane. We'd only been together a short time. What if he left too? The doubt was there, buried deep in my heart, burning a hole through the delicate fabric I'd woven to keep the fragile organ in one piece.

I turned the corner and flew down the two sets of stairs, aiming for the adjoining door to the building next door. I needed to be alone in my apartment, with my things. Away from everyone who could hurt me. Away from the truth I didn't want to know.

I was flying up the second set of stairs when I heard the pounding behind me.

I whirled, finding Meri breathless and red-faced. "Dammit, Jade. Slow down, would ya? Even angels can't keep up with that pace."

My blood pumped rapidly through my veins, making my muscles twitch. I wanted to strike out, or scream, or run until I collapsed, but something switched in my brain as I caught her staring at me as if I'd lost my mind.

What was I doing? I was supposed to be sticking by her side. It didn't matter that the only thing I wanted was a moment to collect myself. Not if I wanted to survive this anyway. "Sorry. I had to get out of there."

Stifling a sigh of frustration, I turned and trudged up the third flight of stairs. Once we reached my door, I produced a key and waved her in.

Two suitcases lined the wall, along with haphazard piles of Gwen's and Mom's clothes. My apartment was barely big enough for one person, let alone two. They'd each been in New Orleans for over two months, dealing with my crap. It was another reason Kane and I were trying to push up the wedding. Gwen needed to get back to Idaho to start the spring farming.

Kane.

A tiny bit of the pain in my heart soothed. He wanted me. He hadn't left me. Not yet, anyway. *Then when?* The dangerous, self-destructive thought hit and I cringed. When would he decide I was too much trouble, too?

"Jade?" Meri said softly behind me.

I turned, eyeing her with tears burning my eyes. "What?"

"I don't know what thoughts you're having to cause such turmoil, but maybe you should change the conversation." Her tone was soothing, knowing, as if she understood exactly what my feelings were doing to me.

Then it dawned on me, she likely did. She'd spent time waiting for someone to come find her. She knew all about abandonment. Not that I wanted to talk about it. What I needed was space to clear my head.

But there wasn't anywhere to go other than the bathroom. I gritted my teeth and strode into the tiny room. Without a word, I closed the door and headed for the tub.

Forty minutes later, my body was shriveled in a prune-like state from lounging in the bubbles. And peace still eluded me. As I was about to reluctantly haul myself out, a knock sounded at the door.

Just go away. I didn't want to talk to Meri. Or anyone.

"Jade?"

I stiffened in the cooling bathwater. It was Kane.

I longed to see him. But I didn't want to talk. God, I needed his arms around me, my head buried in his strong chest. "Give me a minute." I rose and wrapped myself in an oversized towel. Not bothering to get dressed, I opened the door and stumbled into his waiting arms, relief making my limbs weak. His embrace always made me feel safe, loved, even when I didn't believe it.

He held me close as he undid my hair from my hastily tied bun. "Your mom told me about your fight. Do you want to talk about it?"

I shook my head, still pressed to his chest.

"Okay, sweetheart. I understand." He brought his hand up and ran his fingers through my long, wavy hair, lightly stroking my arm with each movement.

I pressed into him and shut my eyes tight, as if I could block the world out. Somewhere deep inside, I knew I was being melodramatic. Knew I should be handling myself better. Knew this wasn't the end of the world or the end of me and Kane. But my heart didn't. It was the war between my messed-up psyche and my heart that tore me apart.

Gently, I pulled away from him and gave him a tiny smile. "Thanks. I needed that."

Concern laced his features and shone in his dark eyes. He glanced once at Meri, now curled up on my repurposed couch, reading the latest copy of *People*. Gwen must've bought it. The magazine was her favorite guilty pleasure. Then he shifted me backward until we were both in the bathroom again. He shut the door with one foot and leaned in to kiss me lightly.

My smile grew. "What was that for?"

He shrugged. "You looked like you needed to be kissed."

A chuckle bubbled up from my throat, surprising me.

"See? You did." He leaned in again, this time with more meaning, his lips taking my bottom one in his as his tongue tasted and teased.

I sank into him, letting him take me over with the wonderful sensation. When he let go, I opened my mouth to him, but he pulled back.

I frowned. "Where'd you go?"

Pressing his lips together, he tensed as he took a breath. "I think we should talk about what's going on."

"I don't want to talk right now." My heart hammered and I searched his eyes, waiting for the other shoe to drop. He looked so serious and...hesitant. About what? Me? Us?

He sighed.

"What?" I said with a slight tremor to my voice and I hated myself for it. I sounded so weak, so needy. It was disgusting.

He dropped his arms and stepped back.

My body ached with the separation, but I didn't move forward. Why was he pushing me away?

"You're overthinking. I can tell."

I chewed on my lower lip, saying nothing.

"I'd do anything for you. You know that, right?"

I nodded.

"And I'm not going anywhere. You know that too, right?"

Another nod. His words were exactly what I needed to hear right then, but they did little to soothe my anxiety. His actions were saying something else.

"You have some things to work out with your mom, but I can see you're internalizing. I can almost feel you locking yourself away from everyone. It's not healthy."

"No you can't." I jerked my head up, my eyes narrowed in irritation.

"I can." He stepped forward, invading my personal space but not touching me. "I told you before that I could sense you. Not like your empath gift, but your energy. That has never changed. And I feel you pulling away from me. I won't force you to accept me, or what I have to give. That's why I backed away. When you withdraw, I can't force myself on you. I can't be just a person you lose yourself in. It's not who I am. And the woman who wants to get lost? She's not who I fell in love with."

My heart started to hammer and tears rolled unchecked down my cheeks. I couldn't deal with this now. My emotions were too raw.

"Aw, sweetheart." He brought his hand up and gently wiped the tears away. "I know you're hurting. All I'm asking is for you not to shut me out. I can't help you when you shut down."

Shaking my head, I stumbled past him. I'd heard him and understood what he was saying, but a voice in the back of my mind whispered, "You're broken. He sees it. Eventually, he'll get tired of the drama and leave just like everyone else." I ran to my closet and pulled out a faded pair of jeans with ripped knees and a stained sweatshirt. All of my regular clothes were at Kane's house.

He didn't follow, just leaned against the kitchen counter, watching as I tugged my clothes on. Once I was covered and feeling more secure, I wiped away my tears and raised my gaze to his unflinching one. "I think I could use a little time to… decompress."

His eyes stayed glued to mine, his attention searching for the emotions he must have known were struggling to come out. But I held them in, not wanting him to see me break down.

He shifted his weight and took a step closer. I stiffened, not sure I could stand it if he touched me again. He stopped, let out a haggard breath, and inclined his head. "I'll be downstairs if you need me."

I gave him a short nod and held my breath as he left. The door clicked softly, and I let the air go, easing the pressure in my chest. Moving to the window, I ignored Meri's curious stare and glanced down at the barren courtyard. The day was chilly, gray, and bleak, just like my mood.

"Want to talk about it?" Meri asked softly.

"No."

"Didn't think so. I'm here if you change your mind."

Of course she was there. And while I appreciated that she was keeping me from being possessed, I resented the fact that I needed her. Resented the fact that she had half my soul and that if she'd never come into my life or my mother's life, none of this would be happening. Knowing she was a victim herself didn't seem to matter much anymore.

Across the room, I heard the soft click of my bathroom door closing. I glanced back to the couch to find it empty. Finally some time to myself. But I knew it wasn't enough. I glanced at the balcony and then back at the bathroom door. Surely the proximity was close enough I could climb outside for some air. The bathroom was less than ten feet away.

Lifting the window, I peeked out at the gray skies. No rain. Yet. I grabbed the throw blanket from the couch and climbed out onto the balcony. New Orleans rarely got really cold, not like Idaho cold, but since I'd acclimated, I wasn't used to the January chill. I wrapped the fuzzy blanket around my shoulders and sat on one of my plastic chairs, content with the courtyard silence.

My anger and frustration seemed to seep away into the void as I sat there, not thinking, not feeling, only taking in the brick courtyard.

Minutes passed. I forgot about Meri, my mom, my dad, Camille, everyone. I let my mind go blank, refusing to think or feel anything. I was blissfully numb.

Then I heard Meri striding across my apartment, her footsteps echoing off the wood floors. "Jade?" Her voice sounded panicked.

I stifled a sigh and stood. As I moved toward the floor-length window, I heard my door bang open.

"Meri!" Pyper's voice was high-pitched, frantic. The sound disturbed me on a cellular level. Something was off, and it wasn't the desperation in her tone.

"Where's Jade?" Meri demanded.

"This way."

I shifted to angle myself back inside, but the curtains were obstructing my view. Gripping the blanket with one hand, I swept the curtains aside with the other just in time to see the pair of them disappear out my front door.

"Hey!" I called, but the door slammed a moment before my outburst. Neither of them had heard me.

I scrambled back into the apartment, dropped the blanket on the couch, and stuffed my feet into a pair of clogs before tearing out the door after them. But I wasn't fast enough. At the top of the stairwell, the ice started to creep up my arms.

"No!" I flailed, almost tripping down the stairs in panic. The ice took over, pushing me back into the far corners of my mind. *Camille, stop this. Just tell me what you want, and I'll do my best to help you.*

The image of the dead girl flashed through my mind. Rage mixed with deep-seated sadness flooded me. Camille took total control, straightened, and then headed back into my apartment. She paused in the middle of the room, glancing around. Her focus narrowed on the bathroom door.

What was with that bathroom? Ghosts seemed to follow me in there. One had even joined me in the shower once.

With a nod, she strode across the room with purpose. Behind her, a low growl snarled, vicious and mean. She spun and narrowed in on her stalker.

Duke. My golden retriever ghost dog stood in the middle of the room, his hackles raised and teeth bared. If I'd had control of my body I would have shivered, he looked that scary.

Camille stared him down, never breaking eye contact. The dog snarled louder.

Good dog. Some part of me was relieved he knew I was possessed. He'd known when Roy was terrorizing Pyper, too.

"Hush," Camille demanded. "Bad dog."

Duke only snarled louder. I smiled inside.

Camille gave a grunt of disgust and strode into the bathroom. She stopped in front of the mirror, inspecting my face, running her hands through my hair, and twisting to absorb all my features. Then her eyes narrowed as she took in my tattered outfit.

"How awful," she said in her high-pitched tone. "A lady would never wear such rags." She ripped the sweatshirt off and stopped suddenly as she took in my torso in the mirror. She raised my hands tentatively and cupped my breasts. Revulsion overtook me, and I longed to hide my eyes, but I couldn't. I was seeing through her but had no control over anything she did.

Pressing my breasts together to create even more cleavage, she smiled. "These will do."

I wanted to throw up. She was touching me. Somehow that knowledge seemed even more invasive than the total body possession.

She brushed my hair until it fell in soft strawberry-blond waves past my shoulders. With deft hands, she quickly pinned the mass into a fancy bun, leaving tendrils hanging on either side of my face.

I hated it and longed to rip out the bun just to spite her.

She smiled at my reflection and picked up a tube of bright red lipstick. By the time she was done, I was painted with rosy cheeks and bright red lips, my eyes shadowed in cinnamon and gold.

With a nod of approval, she headed to my closet and proceeded to tear every last piece of clothing out. All the while Duke growled and barked, but she pretended to not hear him. It's not like he could do anything. He was a ghost dog. He couldn't bite me. He'd slip right through. Unless he could possess me, too. Except there probably wasn't room for two ghosts.

Piles of Mom's, Gwen's, and my old clothes grew up around her until finally she chose my black jersey pencil skirt. She stepped back, placed my hands on my hips and eyed the rest of the clothes in my closet, frustration seeping from her into my consciousness. Seems she didn't like what I had to offer. With a disgusted sigh, she paired the skirt with my one clubbing shirt, the one with the deep V that dipped between my cleavage, the one I never wore because I had to use body tape just to keep it in place. What could I say? It had been a gift from Pyper not long after I started working at Wicked. She wanted me to feel comfortable.

The only way I'd felt truly comfortable was by not working there at all. The energy was just too much to take most nights. Well, at least while I'd been an empath.

Camille stepped into the high-class, call-girl slut outfit, uncovered my strappy black heels, and checked my reflection out in the mirror one last time. Grimacing with what appeared to be disgust, she left the apartment and took off down the stairs with a lot more grace than I'd ever managed wearing those particular shoes. If she hated the way I looked so much, why did she choose the one outfit that could get us arrested if we suffered a slight wardrobe malfunction?

Halfway down the stairs her demeanor changed and she practically sauntered, as if she'd lived her entire life in three-inch heels. When she reached the bottom, she glanced left and right, spotted the exit and took off.

Oh hell, where was she taking me?

She burst through the door into the courtyard and took off through the narrow alley that led to Bourbon Street.

Despite the overcast January day, plenty of tourists crowded the street. She wove between them, instantly losing herself among the partiers. Moving like she owned the street, she ignored the females, but interestingly she studied every male who came into view. A few she even went so far as to rub my breasts on their arms as she passed them. My insides churned with each stab of her disturbed pleasure. When I got control of my body again, she was so on her way to Hell.

Both men gaped, until their significant others cast me a death glare and tugged their men out of Camille's path. What was she doing? Sex-crazed much?

She stopped abruptly and stared up at the Royal Sonesta Hotel. Squaring my shoulders, she nodded at the doorman and glided inside, heading straight for the bar. She stood in the middle of the room, scanning, and then settled on a stool at the bar, one that gave her a view of the room.

"Good afternoon." The bartender eyed me appreciatively. "Can I get you something?"

Camille licked my tongue slowly over my bottom lip, ending with me biting my lip with seductive prowess.

Seriously? The dude couldn't have been a day over twenty-two. Camille was ninety-something years old. Sort of.

Of course, he didn't know that. All he saw was a twenty-something-year-old woman, showing off most of her assets as she practically gave him an open invitation. He leaned down on one elbow, staring down my shirt, getting more than a peek at the goods covered in a see-through lace bra.

"I have a break coming up in ten minutes."

"Is that right?" She ran my finger over the rim of the ice water he'd set in front of me. "How long of a break?"

"As long as it takes, sugar."

Oh, my God! She was really going to do this…use my body to have sex with some random stranger. For sex magic. *Shit!* But for what spell? What did she want so badly? The dead girl? Could a ghost come back from the dead? A shudder ran through my mind. Was that what she wanted? I had to do something— expel her, fight off his advances, something. Anything. But I didn't have any control. I was helpless. At her mercy. Hatred coiled inside me. How was I going to get out of this?

Camille gave him a soft giggle and followed up with a sigh. "I bet a man like you knows his way around…uh…"

His eyes glowed with excitement. "Yeah. I know my way around." His gaze fixated somewhere around my navel, the very spot the V ended on the halter top. "I know what to do once I get there, too."

"I bet you do," she said softly, batting *my* eyelashes at him. The slut.

"Jade?" a familiar voice called from across the room.

My mind whirled. Ian. Thank God. He'd know it wasn't me and find help.

Camille turned, and her lips formed into a seductive smile. Her intense satisfaction seized me. Oh, no. What was she going to do?

"Ian?" she said in a lower register and a bright tone. Her voice didn't sound at all like me, at least not that I could tell, but Ian didn't seem to notice. He was too busy staring at my chest. Damn Pyper and her need to make me "comfortable."

"Look at you, all dressed up." His face eased into a relaxed smile. I had an intense desire to smack him silly. Why the hell was he looking at me like that? What about Pyper? Too bad I didn't have use of my arms. "Going out?"

Camille shook my head. "No."

Ian's eyebrows drew together in confusion. "Working…at the club?"

Camille stood and pressed my body up against him. Ian stiffened as if startled by my actions, but as he glanced down, straight into my shirt, he showed no desire to move away.

"No work tonight." Camille slid my finger lightly down the middle of his chest. "In fact, I was hoping to get a chance to play."

"Umm…"

She giggled that high-pitched irritating sound, and once again, I wanted to smack the crap out of Ian for not noticing I wasn't me. He did back at Bea's shop. What was different now?

"Don't think, Ian. Just kiss me." She tilted my head up, gazing into his pale blue eyes, imploring him to do as she commanded.

Ian took a step back, but she followed, keeping my breasts in contact with his chest.

"I know you want me." She leaned in, so close he had to feel my breath on his lips.

He clenched his fists as if fighting for control, but as she gently brushed my lips over his, he let out a strangled moan and crushed himself to me.

Chapter 18

Camille placed my hands everywhere. In his hair, on his thighs, cupping his ass. He met her fervor, right there in the bar of the hotel. A few catcalls faded into the background as I curled into my mind, horrified by what was happening with my body and friend's boyfriend. Once I had control again, I was going to kill him, carve him up as if I were Dexter and feed him to the alligators out on the bayou.

The fucking bastard!

Kane would kill him for me. I wouldn't even have to lift a finger. Panic took over as I envisioned Kane walking in on this scene. Would he know it wasn't me? Would he stick around long enough to find out? I doubted I would. I hadn't the time I'd caught him with Lailah. Meri had been in control of him then. Surely he'd understand I was possessed. That wouldn't help Ian, though. Not only was he touching Kane's fiancée, Ian was cheating on Kane's best friend.

Ian is a dead man walking

Rage filled every last crevice of my mind, almost but not quite blocking out the interaction I had no control to stop. I didn't want to know Ian in his lust-filled haze, nor feel the heady desire and excitement Camille was generating.

Someone would stop them before clothes started to come off, right?

Ian broke away, breathing heavily. He stared down at me, desire and wonder swimming in his eyes. He grabbed my hand and tugged. Camille followed, all too willingly.

"Where are you taking me?" she asked, huskily, her high-pitched tone gone.

Ian paused in the hallway, glanced down at me, and then pressed me up against the wall. His lips met mine, and I could sense Camille's thrill of being devoured by his kiss as he leaned into her, his body hard and alive with excitement.

She nipped at his lips, sighing with desire.

"Jesus, Jade, I've dreamed of this night after night." His hands came up, cupping my breasts, kneading them with his long fingers.

I recoiled in my mind, trying and failing to think of anything I could do to stop the pair of them. Saying no was impossible with Camille in charge, and it was clear she wasn't going to do anything of the sort. She leaned into his touch and ran my tongue over his neck, biting and nipping until she closed in on his ear. Then she lifted my leg through the long slit of my skirt and wrapped it around his waist, pressing into him.

"Take me," she growled.

He pulled his head back but didn't allow any space between our tight bodies. "Right here?" he asked in a strangled voice.

"Anywhere," Camille said breathlessly as if she'd die if he didn't obey her command. "I've been waiting far too long."

Something settled over him, and he stiffened again, this time jerking back out of Camille's grasp. "Wait. What?" he glanced around the hallway, blinking to regain his focus. "What's going on?"

A tiny seed of hope blossomed. Ian had come to his senses. If it were possible, I would've breathed a huge sigh of relief.

Camille sauntered up to him and ran my fingertip down his chest once more. "We're doing what we've both been dreaming about since the first night you took me out to that club. You remember, don't you? I never got my kiss, and I've been dying for it ever since." My hand came up, and my index finger caressed his lower lip.

What the hell? How did Camille know about that night? Could she read my mind? Or was she reading Ian's? I hadn't thought I could feel more violated. I was wrong. She'd taken everything from me and now maybe my private memories.

A low moan escaped Ian as his eyes once again glazed over with lust. "This way." He wrapped an arm around my body and whisked me into an open elevator a few feet down the hall. As soon as the doors shut, he was on me, taking my hips in his hands and yanking me to him.

Effing Camille! She'd somehow turned Ian into a total slime bucket. My rage slowly turned to terror as the reality sank in that I wouldn't be able to stop whatever happened between them. She was about to force me to cheat on Kane, and I couldn't do anything about it. Would he think to use protection? What if he got me pregnant, or worse?

Camille's desire started as a faint tingling at the edge of my mind then slowly wound its way through my body into each cell, sparking to life with each heightened moment of lust between them. Heat pooled at my center.

The odd sense of arousal and disgust sent me reeling further into my mind.

A bell rang, and the elevator doors slid open. Ian's hands and mouth were everywhere as he maneuvered me backward through the hall until he pressed me to a door. A second later, he whipped out a cardboard key and pushed us into the empty room.

The door slammed closed with an ominous click I was certain no one but me heard.

This time, Camille pressed Ian up against the wall, her hands curling in his black button-down shirt. She moved in to nip his neck and growled. In one swift movement she tugged, and the buttons of Ian's shirt popped off, leaving the fabric dangling at his sides.

His eyes went wide for a nanosecond. Then he whirled, forcing me against the wall, his hands dipping into the slit of my skirt. Flesh met flesh and he grasped, hard enough to leave bruises. I would've yelped if I could have. My mind screamed to get away, to force Ian and his grabby hands out of the room. For me to run as far and as fast as I could. But that tendril of energy was still spilling from my mind, keeping me connected to Camille as she writhed under his touch.

A pulse that had nothing to do with lust throbbed through her. A tingle so faint, yet familiar. Then it started to build.

Clarity lifted the fog on my brain and I knew. She was using sex to steal my magic. She was grabbing hold of Ian's desire and using his energy to steal the magic from me. And I was powerless to stop it.

My skirt was hiked up over my thighs now, my legs wrapped around Ian's waist as he thrust against me, the fabric of his jeans rough against the tiny layer of silk coving my sex.

Please, I silently pleaded to no one. *Make it stop.*

I longed for a detached numbness, but as Camille pulled more and more magic from my soul, my awareness heightened and all of her emotions flooded into me. Hot, desperate lust boiled inside her as she grappled with his belt buckle, followed by gleeful anticipation to use the full force of my magic, and then righteous anger. I couldn't pinpoint what it was she was so furious about, but underneath the dance of emotions gripping her, it was the driving force to her actions.

Camille slipped my hand into Ian's open jeans and palmed his full length. He moaned, thrusting against me as he buried his head into my neck, scraping his teeth down my sensitive skin.

In my mind, I struck out at both of them, wanting to wretch or maim or just curl up in a ball and die. I was so utterly helpless to stop any of it. A dangerous thrill coiled within Camille. Ian's hands were under my shirt, cupping and kneading my now-bare breasts.

"Jade," he said, his voice low and tortured, "I've wanted this since the day we met."

Releasing him, Camille stepped back. Without saying a word, she slowly tugged my silk panties down, letting them fall at her ankles.

Ian's smoldering eyes traveled the length of my legs, pausing to memorize the fabric pooled at my feet, and then he jerked his gaze back up.

She licked my lips. "Come to me."

As if in a trance, Ian moved forward, grasping my hips and jerking me against him. His hands slipped under the skirt again, this time meeting bare skin. "Oh God," he moaned, pressing himself against my mound.

"Take me," Camille growled. "Right now. Right here."

No, no, no, no, no, I screamed in my mind. This was not happening. Ian would not do this to me.

But he was. And as far as he knew, I wanted it. Hell, I was demanding it.

I recoiled into my mind, reciting the lyrics to "Song Bird," by Fleetwood Mac, the one my mom used to sing to me after a nightmare when I was young. Anything to retreat from what was going to happen to my body. I imagined myself curled in a corner with my fingers in my ears and my eyes squeezed shut, oblivious to everyone and everything. *I am not here. This isn't happening.*

The magic was building all around me, pressing in on my imaginary body rocking back and forth. Power. Everywhere. Camille's excitement smoldered hot, burning and searing through her, ratcheting up until it sang in a crescendo of pressure and pleasure.

The sensation of skin on skin entered into my shell of awareness. I pressed my imaginary palms to my imaginary eyes, praying for numbness.

"Now," Camille commanded. "Fuck me."

No!

The door slammed open, wood splintering across the room. Ian froze, his half-naked body hovering over mine on the bed.

The icy fire fled my body, and I slammed back into my flesh.

"Get off me!" I screamed, shoving Ian with enough force that he tumbled right off the side of the bed. I curled to my side, wrapping myself in the comforter as tears spilled unchecked down my cheeks.

I gasped, almost choking on the sob clogging my throat.

"What the fuck are you doing?" Kane's fury reverberated through me.

I scrambled to my knees, clutching the blanket around me just in time to see Kane's fist slam into Ian's face. A sickening crunch filled the room, and blood gushed from Ian's once perfectly straight nose.

Ian seemed to fall in slow motion against the nightstand, his arm sweeping the lamp to the floor. It shattered with a spectacular crash, and Ian landed sprawled among the ceramic shards, tiny cuts seeping all over his torso.

Meri stood just inside the room, shock and fear clear in her wide eyes. Kane reached for me, his face full of concern, but I jumped from the bed and ran into the bathroom. My fingers shook as I fumbled with the lock. Turning, I pressed my back against the door and took a deep breath. Oxygen rushed to my brain, and my head spun. My knees gave out; trembling, I sank to the floor, burying my face in my hands.

Through the door, I could hear a renewed rustling. Flesh met flesh, followed by grunts of pain and growls of frustration. I tucked into myself, rocking in place just as I'd imagined in my mind, and covered my ears.

I fully retreated into myself, and everything went silent. All I could feel was the very real violation of being sexually assaulted. Could you call it assault if the ghost possessing you not only seduced the man, but tortured him beyond desire? It didn't matter. I'd been invaded, heart, soul, and body, and no amount of rationalization could make it better.

Curled up on the floor, I concentrated on the diamond tile pattern, trying not to think of anything. One black diamond tile sat surrounded by eight white tiles. The pattern repeated, perfectly throughout the small bathroom. I counted nine black tiles across. The second row eight black tiles. Nine black tiles. Eight. Nine. Seven. I narrowed in on the odd row, trying to find the missed beat.

"Stop it! Get off him. Kane, stop it. That's enough." Pyper's voice filtered through my fog.

The noise stopped, and muffled voices rumbled in the other room.

I stopped counting tiles and curled into a fetal position again, squeezing my eyes shut, wishing I were anywhere but here. What would Kane say?

Moments later, someone knocked softly on the door. I flinched and wrapped my arms around myself tighter.

"Jade?"

It was Kane. And though I longed to be wrapped in his safe arms, I couldn't bring myself to move. He'd seen me with another man. One I'd almost dated. I couldn't face him. Couldn't look him in the eye after what he'd seen. I couldn't even form words, much less explain myself.

"Jade," Kane said again, softly. "Please, open the door." He didn't sound mad. His voice was soft, tentative. But he'd still ask questions. Ones I didn't want to think about.

Flashes of Ian touching my bare skin, running his tongue and lips over my breasts, and his obvious pleasure from my Camille-controlled touch made me want to gag. I scooted toward the waste bucket in case my stomach decided to purge itself.

Kane's knocking became more insistent and his tone more and more panicked as he called my name through the door. I just wanted everyone to leave so I could get dressed and quietly go home. But which home? Not Kane's house. I just couldn't…

"Jade." Kane's strangled voice pleaded from the other side of the door. "Please, baby, I need to know you're all right."

I still didn't move, despite the anguish that ate away at my heart. My pain was too fresh, too raw. I was certain my soul would crack apart if I had to face Kane right then.

The voices in the hotel room lowered then eventually faded away.

They'd left. *Oh, God. They'd left. What would Kane do now?*

My eyes blurred. Tears ran in a steady stream and pooled on the tile. *Why is this happening to me? Why now?* The life I'd dreamed for myself was slipping away right before my eyes. Through my muffled sobs, I heard the distinct sound of the door opening.

I froze and stifled a cry.

Kane's fresh rain scent washed over me. "Jade?" His voice was so low, I almost didn't hear him.

I squeezed my eyes shut and willed him to go away. I knew he wouldn't, but anything was better than facing him.

His scent faded and a second later, the pipes groaned and water rushed into the shower. I curled the blanket around me tighter.

The room filled with steam then Kane gently tugged the blanket from me. I resisted for a moment, but the lure of the shower won the battle. I had to scrub the day's events from my body.

But as soon as the blanket lifted from my naked body, I recoiled again, ashamed and terrified to look Kane in the eye.

He didn't say a word as he lifted me gently and carried me into the bathtub. Placing me directly under the stream, he stood behind me, fully clothed, making sure I was steady on my feet. The hot water scalded my tender flesh, but I welcomed the pain, letting it drive away the recent memories.

"You're doing fine now," Kane whispered in my ear. "Everything's going to be all right. I've got you."

The tears fell faster and I sucked in a breath. "You're..." The words got caught in my throat.

"I'm what?" he asked.

I shook my head and swallowed. "Don't leave," I forced out.

His hands tightened on my shoulders. His breathing hitched with emotion as he leaned in. A few seconds went by. Then he gently kissed my cheek. "Never," he said, his tone almost strangled. "Never again, Jade."

Chapter 19

With Kane behind me, we stood in the shower until the water turned tepid. He reached around me, shut off the taps, and then wrapped me in an oversized white towel. I stared at my feet, afraid to look him in the eye.

Carefully, he shifted and stepped out of the tub. Once he was stripped out of his wet clothes and wrapped in his own towel, he moved in front of me but didn't say a word. I knew he was waiting for me to look up at him. I just couldn't. I wanted to. I wanted to gaze into his understanding eyes and get lost in the toffee flecks I knew would be there. Sighing, I turned away.

From the corner of my eye, I saw Kane reach for me and forced myself to stay still, to not flinch from his touch. Sweat broke out on my brow and I bit my lip. I clutched the nearby towel rack to keep myself from running.

Barely touching me at all, he tucked a lock of my wet hair behind my ear. "I'll be right back."

As soon as the door closed behind him, I stepped out of the tub and ran the water in the sink, splashing the cold water on my face. Bile rose in my throat; I couldn't even let him touch me. The crack in my heart deepened.

The door opened, and Kane slipped in, careful to close the door behind him. I glanced at his hands and let out a tiny gasp of relief. "Where did you get those?"

He handed me a pair of my jeans and a sweater, along with my undergarments. "Pyper ran to the house and picked them up. Your other…well, we thought this would be more comfortable."

More tears welled in my eyes, but I blinked them back. I clutched my clothes to my chest and met his beautiful, kind eyes. The compassion I found there nearly broke me all over again. "Thank you."

Kane's eyes went soft as he gazed at me, and I forced myself to not look away. Not for him, but for me. To prove I could.

His eyes turned concerned as he searched for something in my gaze. I glanced away, not ready to be scrutinized. He let the moment pass and quickly changed into a fresh set of his own clothes. I stood still, clutching mine, too nervous to do anything.

Fully dressed, Kane turned to me. "Jade?"

"Yeah?"

"As soon as you get dressed, I can take you home."

The lump was back in my throat. I didn't look up.

"Our home," he said, answering my unspoken question.

Relief flooded through me. He still wanted me there.

I nodded, my hands trembling.

A tortured sigh escaped Kane's lips, and he wrapped his arms around me, pulling me to him until my head rested on his chest. He kissed the top of my head. "I love you, pretty witch."

My heart stopped, and my mouth opened to utter the words back to him, but no sound came out. Instead, I gripped the back of his shirt and held on with everything I had. His arms tightened around me, and we stood there for what seemed like hours, though only moments passed.

I pulled away and stared at his chest. "I'm sorry."

Kane didn't move. He barely even breathed. His hand slid up my bare arm, over my neck, and ended with two fingers tilting my chin up to meet his steady gaze. "You have absolutely nothing to be sorry for."

My pulse pounded in my throat as I tried to hold back another onslaught of tears.

"Understand?"

I lost the battle and squeezed my eyes shut.

"Jade?"

I nodded and choked out, "I understand."

He pulled me to him once more, hugging me briefly. "I'll be right outside. Take as long as you need."

I nodded again, clutching my towel around me. The door shut, and quiet voices murmured from the other room. Leaning against the vanity, I concentrated on the air inflating my lungs. I wasn't okay, not by a long shot, but my relationship with Kane wasn't in jeopardy. And that was enough to put me back on solid ground.

Once dressed in my regular clothes and fully covered, I almost felt normal again...until I walked out of the bathroom and spotted the bed. I stumbled back, pressing my palms to my eyes trying to block out the memories of Ian groping me and Camille urging him on.

A hand landed on my back. "Let's go." It was Kane. "Time to get out of here."

I let him lead me out of the room and down the hall, but when we got to the elevator, I shook my head. "Stairs."

Meri and Pyper met up with us, but neither said a word, only followed us down the stairwell. Tourists bustled past, and thankfully, the bar was packed with a line waiting at the entrance, blocking the area where I'd kissed Ian. A tremor ran through me at the thought.

When the door opened and we spilled out onto Bourbon Street, I stood in the street, dazed and almost paralyzed by the crowd. Tourists swarmed, jostling me into drunken coeds.

My eyes glazed over, and the next thing I knew, Kane was leading me up the steps of his shotgun double. It was the middle of the day, but I headed straight for his bedroom, closed the door behind me, and crawled into bed, burying my head in a pillow. I closed my eyes, wanting only to sleep, but I couldn't turn off my mind. Ian was everywhere. Camille, the magic that had swirled in me and her disturbing need to have sex with Kane the night before, and how she'd compelled Ian to act in a way I couldn't believe. How could he have done that?

I tossed and turned, trying to clear my mind. Eventually, I sat up and stared at the opposite wall and the bright painting depicting a flooded New Orleans with houses in treetops. It was sad and hopeful all at the same time. My gaze flicked to the wing chair in the corner, the one Ian and Pyper had fallen asleep in one night while watching over me.

Ian and Pyper. How was she doing? My hand automatically landed on the nightstand and wrapped around my phone. I tapped out a quick message and waited. A few moments later a light tap sounded on the door.

"Pyper?" I called.

The door opened, and her dark head floated in the opening. "Hey." Her eyes were wide, her tone tentative.

"Come in." I patted the bed next to me.

She pasted on a fake smile and slipped into the room. "Can I get you anything?"

I shook my head.

The bed dipped as she crawled across the king-sized bed and sat cross-legged beside me. She smoothed the bed, concentrating on the subtle geometric pattern. "Can I do—"

With someone else to focus on, my bravado returned, and I held up my hand. "I'm fine."

She let out a dismissive snort.

"Okay, maybe I'm not fine, but I think I will be."

"Of course you will."

I smiled at that then sobered. "And what about you?"

She shrugged.

"Pyper?"

Her eyes softened, and then she grimaced. "Please don't do that. Don't feel like you have to talk to me about this. I'm not the one who…never mind. I'll process my own feelings later. Right now, Meri's in the hall. We have something to tell you."

The tiny amount of relief at not having to discuss what happened with her boyfriend fled. "What is it?"

"I think Meri needs to explain it." Pyper opened the door, and Meri, along with Kane, entered the room.

Well, wasn't this just a great big slumber party? Kane perched on the side of the bed, his hand resting lightly on my thigh. His solid presence helped to soothe my unease.

"What's going on?" I asked, noting Meri's hesitant expression. "Where did you go earlier?" My mind whirled with a faint memory of Pyper leading Meri away right before Camille possessed me. I turned to Pyper. "Why did you tell her I was downstairs?"

She winced.

"Jade," Meri started, "Pyper was compelled to do that."

I stared at her, mouth open. "What...?" I trailed off, realizing exactly what that meant. "She was possessed?"

Meri nodded slowly. "That's what we think. It was a mild possession."

"What does that mean? Mild? How can someone be *mildly* possessed?" I gripped the bedspread to keep myself from punching something.

Meri gave me a sympathetic smile. "I know. All it means is the hold wasn't that strong. Camille was able to control Pyper for a very short time—"

"Camille? How? I thought I was the only one at risk."

Meri nodded. "For the most part, you are. But you seem to have a connection to Kat and Pyper—"

'Wait! What? Kat's involved in this too?" My head was spinning. Pyper and Kat had been possessed? I thought back to the night before, when Lucien had to calm her down. "Shit," I said, catching on. "Camille possessed her when she was with Lucien, right?"

Meri nodded. "We think so. I talked to Bea a little while ago and that's what she suspects. Because you've been known to transfer energy to your friends, and apparently you had some trouble with transmitting your essence, they have enough of you in them that Camille is able to control them. Kat more so than Pyper because she's spent a lot more time with you."

Holy fuck. That was all true. I had used my empath gift to help ease my friend's moods when I could. And I'd been doing it wrong for years. "Oh, no."

Pyper grabbed my hand. "It wasn't for long. It's like I lost five minutes of my life, wandering around the club. No trauma. No flashbacks. Nothing odd except I wasn't in control."

Of course it was only for a few minutes. Camille had used Pyper to lure Meri away and as soon as she'd seen her chance, she'd taken me over and turned me into a sex-crazed, psycho bimbo. Ugh.

"And Kat? Is she doing okay?"

"She's still at Bea's. She's perfectly fine, but after today's turn of events, Bea didn't want her to be subject to the ghost again. She's keeping an eye on her."

I held my head in my hands, trying to make sense of everything. Why was Camille trying to possess anyone at all? To save her daughter? But how? She was fixated on me because I was the easy target. But why Kat? Was she drawn to her because of my energy transfer? Did she think she could take her over? I'd have to talk to Kat about what exactly happened. With Pyper, it was clear what Camille had done.

"No one is safe until I get my soul fixed," I said.

Meri got up and headed toward the door. She paused with her hand on the knob, her head tilted forward. "I love your mother. She's been a friend to me when I had no one else. But she's wrong to have kept the identity of your biological father from you. How long are you going to wait until you take matters into your own hands?"

Chapter 20

Meri's words set a fire in my belly. As soon as she left the room, I grabbed my phone and dialed Mom.

Gwen answered on the second ring. "Jade! We're so worried. Are you okay, sweetheart?"

"Put Mom on the phone." My tone was icy, and I winced at the sound. Gwen hadn't done anything wrong. "Sorry, I didn't mean to snap at you. I'm just…stressed."

She hesitated. "Perfectly understandable."

They way she said the words implied she understood, but I'd still hurt her. I frowned, feeling even worse. "Gwen?"

"Yes?"

"You didn't deserve that. I really am sorry." I clutched the phone. "Mom's keeping something from me. Something important."

"You know I don't want to get in the middle."

I bit down hard on my lip. Why was everyone walking on eggshells around Mom? My life was the one at stake. It was really starting to piss me off. "I know."

"But…" There was static on the end of the line and a mumbling of voices. I had the distinct impression Gwen was covering the mouthpiece of her phone. The line cleared. "It's time, Hope."

Silence.

"Jade?" Gwen came back on the line.

"Yes."

"Your mother just went to shower. If she doesn't tell you by the end of the day, I will. But I'd rather it came from her."

I was twenty-seven years old. Why the hell couldn't they just tell me who my father was? I clenched my fists in frustration and ground out, "How long have you known?"

She sighed. "Just a few days, sweetie. I swear."

My fingers relaxed. That was why I loved Gwen so much. She was loyal to a fault and good all the way to her bones. She'd give Mom every chance in the world to do the right thing, but if someone Gwen loved was at risk, she'd take matters into her own hands.

"Okay," I said.

"You know I'm telling you the truth, right?"

"Of course. You don't lie." And she didn't. She'd kept her mouth shut, but she'd never blatantly lied to me about anything. At least not as far as I'd known.

"Good."

"Gwen?"

"Yeah?"

"Where are you? Back at my apartment?"

"No, we're at Pyper's. After what happened today at your place, your mother didn't feel comfortable going there."

"You mean after I was possessed?"

"Yes. It's disconcerting."

Tell me about it. "Do me a favor?"

"Anything."

"Keep her there. I'll have Kane pick up some takeout, and we'll meet you in an hour."

Silence.

"Gwen? Can you do that?"

"I'll try, but you know how she is when she gets something stuck in her head."

"Yeah, she's exactly like you…and me, for that matter. We don't let it go." I rubbed a hand over my throbbing forehead. "Does she have something in mind? Somewhere she thinks she's going?"

"Maybe." Gwen said the word slowly as if she wasn't sure how to answer me.

I knew that tone. She used it every time she didn't want to talk about one of her visions. "You saw something?"

"Yes, but you know I'm not going to say anything about it."

I shook my head. "Of course not."

Gwen chuckled. The conversation was a familiar one.

"See you soon." I hung up and turned to Pyper. "They're still at your place. Is it okay if we pick up dinner and head over?"

"No problem at all." She followed me to the door and laid a gentle hand on my arm. "Are you sure you're ready to deal with everything after what happened this afternoon?"

My mind whirled once again from the memories. I forced a bright smile. "Better than sitting around here thinking about it."

"Fair enough." She held the door open and swept an arm out. "After you."

Forty-five minutes later, with a sack full of po'boys and steaming French fries, Kane pulled into the parking spot behind Wicked. During the short ride and wait for the food, my frustration with my mother had kept me sane, as if anger were holding me together. But as soon as I saw the building, apprehension filled me.

Kane must've felt the shift in my emotional armor because he placed a hand on my knee. "You don't have to go in. I can go get them, and we can go somewhere else."

I shook my head, but everything inside me was screaming, *yes*.

Kane narrowed his eyes and studied me. Then he shook his head. "No, I don't think so. Wait here with Meri, and I'll be right back."

His door slammed and Pyper, Meri, and I glanced at each other.

Pyper grinned. "I guess we're going to have a night picnic." She reached into the bag and drew out a steaming French fry. The starchy smell made my stomach growl. When was the last time I'd eaten? She reached in, grabbed a few more, and passed them to me.

The salty shoestring-cut fries practically melted on my tongue. "Oh, that's good."

Her lips turned up in a satisfied smile. "Told ya."

She'd dragged us to some hole-in-the-wall local joint that was fifteen minutes out of our way, singing the praises of Loletta's Po'boy shack. If the sandwiches were as good as the fries, we were going to be daily customers.

Kane emerged from the back of the club with Mom and Gwen in tow. I glanced at the backseat. Kane's car really only comfortably fit four people. I frowned.

Pyper opened her door. "I'll just wait here. I'm sure Charlie could use some help in the club. Unless you need me for something."

I bit my lip. "Actually, if you don't mind, can you go check on Kat? I haven't been able to see her today, and I want to be sure she's okay."

Pyper's brows furrowed. "She's at Bea's, right?"

I nodded.

"Then I'm sure everything's fine. Bea would've called."

"Maybe, maybe not. I'm not sure she knows what happened." I gritted my teeth. "If she does know, and Kat took a turn for the worse, do you really think she'd bother me today?"

Pyper smoothed her hair from her eyes, her black locks shining in the late afternoon sun. "You might have a point." She stood there, clutching the food bag. "Ian could be there."

The blood drained from my face. Hearing Ian's name made my stomach turn. I'd been fine with talking in a general sense, but I couldn't do this.

Understanding and then anger rolled through Pyper's bright blue eyes. "That doesn't make one bit of difference. Kat is my friend, too. I'm not going to let him stop me from seeing her."

"Okay. Thanks." I took a deep breath, trying to expel the unease claiming my body.

She trotted off to her red Bug.

Gwen glanced once at me then at Pyper. I waved for her to go with my friend. Gwen had already said she'd tell me by the end of the day if Mom didn't come clean. She'd keep her word. "Take care of Kat for me."

"Of course, honey." Gwen grabbed one of the bags of food and smiled at me as she climbed into Pyper's car.

Kane held the back door open for Mom, and she took Pyper's spot.

Mom studied me, her gaze concerned. "Are you okay?"

No, I wasn't okay. What kind of question was that? I'd been sexually assaulted and she was making me crazy keeping secrets. "I'm fine, or I will be once you tell me about my father."

She sucked in a breath. "It's only been a day. Give me some time."

"It's been twenty-seven years."

Silence filled the car.

When it appeared Mom wasn't going to respond, Kane cleared his throat. "Where to?"

"The coven circle," I said, not knowing why I was choosing that place. Maybe it was the large oaks. Maybe it was the feeling of being surrounded by a buzz of familiar magic. But I didn't want to be indoors anymore, even if the temperature was dropping fast into the low forties. My lungs just didn't feel like they were getting enough oxygen.

"Jade—" Mom began.

Meri cut her off. "The circle is fine. If anything goes wrong, all three of us have magic to fall back on."

Kane didn't question anything as he took off down the street toward uptown, where the coven circle was. Goddess, I loved that man.

Mom shook her head. "Never mind."

"Hope," Meri said with a frustrated sigh. She turned to me. "Not that I want to get in the middle of any of this, but your mom isn't exactly a fan of coven circles these days."

"No?" I raised my eyebrows. "Well, I'm not a fan of being lied to, so I guess we're even."

I tore open the bag Pyper had left behind and grabbed an oyster po'boy. My rage started to fuel my hunger, and it was all I could do not to tear through the white wrapper with my teeth. I knew I was being unfair. After all, Mom had been taken by a demon while in a coven circle—by Meri, one of her best friends, no less. None of that could be easy for her. And I couldn't even say why it was so important I go to the circle tonight. It wasn't really a place I usually longed to be. Sure, I craved the heady mixture of magic and the strum of feeling all the members together, but I wasn't even the coven leader anymore. It wouldn't feel the same.

I stopped mid-bite. That was it. I was craving my connection to the coven. Ever since I'd given the title to Bea, I hadn't felt that constant undercurrent and it was making me antsy. Going to the circle wouldn't change that. I opened my mouth to tell Kane we could just go to Carrolton Park, but Mom spoke before I had a chance.

"You're being unreasonable, Jade."

"What?" I twisted in my chair, trying to hold back an accusation of my own.

"It's not time yet. Maybe after we sort this out. And the circle isn't going to do you any good. If you think for one moment—"

"Whoa, whoa, whoa." Meri waved her hands. "That's enough. You two can talk when we get there and have this out." She glared at Mom. "And you know as well as I do that now is the time. Stop taking your insecurities out on Jade. If you'd told her years ago, she would've been prepared for this."

"Meri!" Mom scolded. "This isn't your place."

"We'll have to agree to disagree on that point." Meri gave me a sidelong glance.

I sent her a tiny smile and went back to my sandwich. I could've let Mom off the hook about the circle, but she was being so unreasonable, I decided I'd stay in childish mode just to spite her.

But as soon as we parked in the parking lot and Mom's eyes went wide with fear, my resolve faltered. I placed a hand on Kane's shoulder. "Go to Carrolton. We don't need to be here."

"Actually," Meri began, "I think it's a good idea. We might need to...ah...summon someone. If we're here, it'll be more convenient."

Mom shot Meri another look of disgust but didn't say anything else. In fact, she opened her door, got out, and headed into the trees.

I glanced at Kane. He shrugged and put the car back in park.

"Let's do this," Meri said, standing beside my door.

I tossed my half-eaten sandwich back into the bag and grimaced at the heavy weight of grease rumbling in my stomach. Maybe that hadn't been the best plan. I reached down and grabbed two bottles of water and joined Meri.

"Want me to wait here?" Kane asked from the other side of the car.

"No." I met him halfway in the front of his car and slid my hand into his.

"Good. I don't think I could've stayed away anyway."

I smiled up at him. "I know."

Meri's phone buzzed. She rapidly tapped out a message. Another buzz. More typing. Three rounds later, she slipped the phone into her pocket.

I raised my eyebrows. "Everything okay?"

"Fine." She joined us and started walking toward the trees. "That was Dan checking in on me."

The three of us walked in silence through the oaks, our feet crunching on fallen twigs and dried leaves. Kane kept one hand on the small of my back, his touch making me feel comfortable and safe.

Ahead of us, Meri passed through the last of the trees and came to a sudden stop.

"What is it?" I called and ran to catch up with her.

She stared at the clearing, her mouth open in surprise.

I followed her gaze, and my heart stopped at what I saw in the middle of the circle. A strangled cry came from my throat as I broke into a run.

Chapter 21

An odd mix of joy and trepidation seized me as I stared at the man directly in the middle of Mom's circle. His golden locks had turned silver over the years and despite a few age lines, he looked exactly as he had the last time I'd seen him standing by that old green truck of his.

"Why is he here?" I demanded as I slowed to a walk.

"You wanted to know about your father, so I summoned him," Mom said. "He's the only one you've ever had."

I wanted to shout at her that I needed my biological father. That without him and part of his soul, Camille could come back and do Goddess knows what else. Unspeakable, awful things. Maybe next time she'd succeed. But I couldn't bring that up in front of Dad. I wasn't sure I could bring it up at all.

He turned, and a smile curled his lips, but it didn't reach his eyes. Until that moment, I hadn't realized how much his absence had affected me. The sad, lonely little girl inside me wanted to cry with both anger and relief at his sudden reappearance.

I stopped at the edge of the circle, my hands on my hips, fighting the urge to run into his arms and bury myself in one of his bear hugs. My inner little girl wanted that more than anything, but my adult self held her back. I couldn't trust this man. He'd hurt me. I wouldn't allow him to do it again. "Where the hell have you been for the last seventeen years?"

His gaze flicked to Mom. She turned away and stared in the direction of the Mississippi, just on the other side of the levee.

"Well?" I demanded, irritated at myself for wanting anything from him. He'd abandoned me, left me and Mom and never even came back when she disappeared. So what if he wasn't my real dad? He was the only one I knew.

His legs shifted as he tried to step forward, but his body didn't actually move from his spot. That was when I noticed he was floating just above the ground.

I eyed the ground. It was void of any markers or maps, two standard tools normally needed for summoning individuals. "She knew where you were the entire time, didn't she?"

Dad turned his attention to Mom. "Hope? Are you going to tell her now?"

Mom shrugged. "She wants to know why you left." She spun around, glaring at him. "Go on. Tell her."

He closed his eyes and sighed. "If that's the way you want to play this." He paused, seeming to give her one last chance to change her mind. When she didn't respond, he turned to me and held out his hand.

I stared at it as if he'd just tried to hand me toxic waste.

Slowly, he lowered his arm then rubbed his hand over his jaw. "You probably can't touch me, anyway."

This time I shrugged. I had no idea if I could or couldn't. The last time I'd done a finding spell, I'd actually transported two angels into the circle instead of just their images. I'd been able to touch them. But then again, they'd been completely solid. I couldn't tell if Dad was or wasn't. It didn't matter. Until I got answers, I wasn't going anywhere near him.

His eyes, so sad and tortured, met mine. "I'm so sorry, baby. I never wanted to leave you."

My breath got caught in my throat, and I swallowed the raw ache coming from the depths of my core. *He hadn't loved me enough to stay.* I could not break down. Not now. Not in his presence. "Why did you then?"

"I didn't have a choice."

Mom snorted.

"Hope, not now," he said, his tone full of anger. "This never would've happened if you'd allowed me tell her the truth years ago."

Her head snapped up, and her green eyes flashed with a dangerous challenge. "Don't you put this on me. A ten-year-old was not ready to know she was a white witch."

"If she'd known, she could've started learning all the skills she needed to help with everything she's facing now," he shot back.

He'd wanted to tell me about my powers? That was what they'd fought over? I glanced between them, angry at both of them now. Dad was right; Mom should've told me. But why did he leave me on my own? Who did that?

"Oh," Mom mocked, "and you're just the person who would've taught her everything she needed to know? The one who worked overseas for years at a time? The one who was never there when we needed you? The one who left my baby in *foster care* after I was abducted to *Hell*?"

"Yes, me!" He moved one foot in front of the other as if stalking toward her, but he stayed suspended in the middle of the circle. "If you hadn't forced me to leave, I never would've disappeared from your lives. If you'd been honest from the start, none of this would've happened. And if you hadn't called the damned council to get me out of Idaho, I sure as fuck wouldn't have left Jade."

"What?" Mom and I said together.

I jerked and turned to her, anger seizing me. She'd kept him from me? How could she? "You forced him to leave?"

Kane and Meri stepped close, standing behind me as if to back me up if I needed them.

Mom tore her gaze from Dad, and trembling, she met my hard stare. "I couldn't do it, Jade. You weren't ready. I knew you were powerful. You showed all the signs of a white witch. When you uttered my spells with me, they always worked ten times better than when I did them alone. You even worked some of them on your own a time or two. I was terrified that if I told you what you were, it would be too much for you to handle."

"You knew?" I gasped. "All those years, you knew I held this power, that darkness would follow me because of it?"

She nodded, her expression devastated. "I was going to tell you after you turned sixteen."

"You should've told her when she was a kid!" Dad bellowed. "Look at what you let happen!"

"And where were you? Off working undercover for the witches council? If you'd cared, you wouldn't have left."

"You know you gave me no choice." Dad clutched his fists at his sides as he shook in unbridled fury.

"You had a choice, you bastard. You chose the council over us."

"No, Hope. You lied to me," he said in a quiet, controlled voice. "Left me in the dark, made me believe she was mine. And when you didn't agree with my parenting choices, you threatened to have me removed from her life. I love that girl. Do you have any idea what that did to me? What *you* did to me?"

I froze. "What did you just say? Mom made you believe I was yours?" I turned pleading eyes on her. What was wrong with her? How could she treat the people she loved with so little respect? And she'd made me think everything was his fault. This wasn't my mother. Not the one I thought I knew. Betrayal clutched at my heart and a pit formed in my stomach. "You lied to him, too?"

Kane stepped up beside me and wrapped his large hand around mine, letting me know he was still there.

Tears filled Mom's eyes. She angrily brushed them away and glared at Dad. "What the hell is wrong with you, Marc?"

He threw up his hands. "You can't keep lying to your daughter."

I tore my gaze from Mom and turned to the man I'd loved and resented as my father all these years. "You're not...I mean, you don't think of me as your daughter?"

He took two steps toward me and then scowled in frustration. Tears glistened in his eyes as he turned his attention to Mom. "Couldn't you have called me? Jesus. I would've caught the next plane."

Mom shook her head and backed up, clutching her hands to her chest. "That wouldn't help anything."

"It would've given me a chance to hold the little girl I helped raise for eight years before you ran me off." He let out a grunt of frustration and faced me. "Jade, my darling, you will always be mine in every way that counts." He touched his chest. "You live here with me every day."

I clutched Kane's hand. "But you're not my biological father." It wasn't a question. I already knew the answer.

He shook his head. "God, how I wish I was."

Something sharp and painful tore through my chest. I ripped away from Kane's hold and stalked forward. "Then why did you let her make you leave? We needed you! And when Mom left…" I paused to collect myself. "You have no idea what I went through. Even if you weren't my father, you could've been my dad. But you weren't. You let her send you away." I spun and ran back to Kane's side. "Let's go."

"Jade," Dad—no, *Marc*—called. "Please, give me a chance to explain."

I cast him a scathing glance over my shoulder. "You've had seventeen years to explain yourself." I jerked my head in total frustration and faced him again. "I have a damn online store in my name. One Internet search and you would've found me."

Kane stood behind me with his hands on my shoulders, supporting me.

"You're right," Marc conceded. "And I did look for you. I've known you've been living in New Orleans for the last several months. I knew your mom disappeared, but I didn't find out until after you were living with your aunt."

"And?" Why? Why had he left me? Why hadn't he gotten in touch? If Mom was the problem… None of this made sense.

"I didn't want to disrupt your life. By then, I hadn't been a part of it for the better part of eight years. You had healing to do and, as I understood it, a deep-seated hatred for all things related to witchcraft. That's what I am, sweetheart. My whole life is and was the council. I'd only have brought you pain."

I squeezed my eyes shut, not willing to listen to his ratio-nalization. "I waited for you," I said so quietly I thought only Kane heard me.

"Jade." Marc's voice cracked. "I'm so sorry. If I'd known, if I'd thought even for a moment my presence would help, I would've been by your side."

I pressed my lips together and shook my head, trying to stave off more tears. I'd had enough.

"Who's my real father?" My tone was low, demanding.

He shook his head. "I don't know. She never would tell me."

Hatred formed a ball in the pit of my stomach for the woman I'd adored, grieved over for twelve years, and then risked my life to save from purgatory. The powerful emotions made me sick.

I turned to her, my body trembling. "No more lies, Mother."

She stood frozen in the twilight, her mouth partially open. Slowly, she shook her head. "I've wanted to tell you." Her voice dropped to barely a whisper. "It's too dangerous. He'll hurt you."

Ice formed a thin layer over my heart. "It's too dangerous not to. Let's go," I said to Kane. "We'll find out another way."

We took off without looking back. Thankfully, Meri fol-lowed without being asked. When we got to the trees, she said, "Jade?"

I paused, staring at a water oak, concentrating on the pat-tern of its intricate bark. "What?"

"What about Hope?"

"What about her?"

"Are you going to wait for her, or is she finding her own ride home?"

I gritted my teeth. I didn't want to be anywhere near her, but I couldn't just leave her there. I didn't even know if she had her wallet or cash for a cab. "Tell her to meet us at the car."

Kane and I waited at the edge of the trees while Meri returned to the circle. They exchanged a few words that had Mom shaking her head and frowning. She waved Meri away and turned back to Marc, obviously giving him a piece of her mind, judging by the angry expression on her face.

Meri returned and shrugged. "She says she'll meet you later."

An all-encompassing anger took over, and I had to suppress the scream clawing at the back of my throat. It came out in more of a strangled cry. "Goddammit."

I stalked off through the trees. Who did she think she was? Yeah, I was pissed at Dad—Marc—but she'd set the events in motion. She'd lied. She was hiding who my real father was from me and Marc. Gwen said she'd known for only a few days. I believed her. But had she known where Marc was all those years? A tiny seed of doubt planted itself in the middle of my chest. Marc said he knew where I was after I went to live with Gwen. Had she kept him informed?

And with that one thought, my entire life became a lie. I couldn't trust any of my parental figures.

We came upon another water oak. One of its massive limbs was growing right into the ground. As I passed it, I struck out my leg, needing to kick something.

Pain engulfed my foot, and I let out an agonizing cry. Half hopping, half limping, I clutched Kane's arm as tears of pain stung my eyes. I blinked them back, determined to not let anyone see me cry. I was too pissed off. All I wanted to do was kick something else.

I didn't, though. My toes throbbed entirely too much. I dug around in my pocket and came up with one of Bea's healing herbs.

Kane gave me a small smile. "Not too long ago, if I'd tried to take one of those, you would've slapped it out of my hands."

"True," I said. "I've evolved."

He shook his head, his eyes worried. "I can see that. You okay?"

"No, but I will be as soon as we get to Bea's." And perform that finding spell.

Chapter 22

The car bounced over the rough road as we made our way to Bea's house. The potholes in the streets were getting worse. Turning into her long driveway, I held my breath. I didn't really want to see anyone except Bea, but all too often her small carriage home was the gathering place for all things paranormal. With her acting as the coven leader again, anyone could be there.

I blew out a breath and shook my head. Who was I kidding? I didn't care if any of the coven members were there. The only person I really didn't want to see was her nephew, Ian. There was a good chance he'd come to Bea for healing herbs after Kane had broken his nose. Would he tell his aunt he'd almost had sex with me while I'd been possessed? A cold sweat coated my body, and I sucked in a deep breath. I could get through this. I had to. As long as I stayed in possession of my body, everything would be fine.

Kane squeezed my hand. "Try not to worry so much. Everyone here loves you."

I gave him a small smile. Easier said than done.

We rounded the bend in the driveway, and Bea's bright yellow carriage house came into view. The tension eased out of my shoulders. Two cars sat in front: a Prius and a Bug. Bea's and Pyper's.

We climbed out of Kane's car, and a second later, Kat flew out of the door and ran straight for me. She caught me in a giant hug, nearly knocking me over. "Jade! Are you okay?"

Tears sprang to my eyes. "Yeah," I forced out on a sob.

"Oh, no." She pulled back, holding me at arm's length. "You're not." She tugged on my hand. "Come inside so we can talk."

I shook my head, fear keeping me rooted to my spot. If I went inside, I'd have to see everyone. I longed to be cuddled up in Kat's apartment, drinking hot chocolate and listing to eighties music while we ate Chinese food and talked about nothing and everything at the same time. When was the last time we'd done anything even remotely normal like that? Not since before I'd moved to New Orleans. "Can we stay out here? I'd rather sit on Bea's back porch."

"Sure. I'll just get Gwen and grab us something to drink. Meet you there in a few." She turned to go, but I grabbed her arm.

"No. Not Gwen. I'm not ready to talk to her yet."

Kat's hazel eyes went wide with curiosity, then cloudy with worry. "Something else happened, didn't it?"

I gave her an incredulous look.

"I mean after what happened…umm, since Gwen and Pyper came over an hour ago."

"You could say that." I stepped away and glanced at Kane. "Can you fill Gwen and Bea in? I'm pretty sure Gwen knows about Marc, but I'm not ready to face Bea."

He nodded and swept me into a hug and whispered, "Anything, love."

I hugged him back, not wanting to leave the comfort of his embrace, but if we stood there any longer, I was sure the rest of the house would come to investigate.

"Go on to the back," Kane told Kat. "I'll bring you three some dinner."

Meri, who'd been standing off to the side, said, "I'd appreciate that. Thank you."

Kat and I nodded, staring at each other. Her eyes gleamed and she raised one eyebrow, barely tilting her head in his direction. I knew she was thinking the same thing I was. Where did this man come from? Despite all the shit that kept going on around me, he was always there for me. It was almost scary. No one was that great.

The three of us walked around the house and settled at the patio table. Bea's screened-in porch overlooked her garden, and her freshly planted annuals. The bright pink flowers were a welcome reprieve in the shit storm my life had become.

"Okay, spill it," Kat said, cutting to the chase. "What did your mom say?"

"Not much." In the middle of the table sat an unlit candle, and just for something to do, I concentrated and muttered, "*Flama.*"

The wick smoldered, then a flame rose tall and strong.

Kat frowned. "Stop that."

"Why? No one said I couldn't use my magic."

"Not that." She waved at the candle. "Your avoidance. How can I help if you don't tell me what's going on?"

Meri leaned in. "Actually, it's probably better if you conserve your strength and not use magic right now."

I scowled but chose not to respond. I'd use magic if I damn well wanted to. It was just about the only thing left that I had any control over—sort of, as long as Camille wasn't in my body.

Not ready to talk about Marc, I asked Kat, "How are you?" I studied her bright eyes, rosy cheeks, and full red lips, all void of any traces of makeup. "You look fantastic." Not even a hint of what she'd gone through the day before remained. "I take it you're feeling better?"

"As good as new. Bea plied me with her healer drugs, and today, I feel like I could almost fly. Those pills are amazing."

My lips twitched at the wonder in her eyes. "Totally addicting," I agreed then sobered. "And Lucien? Any word on what's going on with him?"

Kat frowned. My heart weighed heavy in my chest. I should've called to check up on him. I'd been a complete bitch the last time we'd spoken. I knew he'd never do anything to intentionally hurt Kat or anyone else. If he'd thought for one moment a spell he cast would harm anyone in the slightest, he'd give up witchcraft altogether.

"Yeah," Kat said quietly. "He's not handling this well."

Damn you, Jade. My behavior must've made him feel infinitely worse. "Did you find out anything else about his curse?"

She nodded slowly.

"Well?"

Grimacing, she sent me an apologetic look. "It's not really for me to say. I'm sorry. But Bea knows, and she's working on it."

A low, angry buzz started in my head. She couldn't tell me? Bea knew? What the hell? Up until yesterday, I had been the coven leader. But I was stripped of my title due to no fault of my own. Kat was my best friend. She'd almost died, and now she wasn't allowed to tell me why. "Does no one trust me around here?"

She reached across the table to take my hand. "I'm sorry. You know I don't like to keep things from you, especially these kinds of things, but it's personal. It really should come from him."

I gently released my hand from hers and reluctantly nodded. It wasn't like he could do any magic right now anyway. "Okay. Since that subject is off limits, did anyone tell you what happened to you? Why Lucien had to spell you in the first place?"

"Yeah." Kat glanced down at her hands.

My heart just about broke in two. She'd been possessed because of years of being subjected to my magic. And though I hadn't known what I was doing at the time, it still didn't mean I wasn't ultimately responsible for the invasion and her near-death experience.

"I'm so sorry," we both said at the same time.

"What? You have nothing to be sorry for," I said.

Meri quietly got up and moved to the other side of the porch, clearly picking up on the turmoil running between

Kat and me. She curled up in another chair and rubbed her forehead, a sure sign of a headache. More guilt shot through me. It was the empath gift again. After living with it my whole life, even I would've had trouble after a day like today.

"Stop feeling guilty," Meri called. "It's not your fault. I took your soul, remember? None of this is your fault."

"She's right," Kat said softly. "I said I'm sorry because I'd only been possessed for a short while. And Jade, it truly was horrible. I didn't know what was going on at the time. I thought I was having some sort of stroke or schizophrenic episode or something. Then after what happened with Lucien, everything was so confused I didn't know what was real and what wasn't. The point is, you've been through so much, and yet you continue to worry about me and be here for me, even when your life is falling apart around you. After what happened today at the hotel…" She shuddered. "I don't even know how you're functioning."

I sat there, stunned by both of them. Neither blamed me? I was at the center of all of this.

"We're in this together." Kat scooted closer and brushed her shoulder against mine.

A weight lifted off my chest. There was still a lot wrong, but with my friends by my side, I could get through it. We just needed to find my father. Whoever he was.

A shout came from inside the house, followed by shattering glass. I sprang to my feet, knocking over my chair.

Kat jumped up and ran to the door, covering her mouth with her hand. "Oh, no."

High-pitched screaming floated through the closed door, too muffled to make out the words.

I took two steps to join Kat, but she whirled, blocking my view. "No. Do not go in there."

"Why?" Something was very wrong.

She took me by the hand and led me back to the table. "Trust me. Not now. I'll be right back."

Kat disappeared into the house. Pyper's voice carried out the door. Something about consequences. Who was she yelling at?

Meri took Kat's spot by the door. She glanced back at me and frowned. "Maybe we should take a walk."

"What's going on?" I shifted, trying to peer into the window, but Bea's drapes were blocking my view.

Meri pursed her lips and glanced back into the house. Then she shrugged. "You'll find out eventually. Your mom's here. She brought Ian."

"What?" I barked and stalked to the door. My entire body shook with anger. What was she doing? Had she lost her mind? First the lies and now this? Nudging Meri out of the way, I yanked open the door and strode in. I made a beeline to Ian, stopping behind him. "Get out."

Pyper stopped chewing him out, and everyone seemed to freeze. Ian turned slowly and looked down at me with a crooked nose and anguish-filled eyes, one black and blue and swollen shut. Jeez, Kane had done a number on him.

I took a step back and blinked. He had his hands stuffed into his pockets. His shoulders were hunched, and he was white-faced. He looked...haunted.

He closed his good eye and took a steadying breath. "Jesus Christ, Jade. I'm so, so sorry."

I took another step back, and Kane moved to stand in front of me, blocking my view of Ian. The tight ball of panic in my stomach eased slightly.

"Ian," Kane said, his voice vibrating with anger, "leave. Now."

Ian nodded solemnly. "Yeah. Sorry." He turned, gave Pyper a pained look, and strode toward the door.

Kat sent me an apologetic grimace and ran after him. The pair disappeared onto the front porch.

"Why?" I asked the room.

Everyone turned to my mother. She had circles under her eyes and locks of her dark hair had fallen from her signature low ponytail. In a defeated voice, she said, "I was walking along Saint Charles and he drove by. He insisted on taking me home.

I told him I didn't want his help, but he was blocking traffic and wouldn't take no for an answer. Short of spelling him, I didn't know what else to do. So I told him he could take me here. I'm sorry." She took off up the stairs to Bea's second floor.

"Hope," Meri called after her. The angel glanced at me once then followed Mom.

I didn't care. I was beyond worrying about what Mom did or didn't do. If she wasn't going to be honest with me then there was nothing for us to talk about. I stood in the middle of the room with Bea, Gwen, Pyper, and Kane. These were the people I trusted most in the world, but an overwhelming urge to go back outside seized my gut. The walls were closing in on me. But Meri was upstairs, and I couldn't risk being taken over by Camille yet again.

Waving a hand at the front door, I glanced at Bea. "Is Kat safe out there?"

Bea frowned with disapproval. "I know you've had a terrible day and you don't trust Ian, but he's still my nephew. He won't hurt Kat. If I thought for a moment—"

I held up a hand to cut her off. "That's not what I meant." Even though I felt utterly violated, in reality, Ian hadn't done anything wrong. Camille had come on to him. The only thing he was guilty of was trying to have sex with an engaged woman, one who had seemed more than willing. Last I checked, that wasn't against the law. In my heart of hearts, I knew he'd never intentionally hurt any one of us… not that way. Cheating on his girlfriend was an entirely different matter. "I was referring to Kat being possessed. How likely is it Camille will strike again?"

"Oh." Bea sank down onto her couch. "Sorry, dear. It's been a trying day for everyone."

I nodded my agreement.

"Not likely at all since she's here. The wards in and around the house can protect both Kat and Pyper."

"What about the ghosts I saw on your porch the other day? Could they hurt her?" My heart started to hammer, and I moved closer to the door.

Bea shook her head slowly. "I don't think so. I strengthened the wards around the house, and she's been spending time outside all afternoon. It hasn't been an issue."

"Strong enough to protect me?" If I could stay at Bea's, at least Meri could get a break if she needed to do anything besides babysit me.

"From what I've heard, your possession is much more complete. Now that she's so familiar with your body, I doubt it," Bea said with no small amount of frustration. "We really need to find your father. Until we do, you and everyone you've shared energy with are at risk."

Kane stilled beside me. "Everyone? Even complete strangers Jade may have nudged a little emotional energy to in passing?"

My body went completely cold. It wasn't as if I'd been in the habit of passing out my emotional energy, but I'd done it more than a few times when needed: to help a neighbor recover after she'd been assaulted, to ease the suffering of a friend in college after a horrific break-up, to calm a baby who was crying on a plane. Oh, Goddess. The baby.

My stomach churned, and I almost gagged. "We have to do something about this. Now. Too many people are at risk."

"Agreed," Bea said. "We have to find your father. It's the only way."

"Mom hasn't exactly been forthcoming in that department."

Something banged against the front door, making it rattle. We all turned to stare at it.

"Kat!" I cried, sick all the way to my bones. Something was wrong.

Gwen, who was the closest to the door, flung it open.

"What the fuck?" Pyper cried, her face turning a dark shade of crimson.

I gaped. Standing in the threshold were Ian and Kat wrapped in an embrace, making out like two teenagers at prom.

Chapter 23

"Ian!" Bea stood a few feet from them on her porch.

He ignored her, burying his hands in Kat's red curls. His eyes were glazed as if he wasn't even seeing her. The vision tugged at the recesses of my mind. I hadn't registered it at the time, but I'd seen that exact same detached expression earlier that day.

"Holy shit," I said, clutching Kane's arm. Blood rushed to my head. "That's not Ian." The man I knew was easygoing, playful, engaged. Intense, even. But never detached.

"What are you talking about? Of course it is." Kane scowled, his muscles flexing as he shot past me to go out the door.

"No!" Without thinking, I followed him and grabbed his arm before he pummeled Ian for the second time in twenty-four hours. "I mean, something's seriously wrong. Ian is being controlled somehow." He had to be. Why else would he be trying to make out with every female within a ten-mile radius?

Kat, oblivious to the crowd, gasped out in that all-too-familiar high, tinkling voice, "Ian, take me home."

"Oh, my God!" I ran forward, pushing my hands between the pair to break them apart. Kat had spoken in Camille's voice. I'd know it anywhere.

Kat stumbled back and then grinned at me, her face contorted with a shameless glee. "It's you again." Camille used Kat's body to slink toward me. "I knew if I could find a way into this one, you'd come running." She reached out Kat's slender arm and ran her red-tipped fingernail down my cheek.

I backed up, only to realize I was moving further away from the door, from the inside of the house where Meri was upstairs. Shit! I'd done it again.

"Meri!" I cried, frantic and pissed off at my own hasty stupidity.

I glanced at Bea hovering in the doorway. She'd said Kat was safe here. She'd been wrong. Either Camille was much more powerful than we'd given her credit for, or Bea's wards weren't as strong as she thought. The difference had to be Camille. Bea's wards had never failed before.

"That's right, witchy girl. Sex magic," Camille said with a sly smile. "Today's events left me hopped up with no release. If tall, dark, and jealous over there hadn't interrupted, I'd already be out of your life. Instead, I'm forced to hang around and wait."

Out of my life? What did that mean? Was she just after an orgasm? Bile rose in my throat.

"Tell you what. I'll let you choose which one this time." She waved at Ian. "Eager Beaver over here," she said and then turned to Kane, "or Mr. Sexy Pants." Kat's eyes filled with lust as she gazed at Kane. "Umm, I sure do hope you choose that one. I'm really up for the challenge."

I glanced at Kane. His eyes were a stormy mix of rage and helplessness. His natural inclination to fight for me was totally useless. There was nothing he could do. Camille used Kat to head in my direction.

My magic sparked just as Camille seized my body. Her icy signature slithered through me. My magic sprang to life and heat shot through my veins to hold her off. Cold against heat slammed together, raging a war as she tried to possess me, and I used all my strength to keep her at bay. Her frustration washed over me, prickling my skin the way it used to when I'd been in possession of my empath gift. It felt irritatingly familiar and served only to make me angrier. I did not want to know what this ghost was feeling, especially not the residual lust that was streaming off her in waves.

My magic pulsed just beneath my heart, the pressure straining to release from the center of my chest. I grabbed on to it, holding it in my mind, and then sent it rushing into her like a full-out mystical punch.

Camille only laughed and absorbed the magic as her essence slipped into my body and strummed with the power I'd just given her.

How could I be so *stupid?* I should've known as soon as I felt her emotions that she'd already taken hold of me. How else would I feel them?

Bea chanted softly in Latin, power sparking in electric currents from her hands. Camille turned to stare at her, curiosity and wonder pressing on my mind. And something else that felt suspiciously like respect.

Without warning, Bea's magic hit us like a jolt of lightning. My body spasmed, and someone screamed, but it wasn't Camille. Kat, maybe. Bea's electrode-like magic sizzled through my limbs, heading straight for my chest, slamming into my magical source. I sucked in a gasp as the pain reverberated through me. Holy beeswax! What had Bea done? Once again, I was stuck in panic mode without any way to react. Goddammit, I was getting tired of this. Had Bea just tried to render my magic useless?

Camille didn't attempt to fight whatever Bea had done. Instead, she welcomed Bea's magic, using my—no, *her* own magic to probe and test the sparks as they crept closer to my center. Then I felt Camille grin. Bea's magic stalled, and Camille's took over, wielding it into something dark, erotic, and twisted. She spun and tossed the magic, hitting Ian square in the chest.

His one good eye went round with shock then narrowed as he scanned my body from head to toe. "I liked the skirt you wore earlier." His tone was low and gravelly, as if he wanted to ravish me right there.

Kane growled, ready to tear his head off, and tried to jump in front of me, but Bea held him back.

"No, Kane," she said. "Camille's magic is too strong. Touch her, and she'll claim you too if she wants."

I screamed inside my mind at the moment of sudden clarity. Camille was well versed in sex magic. She'd been controlling Ian all along. And Bea had just figured it out.

"Come." Camille beckoned to Ian with my finger and walked off the porch. He fell in step beside us and placed one firm hand on my ass. I longed to punch him in the nuts, even though I knew it wasn't really him.

"Get off her, you fucking tool!" Kane bellowed and jumped over the railing of the porch. In two strides he was on us, throwing his arm around Ian's neck, holding him in a headlock.

Camille cried out in rage, "Let him go, dreamwalker, or my magic will be burning a hole in *your* heart instead of the ghost hunter's."

What? Was she slowly killing Ian? Shitballs. This ghost was eight different kinds of crazy. What had happened to her in life to mess her up so badly? And Ian. Oh, God. Kane was going to kill him, and none of this was his fault. His haunted face swam in my mind. He'd been used just as I had.

Kane ignored Camille as he dragged Ian back toward the house.

Everyone else eyed me warily. What the hell? Were the rest of them going to let Camille walk off with my body? Couldn't someone try to block her way or something?

Out of nowhere, a battle cry came from behind me. Someone jumped on my back, knocking me forward. Pain exploded in my knees as my limbs came to life, my nerve endings overly sensitive and raw. I sprawled, and gravel cut into my arms and face. Camille had vanished from my body.

"Hey, get off," I muttered into the rocks, squeezing my eyes against the pain.

My attacker rolled off and peered down at me. "Is she gone?"

I stared up into Meri's worried face. "Did you have to tackle me?" I moved my jaw around, testing to be sure everything still worked correctly.

"Sorry. I panicked." She smiled. "Worked, though. She had a really tight hold on you. I expected her to vanish when I stepped onto the porch. When she didn't, I wasn't sure what else to do."

I rolled over and pushed myself up onto my knees. Across the driveway, Ian was still struggling to get out of Kane's hold. I sighed. "Bea, is he still spelled?"

She glanced at Ian, held out her hand, and sent a jolt of magic in his direction. The white light hit Ian in the chest. His body went limp in Kane's arms, then he took a deep breath and glanced around, clearly unaware of what had just happened.

"Hey, let go, man," he said to Kane, grimacing in pain.

Kane met my eyes, and I nodded. "Camille's gone. It's all right now."

Pyper stalked toward Ian, placed a possessive hand on his chest, and announced, "Mine."

"Maybe not quite gone," Meri said, eyeing Pyper. "I think she jumped bodies."

Bea's face contorted into a snarl, something I'd never before seen from the normally pleasant southern woman. Wind picked up behind her, seeming to come from the house. Pyper went rigid, but her wild eyes bored into Bea's. Somehow Bea was holding her in place.

"Whoa," Kat said, moving toward me.

"Get inside," Bea commanded us. Everyone moved except Ian. He stood frozen, staring at his aunt and Pyper. "Ian, move," Bea yelled.

Bea's direct demand propelled him into motion, but he kept his eyes glued to Pyper as he climbed the stairs.

Once we were all safely inside the house, we watched from the open doorway as Bea's magic spun around her, white sparks shooting off her like fireworks. "Camille, get your bony ass out of Pyper's body, or I swear to all that's good in this world, I'll send you to hell right now, consequences be damned."

Pyper's lips moved, and Camille's high voice flowed from her, making me want to crawl out of my skin. "You wouldn't dare open a portal here."

"Don't test me."

"I'll take pieces of her soul with me." Camille lit up Pyper's face with a cocky grin. "That will make the rest of her damned. You know that."

Bea's magical sparks turned blood red as she narrowed her eyes at the ghost. "I'm willing to risk it." Her tone was so frighteningly steady, I believed her. Bea was downright scary in this state. Gone was the sweet southern lady, replaced by a magic-wielding warrior, willing to do whatever it took to take down the evil spirit…including risk Pyper's life. Had Camille become that much more dangerous?

Camille's cocky smile wavered, and then she took off running toward the street.

Bea swore under her breath, raised her arms and shouted, "*Risisto!*"

Pyper's body froze in place, one foot in front of the other, her arms stuck in a pumping motion.

Bea glanced at us. "Do not move."

No one said a word as Bea took off down the stairs to retrieve Pyper. The instant Bea touched her, Pyper crumpled, but Bea's arms wrapped around her tiny body, saving her from collapsing in the gravel.

"At least someone is thoughtful," I said to Meri. "Those rocks hurt." I ran a hand over my cheek, inspecting the damage once more.

"Get a grip. I saved your ass. Why the hell were you outside…again?"

I turned away from her accusing eyes. "Kane was moments from killing Ian, and Camille was possessing Kat. I tried to help."

"Way to jump in without thinking, as usual."

I turned and strode into the kitchen where Kane was gathering ice into a compress. I raised an eyebrow. "Who's that for?"

He held it up to my face. "You. You're going to have quite the color there tomorrow."

Perfect. Not only was I mentally battered, I was going to have a black eye, too.

Bea helped a white-faced Pyper back into the house. The moment they stepped through the door, Ian whisked her into his arms and gently placed her on the couch. "Pyper, are you all right?"

She ran a trembling hand over her forehead. "I think so." Her voice was low and shaky.

Mom stood at the base of the stairs, her hand at her throat. Meri joined her and bent her head in confidence.

I ignored them and headed for the kitchen to grab some fresh orange juice. Kane, on the other hand, stepped in front of Ian, forcing him away from Pyper.

Ian stumbled back, appearing frustrated and lost at the same time. I waved him over. He stared at me, his lips pressed together and his jaw tense.

Kane sat on Bea's coffee table, leaning forward, talking to Pyper in a low, calming tone.

"Ian," I demanded in a whisper, "come here."

He glanced back at Kane and Pyper, shook his head, and retreated to the kitchen.

"What happened?" I forced out, ignoring the ache in my stomach from being near him. Memories overtook my mind, but I shoved them aside. I had to get through this.

He scoffed. "You were there. Camille bounced from Kat, to you, to Pyper, and I was Camille's boy-toy." He spat out *boy-toy* with no small amount of disgust. "Just like this afternoon." His entire face went red with what I'd bet my last dollar was shame, and he took two steps back.

"I realize that." I poured a tall glass of orange juice and struggled to keep my arm steady. Being near him was making me sweat. My hands trembled, and my heart raced.

Stay calm. I sucked in the cool air, trying to disassociate my own panic so I could understand exactly what was actually happening to Ian. "What I mean is, what happened to you? Start with last night at The Herbal Shop."

He ran an unsteady hand through his shaggy blond hair. "I don't even know."

Just breathe. "Can you try to describe what was going on in your mind?"

He let out a frustrated huff. "That's just it. I remember everything, but I wasn't in control of my actions."

Blood rushed to my head. "You mean…you might've been possessed?" Jesus effing Christ. Were there two ghosts?

He shook his head. "No. As far as I know, I've never been possessed before, so I don't think so. More like I was compelled."

"Like you were spelled to kiss me?"

He nodded slowly.

Over his shoulder, I caught Kane's steely gaze. He rose, his fists clenched. I shook my head and gave him a pointed stare. *Not now*, I mouthed.

Ian spun, and Kane glared at him.

"Oh, dammit." I ran in front of Ian and pushed him deeper into the kitchen. Then I strode over to Kane. "Cool it, okay? I'm finding out what happened."

Kane put a possessive hand on my shoulder, the weight of it practically pinning me to my spot. "I don't want you anywhere near him."

I shifted and grunted as I pushed his hand off me. "Understood, and I normally wouldn't either, but I saw a distinct shift in his personality while we were outside. I think it doesn't have anything to do with him and everything to do with Camille. I need to find out what happened."

Kane's nostrils flared.

I had to bite back a chuckle. He was trying so hard to stay calm, but he was losing the battle. I placed a hand on his chest. "It's okay. I'm fine. I promise."

He gazed down at me, eyes going soft. "You're sure? It might be better if Bea talks with him."

I nodded toward Bea, who was across the room, digging through her spell books. "She looks a little busy. Really, I'm fine. I'll yell if I need anything." I grabbed the glass of orange juice and slipped my other hand into his and led him back to Pyper. "Hey, you." I handed her the glass. "You look like you could use a pick-me-up."

A bit of color had returned to her face but not much. The orange juice sloshed in the glass as she brought it to her lips. I gave Kane a worried glance. He frowned and took the glass after she took a few sips.

"Thanks," she said to me and slumped back into the couch. "How do you survive this?"

I grimaced. She did look a lot worse than I usually felt after a possession. I glanced at Kat. She was also a little shaken, but not as bad as Pyper. "I bet it was Bea's magic that caused this. She had to do something to keep Camille from running off with your body."

Pyper groaned.

"Don't worry. I'm sure one of Bea's herbal pills will do the trick."

"Or three." She sent me a weak smile.

My heart lifted. A joking Pyper meant she'd be fine. I left her in Kane's capable hands, my heart warming at the attention he gave her.

I joined Ian in the kitchen, still keeping my distance, taking note of the jealousy etched all over his face as he watched the two of them together. "They really are just friends."

He flinched. "I know that."

"Then why the face?"

Ian shook his head. "He has a piece of her she keeps hidden. That vulnerable place deep inside. At first, I thought she never let anyone in, but when they're together, I see it."

His obvious pain made me almost want to reach out for him, but the day's events slammed into me and I held back, fearful of the anxiety making my head spin. Instead, I cut a piece of Bea's carrot cake and passed it over. Hey, comfort food always worked for me.

"They're like brother and sister. Neither of them really has any other family they can count on."

"Except you," he said, not looking at me. He turned his back to me and clutched the counter. "Jade?"

"Yeah?" I shoved a piece of carrot cake in my mouth.

"I apologize for today." His kept his voice low, yet loud enough that I could hear him and the regret behind the words. "I don't even know what happened. One minute, I was in the bar, the next, I was out of my mind, practically mauling you in that hotel room."

The carrot cake turned to sawdust in my mouth. I tried to swallow, choked, and spit it out in a napkin.

He turned to look at me.

"Sorry. Got caught in my throat."

He nodded and went back to studying the granite pattern on the counter. "I don't expect you to forgive me. But I do think I was under a spell of some sort." He shook his head, slowly and deliberately. "I had to be. I was supposed to be monitoring that room for ghosts, not...I'm sick about what almost... could've... Fuck." He hung his head.

I pressed my back to the opposite counter, trying to disappear without having to move. I appreciated his apology and even though I already knew he must have been enthralled by Camille, my insides hadn't yet got the memo. My pulse was racing, and I had to clutch the counter to keep from running. I cleared my throat. "I know, Ian."

His head popped up, but he didn't turn to look at me. He nodded once and moved across the room to settle quietly in a chair as far away from everyone as possible.

I frowned. He needed help, but I couldn't be the one to help him. We had a much more important matter to deal with. I glanced at the stairs. Mom and Meri were gone. They must've retreated to the guest bedroom again to discuss Goddess knows what. I let out a frustrated grunt and stalked to Bea's side.

"She's going to be just fine after a few healing pills," Bea said, flipping through one of her witch's tomes.

"Good, glad to hear it."

"Here." She handed me a book. "Do me a favor and look for a banishing spell."

I took the book but didn't open it.

Bea bent to rummage through her bookcase, but when I didn't move, she glanced up. "What is it, dear?"

"I want to do a finding spell."

"Who's missing?"

"My father."

Chapter 24

She straightened and eyed me. "Your mother doesn't know where he is?"

I shrugged. "I have no idea. She won't even talk about him, let alone tell me who he is. All I know is, the man I thought was my father isn't. I will not put Pyper and Kat in danger again. The solution is to find my father, whoever he is, and convince him to help fix my soul."

Then we could worry about whatever it was Camille was up to before she possessed someone else.

Bea cast her eyes toward the ceiling. "She isn't going to go along with this."

"No, she won't, not if her recent behavior is any indication, but I can't afford to wait any longer." I glanced at Pyper, still shaken from her possession, and Kat, who was wide-eyed and nervously picking at her fingernail polish. "What are we going to do, stay here forever?"

"Maybe not forever." Bea gave me a small smile. "But it's not a hardship to watch over you girls."

My heart swelled and suddenly I was overcome with sadness. Why couldn't my relationship with my mother be as comfortable as the one I had with Bea? At one time, Mom had been that kind of mother. Or so I'd thought. In reality, she'd lied to me my whole life. I shook my head. There were more important things to focus on.

"Can we do the finding spell in here, or do we have to go outside?"

"Outside," Bea said. "We really need that circle."

I let out a heavy sigh. "Okay, but please don't make me go get Meri. If Mom finds out what we're doing, she'll never let me out of that room."

Bea turned to Kat. "Can you retrieve Meri?" My mentor frowned. "And keep Hope occupied for about fifteen minutes?"

Kat sent me a questioning glance. I gave her a reassuring smile, moved to her side, and whispered the plan in her ear.

"Yeah, okay. The sooner we're no longer Camille-bait, the better."

I kissed her cheek. "Thank you."

She waved me off, and not even a minute later, Meri descended the stairs, glancing around. "Kat said Dan was here."

I hid a soft chuckle behind a cough. Kat had found the perfect excuse.

"Sorry." Bea grimaced. "I wish she hadn't said that. We need you for a spell that Hope isn't going to like, but it's imperative we do it as soon as possible. Would you mind joining us in the circle outside?"

Meri's face fell, a mixture of disappointment and irritation. "I really don't want to get involved. They have enough to work out because of me."

I slipped my arm through hers. "This has nothing to do with you, other than that I need you to keep me safe. We're doing this either way." I met her eyes and cast a pleading look. "Please, Meri. I can't have anyone else getting hurt. Mom's been keeping secrets for years. I don't know what to believe anymore."

"You're doing the finding spell, then?"

I nodded. "Do you know who my real father is?"

She took a deep breath. "Actually, I don't."

Kane looked up from his spot next to Pyper. "Really? It sure seems like you know more than you're telling."

Meri bit down on her bottom lip and chewed as if she was deciding how much to say. Then she turned to me. "I knew Marc wasn't your birth father. I also know where he lives and works, but that's all. I've been trying to get Hope to open up. I know how awful this is for you. And since she won't budge, if you need my help, you've got it."

I let out a breath I didn't know I was holding. "Let's do this." I met Meri by the door, and we waited together for Bea.

With her spell book and a candle in hand, she grabbed a ceramic dish and her ceremonial knife from her mantle and handed them to me.

Laughter spilled down the stairwell. I tensed with frustration. What the heck was Kat laughing at? There wasn't anything funny about what was going on.

Bea shook her head, mildly amused. "Kat's been a little punchy all day. That's to be expected after the coma. After a few days of sleep, she'll be good as new. As for now, she's a walking giggle. Let's hurry before she runs out of material."

She was punchy? I hadn't noticed. Crap, had I been that caught up in my own drama? I glanced at Pyper. Probably. Hadn't she said as much the night before? I needed a crash course in observation, stat.

Meri pulled the door open, and together, we stepped out into the rapidly cooling night. I wrapped my arms around myself and shivered.

"It'll be warmer once we activate the circle," Bea said.

My heart thundered with anticipation. Magic. My limbs ached to feel the heady spark coursing through them.

Once on the lawn, Bea raised her arms to the heavens and called, "Coven of the Crescent City, heed my call, fill the circle with your will."

A pentagram lit from the ground, shining through the lush grass. As soon as the three of us formed a small circle in the center of the pentagram, the light winked out.

I snapped my attention to Bea. "What happened?"

She shook her head. "Nothing, dear. Since it's just the three of us, we'll need a boost. Evoking the circle at the same time as the candle will spread our reach."

"Meri." Bea passed her the white pillar candle. "You hold this. When I give the command, you and Jade light it at the same time. Got it?"

The one time I'd done a finding spell, my range had only been two hundred miles with the coven helping me. Bea was going about this much differently. Why? I couldn't resist asking, "How far will our range be?"

She glanced at the knife. "With your blood, that won't be an issue. The DNA will act as the unifier."

"Oh. Great." My stomach flipped over about three times. As soon as Bea cast the spell, I was going to know who my real father was. My heart pounded rapidly, and a cold sweat broke out on my forehead. I wasn't ready for this. Would he know me? A tiny bit of fear crawled its way into my being. Why didn't Mom want me to know him?

"Take a deep breath, Jade," Meri said. "You can deal with all that emotion later. Right now, this is about protecting your friends and yourself."

Deep breath in, deep breath out. I repeated the motion a few times and my heartbeat slowed to a manageable rhythm. She was right. I'd do just about anything to protect my friends.

"Your loyalty is remarkable."

I gaped at Meri. "Look who's talking. You ended up in Hell after sacrificing yourself for Philip. Loyalty doesn't run deeper than that."

She shrugged. "I'm not the same person I was then."

"No? You're here, aren't you? If that doesn't say loyal, I don't know what does. You haven't left my side for over forty-eight hours, and we both know it hasn't been a picnic." God, had it only been that long? It seemed like a week since I'd slept.

She smirked, then her lips settled into a small, pleased smile. "No, but it turns out you're not quite as annoying as I once

thought. I think we might even be able to be friends…once
we get your soul in working order."

I laughed. "Yeah, I think a friendship could be arranged."

"Ladies," Bea scolded us. "It's time to concentrate."

I buttoned my lips but couldn't help my own private smile.
We'd just had a breakthrough in our relationship. Who would've
thought I'd end up friends with an ex-demon, soul-stealing
angel?

Bea lifted her arms skyward. "From Heaven to Hell and all
in between, our circle seeks him who can't be seen." She nodded
at me, staring at the knife.

I crinkled my nose, brought the sharp blade swiftly across
the pad of my thumb, and winced. Blood instantly pooled and
ran down into the white ceramic dish. At Bea's signal, I tipped
the bowl and let the blood seep into the spelled earth. When
the last drop disappeared into the grass, Meri set the candle
in the center of the circle, and the three of us joined hands.

Meri met my eyes, and together, we cried, "*Ignite!*"

Bea's voice joined us, and as the candle and circle flared
to life, sweet magic exploded in my chest, spreading to every
nerve ending.

I vibrated with it. "Holy shit," I breathed.

It wasn't like anything I'd ever felt before. Bea and I had
worked a few spells together, but it had never been this intense.
The sensation was all-encompassing, intoxicating even. I could
swim in the heady power for days, content never to come up
for air.

Bea's amber eyes flashed with light then she closed them
and lifted her head. "Goddesses of this world and the beyond,
we ask of you to accept our blood offering. Live it, breathe it,
and taste it. We seek knowledge of the creator. We ask only
of knowledge, not power. By the power of three to one, may
your will be done."

The candle burned to a bright blue-white, and the circle
mimicked the color, illuminating our faces in the brilliant glow.
The flame pulsed with the power strumming through me. It

filled me up, pressing against my inner walls. I could barely hang on to it as it strained to leave my body, to connect with the witch and angel standing next to me. The power was alive and hungry.

I was hungry. My body ached for the release. I squeezed my eyes shut and clenched my teeth and fists, desperate to keep riding the tide. It was too potent, just *too* much.

"Now, Jade," Bea commanded.

My eyes flew open, and right there in the middle of the circle stood the outline of an angel, one I vaguely recognized from my hearing just a few short weeks ago. If the magic sparking through me hadn't been so strong, I'd have leaped back.

"Release your magic, Jade!" Bea commanded again.

I didn't hesitate. My magic joined with Meri's and Bea's. Bea tugged, siphoning it out of my body, leaving me empty as she twined the tendrils with hers and Meri's. When she let go, the entire pentagram lit with the brilliance of thousands of stars.

"Whoa." I blinked.

Meri stared at the angel, now in full form. His shoulder-length blond hair framed his angular face, and he wore cream linen pants paired with a button-down dress shirt. He looked very old-school New Orleans. "Councilman Davidson?" She frowned and glanced at Bea.

Bea tilted her head and cast her eyes heavenward again.

The angel glanced around Bea's yard and set his lips into a disapproving frown. "Beatrice, may I ask what you think you're doing, summoning an angel from the high council into your garden?"

I stared at him in total confusion, my mouth hanging open. Why had she summoned *him*? Anger made my body practically vibrate. Soul stealer. He was one of the angels who'd voted to give my soul to Meri.

Bea glanced at me then back at the councilman. "My apologies, Drake. We were doing a routine finding spell, using DNA. We didn't know who would show up here. You are bound within the circle for our protection…and yours."

How had this happened? I wasn't related to this guy. Was I? We'd used the DNA spell. I shook my head. Maybe we'd done it wrong, or the DNA had been contaminated. Unless…

My chest constricted, and my lungs stopped working. I wasn't even sure I tried to breathe. The spell couldn't have gone wrong. We'd used my blood, for Goddess's sake. My head spun. This man was the reason Philip had said my aura was like an angel's. He was my *father*. And the reason I'd nearly lost my soul.

A faint recognition dawned in his expression as he noted Meri and me. Then he turned confused eyes on Bea. "Forgive me, but whose DNA did you use? I'm under the impression my siblings and their offspring are living on the other side of the country. Washington State, I believe."

Bea nodded. "They are. I talked to Pamela just last week. They are all well."

I glanced back and forth between them, still in shock. She knew him. So did my mother. *This* was why she hadn't wanted to tell me.

His brow crinkled in confusion. "Then I don't understand."

Bea turned to me, and her eyes seemed to move past me over my shoulder. Her jaw set with determination as she nodded toward the house. "I believe the witch on my porch might add some perspective."

Drake turned slowly. His eyes went wide with shock for just a moment. Then they sparkled, and his tone shifted to one soft and full of wonder. "Hope?"

"Drake?" Bea said.

He tore his gaze from Mom and focused on Bea. "Yes, Beatrice?"

She held her hand out to me. "I'd like to introduce you to your daughter, Jade."

Chapter 25

"No!" Mom flew off the porch and ran toward us.

"What?" Drake eyed me in total confusion. "You're mistaken. This is the witch with the shared soul, is it not? And that's the angel." He pointed at Meri.

"Yes," I spat, my confusion spilling out as anger. He couldn't be my father. He just couldn't. Not him. "And you and the damn council were willing to sacrifice my life for the greater good as if I have no value as a person. Who does that?"

Drake ignored my outburst and raised his eyebrows in Bea's direction.

Coldhearted bastard.

Bea let out an exaggerated sigh and nodded.

Mom came to a stop just on the other side of the illuminated pentagram. It was clear by the frustration on her face that she'd been locked out. "No! You've got this all wrong."

Bea turned to her. "Are you saying Drake isn't her father?"

Mom placed her hands on her hips and scowled. "That's exactly what I'm saying."

My gaze drifted between Mom and Drake. He couldn't keep his eyes off her, and she was shooting daggers at him.

"You don't belong here," she said through clenched teeth.

"I never did," he said quietly.

Mom paced behind me. "Send him back."

"I can't do that." Bea cocked her head to the side. "Besides, Jade needs him."

"No. Not him."

Bea threw her hands up. "What do you suggest she does then, Hope? Are you going to give her your soul? Because she isn't going to survive the week if she doesn't get some help."

"If I have to." She glared at all of us, her dark hair loose and framing her face. "He'll never do the right thing. Look at what he did when she went before the council. He tried to kill her!" Mom's voice cracked, and tears streamed down her face.

Drake turned his attention to me, and something in his expression shifted. Some small piece of recognition lit in his light green eyes. He frowned then turned his attention to Mom. "Hope, is this true? Is this young lady really my daughter?"

She fell to her knees, wiping the tears from her stained cheeks. "Please just go," she choked out. "I don't want you to be her father. Everything about you puts her in danger." Her eyes were swollen and red with anguish as she met mine. "I didn't want it to be true. I couldn't tell you because he'll hurt you. Because he already has. I'm sorry."

I felt the blood drain from my face as my body started to tremble. He was my father—the man who'd signed my death sentence. No. *No.* This wasn't happening. It had to be a mistake. My entire life was a lie. My throat ached with unshed tears. I'd found my father…my angel father.

Hopelessness settled over me, making me almost numb. He'd never give me part of his soul. High angels, for all their soul-saving bullshit, didn't give a damn about individuals. They'd never risk one of their own for a damaged witch.

I turned and took a step toward the house. I didn't want any part of his inevitable rejection. He could keep his damned soul. I'd find another way.

Bea's deceptively strong hand wrapped around my arm, stopping me. "Do not break the circle," she warned.

Her tone and the fury blazing in her eyes stopped me in my tracks. I studied her, noted the way she glared back and forth between Mom and the angel, and decided her fury wasn't aimed toward me. Instead, it was directed at two clueless parents.

Drake tried to move forward, but the circle held him in place. "Beatrice, I demand you release me."

"Not yet." She shook her head. "Not until you hear Jade out."

Oh, crap. She was going to make me explain how I needed part of his soul. My insides recoiled at taking anything from him, of baring any part of myself to someone who cared so little for human life. But my friends' faces materialized in my mind, and I knew I'd do it, no matter how much I wanted to run away screaming. Where was Kane?

As if he'd heard my thought, his steady voice materialized from behind me. "Jade?"

I glanced back at him. "Hi." *Hi?* Jeez. So eloquent.

"What's going on?" Kane stared at Mom and frowned, appearing at a loss as to what to do.

I choked out a strangled laugh. "Summoning my father. The one who ordered my soul be given to Meri."

"What?" His whole body went stiff, and rage blazed in his dark eyes.

Drake was studying me now. "How old are you?"

"How old do you think?" I snapped. "Twenty-seven."

His already pale face drained of all color, the moon making him appear almost translucent. "Hope?" he asked, desperation clear in his voice, "is Jade my daughter?"

"Biologically, but you'll never be her father. Not in the way it counts," Mom said weakly. "You were gone. You left us."

"Us," he breathed. His eyes darted to me, and this time he took me in, as if memorizing every detail of my face.

I stared back at him, uncomfortable and a little bit awed. He was tall, illuminated by more than the moonlight and shining with an ethereal glow. This was no low-level angel like Meri, Philip, and Lailah. He was the real deal, a full-fledged angel who didn't live in our world. Funny, I hadn't noticed the glow while we were in the angel realm. Maybe it was only obvious when he stood among humans.

His eyes turned cold and hard as he pinned Mom with his gaze. "You kept her from me."

A sharp pain lanced through my heart, and I swear it was bursting into a million pieces. That was two fathers Mom hadn't given me a chance to know. I felt as broken as she looked, crumpled on the lawn. If she hadn't kept this secret, would the angel council have voted differently, knowing who I was? Would Drake have? I clutched my chest and concentrated on breathing.

Mom stood on shaky legs. Her hands flexed and then curled into tight balls. "You left me. Didn't want me. You said it plainly enough. 'Hope, thank you for our time together, but you knew all along this was temporary. I have my place, and you have yours.' Then you left. Not an 'I love you' or a kiss goodbye. You just walked out the door and never looked back." She sniffed back the tears and hastily dried her eyes. "I was temporary. *We* were temporary. I wouldn't let you be temporary in Jade's life. Not then, not ever. You never even checked on me. Not once. I gave you four years of my life, and you just left."

"You know why," Drake said, steel in his voice.

"Yeah, I know *all* about why you left," she said, sarcasm dripping from her lips. You weren't going to be there for her anyway. And worse, you would've hurt her the way you hurt me. That's why I never told you. She didn't know either until five minutes ago. And I swear to the Goddess, if you try to take her back to the realm, I'll come at you with everything I have, even if I have to enlist Hell for help."

Whoa. Four years? Mom had dated my father for four years, and I'd never heard one word about him.

He jerked back, shocked by her outburst, then narrowed his eyes. "What do you mean, you know all about why I left? I was called to the order. You know that."

"You *bastard*." Her bravado left her in one fell swoop. "You're lying. I know you found your mate. And I know you left me because of her." She turned on her heel and stalked back to the house.

Drake pressed forward but once again was stopped by the wall of the circle. "Let me out," he demanded, staring after Mom.

"We have some negotiating to do first," Bea said mildly.

He glared at her. "This isn't the time."

"Now is the perfect time," I said, sympathy for Mom thawing some of my anger. Damn angels and their stupid mates. After all these years, Mom was still crushed. No matter what choices she'd made, it was clear she hadn't made them lightly. "Because of you and your council, I'm living with half a soul, which apparently means I'm susceptible to ghost possession. And so are a few of my friends who I've shared some energy with over the years."

His pale eyebrows rose. "Possession?"

"Yes," Bea said. "Since Jade lost Hope for a number of years to Purgatory, she didn't find out about her witch status until recently. But she was an empath and learned she could help people by transferring calming energy. What she didn't know was that she was also giving up some of her essence each time. A ghost has created a bond with Jade, and because her soul is weakened, she can't break it. Now the ghost is taking turns possessing her friends to get Jade's body." Bea placed her hands on her hips. "There's a solution, of course."

Drake frowned. "You're not suggesting...?"

"That's exactly what I'm suggesting." Bea's tone went from patient friend to authoritative coven leader in the blink of an eye. "And judging by the state of things, I'd say you owe this young lady a lot more than a portion of your soul."

Drake shook his head slowly. "This is against council policy. I cannot do what you ask." He cast a pained look my way. "Not even for my only daughter."

"You could ask for a hearing," Meri said, speaking for the first time. "You could bring Jade before them and present her case. There is a precedent of exceptions to the bylaws in certain cases regarding souls."

A terrifying shiver crawled up my spine. Yeah, ones where they gave perfectly good souls to other beings. Another hearing? Had she lost her mind? That was entirely different from having them approve a petition. A trial would be putting my life in their hands. "No!" I shouted. "I'm not going back there."

Every instinct demanded I run far away from all of them and this crazy mess. If I went back in front of the council, they could take away the rest of my soul. I met Kane's eyes and all but passed out from the pain and fear I saw staring back at me. He wouldn't let me go anyway. I could feel it.

But Drake was nodding. "Of course, I could do that."

Bea met my pleading stare. "It's the only way, dear."

I shook my head violently. No way was I going anywhere.

Drake pulled out something that looked suspiciously like a Blackberry, tapped a few keys, frowned, tapped a few more, and then nodded. "It's set. One week from today, the council will hear the motion and vote on what to do."

"What? No! I said no."

Drake turned to me. "My daughter, I do apologize. I would've loved to watch you grow and to prepare you for this separate world we live in. I'll do my best to see you through this, but you must understand. I can't let you walk around with a broken soul, one that could be possessed. This is for the best. Otherwise, it's likely your guardian angel will get orders to bring you in himself. Be ready in seven days. I'll send for you."

"Only if I'm allowed to go with her," Kane said from behind me.

"Who are you?" Drake asked almost dismissively. Then his eyes narrowed. "Dreamwalker?"

"Yeah." Kane tensed, and the muscle in his jaw pulsed.

What did his dreamwalking have to do with anything? And why was Kane suddenly defensive about it? I'd never seen him react that way.

"I'm her fiancé, and I'll be damned if I sit by and watch her disappear for another two months."

"Kane," Meri said quietly, "it's not that kind of hearing."

He snorted. "I don't give a fuck what kind of hearing it is. Jade isn't going without me."

Drake studied Kane with interest. Then he pressed another button on his angel-version Blackberry. Nodding, he said, "Your request has been granted."

My breath caught in my throat. His acceptance of Kane's demands had come too easily. Drake was entirely too interested in Kane. What did the angels want with dreamwalkers? I bit the inside of my cheek to keep from screaming.

"Bea," Drake said, "can you release me now?"

She nodded, whispered something in Latin, and then stepped back, breaking the circle.

Drake gave her a nod of appreciation. His eyes met mine as he held out a hand. "It's nice to meet you, daughter."

I stared at his outstretched hand, not quite sure what to do. Awkward silence fell all around us, but he didn't relent. Quickly, I grasped his hand and shook it once.

He squeezed lightly, dropped my hand, and with a small smile, vanished into thin air.

Chapter 26

Mom stalked off the porch toward Bea and glowered at her with murderous eyes. "If you ever interfere in my daughter's affairs again, you'll regret the day you inserted yourself into her life."

"Mom!" I cried, grabbing her arm and jerking her away from my mentor. "Apologize."

She clamped her mouth shut and glared at all of us defiantly.

"Bea, I'm so sorry," I said quietly and turned back to Mom. "Stop. Bea isn't to blame. I asked for her help."

"It wasn't her place, Jade."

Really? This from the mother who lied to me and both men in her life? She had some nerve.

Bea cleared her throat. "I think I'll go inside and give you some privacy."

Mom scoffed. "As if any of that matters now." She spun on her heel and headed back into the house.

Bea frowned, watching her go.

I waved an impatient hand and shook my head. "Forget it. You helped me do what she refused to do. Thank you."

Bea's frown deepened. "She had a very good reason." Her amber-brown eyes locked on mine. "Do you not understand what just happened?"

Biting down on my lip, I nodded. "Yes." I knew exactly what had happened. "My father is an angel, and in one week's time, my life will yet again be in the council's hands." My voice cracked, and I swallowed the lump clogging my throat. Fear rose up, threatening to strangle me. I pushed it down, refusing to be beaten. "I understand the consequences, but it isn't something that can be helped. You know I won't stand by while my friends are in danger. Just like Mom wouldn't. You'd think she'd understand my deep-seated need to do what's right by them."

Bea nodded as her gaze landed on Meri. "Yes, you'd think so. But letting your daughter put herself in danger is much harder than putting yourself on the line." She cut her eyes to the house and then back to Kane. "I suspect you know a little something about protecting your loved ones."

A shiver ran up my spine. Yes, I did.

Kane held his hand out to me. "Come here."

I gladly wrapped my arms around him and buried my head into his chest. "Take me home?"

He gave me a squeeze then released me. "Let's go."

Not even bothering to walk back into the house, Kane deposited me and Meri in his car and got into the driver's side. "Do you need to tell anyone we're leaving?"

I shook my head and pulled out my phone. One group text later, I nodded, indicating we could go.

No one spoke on the fifteen-minute ride back to Kane's house, not when he parked and not when we shuffled through the door. Meri headed straight for the guest room, only pausing to say goodnight just before she disappeared behind the closed door.

Kane ran a reassuring hand down my back, a caress he'd given me a thousand times before. Standing alone with him in his house, I stiffened and took a small step forward. All of a sudden, his touch was too personal, too intimate after the day's events.

He moved with me, wrapping that same arm protectively around my shoulders.

My thoughts jumbled, and somehow, I was transported back to that hotel room. The memory of the cool tile echoed on my skin, and all I saw were black and white squares. My shoulders hunched as I longed to curl once again into a ball and slip away into the safety of my numbed mind.

"What's wrong?" He tucked me tighter to his chest, his warm breath caressing my ear.

"Let go!" I jumped from his grip and took a deep, steadying breath.

He held his hands up in a surrender motion. "Whoa. What's wrong?"

"I…" Another deep breath. I ran a hand over my forehead. "Nothing. Sorry. I just need a minute."

What the hell was wrong with me? My skin was crawling. Ian's face, dazed and out of control, replaced Kane's. Something broke inside me, and I ran. He called after me, but I didn't stop until I was safely locked in the master bathroom.

My knees buckled as the memory of Ian's touch slithered over my body, greedy, heated, and utterly repulsive. I slid to the hard tile floor, shaking.

A soft knock sounded behind me, and I jumped away from the door, wrapping my arms around my middle as I continued to struggle to breathe.

"Jade," Kane said through the door, "what happened?"

I didn't answer, only backed up toward the tub. The words were frozen in my throat.

"Love, I'm worried. Please open the door."

My heart started to crack. I couldn't. I just couldn't talk to him right then. My body was betraying me. My head screamed for me to open the door, to wrap myself in his safe arms, but the cold sweat covering my skin held me prisoner.

"Jade…please," Kane pleaded. The doorknob rattled. "Unlock the door."

The worry in his voice spurred me into action. This was Kane. Not Ian. He wasn't controlled by a ghost. And I wouldn't let what happened control me. Besides, if I didn't answer soon, no doubt he'd find a way to pop the flimsy lock. I reached down and turned the knobs in the tub until the water sprayed full blast.

"Shower," I called over the rushing noise.

"Just tell me you're all right." Frustration overshadowed the concern in his tone.

I moved to the door, cursing myself for pushing away the one person I knew without a doubt I could trust. But could I trust myself? My reaction to his touch had been too visceral. I needed time. I wasn't ready to face him.

Not until the trembling stopped.

I pressed my shoulder to the door. "I'm okay." I sucked in another breath, trying to control the quaver in my voice. "I'm getting in the shower. I'll be out soon."

He was silent so long, I wondered if he'd left. Finally he answered, "All right." His footsteps echoed off the wood floors as he retreated from the room.

In a trance, trying very hard to not think about the last time I was naked, I stripped my clothes off and stepped into the steaming shower. The scalding water seared my skin, turning my flesh bright red. A dam broke, and imaginary hands twisted in my hair. His pale blue eyes smoldering with passion. His heated skin pressing against mine. And my hands running over his lean muscles. My lips eagerly seeking his. Touching him intimately…in places I should only ever touch Kane.

A sob broke from my throat and I grabbed a wash cloth, frantically scrubbing away the fear and shame clinging to what was left of my soul.

When the water turned tepid, I forced myself to step out of the shower and wrapped my raw body in an oversized bath sheet.

Shit.

I hadn't brought any clothes into the bathroom. I glanced at the pile on the floor and winced. No. Even the clothes Pyper had brought me earlier were tainted now.

At least my heart wasn't racing anymore. The scalding water had managed to chase away my panic attack. Still, I didn't know what to say to Kane. How could I tell my fiancé his touch caused me to run? That when I felt his fingers on my skin, I was reliving a horrible nightmare?

I sighed and slowly opened the bathroom door, peeking into the room. The muscles in my shoulders eased as soon as I realized Kane had left. And on the bed, my favorite and most modest jersey pajamas and a pair of fuzzy socks were folded neatly, waiting for me.

My eyes misted. *Kane.*

I snatched the clothes, hurried back into the bathroom, and took my time dressing. Then I engaged in a marathon teeth-brushing session. When there was nothing else to clean or groom, I tiptoed back into the bedroom and crawled into bed, praying I'd go to sleep before Kane returned.

The door creaked, and he appeared, closing the door with a soft click.

I eyed him through lowered lashes, my pulse quickening. Would he want to talk? To touch me? I wasn't sure I could handle it.

"Hey," he said softly.

The sound of his voice seemed to melt a tiny piece of my anxiety. "Hey."

He leaned against the door, keeping his hands tucked into his pockets. His expression downcast, he appeared hesitant. Unsure. "Do you want to talk about it?"

Keeping eye contact, I shook my head.

He nodded. "I understand."

Something loosened in my chest and my breathing became easier. If he didn't try to force anything, I could get through this. "Thank you," I whispered.

Kane blew out a breath and ran a hand through his hair. "Every instinct is screaming for me to crawl into that bed and hold you in my arms for the next week."

I closed my eyes, wishing…praying I could let him do just that. I wanted him to. More than anything. To feel him beside me, to lose myself in his familiar scent. And sleep soundly, safe in his loving arms.

What if I freaked out?

No. I can't take it. Not tonight.

I couldn't turn him away, either. I was frozen in fear of the unknown and my own irrational reactions. This was *Kane*. My best friend. The love of my life.

"I want that, too," I finally said, my voice trembling with emotion.

Kane didn't hesitate. In three steps, he was next to the bed, but instead of undressing, he crawled right in and pressed up against my back, wrapping those strong arms around my middle.

I tensed.

"It's okay, love. It's just me. I'm only going to hold you." He pressed his cheek to mine. You're safe now. I won't let anything happen to you. I promise."

We lay there like that for what seemed like hours, him reassuring me and me concentrating on breathing. Eventually, my body started to relax, and my world faded as I drifted off into oblivion.

I awoke to the sun streaming into my eyes and a very warm Kane still plastered to my back. My neck and shoulder ached from sleeping in the same position for eight hours. I slid my hand over Kane's resting on my stomach and reveled in the joy of having him near, wrapped around me, keeping me safe.

He shifted, and cool air seeped between us, chilling me. I shivered and gently slid out from under his arm. He reached for me, pulled me back. "Too early," he mumbled and tightened his arm around me.

I sucked in a breath, fighting the rush of anxiety trying to set in. Dammit! He'd held me all night without incident. Was I going to forever flinch every time he grabbed me?

He awoke with a start, tearing his hand from me. "Jesus. Sorry, Jade. I didn't mean to scare you."

"What?"

"You were trembling again."

I took a moment to collect myself, consciously letting go of the anxiety and forcing myself to relax. I had nothing to be afraid of. This was Kane in my bed, not an enemy. He would never, ever hurt me. I turned and smiled as I pushed a lock of his dark hair out of his eyes. "No, I wasn't. I was shivering. It's damn cold in here."

He blinked the sleep from his eyes and scanned my pajama-clad body. "You're cold?"

"Yes." I forced a laughed. "My heater rolled away and stole half the covers."

He pulled the blankets up to my chin and tucked them around me. "Can't have that."

I snuggled in next to him, grateful I was able to overcome my freak-out.

"We'll work it out, you know."

"I know." I raised my chin and stared into his determined gaze.

His expression softened and he moved in, his lips gently brushing over mine. "I'm never going to let anything come between us. You know that too, right?"

I returned his kiss and murmured against his lips, "I'm counting on it."

An hour later, Kane's small house filled with voices. I'd just emerged from the shower and finished getting dressed when Lailah barged into my room.

"You ready?"

I frowned. "For what?"

"Wedding planning. Come on. They're waiting." She grabbed my hand and pulled me to the door.

I clutched the doorframe and planted my feet. "Whoa. What? We can't go out."

"Sure we can. I called Ms. Bella, and she squeezed us in. She's waiting at her shop. I also made appointments with the caterers and a wedding planner to get everything else done. Bea, Pyper, Meri, and Kat are waiting. Your mom and Gwen, too."

"Wait. A wedding planner?" What was she talking about? Kane and I hadn't discussed that.

She flashed me a silver credit card. "Kane gave this to me. He said with everything going on, he didn't want you to have any more stress than necessary. Now come on. The mimosas are waiting."

I let her tug me out of the room, but instead of following her to the living room, I took a detour to the kitchen, finding Kane leaning against the counter with a mug of coffee.

He smiled at me and grabbed a paper coffee cup from the counter that had The Grind logo scrolled across it. "Pyper brought you chai."

"That was kind of her." I moved to stand next to him. "I hear you orchestrated some planning today."

His hand grazed my wrist and when I didn't pull away, his fingers twined with mine. "I know you said you didn't need a wedding planner. And you know I don't care if we get married by a justice of the peace or by Elvis. I'd marry you anywhere, at any time. Right here right now, if I could. But you want something a little more traditional."

"Is that a problem?" My formative years hadn't been rich with friends and family. It was now, and I really wanted the fancy dress and big day to share with them. Though, when it came down to it, I'd marry Kane anywhere, anytime as well. I just wanted my fairy tale day. I hadn't had many of them.

"Not at all, love. Lailah has my card. Use it with Mamaw's blessing. She'd have loved to have been here for this."

"I wish I could've met her."

Kane leaned down and brushed a light kiss over my lips. "Go with your friends. Let them plan this with you."

"I don't want to leave you," I said staring at his chest. Fear started to seep its way into my heart. In six days, I had to go before the angel council. As much as I tried not to think of what the consequences of that visit might be, the fact remained that the last time I asked them for help, they tried to give my soul to Meri. What if they did it again?

He pressed his cheek to the top of my head. "And I don't ever want to let you go, either. But for today, let's pretend our life isn't a supernatural roller coaster and plan for the future. Isn't that what you've always tried to live by? To look in the direction you want to go?"

"Yeah."

"Then let's look to our wedding day and our future."

I hugged him, letting his scent fill my senses, and then pulled back and smiled up at him. "I love you."

A slow grin spread over his face. "I never get tired of hearing that."

Chapter 27

"How's this going to work?" I asked Bea. "I know with Meri around I should be okay, but what about Pyper and Kat? Is Camille going to come after them again?"

"I don't think so." Bea picked up her Ralph Lauren handbag and rummaged around until she pulled out two tiny dolls.

I raised my eyebrows. "Voodoo?"

She smiled. "Not exactly. I've been talking to some colleagues and a contact in Salem recommended these. They're similar, but only because they represent a person. I've infused a protection ward on them. All Kat and Pyper have to do is keep them on their person. It should be enough to keep Camille out."

"How can we be sure they'll work?" I tried very hard to keep the skepticism from my voice. The solution couldn't be that simple, could it?

"She's very experienced in this sort of thing." Bea patted my arm. "Don't worry. I trust her. She says the ward is temporary. They should be good for the next three or four days, at least."

I sucked in a breath. "Okay, as long as you're sure they'll be safe."

Bea waved a hand, her perfectly manicured pink nails pointing toward the living room. "They're fine now, right?"

I eyed them both. Kat was busy texting someone, and Pyper was grilling Kane on wedding flower preferences. I almost laughed at his deer-in-the-headlights look. "Yeah, I guess so."

"Okay then. Grab Meri, and let's get this celebration back on track."

Ms. Bella's shop was in downtown Cypress Settlement, the small town that was home to Summer House. As we neared her gingerbread Victorian shop, I started to fidget. Even if we managed to get my soul fixed, would we still be able to hold the wedding at the house? Would Camille be a major nuisance? Would Kat and Pyper be safe?

"What's bothering you?" Kat asked, sending another text while eyeing my ruined fingernail polish. I'd picked most of it off during the trip from Kane's to Cypress Settlement.

Pyper steered Kane's Lexus down a side street and glanced back at me. "You okay?"

"Yeah. I'm just worried about holding the wedding at the house. It's Camille's home. Even if we do solve the soul issue, there's no guarantee she won't ruin the wedding with her antics like she did at the Christmas party."

"Don't worry," Kat said as her phone buzzed. She frowned and typed in another message. "Bea already said we could banish her once your soul is solid again. Right now, she's too attached to you."

Bea, Lailah, and I had banished a ghost to another dimension once, with the help of our friends. If we could do it once, we could do it again. I nodded. "Who do you keep texting?"

Her face flushed as she bit her lip.

"Lucien?" I guessed.

"Uh…yeah." She gave me a tentative smile.

"Is he okay?" I'd been really hard on him the other night, and I, more than anyone, should know how awful he felt. While I'd never almost killed anyone, I'd certainly had my share of fuck-ups.

Kat put her phone in her purse and turned to me. "No. Not really, but Bea and Lailah are researching a solution to his curse."

"That's good."

She nodded then blew out a breath. "Listen. You need to talk to him and apologize. I'm not mad at him, and you shouldn't be either."

I took her hand and squeezed. "You're right. He didn't deserve the way I treated him." My voice hitched. "I was scared, and I lashed out. I'll talk to him. I promise."

Her shoulders relaxed, and she gave me a small smile. "That's the girl I know and love."

Pyper pulled into a parking space in front of La Bella's. "Enough of that. It's time to see Jade in that gorgeous dress of hers."

I grinned as we filed out of the car, meeting Bea, Gwen, and my mom on the sidewalk. Finally, we were going to tackle the wedding planning. A day with the girls and all things bridal was just what I needed.

Everyone was in high spirits, chatting and laughing as Ms. Bella greeted us at the door. Except Mom. She hung back, quiet and withdrawn. I didn't even know what to say to her. She'd lied to me. If I'd known about my angel father when she'd been taken, maybe I could've found help for her sooner. And not felt so abandoned half my life. Keeping me in the dark was not okay. But now wasn't the time, so I gave her a tight smile and let my friends usher me into the shop.

Ms. Bella directed Kat, Lailah, and Pyper to their dressing rooms. She also had dresses lined up for both Mom and Gwen to try on. Then Ms. Bella's assistant hurried over and grabbed my hand. "We're ready for you, too," she said with a bright smile.

I waved at Bea and let Judy pull me to the oversized dressing room, where my pale silver gown waited for me. Five minutes later, Judy led me out of the room and onto a raised platform in front of the three-way mirrors. I stared at the misty-eyed woman gazing back at me in her intricate silver dress, the bodice adorned with delicate crystal beads. Elegant and strong, the girl who'd lived through the last few days had transformed into someone entirely different. I didn't even notice the pale bruising on the left side of my face. All I saw was a radiant bride who would knock Kane to his knees. He was going to love it.

"You look beautiful, shortcake," my mom said quietly from behind me.

I twisted to find her beaming at me with tears in her eyes. "Thank you." I turned back around and swallowed. I didn't know what else to say to her.

When I looked again, she was gone. I squeezed my eyes shut, trying to block out the waves of emotion crashing through me. I didn't want to be mad at her. But we needed to talk before we settled anything. I scanned the room and found her standing next to Gwen as my aunt pulled out dress after dress, holding them up to Mom. Armed with four of them, Mom headed off into a dressing room.

Gwen met my eyes, and the understanding there almost broke me. Aunt Gwen was so much more my mother figure than Mom was that it was heartbreaking. Would Mom and I ever reach a place where we didn't feel like strangers?

Ms. Bella arrived with a pincushion strapped to her wrist. "Oh, lovely!" She clasped her hands together, inspecting the dress, pulling and pinching as she pinned.

Slowly, my wedding party started to gather around me, Lailah and Kat wearing deep plum dresses and Pyper in her feminine tux. My heart swelled. This was really going to happen.

Ms. Bella stepped back, inspected her handiwork, and nodded. "Yes. I believe that's it." She turned to my friends and gestured toward my dress. "Ladies? What do we think?"

Pyper let out a catcall, while Meri and Lailah grinned.

Kat's eyes misted. "Oh, my. It's just…" She wiped away a tear.

"You look pretty good yourself," I said, blinking back tears of my own.

"You need a veil," Pyper declared and moved to a rack to pull some samples. We spent the next ten minutes debating veil length and style, until I was sure I'd gone through every one in the store. I frowned, totally confused.

"I like the piped one with the lace," Bea said.

I glanced at it and tried not to grimace. Lace wasn't really my thing.

"No, the one with all the tulle," Kat said.

I liked that one, but it really didn't go with my dress.

"She needs a beaded one," Lailah said.

I nodded. "I think she's right." I glanced at the two that would go nicely with my dress, but one was entirely too voluminous and the other seemed four miles too long. I sighed. "Ms. Bella, do you have any that are a little more understated?"

"Judy, can you check in the new shipment?" Ms. Bella asked, adjusting a strap on Kat's dress.

Her assistant scurried away, and everyone went back to chattering.

"Jade?" Mom asked, holding something behind her back.

"Yeah?"

"How about this?" She produced a low-profile tiara, adorned with the same beads that decorated my dress. "I know it's not a veil, but I thought…well, I wore one similar when I married your fa—I mean, Marc." She climbed up on the raised platform and settled it on my head, adjusting my hair into a stylish bun.

Before I turned to the mirror, everyone stopped talking. I stared at them. Kat clasped her hands together. "That's it, Hope. It's perfect."

"I agree. It's gorgeous, but not too over the top," Lailah said.

"You don't think I look like Cinderella?" I asked.

"Hell no," Pyper said. "In that sexy dress? No way." She grinned.

I turned to the mirror, taking in my elegant gown, the fitted mermaid skirt and the understated tiara. I loved it. No veil needed. "It's perfect."

"Yes! Another task checked off the list." Kat made a big show of scribbling in her notebook and then tucked it away to answer another text.

I rolled my eyes but couldn't get the stupid grin off my face. My anger melted when I saw the pride shining in Mom's eyes. She was my mother. I knew she'd been ruled by her fears and that's why she'd kept secrets. We'd work our problems out later. Right then, I wanted to share this joy with her. I opened my arms, and she stepped into them. She hugged me tight, and I prayed one day we'd find our way back to that easy mother–daughter relationship we'd once had.

After that, the day flew by while we met with the wedding planner and went over every last detail, from the invitations, decorations, and flowers to the band, the entrees, and the photographer. Our final stop was the bakery to decide on the cake. I was exhausted but ridiculously happy with our progress.

I still had the desserts in Kane's refrigerator at home. It was a true testament to how horrible the last couple of days had been that I hadn't even tried one of them. I shuddered at the thought. Dessert never lasted long in our house.

Despite my running out on her a few days earlier, the bakery owner greeted us with warm smiles and understanding. Her dark hair was pinned up, and she wore a crawfish-covered apron over her jeans and work shirt. Across the top of the apron, someone had embroidered *Stella, Head Cookie in Charge.*

"I'm so sorry I missed you the other day. Uh…something came up," I said, shaking the woman's hand and smiling at the flour smudged across her forehead. I liked her instantly.

"Don't worry about it, hon." She flashed a brilliant smile. "After twenty-five years in the wedding business, we've seen it all." She led us to the back of the shop and through an intricately carved door into a tasting room. Three cloth-covered tables sat in the middle of the room with velvet-covered pink seventeenth-century chairs. A matching settee lined the wall. But the real show was the dessert trays set up at each place setting. There were no less than seven of the most beautiful confections I'd ever seen.

My mouth watered just looking at them.

"Oh, wow," Kat said with her eyes wide. "Any of them cheesecake-flavored?"

Stella laughed. "Three of them. We heard the bride is a fan."

"Stella, you just became my new best friend." I winked.

An hour later, my mouth happier than I'd ever imagined, I chose the mocha cheesecake-filled butter cream cake and sat back to watch my friends devour as many of the samplers as they could possibly stand.

"Excuse me," Kat said. "Restroom time." She hurried out of the room, almost waddling from the decadent desserts.

Laughter rang around me, all my friends in good spirits from the productive day and the lack of drama. It almost seemed unreal that we'd survived a whole day without any hiccups.

I pulled my phone out to call Kane but got his voicemail. Instead of leaving a message, I hung up and sent him a quick text. Placing my phone on the table, I dug into my cake of choice one last time, letting the creamy goodness melt in my mouth. Good Goddess. If I hadn't been surrounded by my friends and family, I might've orgasmed right then and there, it was that good.

My phone buzzed. I grabbed it, smiling, until I read the text. It was from Ian.

Text me after you talk to her.

I frowned. Talk to who? About what? I scrolled up, finding a string of texts from throughout the day, but they weren't from me.

Another phone buzzed on the table. My gaze landed on it, and that was when I realized I was holding Kat's phone, not mine. It took all my willpower to put Kat's phone back on the table and not read the exchange. I stared at it, watching it buzz with another incoming message.

I shouldn't read her private texts. No matter how much I wanted to. Who was she supposed to talk to? Me? Pyper?

I grabbed my phone and smiled at Kane's enthusiasm for the cake I'd chosen.

Bring some home, so I can feed it to you and watch your magical lips do unspeakable things to the fork.

I couldn't hold back the laugh. On our first date, he'd found my sexual weakness while feeding me cheesecake.

Kat reappeared. Her phone buzzed again. She snatched it and frowned.

I stared at her expectantly. She stuffed her phone in her pocket and pretended not to notice.

The chatter of my wedding party rose, and laughter rang through the room at something Ms. Bella said.

Even though I knew I should, after everything that had happened I couldn't let it go. I leaned in close to Kat. "You've been texting with Ian all day."

She cut her eyes to me. "So?"

"You said Lucien."

"No, you said it was Lucien. I didn't disagree with you."

I raised skeptical eyebrows. "You confirmed it was him. Why did you lie about it?"

She sat back down but pushed her chair a few feet away, as if that was going to stop my questioning.

"Kat? What's going on?" I asked quietly, trying to keep our conversation somewhat private.

She closed her eyes and sighed. "I don't want to bring this up here. You're having a good day. I don't want to ruin it."

The familiar panic flooded my chest, and I stood up, almost knocking over my chair.

Bea, Pyper, and Meri, all looked up at me, concern lining their eyes.

"Everything all right, dear?" Bea asked.

I nodded and glanced at Meri. "Can you join me and Kat outside for a minute?" This couldn't wait. If something was wrong, I needed to know.

Meri nodded and came around the table to join us. I grabbed Kat's arm, smiled at the others, and said, "We'll be back in a minute. Just need some fresh air after all the gluttony."

They laughed and continued to chatter in high spirits.

"Jade." Kat sighed as I pulled her out onto the street.

"Kat," I mimicked. "What is going on?"

She met my eyes, with compassion shining in hers. "I know you're having a hard time with all this, but you need to talk to Pyper about Ian. What happened isn't his fault."

Meri stood beside me, leaning against the brick wall. "Why does she need to talk to Pyper? Shouldn't Ian be the one doing the explaining?"

I nodded, wondering the same thing.

"Pyper won't talk to him. She thinks he still has feelings for Jade. But he doesn't. Plus she's convinced he has something with that reporter chick, Sybil. That piece of work has been all over him, thinking she can hitch her star to his with the ghost hunting. He isn't into her at all. In fact, he's disgusted by the way she's behaved around him. But that's for them to discuss. What's important is that he's beside himself with what happened." Kat shoved her hands in her pockets and met my eyes. "Honestly, he's not doing well. Way worse than you are."

"Hey!" I stiffened. "You don't know what I'm dealing with."

"You're right. I don't. But I do see you out with all of us, managing to at least put part of this behind you. I'm sure it's hard. God, I can't even imagine how hard it is. But you have all of us and Kane." She shook her head. "Ian has no one except me right now. He can't talk to Bea about this, and Pyper, who's become his best friend, won't take his phone calls."

What must it be like for him? Feeling like he'd assaulted one of his friends against his will and losing the one person he trusted most because of it? Understanding and compassion consumed me. He was the victim and villain rolled into one.

I nodded to Kat. "I'll talk to Pyper."

Chapter 28

The rest of the week flew by with Meri and me spending hours every day dealing with questions from the wedding planner. I'd tried twice to talk to Pyper about Ian, but she'd shut me down both times.

The day before the council hearing, we stopped at The Grind as the last of the day's customers were leaving. I'd taken the week off, mostly because it was awkward having Meri hang around the cafe all day while I worked. The fact was, Kane had made it clear I didn't need to work anymore, so it wasn't as if my pocketbook was taking a huge hit. Once I'd moved in with him, he'd stopped accepting my rent check for the apartment, even though most of my stuff was still there.

It wasn't as though I planned to be the little wife. I still had a teaching commitment at the glass studio. As soon as life got back to normal, I'd get back to working in the cafe and making the intricate glass beads for my online store.

Pyper glanced at the clock. "Just in time. What can I get you two?"

I smiled. "I'll get it." I whipped behind the counter and made two iced chai teas. After placing the money in the register, I slipped the change in her tip jar and then leaned against the counter to wait.

A few minutes later, she flipped the lock on the door and announced, "Closing time."

"Good." I pulled out a chair. "Sit."

She quirked a skeptical eyebrow at me.

"Please? It's important."

She pursed her lips and pulled her freshly dyed hair into a bun. This time around, she'd layered streaks of ash blond through her black locks. "If this is about Ian—"

I cut her off. "It is, but it's also about me. Please, Pyper? Just hear me out, and I won't bother you about it again."

She eyed the swinging door to the backroom as if she was considering bolting, but I placed a soft hand on her arm.

"Please?" I said again.

"Fine," she huffed and reached over the counter to pull out a small bottle of chocolate liquor she always kept there. After dousing her coffee with a generous shot, she sat and crossed her arms over her chest. "I'm listening."

I blew out a breath, not sure where to start. I glanced at Meri. She shrugged.

Okay, maybe it was best to jump right in. "Can you explain to me how you felt when Camille took over your body?"

Pyper's eyes went wide. I'd caught her mid-gulp, and she started to choke. "Excuse me?"

"When you lured Meri away from my apartment that day, do you remember what it was like to have Camille controlling you?"

She put her coffee cup down. "Yes. Of course I do."

My fingers drummed on the tabletop. Staring at them, I stopped the motion, forcing myself to calm down. "Can you explain it?"

"Why?"

I leaned in. "I'm trying to understand something."

Her nostrils flared, and I recognized her attempt to control her temper. Pyper wasn't known for over-sharing. "Fine. I was myself, then it was like I had a brain reset, and I couldn't control what I was doing."

"Were you conscious of your actions?"

"Yes," she said through clenched teeth.

"And did you try to stop it?"

"Yes."

I softened my voice, hoping I was coming off as understanding. "But you couldn't, right?"

She leaned back, her shoulders slumped. "No, I couldn't." Closing her eyes, she took a deep breath. "I'm sorry. It was my fault what happened to you."

I slammed my hand down on the table in sudden anger. "No, it wasn't. And that's the point, isn't it?"

Shock flickered over her face and she sat up. "What do you mean?"

"Camille was controlling you. You had no way of stopping her. I don't blame you. I never have."

"Yeah, but—"

"No, Pyper. No buts. This is a ghost possession we're talking about. And the same thing happened with Ian."

"He wasn't possessed!" she cried and stood up. Suddenly, her body went rigid, and her eyes rolled back in her head.

"Pyper?" I jumped to my feet and took her arm at the same time Meri did. "What's happening?" I asked the angel.

Meri shook her head. "I'm not sure."

Pyper relaxed, and her eyes focused on me. A slow, satisfied smile spread over her face. "Hello again, Jade."

The high, tinkling voice made my ears ring. I shook Pyper's arm. "Get the hell out of her body, Camille! You aren't welcome here." I pivoted toward Meri. "How is this possible?"

"She's too vulnerable. Camille might be going after her again because you're here, trying to use her to get to you." Meri let go of Pyper's arm and ran behind the counter, frantically searching the shelves.

Because of me? I dropped Pyper's arm and backed up, my entire body cold with fear. This was happening because of me. It had to be. Pyper had been fine all week. "What are you looking for?"

"Her charm!"

Of course. "Check in the back. She has a shelf she keeps stuff on."

I backed up, blocking the front door to ensure Camille couldn't get away. "What do you want?"

Pyper's eyes narrowed. "Isn't it obvious? I want my daughter back."

I scowled. "Then why have you been trying to use my body to have sex with anyone who'll move?"

Camille's humorless laughter rang through the cafe. "You're the worst witch I've ever met. Don't you research anything anymore?"

What the heck was she talking about? I leaped forward and shook Pyper's arm. "Just tell me why, dammit! We could've helped you if you'd just tell us what you need."

Pyper's face fell from righteous indignation to desperation. "You'd never help me. No one helps witches who use sex magic."

"What?" I cried. Who cared if she was skilled in sex magic?

"I needed the spell to bring back my daughter." Tears formed in Pyper's eyes. "She's being held captive by another spirit. If I could free her, I'd leave everyone alone. I just want to free her soul."

Her daughter's soul was what she'd wanted all along. She hadn't wanted to bring her daughter back to life, just free her. Why hadn't we tried to figure that out? The last time we'd had a ghost, I'd researched as much as I could. With Ian's help—

Ian.

He was the ghost hunter and the one person I hadn't been able to even think about, the one who would've put me on the path to uncover the mystery. If Camille hadn't chosen him, we might have figured this out sooner.

The back door swung open, and Meri burst through. Within moments, she had the charm pressed into Pyper's hand. Pyper's eyes rolled into the back of her head again. She slumped into my arms as Camille left her body.

"Pyper?" I stared down into her pain-filled face.

"Yeah," she whispered, and tears filled her eyes. "It really wasn't Ian's fault, was it?"

I let out a huge sigh of relief. "No. He was spelled."

She steadied herself and walked over to the bar, gripping the counter to hold herself up. "Did he know what was going on and couldn't stop it? Just like I did?"

I nodded.

"Oh, God." She placed a horrified hand over her mouth. "He must feel terrible."

I nodded again. "I think he could use a friend besides Kat." I stared pointedly at her.

"Have you spoken to him?"

"No." I swallowed and moved to stand next to her, staring at the floor. "It's too hard. I don't blame him. I really don't. But I can't seem to let it go either. I'm sure in time…"

Pyper squeezed my hand. "I understand." Then she pulled me into a hug. "I'm so sorry. I know this is hard. I didn't mean to make it harder."

I let out a relieved huff of laughter. "You don't need to be sorry, but we have to find a way to move past this." I gulped in a welcome breath of air. She'd scared the crap out of me. "Tomorrow's the hearing. After that, everything will be better." I hoped.

"Yes, it will," Meri agreed. But I saw the unease in her eyes. Whatever happened, one way or another, we'd keep Pyper and Kat safe.

"Why did Camille show up now, when we haven't seen her all week?" I asked Meri.

She frowned. "My guess is the spells on the voodoo dolls are fading. With the high emotion running between the two of you, Camille gathered the strength to invade Pyper. But not you, because I'm here."

"Crap," I muttered. Tomorrow couldn't come soon enough.

I awoke the next morning wrapped in Kane's arms, wishing for more time. I'd been waiting impatiently all week, but now that the day was here, all I wanted to do was stay in bed, content with the illusion of safety.

He shifted beside me and then ran a careful hand over my cheek. "Morning."

"Morning," I said, and he wrapped his arms around me tighter. I could feel his arousal on my back, just as I had all week, but I didn't turn to him as I normally would. We hadn't been intimate since the hotel incident, and to Kane's credit, he hadn't made a move even once. He'd been sweet and gentle, waiting until I was ready.

But each time I even thought about it, I chickened out. What if I had flashbacks? Or if all the helplessness came back? I never wanted to feel like that with Kane. Instead, I snuggled into him, hoping it was enough.

A knock sounded on the door. "Jade? Kane? Lailah called. She'll be here in an hour," Meri said.

"Damn," I murmured.

Kane's warm breath heated my skin, and he pressed a slow kiss to my neck. "Let's get this done, pretty witch, so I can bring you home and marry you."

I smiled. "I like the sound of that."

He rolled away and disappeared into the bathroom.

I suppressed a shudder, trying to ignore the apprehension building in my chest. What if these were the last moments Kane and I had together? What if the council put me back in the room where time stood still? Or worse? My feet hit the floor, and before I lost my nerve, I stripped, and headed into the bathroom. With my body and soul exposed, I pulled open the shower curtain.

"Hey," Kane's face blossomed into a slow smile. "Want to join me?"

I nodded and stepped into the clawfoot tub. The hot water hit my back, cutting off Kane's access. My heart raced with a painful combination of fear and excitement. I lifted my head and pressed a kiss to his open lips. He held perfectly still, letting me move over his lower lip, and when I flicked my tongue into his mouth, a soft moan escaped his throat.

It was a familiar, welcome sound, and my body responded instantly to his desire, heat pooling in my belly.

His arms came around me, and I pressed into him, smiling when I felt his erection on my stomach. Standing in the shower with the water sluicing over us, no other thought entered my mind except for touching this man, the one I loved and trusted above all others.

Kane pulled back just enough to look down into my eyes. "You don't have to do this, you know."

I ran my hands over his soapy chest and nodded. "I know."

"We can wait." His chocolate eyes searched mine. "This won't be our last chance, love. And even if it was, none of that matters. You've given me more than I could've hoped for." He touched his heart. "It's all right here. Your love and mine."

Tears of happiness filled my eyes and I blinked them back. "Me too."

I turned to let the water wash the soap from his body and then tugged him gently from the tub. With both of us wrapped in towels, he stood there as I dried him off, and didn't protest when I nudged him into our room.

The morning light streamed through the windows and shone on his glorious chest. His wide shoulders, slim waist and narrow hips made my mouth go dry. I licked my lips and pressed my palms to his torso, running light hands down the firm planes of his stomach.

He sucked in a ragged breath but said nothing and didn't try to touch me. I understood he was letting me do what I would without interference from him. I could go as far as I wanted and stop at anytime. And right now, I wanted everything. All of him. Pressed against me, inside of me.

I kissed the nape of his neck, flicking my tongue across his warm skin. He tasted like salted caramel, sweet and tangy at the same time. My stomach clenched in anticipation.

His muscles rippled under my touch. I tugged at the towel, letting it drop to the floor, and he closed his eyes. I knew he was struggling for control and I loved it. Still he stood there, waiting for me to reacquaint myself with his body.

My towel fell, joining his on the floor, and I pressed my pebbled nipples to his chest, smiling at his sudden intake of breath. He was almost trembling with need. A surge of heady power rippled through me, fueling my newfound confidence.

Standing on my tiptoes, I pressed my mouth to his and licked at the seam of his lips until he opened to me. Teasing his tongue with mine, I lowered my hand, wrapping it around his velvety length.

He pressed into my palm but stilled himself as his tongue plundered my mouth in a frenzy. Still, his hands stayed at his sides.

I stroked the length of him, my excitement growing with each gasp and groan he muttered into my mouth. Jesus, how was he maintaining his control? He wasn't even touching me and I was ready to explode. I released him and placed his hands on my hips as I backed him up against the bed.

His knees hit the side, and I pressed my palms to his shoulders, nudging him down.

"You're sure?" he whispered between kisses.

"I'm sure. Now lie down."

He nipped my lower lip and smiled. "Gladly."

Stretched out on the bed, Kane watched me, desire and love radiating from him. My entire body quivered as I gazed at him. He was so beautiful, inside and out.

I climbed onto the bed, lying next to him, my leg draped over his. "Wrap your arms around me," I whispered as I trailed kisses down his neck.

He did as I said, lightly caressing my goose-pimpled flesh. "You're cold."

I chuckled. "Not even close." Then I climbed on top of him and slowly lowered myself until his thick length filled me.

His strangled groan matched mine as I started to move.

Chapter 29

Kane and I emerged forty-five minutes later, freshly showered and sharing secret smiles. Okay, maybe not so secret, but Lailah and Meri were too tense to notice.

"What's the procedure?" I asked and sipped at my coffee, my happiness vanishing as reality crashed around me.

The front door burst open, and Mom flew into the house. "Am I late?"

We all stared at her.

She slammed the door shut, spotted me, and let out a relieved sigh. "I guess not."

"Hope," Meri said gently, "you're not allowed at the hearing."

Mom's face scrunched up in confusion. "What do you mean? She needs part of my soul."

Lailah shook her head. "If they decide to take that course of action, you'll be summoned. Until then, it's best if you wait here."

Mom gaped then turned to look at me. When I shrugged, she stormed off into the kitchen.

"Shit," I said and picked up my phone. Just as I dialed Gwen's number, she strode through the front door, wearing all white, as if she were an angel herself. Her gauzy blouse billowed over white jeans. I raised a suspicious eyebrow, put my phone away, and went to hug her. "Thanks for coming. Mom's going to need you."

She nodded knowingly and glanced away. "Yeah."

"Gwen? What's up?"

She shook her head. "I don't know yet…exactly."

I narrowed my eyes. She was being purposely vague as she always was after she had a vision.

She touched my arm, and then disappeared into the kitchen with Mom. What happened to her regular uniform of blue jeans and a T-shirt? I tried not to read anything into her reaction or her outfit, but I failed. Surely she would've been more upset if she'd seen anything terrible. But she sure appeared as if she planned to address the angel council.

Before I could follow her and pry even the tiniest bit of info from her, Philip arrived. He was already dressed in his white angel robe, his emerald eyes bright against his fair skin. Jesus on a cracker, I hadn't known he was coming. I hid a scowl and clutched Kane's hand.

"Ready?" Philip asked.

Lailah gave him an odd look, taking in his attire. She'd dressed in her regular uniform of a long skirt and form-fitting T-shirt. Who was he trying to impress? The council or Lailah?

She nodded. "Yes, you can answer the call."

Philip uttered an incantation, and a bright light materialized all around us. I recognized it as the portal to the angel realm. A moment later, I woke up on gold and white tile. The stark sanctuary sent a tremor through me. It was exactly like the Saint Louis Cathedral, only all the murals were washed out in shades of white and gold.

My muscles spasmed, and I clutched my chest, trying to block out the memories flooding back, the way my soul had almost been stolen from me right before it was torn in half.

No. I wasn't going to live through that memory again. Not today. Not ever. Scrambling to my feet, my heart racing, I clutched the person nearest me. The tall, pale-haired man studied me through hooded eyes.

I let go of Drake and jumped back. "Where's Kane?"

"Hello, daughter," my father said, his voice smooth and authoritative.

"And Lailah?" Ignoring him, I glanced around and found none of my friends, only a panel of council angels. They all stared at me with open curiosity. It was as if a spotlight had shone on me, and I longed to creep back into the shadows. I wasn't supposed to be standing here alone with an angel who'd sentenced me to death once. My flight instinct kicked in, but I forced myself to stand still and face them.

"Both Lailah and the dreamwalker are here. The council wants to speak with you first before they call for testimony." He wrapped his large hand around my arm possessively and moved me forward to a podium directly in front of the council.

Scowling, I shrugged him off. "Let go."

His eyes clouded with irritation. He lowered his head and whispered, "Be careful, daughter. I might be your only ally here."

The way he said "daughter" repeatedly was really starting to get on my nerves. "I can take care of myself."

One eyebrow rose as he frowned at me. "I'm certain your mother did not raise you to be so disrespectful."

He did not *just say that.* He had left her, after all. I had some sympathy for the fact that Mom had kept him in the dark about me, but I was twenty-seven years old. Scolding me was unacceptable. Just because we shared DNA didn't mean we had a relationship. "How she raised me is none of your damn business," I whispered.

A collective gasp rose from the angel audience. Holy crap! *They heard that?*

"Watch your tone, daughter," my father said. "Disrespecting the collective will not help your cause."

I bit the side of my cheek to keep from verbally lashing at him again. I did need his help, if only for part of his soul. "I'd like to see Lailah."

"You will."

A gavel hit the high council table, and an older, silver-haired angel I recognized as Madeline took Drake's place as the hearing facilitator. "Ms. Calhoun. It is…unexpected to see you here again before the council. You seem to be making a habit of taking up our time."

I suppressed a snort of disgust. *Their precious time?* How dare I want to live my life without being possessed?

When I didn't answer, she turned to Drake. "I understand you have a personal involvement with Ms. Calhoun?"

He nodded, his long pale hair slipping forward so I couldn't see his expression. "I have recently learned Jade is my daughter. She is petitioning for a sliver of my soul to help heal her torn one."

A pin drop could've been heard after my father's announcement. No one even breathed, especially not me. The clarity of my situation settled over me, and at once, I knew I was wasting my time. They would never compromise an angel's soul…even if he were willing.

Madeline cleared her throat and addressed my father. "You know our policy as well as the rest of the council, Drake."

He nodded. "I do."

"And you still brought her here, knowing the answer?" The disapproval rang loud and clear.

Yeah, this was never going to work. Why had he bothered?

Drake appeared unconcerned with her subtle censure. Slowly, he scanned the council's faces, making eye contact with each one. Then he cleared his throat. "I am aware of the council's policy, having been one of the committee members who drafted the original language of the directive."

Madeline's face pinched in disgust. "And yet you feel because Ms. Calhoun is your daughter, we should ignore our laws?"

Drake's eyes narrowed, and his voice held a warning, "Madam, you forget yourself."

The effect was immediate. Madeline bristled and glanced away, a bright blush rising on her pale cheeks. "My apologies, Councilman Davidson. I meant no disrespect."

A rumbling murmured through the rest of the council.

I turned to Drake. "What's going on?" I whispered. Their reaction indicated he was high up in the chain of command. Judging by the sidelong glances they were sending his way, I was pretty sure that wasn't a good thing. Was there some kind of power play going on here?

He ignored me as if I hadn't even spoken. "I'm not petitioning to have Jade take part of my soul."

I sucked in a sharp breath. What. The. Hell? How was I going to recover? I turned blazing eyes on him, ready to verbally tear him to shreds, when the side door opened, and my mother, followed by Gwen, Lailah, Philip, and Kane, filed in.

My mouth fell open. Kane nodded to me as he took a seat to the left of the dais. I'd never been more grateful to see another person in my life. His presence called up a strength from deep in my core. It always did. "Lailah said Mom wasn't allowed to come," I said to Drake. "And what about Gwen?"

He stared straight ahead, glowering at Madeline, who was shooting daggers at him with her eyes. "The council made an exception upon my request."

Okay, maybe having a high-ranking father was a help with the council, as long as no one lost a soul or ended up in the room where time stood still.

Philip left the group and came to stand beside me. I took a step away and turned pleading eyes on Lailah. She gave me a reassuring smile and nodded in Philip's direction. Was she seriously suggesting I trust that guy?

"Ladies and gentlemen of the council, I wish to request permission to speak on Ms. Calhoun's behalf," Philip said.

I took another step back, thoroughly confused. What had changed Philip's mind about me? He'd never been particularly helpful when it came to what was in *my* best interests. Only my soul's.

"You may speak," Madeline said.

Philip walked to the center of the room, nodding an acknowledgment to each of the council members. "Thank you. As you may recall, less than a month ago, I stood here advocating for the angel Meri to receive Ms. Calhoun's soul."

A murmur of agreement ran through the court.

"At the time, we were under the impression that neither could live with a partial soul, so we chose who should be the recipient. What we did not know was that Ms. Calhoun is a direct descendant of an angel. She had the capacity to manipulate her soul—enough so that she even managed to retain part of it during the soul transfer to Meri."

"Her connection to Drake does shine a light on her abilities," Madeline said. "However, I'm sure the council will agree when I say the deliberate sharing of souls is not acceptable. Especially angel souls. Ms. Calhoun will have to find a way to battle her possession on her own."

Mom stood from her chair, her eyes wild with anger. "What happened to my daughter is your fault, all of it: the fact that her father is an angel, that he left, and that she lost part of her soul. Your damn rules ruin lives. How dare you sit there in judgment of what is right and wrong? She deserves a chance at a life. A good, solid one. The one I sacrificed for *the greater good.*" She said the words 'the greater good' in disgust. "Who are you to judge who is worthy and who isn't? Her soul should never have been taken from her in the first place."

What did she mean, it was their fault my father was an angel?

"Ms. Calhoun—" Madeline scolded.

"Stop!" Mom shouted. "I know you won't do anything about that decision now. But you can and will do something to fix it. Give my daughter as much of my soul as she needs in order to heal." She turned to Drake, her words clearly meant for him and not the council. "You owe me that much."

He met her tortured eyes. "They won't let me sacrifice part of my soul. You know that."

"But they'll take mine." Power built around her, magic so white it almost blinded me.

"Hope, no!" Drake shouted and ran forward. Her power lashed out, striking him, leaving an angry red welt across his handsome face. He jerked back, clearly stunned.

"Seize her," Madeline demanded.

Guards materialized from the wings and surrounded Mom. Their collective power quickly squashed the impressive magic swirling around her. Her knees buckled, and she fell to the tiled floor, pain etched on her weary face.

"Stop it!" I ran forward, trying to get to her, but the guards tightened formation, and Drake pulled me back. I jerked my arm away from him. "Let me go. She's my mother."

"One who is willing to die to save you," Drake said into my ear. "You know what it's like to be at the council's mercy. Step back now, and we may be able to salvage things before they lock her up."

I froze, my blood running cold in my veins. If they locked her up, years could pass before I saw her again.

"I will do my best, but I need you to cooperate. Can you do that?" His breath tickled my ear as I nodded. "Good. Now stay quiet." He walked to the circle of guards and waved a hand. They parted just enough to let him through. "Stand up, Hope," he commanded.

Mom did as he said, glaring at him.

"What were you trying to do?"

She took a deep breath, her jaw tense. "What you should be doing right now. I was going to give half of my soul to my daughter."

My eyes bugged out. "No! She can't do that."

Drake didn't acknowledge my outburst and nodded in her direction. "I see."

"Wait." I ran forward. "She'll be compromised if she does that. No. I won't let her."

Mom's expression softened as she found me among the guards. "And I won't let you go on living this way. I'd rather sacrifice myself than risk losing you."

"It's very dangerous," Drake interjected. "And not sanctioned."

I shook my head, my heart weighing heavily in my chest. "You know I can't let you do that, Mom."

"Jade—"

"I think we've heard enough." Madeline glanced at the council members and pressed her lips together in a thin line. "Guards?" She beckoned them with the wave of one hand. "Show them to their accommodations. We'll discuss what, if anything, we should do about this later in the week."

My peanut gallery jumped to their feet.

"I'll share my soul," Gwen said, panic filling her voice. "If Hope and I both give a little, not half, we should be fine. No one would be in danger."

"They share DNA," Lailah reasoned. "Giving a small piece has been done before to help heal another. This situation isn't any different."

Kane gazed at me, his eyes intense and filled with worry.

"Quiet!" a voice boomed. From the shadows of the dais, the most beautiful and intimidating angel emerged. She moved her long limbs with assurance and grace as she commanded the attention of everyone in the room. Her onyx eyes settled over the council, piercing them with an air of authority. Everyone, even Madeline, bowed their heads in respect.

"Chessa," Drake said reverently, "it's kind of you to join us. I didn't think you'd be back for another few days."

She smiled at him warmly. "My trip went better than planned."

Mom's face tightened, and her eyes squinted as she stared at the chestnut-haired beauty in front of us.

"Hope," Chessa said coolly to Mom.

Mom bowed her head slightly, though it was clear by her grimace she loathed the action. "Chessandra."

Chessa glanced around at everyone then narrowed her attention on Drake. "You have a daughter."

He inclined his head. "I wasn't aware until last week."

"And you very much want to save her soul." It wasn't a question, but a statement, as though she was seeing right inside his heart.

"Yes, I do."

My breath clogged in my throat. He wanted to save me. They'd both confirmed it. A tiny spark of hope blossomed in my chest—not only for my soul, but for that little abandoned girl I kept locked away. Her small voice spoke to me from the very back of my mind. *My father wants me.*

"And the council isn't prepared to sacrifice a piece of your soul to save her." She drummed her fingers on the podium. "I can't say I disagree. It's far too dangerous for all of us." The angel turned to me. "The last thing I want to do is deny you and Drake help, but you see, the council's souls are bound. It's part of a ritual we angels undertake when we commit to the century-long position of councilmen." She winked, and I almost fell over from surprise at the shift in demeanor. "It's to keep us honest. When you're bound to someone, you know what's in their heart. To give you a piece of Drake's soul would mean giving you a tiny piece of the souls of everyone on the council."

I stared at her wide-eyed, angry, frightened, and awed all at the same time.

"This hearing is over," Chessa commanded and waved a dismissive hand at the dais.

"Wait. What?" I turned to my father. "It can't be over. My friends are in danger." I pivoted, pleading my case to Chessa. "Please, my friends are being targeted by a ghost. This isn't just me we're talking about here."

"I'm aware." She glanced at the council members. "You may go. I'll handle it from here."

"Yes, your highness," a few of them mumbled as they stumbled out.

Your highness? Oh, shit. It was over. The ruler of the angel realm had already said my father giving up a piece of his soul was impossible. Without it, my soul would never fully heal. My shoulders slumped as I prepared myself for the inevitable.

Chessa pointed at Gwen and then Kane. "You two, come with me."

Gwen and Kane glanced at each other then carefully made their way toward us.

Chessa stared at Drake. Even though they didn't speak, I got the distinct impression they were communicating. They held each other's gazes for an intense moment until finally my father gave a short nod and stalked over to Mom, placing a firm hand on her upper arm.

She glanced at him in total irritation and tried to shake him off.

"Drake will wait with you here," Chessa said to Mom. Then she turned to me, Gwen, and Kane. "You three, come with me to my chambers."

Chapter 30

Lailah positioned herself next to Mom and sent me a reassuring smile as I followed Chessa out of the room.

Take care of her, I mouthed.

Lailah nodded, and her expression sobered as she glanced up at Drake.

The knot in my chest tightened. Kane's hand slipped into mine, a reassuring gesture that meant nothing when angels were in charge. Was this it? Were we going to find out my fate? My hand tingled against the weight of his. My fingers curled, digging into his flesh. I'd never let go. I'd fight for me. For Kane. For us and what we had. Soul or not. I wasn't giving up. With renewed determination, I stepped through the double doors of Chessa's chambers.

The warm wood tones and volumes of leather-bound books took me by complete surprise. Were we still in the same angel realm? The one that seemed overrun with tile and marble?

"Have a seat." Chessa nodded to the ornate wing-backed chairs in front of her desk.

Gwen and I sat, but Kane stood behind me, his hands on my shoulders.

Chessa raised one eyebrow at him then shrugged when he didn't respond. Her bottomless onyx eyes met mine. "I have a solution for you, but there's a cost."

Kane's grip tightened on my shoulders.

"What's the cost?" I asked, proud my voice didn't shake. I knew I should be intimidated, but for some reason, the high angel put me at ease. How did she do that?

"Using your parents' souls to help heal yours is out of the question."

"But—"

She held up a hand. "If Drake wasn't a member of the council, we'd consider transferring a portion of his soul. But he is, and his term isn't up for another eighty-two years. We can't use your mother's soul, either. Her soul is too fragile after spending all those years in Purgatory. If we took any from her, she wouldn't just be susceptible to possessions, she might lose herself altogether."

My stomach ached. My perfect solution had just flown out the window. I couldn't care less about the council and their rules. As far as I was concerned, my father was obligated to help me. It was the least he could do after abandoning me. He'd helped create me; he could damn well heal me. He owed me that much. But Mom was another story. I wouldn't take part of her soul if it put her at risk.

"You know, he really didn't know you existed," Chessa said, studying me with concern in her eyes.

I glared at her. "Are you reading my thoughts?"

She smiled. "Not on purpose. But your soul is weak, and you're Drake's daughter. Both of those things make your mind more open to me."

Suspicion settled over me. She had some sort of relationship with my father.

"We're mates," she confirmed.

Holy shitballs.

Chessa chuckled. "Yes, I suppose that's a shock."

Kane and Gwen stayed silent, and I was grateful. My heart hurt for Mom. This was who he'd left her for.

Chessa sobered, as if my thoughts were making her uncomfortable. "Now, the deal."

"What is it?" I asked flatly.

She stood and then sat on the corner of her desk. "We can restore your soul by using small pieces of your mate's." She gestured at Kane then nodded to Gwen. "And a bit of your aunt's."

"And that would actually work?"

"Yes. Your aunt's takes the place of your mom's and will give you enough DNA to heal. Your mate's is special. His will strengthen you due to the bond you already share."

I glanced at them both. Each nodded their agreement, but I wasn't so quick to take them up on the offer. "What's the catch?" I crossed my arms over my chest.

"In exchange for our help with the transfer, you'll be required to work for the council."

I narrowed my eyes. No point in being diplomatic. She'd already said my mind was open to her. She'd know what I was thinking anyway. "I assume there isn't room for negotiation."

Chessa shook her head.

"Because angels are all about that greater good bullshit."

Her lips curled into an amused smile. "You could put it that way."

"And Gwen and Kane? How would they be affected?"

Her smile widened. "You're smart to ask questions. Most don't when they're seeking help from the council."

"I've had experience with your brand of help before."

All pretense of amusement vanished from Chessa's face. "Yes, you have. That's precisely why I think you'd be a good fit for this assignment."

I peered at her, holding her gaze, and waited.

"Your aunt will not be affected after the initial discomfort of the soul transfer. The dreamwalker is different. You're mates, are you not?"

"Yes," Kane said at the same time I said, "No."

I glanced back at him, wincing, and rushed to explain. "Not the way she means." Turning around, I waved an arm around the room. "Humans don't have mates the way angels do."

"I am well aware of that fact, Ms. Calhoun." Chessa pulled out a thick folder and opened it. "A mate can mean many things, but in this case, we're talking about a mystical connection. It says here in your file that Mr. Rouquette can sense your energy when he's around you. Is this correct?"

"Yes," Kane said. "It was stronger when she was an empath, but even now I can sense her and know when she's around."

Chessa nodded and gave me a pointed stare. "And he is able to dreamwalk you?"

"He can dreamwalk almost anyone he knows," I said stubbornly. I wasn't sure where she was going with this, but I didn't want her pulling Kane into any crazy angel business.

"That's true, but he isn't quite able to control his ability around you."

"What does that matter?"

"It means that, on some level, you draw him to you, that you are partially responsible for him entering your dreams. Otherwise, he would've been able to stop himself when you first met."

My mouth hung open as I twisted to look at Kane. He had invaded my dreams right after we first met and insisted it wasn't intentional. He raised his eyebrows as if to say, "I told you so."

Closing my mouth, I turned back to Chessa. "You're saying we have some sort of mate connection. Okay, so what?"

She stood. "It means you feed off each other. It also means you're the perfect partners for the job I have in mind."

"Partners? No way. Not happening." Shaking my head, I clutched the arms of the chair. "I don't want Kane mixed up in any of this."

He moved from behind me, and I stood, not liking the fact that they were both towering over me. "I'm already involved," he said to me, softness radiating from his eyes. Damn, he'd do it no matter what I said. He turned to Chessa. "What's the job?"

"I'd like you both to be shadowwalkers."

Kane and I shared a confused glance. "Which is?"

"A shadowwalker can walk the lines between dimensions," Gwen said. "Chessa wants you to help them save souls that have been lost between worlds."

The angel rose from the desk and retreated to her leather chair. She grinned at Gwen. "Yes, that's exactly what we would like."

Kane gripped my hand and my shoulders tensed. "For how long?"

She brought her fingers together, tenting her hands in front of her. "What would you give to save your soul? Your life?"

Son of a bitch! I knew this was going too easily. She was just as bad as the rest of them. "Yes, but not Kane's."

"Ah." She leaned back, looking thoughtful. "But I bet he'd be willing to give his for yours."

A storm brewed inside me, and the way Kane's fingers were pressing into my flesh, I knew she was right. He would give his life for me, just as I would for him. But I'd never be able to live with myself if he sacrificed himself for me.

I shifted and met Kane's rich chocolate eyes.

"Jade." His voice was soft but full of determination. "I won't stand by and watch you fade into oblivion."

There was no point in denying his devotion. Chessa could read it all over both of us, and considering she was an angel, I knew she wouldn't stop until she got what she wanted from us.

This moment, even more so than our wedding day, meant we'd be committing our lives to each other forever. The angel was asking us to form a mated bond, one that would be unbreakable.

"Are you sure? This is more than a lifetime commitment," I said.

"I've already committed my life to you."

"I know, but this is so much more permanent."

He chuckled. "Do you really believe I ever thought our marriage would be anything except permanent?"

"You know what I mean. Not only will we be tying ourselves together, but to the angel realm. This isn't an 'until death do us part' thing. This is eternal." Biting my lip, I nodded toward Chessa. "This is an ongoing payment for my soul. In essence, we'll belong to them. Forever." My heart pounded with the realization that if we said yes, I'd be getting everything I ever wanted—someone who couldn't ever leave me. We'd be bound in life and death. I'd never be abandoned again.

Then a sickness took over. I didn't want him like that, forced to be with me by a higher power. Shaking off the thought, I focused on the fact that he'd already chosen me.

Kane stared down at me, his expression calm, thoughtful. Then he smiled and faced Chessa. "I want to negotiate terms."

She frowned. "What terms?"

He motioned for me to sit and took the chair beside me. "Everyone in this room knows I'm going to say yes, but I'm not willing to let the realm have complete control over us. If we were to become slaves to you, our lives would hardly be worth living anyway. So my offer to you is this: the pair of us will accept your condition of becoming shadowwalkers, but we want to be compensated as a low-level angel would. We also want all the benefits and rights that they have under your laws. There will be no exceptions because we are humans."

Whoa, this was businessman Kane in action. I had no idea he knew so much about angels, but then, he had dated Lailah a while back. It made sense he knew about their world. I couldn't help but smile. He could be my negotiator any day…or night.

"We will not be at your beck and call, and we will not be expected to run down cases that are suicide missions," Kane added.

Chessa made a note in the file. "Who do you propose decides the danger level of the missions? The shadowwalkers who work for us report directly to me. Always have."

"We will." Kane never broke eye contact with her. "If you disagree, we can bring it up before the council for an inquisition."

"And the witches council," I interjected.

Chessa's eyes narrowed into thin slits. "The witches council has nothing to do with this."

"No, they don't," I agreed. "But I'm certain my coven will end up involved. They would never sit by and let something happen to me if a mission goes wrong. Plus the witches council will act as a balance in case the angel council becomes…how should I put this? Corrupted by their power."

"Absolutely not," Chessa said. "Unacceptable. Witches are not welcome in the business of angels."

"Yet you want to employ me in your search for lost souls."

Gwen cleared her throat. "May I make a suggestion?"

All three of us turned to stare at my aunt.

"Yes, you are allowed to speak," Chessa said.

I bit back a snarky reply. Who did Chessa think she was anyway? Just because she was a high-ranking angel…

"Perhaps you could put together an appeal board made up of witches who are familiar with angels and their ways."

"And who would these witches be?" Chessa asked suspiciously.

"The ones who bore angel children seem the best candidates. They have the most knowledge."

"No." Chessa closed the file in front of her. "That's a deal-breaker."

"Then I refuse to give Jade part of my soul." Gwen sat back and crossed her arms over her chest.

"What?" I asked in a low harsh tone.

She ignored me.

"You've seen something," Chessa said with certainty. Was she reading Gwen's mind too? Most likely.

Gwen shrugged noncommittally.

"You'd really condemn her?"

"It's my belief that if there aren't checks and balances, her life will no longer be her own. That isn't something I can contribute to, so yes. If you refuse to offer her a way to appeal life-threatening situations, then I refuse to give her a piece of my soul, which I'm certain you need."

Chessa sucked in air through her nose, and her face flushed.

She's just as desperate for us to agree as we are to fix my soul. Why? Did it matter why if I came through this alive? The tension eased from my shoulders. She wasn't going to roll over and let us have our way, but she would bend.

Now was the time. "I agree," I said. "If the review council of witches is ignored, I'm going to have to refuse this offer."

Gwen's lips twitched, and I knew she was hiding a smile.

Chessa studied me. I made no effort to hide my contentment with my decision. She blew out a breath. "Fine. I'll set one up."

"With witches who are in no way affiliated with the angel realm except that they have an angel child," Gwen said.

Chessa leaned forward. "Are you implying I'm dishonorable?"

Gwen mirrored her action. "No. Not at all. I'm just looking out for my niece."

The angel hit a button on a speaker and demanded her assistant write up the contracts and clipped out the instructions for a witch's appeal board. There was silence on the other end of the intercom and then finally her assistant cleared her throat. "As you wish, Ms. Ballintine."

Chessa glared at us. "The contracts will be ready in ten minutes."

Chapter 31

An hour later, Mom, Lailah, and Philip were dismissed. The contracts were signed, and then Gwen, Kane, and I were strapped into reclining chairs, waiting for our souls to be altered.

Chessa hovered over me. "You'll be given a few weeks to recover, and then a directive will be sent with your first mission."

"Fine." Honestly, I was too nervous for Gwen and Kane to care much about my new job. I knew exactly what it felt like to get part of your soul ripped away. It made my stomach turn just thinking about it. I glanced at the lab technician. "Can you give them painkillers?"

He shook his head. "They need to be alert. Besides, it won't hurt that much anyway."

I scoffed. *Right.*

"We'll be fine, sweetie. Don't worry," Gwen's voice drifted from my left.

Kane's hand tightened on mine. We were in separate chairs but close enough our hands could touch. "You lived through it once. We'll live too."

"But I was unconscious for days afterward."

"It won't be anything like that, Ms. Calhoun," the kind-eyed technician assured me. "Your soul was ripped in two. This is closer to a medical procedure. Much less messy, much faster healing time. They'll both be conscious, just a little weak for a few days while they recover."

A small sense of relief fluttered in me. As long as they were okay, I could get through this. With Kane by my side, I could do anything, and now he'd be by my side forever. I tried not to be too grateful for that fact. Certainly there'd be consequences to walking the shadow world.

Gwen reached out and grabbed my other hand. "It'll be fine, Jade."

I let out a slow breath. "What happens after the transfer?"

"The three of you will be sent back to New Orleans. I'll be in touch." Chessa spun on her heal and left the room.

"Okay, you three," the technician said. "I'm going to count back from three. On one, you'll start to feel the transfer. Three, two, one."

Gwen sucked in a sharp breath at the same time that Kane's fingers jerked in my hand. I squeezed my eyes shut, praying their pain would be over soon. My own experience had almost killed me.

My hands started to tingle, and a jolt suddenly raced through both limbs, shooting straight for my chest and then sinking lower, filling my torso. The two sparks collided, and my back arched right up off the table in a bone-jarring spasm. Ecstasy burst through me, heightening every last nerve ending with sweet pleasure.

"Jade!" I heard the faint cry, knew it must be Gwen, but I couldn't respond. I was all but suspended over the table as pure magic filtered right into my soul. My eyes watered at the intensity of emotion running through me. Love, fear, overwhelming protectiveness, and determination.

Kane's signature mixed with Gwen's and then faded as the magic collided with my own soul, filling me up, making me vibrate with power. My soul pulsed in my gut, new, raw and powerful. The straps holding me in my chair slipped away and the room turned first white, then black, and then blinding.

I squinted into the sunlight, dampness seeping in through the knees of my jeans. The sweet scent of grass and damp earth invaded my senses.

"Jade?" This time it was Kane's voice.

I turned my head toward the sound, blinking to clear my vision. As my eyes adjusted, I made out a large moss-filled oak tree and realized we were sprawled on an immaculately manicured lawn. The damp lawn and earthy scent indicated it had rained recently. Glancing around, I took in the large Victorian home. "What the hell?"

"We've been sent back to Summer House," Kane said and lifted me to my feet.

A surge of power gripped me, and the world faded into various shades of gray. The shadows started to move, becoming more and more solid the longer we stood there. Near the base of the oak, movement caught my attention. The shadow morphed into a silhouette outline of a man and as I studied him, his round, pudgy face came into focus. He brought his hand up, tipping his bowler cap, and turned, walking directly through the trunk of the tree then disappearing into the earth.

"Let go!" I shouted at Kane and moved away.

Bright sunlight streamed back into my vision, and I let out a long sigh of relief. "Holy shit. I think I just got my first taste of what it means to be a shadowwalker."

Kane's face was white. "Wow."

"You saw it, too?"

He nodded and moved toward me with his hand outstretched. But then he dropped it, his jaw tense with frustration.

My heart sank, and horror ran through me. Would this always happen when we touched? I closed my eyes and took a deep breath. "I'm sure we can learn to control it." I said the words, knew I meant them, but everything was too raw for my heart to believe it.

"Yeah. I'm sure we will." Kane's voice shook.

"You will," Gwen assured us.

I glanced her way, grateful to see she didn't look near as shaken as Kane. "You're okay?"

She nodded. "Tired. But I'll survive."

Tentatively, I put an arm around her. The panic running through me eased when my world didn't shift. "Why did they send us here?"

The three of us headed toward the house. I eyed a silver Prius. "Bea's here."

"She's not the only one." Kane gestured toward a line of three familiar cars parked farther down the driveway.

"It's the coven." I took off in a sprint, heading for the back of the house. If they were working a spell…then it hit me. Coven magic jolted to life just below my heart, spurring me faster. It surged and waned like a faulty circuit. I *needed* to be in that circle, connected to them. Whatever they were doing, they were straining past their ability. If it wasn't for Bea's magic, they would've already failed.

I rounded the back of the house and almost came to an abrupt stop. In the middle of the circle, Camille was suspended, trapped in a smaller circle. Blue candles barely flickered to life below her. It was almost exactly the same setup Lailah had performed the day we'd tried to free Pyper of her black shadow.

When had they decided to do this? While we were in the angel realm?

What about Camille's daughter?

Would helping her find the little girl put her soul to rest? There was no time to find out. The coven wouldn't be performing the ritual on such short notice unless they felt they had no choice. Had Camille gotten worse? Whatever had happened, I had to help them.

The coven's faltering power spiked back into action, and a moment later, I jumped into the circle, determined to do my part in sending Camille away.

Clasping hands with Bea and Rosalee, I savored the magic pouring into me and then through me and back into Bea. She took in a relieved breath but didn't acknowledge my presence in any other way.

The blue candles burned taller and brighter, acting as Camille's prison. The next step was to open a portal and banish her into another dimension. Only, as I gazed at her, my vision turned once again to the gray shadows.

My heart raced, and I glanced around for Kane. He was near the back door, observing, not even close to me. I sucked in a breath and studied the scene around me. Shadows moved, creeping toward the blue circle. A few grew into solid shapes, and one reached out hungrily grabbing at Camille. I suppressed a shudder. What were they? Why did they want her? If we banished her, would she become one of the faceless shadows?

Did I care? The memory of ice crawling up my limbs as Camille seized my body and Ian's dazed, lust-filled face filled my mind. No, I didn't.

"Goddess of the afterlife," Bea cried into the wind, "hear our call! The ghost Camille is not for this world. Heed our sacrifice and take her where you will!"

The ground rumbled beneath our feet. A faint trace of fear ran through the coven collective.

"Stand strong!" Bea called. "The Goddess has responded."

The ground continued to rumble. Two shadows morphed into solid form, their features becoming clearer with each passing moment. One was small, the size of a child, her face fresh and full of life. The other was Camille's age, his expression set in anger. Something menacing streamed from him, curling around me, pressing on my skin.

I glanced around. Could anyone else see them? They were all chanting along with Bea as the ground slowly started to open just beneath Camille. Camille glanced down, her eyes wide, and then she latched onto my gaze. Fear rolled off her in waves. Heartbroken and terrified, tears spilled down her pale face.

Heartbroken? Terrified? Those were not the emotions I'd expect to feel from a ghost intent on bringing pain to anyone. Desperation clung to me, the emotion clear even though it wasn't my own. I tilted my head heavenward, awe filling me. The soul transfer had given me more than a whole soul. My empath gift had returned.

I clamped down on my wonder and focused. Nothing sinister came from Camille, only desperation and fear, but not for herself.

The child moved closer, standing right next to the blue candle circle, and reached a hand up. Camille stifled a cry and pounded on an invisible wall, trying to get to the little girl. They both pressed their hands flat against the barrier, palm to palm, as if they were touching.

Tears filled my eyes as their mutual heartache crashed into me. Their separation mirrored the one Mom and I'd suffered all the years she'd been in Purgatory.

The man reached down and grasped the child by the middle, tearing her away from her mother. Pure hatred and glee sparked off him as he reveled in Camille's pain.

"No!" I cried. "Stop."

The coven went silent.

Bea's hand tightened around mine wariness radiating off her. "We can't stop now, Jade," she said calmly. "Once Camille is gone, we'll all be safer."

"You don't understand," I forced out through the emotional agony tearing through me. She'd told me before all she wanted was to find her daughter. She'd only used me because she'd been desperate to save her from the man who was somehow responsible for her death. Even in the afterlife, he'd managed to keep them apart. No wonder she'd gone crazy. "There's someone much worse feeding her behavior. I can see him, feel him. We have to help her."

"Jade?" Bea's voice faded into the wind as it picked up and the portal started to grow.

"Release her!" My voice came out deep and commanding. Even with all the pain Camille had caused, I couldn't condemn her to an eternity in Hell.

A murmur went through the coven. Everyone fell silent, and then Bea shouted, "Unlock!"

The candles extinguished, and the wall rippled into nothing. Relief crashed through Camille, and she flew with furious determination at the man clutching her daughter. She rammed into him, and the little girl fell to the ground. His lips curled into a snarl as his hands shot up, wrapping around Camille's neck, trying to choke the life out of her.

Good thing she didn't need to breathe. Confusion ran rampant through the coven, and I realized they couldn't see the man, only Camille. "She's fighting the ghost who killed her daughter. He's the one we need to banish."

Bea didn't hesitate. She started to chant. The coven followed, and the ground rumbled to life, the portal growing again.

How had the man and Camille's daughter gotten into the circle in the first place? I had no idea, but now that they were there, they couldn't leave until we broke it. Unfortunately, we had no way of forcing him into the portal. Camille needed to do that herself.

The man shifted her into a headlock and dragged her toward the portal. She bucked, clawing at his grip, her eyes bulging.

The protective streak in my heart longed to rush to her defense, but I was bound by the coven magic to hold the circle. Bea, as the coven leader, was directing the magic, and I couldn't do anything but feed her my strength.

Camille forced out a strangled gasp and bit down hard on his hand.

"Filthy wench!" he growled, yanking his hand back and smacking her in the side of the head. "Do that again, and your daughter goes to Hell with you."

Camille went limp, soul-crushing fear slamming into me. "Not Lizzie," she whimpered, pliant and defeated.

His lips turned up in a sinister grin as he lifted her off the ground, her feet dangling in the fiery hole.

"No!" the little girl screamed and ran toward the pair, tears streaming down her anguished face. "Mommy!"

The sound of her daughter's voice stirred a primal reaction in Camille, one that touched me deep in the depths of my newly healed soul. A mother's love. The kind that moved a mother to sacrifice herself for her daughter. Exactly like Mom had when she'd offered her soul, knowing it could mean the end of her life. My eyes filled with tears, and I wished I could do something, anything to help.

At the edge of the portal, Camille kicked out, catching the man on his knee. As he went down, she launched herself over him, barely scrambling from his grasp. She rushed across the grass and picked up her daughter into a fierce hug.

"Now!" I shouted. "Trap him before he gets away."

"Ignite!" Bea commanded.

The blue candles sprang to life around the man, encircling him in the light. The portal continued to grow beneath him. Camille collapsed to her knees, anguish and relief wiping away the last of her energy. My knees buckled from the sheer intensity of her emotion, but I managed to stay upright. I couldn't disconnect from the magic, not now that we were so close to banishing the kidnapper.

My hair blew over my face, partially obscuring my vision as a wind picked up in the circle. The force whipped around the man I realized must've been Camille's murderer. He stayed suspended above the portal, rage shining in his empty eyes, expletives getting lost in the storm.

"Take our sacrifice. Bind him to the fiery realm. Never let us gaze upon his fetid soul again." Bea dropped my hand and raised her arms heavenward, her final salute to the Goddess.

All the wind rushed into the portal, sucking the evil bastard with it. He vanished, and the hole sealed itself, the perfectly manicured lawn appearing unmarred.

Silence filled the yard as Camille and her daughter clung to each other. Camille raised her head, her pointed gaze landing on mine. Gratitude and regret brushed against my psyche. *Thank you,* she mouthed and then the pair slowly faded away. Not one sign of the magic remained.

"Where'd she go?" Rosalee whispered to me. "Camille, I mean?"

I shrugged. "I'm not sure. But she got what she wanted. I'm fairly positive we won't be seeing her again."

Bea's hand gripped mine. "Are you sure?"

Without turning around, I knew Kane was behind me. A smile tugged at my lips. As much as I'd enjoyed being empath-free, I had to admit, having the ability back was like coming home. I turned to him and held my arm out. "Let me check."

Our hands met. I fought the shadow world for just a moment, proving that I could, and then let the grayness rush in. Slight movements danced at the edge of my vision, but nothing turned solid and more importantly, I felt nothing. No grief. No frustration. And no icy chill. "She's gone," I said with certainty.

Kane pulled me into a bone-crushing hug. The world was still gray, but when I closed my eyes, I only saw him. And that was all I needed.

Chapter 32

I lounged on the cream-colored chenille couch in Summer House's vast library.

Kane sat at the desk, sorting through brochures of honeymoon options. "How about Hawaii?"

I wrinkled my nose.

He laughed. "You have something against the brilliant blue waters and pristine beaches?"

"No, that sounds lovely. But I'd rather go somewhere a little more interesting."

"Like?"

I shrugged. "Italy sounds cool."

"Oh? Let me guess. There's this island not too far from Venice you'd like to check out."

I couldn't help the twitch of my lips. He was on to me. "Well, yes. You know I'd love to go to Murano."

He rose from behind his desk and joined me on the couch, careful to not touch me. I reached out to him instead. We'd learned over the last few days that I had to consciously shut the shadows out before we touched. If he caught me off guard, sometimes it proved too hard to push them away. For some reason he didn't have the same problem. I thought it had something to do with his dreamwalking ability. He had more control than I did.

Our fingers touched, and the familiar spark we shared rushed through my arm, making me tingle everywhere. No ghosts or shadows anywhere.

"We can go check out your cute glass island if that's what you want."

I chuckled. "They're master glass workers. I don't think they'd appreciate their island being called cute."

"It's cute if you're there." He leaned in and brushed his lips over mine. I opened my mouth, darting my tongue over his. He pulled back. "Not sure it matters where we go on our honeymoon. I don't plan to spend more than five minutes outside of the hotel room."

"Why go anywhere?" I murmured. "Seems easier to stay here if you're going to keep me naked for two weeks."

He groaned and pushed me back into the cushions. My arms came around him, and I pulled him closer, pressing my body against his hard form. "Now you're on to something."

My nipples hardened into tight points as his hand brushed over my breast, taking the nub between his thumb and forefinger through the flimsy material of my cotton shirt. I arched into him, heat pulsing between my thighs.

His hand snaked under my skirt and was dipping beneath my lace panties when the doorbell rang.

"Damn it," he muttered into my neck. "This is why we're going away on a honeymoon." He pushed himself up and gazed down at me, molten desire raging in his dark eyes.

My breath caught as it always did when he looked at me like that.

"Give me two minutes to get rid of them."

I nodded, my mouth suddenly dry.

He disappeared, and a few moments later, voices I recognized filled the hallway—Kat and Lucien. I jumped off the couch and busied myself with straightening my clothes.

Kane knocked on the partially open door and poked his head in. "You decent?" he mouthed.

I laughed. "Yes."

The pair filed in behind him. Lucien hung back, leaning against the vast bookshelf, while Kat gave me a hug.

"Sorry to barge in on you," she said. "Hope asked me to drop something off, and I was wondering if we could talk for a minute."

"Sure." I glanced around, noting she wasn't carrying anything but her handbag. "What do you have for me?"

"It's in the car." She sat on the couch Kane and I had just been making out on and perched on the edge.

"Okay."

Lucien shuffled in place, staring at the floor.

"What's up?"

"Actually, Lucien wants to talk to you." She waved him forward.

Shaking his head, he cleared his throat. "I'm good here."

Nervousness spiked off him, and I had the sudden urge to send him calming energy. Whatever it was, he was struggling. But in light of recent events, I'd decided to keep my energy to myself, especially since I now saw into the shadows. Who knew what sort of side effects my new ability would bring?

"What's up?" I asked.

He pushed away from the bookcase, determination taking over his demeanor. "I'd like permission to renounce my membership in the coven."

Shock seized me, and my mouth fell open. "Why?"

His green gaze flicked to Kat. "You know why."

Sadness rippled in my chest. Lucien was a powerful, conscientious witch. And that was why he was trying to quit. He wouldn't knowingly put anyone at risk. I frowned. "Bea's still the coven leader. Shouldn't you be having this conversation with her?"

We'd decided not to transfer the coven back to me until we were certain Camille was out of my life and I had a handle on my new ability. So far, everything seemed normal, but I'd made up my mind to hold off until after the honeymoon. For the next month, the coven was Bea's responsibility.

"I suppose, but I wanted to talk with you about it first." He met my gaze. "We both know Bea is only holding your spot for you. Since I was your second in command, it felt right to talk to you first."

Slowly, I sat in one of the velvet-covered chairs across from the couch. "I'm not happy about the idea, but I do understand."

"I'm not sure you do." He glanced at Kat. Something painful clung to him.

My heart clenched. "I'm pretty sure I do." That pain clinging to him was anguish-filled love. He was in love with Kat, and I was almost positive she didn't know it.

His head shot up as he glanced between us. Then he must have seen the understanding in my eyes because he nodded. "Maybe you do."

Kane shifted behind me. I sensed him but wasn't expecting it when he leaned down and clamped a hand on my shoulder.

The room turned gray and across from me, Lucien's form was solid black.

"I think Kat and I should give you two some time," Kane said into my ear.

I clasped his hand, forcing him to stay connected with me. "Wait!"

He stiffened but didn't move.

I pointed at Lucien. "What do you see?"

He sucked in a breath. "Darkness."

"Does he look solid black to you?"

Kane nodded. "Yes."

"What?" Kat and Lucien asked in unison.

My vision blurred, and I let myself see past the blackness. Lucien's form was outlined in solid gray. It wasn't that he was consumed by darkness; the darkness clung to him. "It's the curse."

"Whoa," Kane breathed.

I let go of Kane's hand. The world turned back to color. "No."

"No?" Kat said, her voice high-pitched. "What does that mean?"

I shook my head. "I'm not letting Lucien leave the coven."

"But Jade—" Lucien started.

"No," I said again. "You've been cursed, and it's clinging to your soul. I refuse to let you renounce the coven. We'll find a way to fix it. One way or another. Understand?"

They were both silent. Kat got up and moved to the door. "I'll give you a minute. I've got to get that thing from my car anyway." She quietly slipped from the room.

Kane nodded to me and followed her.

Weariness radiated off Lucien. "Clinging to my soul?"

"And your heart," I said quietly.

"It's a love curse then." It wasn't a question, only a realization.

"I'm afraid so."

He hung his head. "Then you have to let me leave."

"Why?"

Sighing in frustration, he moved to the couch, taking Kat's place. "It will only go away one of two ways: if I fall out of love with her, or if she dies. I don't think I can do the first, and the second..." He ran a frustrated hand through his blond hair. "I'll never let that happen."

"And what if you fall in love with someone else? What will you do then?"

He shook his head. "I won't."

"You can't control love, Lucien."

"I can, and I will." The pain seeping off him stabbed at my heart and was too much to bear.

I reached out and grabbed his hand. "That's no way to live. If I know one thing about my friend, it's that if she loves you back, she'll fight fiercely for you. Trust me when I say she won't give up. Do you really think you can walk away from that?"

"I have to." His voice broke and he swallowed. "I can't let anything happen to her. I'm a death sentence."

I stood. "Not if I have anything to say about it. I forbid your request, and I'll make damn sure Bea does to. Got that?" I was so frustrated I was shaking. "Don't give up on us. We won't ever give up on you. We'll find a way to break the curse. Hell,

Lucien, we brought Bea back from black magic. What makes you think we can't fight this?"

The muscles in his arms flexed as he fought for control. "Because I've been researching this curse. No one ever survives it. Not one. They all die."

"Kat didn't," I challenged. "We brought her back."

"Yeah, by some miracle. I can't risk it again. I won't."

I narrowed my eyes. "She's my best friend. I'd do anything for her. *Anything.*"

"So would I."

"Except stay and fight for her."

"Dammit, Jade!" His fist came down on the sixteenth-century end table, causing it to creak and bow under the pressure. "I'm doing this for her."

"No, you're not." I lowered my voice "You're doing it because you're scared. Just promise me a month. Bea's staying with the coven for the next four weeks. Give us that long to work on this."

He closed his eyes.

"Lucien?"

"Yeah?"

"Trust me."

His conflicted gaze bored into mine. "If anything happens to her…"

I nodded my understanding, praying I'd made the right decision. Neither of us said another word. I wouldn't let anything happen to Kat, and neither would he. Lucien stared at me, his body tense and filled with unease. Then he turned and quietly let himself out. I sat down behind the desk and let out a shaky breath.

"Jade?" Kat let herself back in.

I forced a smile. "Hey."

"You talked him into staying?"

"For now."

"Thank the Goddess." She slumped into a chair. "I thought he was ready to skip town after what had happened to me."

I nodded. That had been his exact plan.

She pulled an envelope from her purse. "Your mom gave me this to give to you. She said she's never read it and to tell you she's sorry. That she had her reasons."

I took the crumpled envelope from her hands and ran a finger over my name scrolled in jerky cursive handwriting.

"It's from Marc," she said.

I nodded, recognizing the green envelope from memory. "She said she didn't know where it was."

Kat gave me a sympathetic smile. "I'm sure this is hard on both of you. Obviously, she planned to tell you, or she wouldn't have brought this from Idaho."

I nodded again. She must've. I didn't believe for a moment Gwen would've kept this from me.

"She also gave me this." Kat produced a smaller beige envelope and passed it to me.

I recognized the handwriting instantly. It was Mom's.

Kat rose and kissed me on the cheek. "Call if you need me."

My eyes never left the beige envelope in my hand. "I will. You do the same."

"Always." The door clicked softly behind her.

The room was so quiet I could hear the sound of my own breathing. Why did Mom send me a letter instead of speaking to me in person? Anger rippled through me. Damn her. I turned the envelope over and ripped it open. The card that fell out had one of those stupid LOL cats on the front with his head buried in its paws. The caption read, *I screwed up.*

Understatement of the century.

Inside she wrote:

> *I don't have any excuse other than I was scared for you. Council angels have a way of destroying people. I never wanted you to go through that. I should've known there was no escaping it. Your real father—the one who helped raise you, Marc—never agreed with me. My stubbornness eventually tore us apart. I hope*

Angels of Bourbon Street 287

you can forgive me for that too. He's a good man. I should've never kept him from you.

Mom.

Tears pooled in my eyes. After all I'd come to know about the council, I couldn't fault her for trying to protect me from them. They were self-serving and all but void of humanity. I'm not sure I would've made the same choices she had, but I did understand her motivation. And it came from a place of love.

With trembling hands, I carefully tore the seal from Marc's letter.

My darling Jade,

It's been two years now since I last saw you. I can still envision you standing by that stream, a daisy tucked behind your ear as you squealed, trying to bait that hook. As long as I live, I'll never forget the delight I saw on your face when I told you we'd spend the day together. It's one of those precious father/daughter moments that brands your heart.

By now, I'm certain your mother has told you the truth. Otherwise she wouldn't be delivering this letter to you. It's true, you are not my biological daughter, but you are mine in every way that counts. I held you as a baby, watched you sleep, worried when your fever wouldn't break. My heart aches when I think of all the hours we've lost and the thousands more we're bound to miss out on, all because your mother and I are unable to come to a reasonable compromise.

You'll never know how much being away from you breaks my heart. But I also couldn't continue to live a lie. Please understand, I would have gladly gone on being your one and only father, but it became apparent each and every day that your power as a white witch was growing. You were blossoming into a wonderful witch of a woman. And I wanted to nurture that. It's who I am. My entire adult life, I have sat on the witch council. I mentor youth, teach them to understand their gifts. Help them make the world better with the power they possess.

Your mother was never comfortable with the amount of power you obviously contain. I understood her hesitation. Dark forces follow those who are the most powerful. And you, my darling, may be the most powerful witch I've ever met. I wanted to prepare you for the days ahead.

Unfortunately your mother has other ideas. Do not blame her. It must've been very scary for her. There came a day when she no longer trusted me to keep her secret and that was the day she asked me to leave. I never wanted to leave you. Never.

Since you are not legally mine, I didn't have any choice. I'll be here for you always. Only a phone call away. If you need me, I'll be there.

All my love, Dad.

My eyes blurred, and tears stained the letter, making the ink run. I lay my head down on the desk, letting the emotions take me. Sobs rippled through me as joy and frustration fought for dominance in my heart.

Neither of my parents had wanted to leave me, yet both had made choices that kept us apart. I wasn't sure I could ever fully forgive either of them. But at the same time, the hollow ache in my chest seemed to slowly disappear. With each tear I shed, that deep-seated sense of abandonment faded away, replaced by an acceptance I'd never known.

I pressed the sheet against the desk, smoothing the folds, and then wiped the tears from my eyes. The door creaked open, and in walked Kane. He took one look at me and strode over, offering me his embrace.

I willingly stepped into his arms and clung to him.

He kissed the top of my head and ran his sure hands down my shoulders and arms. "What can I do for you, love?"

"You're already doing it," I said into his shoulder.

He wrapped his arms around me and pulled me closer. "Do you want to talk about it?"

I shook my head. "Not much to say, except that they both made mistakes."

"But they both love you."

"Yeah, they do." I pulled back and stared up into his gentle face. "My life's a mess."

"So is mine." He cracked a small smile. "Wait until you meet *my* parents."

"They can't be worse than mine." I laughed. "I mean I have three now, two witches and an angel."

"You think that's bad?" He pushed a lock of hair out of my eyes. "I have a disinterested skirt-chaser of a father and a vodka-guzzling mother who ignores his indiscretions in order to keep up pretenses."

"What?" I made a disgusted face. "I thought they were adventurers."

"Oh, they are. They're also pretentious, spoiled, selfish, and not at all interested in their son's life."

"Kane!" I stepped back. "Then why are we inviting them to the wedding?"

He shrugged. "It seemed important to you." His lips quirked into a sheepish grin. "Haven't you figured out by now I'm only interested in making you happy? You seemed to need family. I was bound and determined to give it to you, even if they are sort of a nightmare."

I shook my head. "I have all the family I need." I pressed my finger into his chest. "Right here with you."

"So I can uninvite the ingrates?"

I laughed. "If you want. All I need is you."

His gaze met mine, intense and smoldering. "You've got me, love. You've definitely got me."

Our lips met, gentle and full of love. When his mouth opened, taking mine, the rest of the world faded away. He was mine and I was his. No matter what happened tomorrow, we'd face it together.

He pulled away and held his hand out. "Let's go."

"Where?"

"Upstairs. Remember that moment we were having on that couch earlier?"

I slipped my hand in his. "Yes."

"We're going to recreate it about six different ways."

Grinning, I let him pull me after him and squealed when he picked me up at the base of the grand staircase.

Oh, yeah. Move over Rhett Butler, Kane Rouquette just stole my heart...again.

About the Author

Deanna is a native Californian, transplanted to the slower paced lifestyle of southeastern Louisiana. When she isn't writing, she is often goofing off with her husband in New Orleans, playing with her two shih tzu dogs, making glass beads, or out hocking her wares at various bead shows across the country. Want the next book in the series? Visit www.DeannaChase.com to sign up for the New Releases email list. Look for *Shadows of Bourbon Street* coming early 2014.

14993497R00169

Made in the USA
Middletown, DE
19 October 2014